PORTRAIT OF THE SPY AS A YOUNG MAN

PORTRAIT OF THE SPY AS A YOUNG MAN

Edward Wilson

A

First published in Great Britain by Arcadia Books 2020
This paperback edition published in 2022 by

Arcadia Books
An imprint of Quercus Editions Limited
Carmelite House
50 Victoria Embankment
London EC4Y 0DZ

An Hachette UK company

A CIP catalogue record for this book is available from the British Library.

ISBN (MMP) 978 1 52942 228 3
ISBN (Ebook) 978 1 91135 087 3

This book is a work of fiction. Names, characters, organisations,
places and events are either the product of the author's imagination
or are used fictitiously. Any resemblance to actual persons, living
or dead, events or particular places is entirely coincidental.

3 5 7 9 10 8 6 4

Typeset in Minion by MacGuru Ltd
Printed and bound in Great Britain by Clays Ltd, Elcograf S.p.A.

Papers used by Quercus Books are from well-managed
forests and other responsible sources.

To our grandson, Jackson Gore-Manton

Ami, entends-tu
Le vol noir des corbeaux
Sur nos plaines?
Ami, entends-tu
Les cris sourds du pays
Qu'on enchaîne?
Ohé! Partisans...

Le Chant des Partisans,
words by Maurice Druon and Joseph Kessel;
music by Anna Marly

Gare de Limoges-Bénédictins: May 1943

It was turning into the worst of all nightmares. As soon as the flow of disembarked passengers ground to halt, William Catesby knew there was trouble ahead – and, when he saw the blue berets, he realised they were in serious danger. The *milice française*, despite their smart new uniforms – blue berets and jackets, brown shirts and boots with gaiters – were not the sharpest of cops, but they made up for stupidity with brutality. They were recruited from prisons and the ranks of unsuccessful petty criminals. Joining the *milice* meant you were exempt from being deported to work in Germany and had plenty of non-rationed food. The most frightening thing was that these ex-criminals had the power to arrest and torture.

Catesby and the new wireless operator, a Frenchwoman recently infiltrated by RAF Lysander, had excellent fake identity cards and supporting documents. He was worried, but hoped they could bluff their way past a *milice* cretin. Stay calm and you can do it. Then Catesby's heart sank. *Oh, shit!* There were other uniforms at the end of the train platform – and they weren't wearing gaiters and blue trousers, but polished jackboots and a black diamond patch emblazoned with SD on the lower left arm of their field grey tunics. *Sicherheitsdienst.* The radio transmitter that Catesby was carrying was disguised by a brown leather case to look like an ordinary piece of luggage. The problem was its weight. It was bloody heavy – more than twenty kilos, which made pretending it was an ordinary travel bag difficult. But that problem no longer mattered. Catesby and his radio operator were about to be arrested and tortured.

He wished he had put his cyanide pill in his jacket pocket. He feared that he would break under questioning. Many stronger agents did. Catesby made a quick mental inventory of those who would be arrested if he broke. If, however, he managed to resist for a day or two, they might be warned and have a chance to go into hiding. But what weighed on him most was the secret that had been entrusted to him during his brief visit to London. Why oh why had the major briefing him at SOE HQ confided such a sensitive and important secret? And to him, Catesby, a mere underling in the scheme of things? The major suggested he needed to know about it to better appreciate the role of the Resistance in the coming months. Or was the major just showing off? The fact that the allied invasion of Europe would take place between June and September 1943 at the Pas-de-Calais was a secret that Catesby would gladly excise from his brain if he had a drill and scalpel. If the Gestapo tortured it out of him, they would have extracted a crown jewel.

Catesby cursed himself for having volunteered for Special Operations Executive – an ordinary death on the battlefield would have been quicker for him and less costly for the allies. An SOE death meant horrific torture – followed by years in a concentration camp and eventual execution. He then made up his mind. It would be his last act of decency before breaking under torture. Catesby whispered to his companion without looking at her. 'Pretend you don't know me. Move forward now. I will lag behind. You must get out of the station before they search me.'

She ignored him and said, 'Put the transmitter on top of your head.'

'What?'

'Don't argue. Do as I say and do it now!'

The new radio operator, who looked about forty, was old enough to be Catesby's mother – and radiated both sensuality and authority. She was stunningly beautiful with expensively coiffured blond hair. Something in Catesby instinctually obeyed and he hefted the radio on to his head. It was, actually, a lot easier carrying the heavy lump of coils, batteries and accessories this way than by his side. For a second he gave a grim smile at how silly he must look.

Meanwhile, the wireless operator was shouting her head off in fluent German. '*Schnell!* We have a captured terrorist radio transmitter and need to get to Abwehr HQ immediately.'

Catesby had to run to keep up with her as she hurtled towards the German security police with an angry frown. The NCO in charge bore a confused look on his face. One of the *milice,* who obviously didn't understand German, seemed to be asking what was going on. The German NCO gestured him away and addressed Catesby's companion. 'How can I help? My superiors told me nothing about this.'

'They said there would be a car waiting. We're already late – and this transmitter has an encryption device that urgently needs decoding. Where is that fucking car you promised?'

The NCO was clearly intimidated.

'Who is your immediate superior?' shouted the woman.

The NCO whispered the name of a Gestapo junior officer.

'I know that name. Captain Barbie mentioned him to me when he said he was arranging a car.'

The NCO visibly shook at the mention of the name Barbie. 'I think it best,' he said, 'that you take our car to avoid further delay.'

The woman nodded her head in exasperation. 'Yes, that would be a good idea.'

The NCO summoned a tall languid soldier who wore ordinary *Wehrmacht* field grey without a *Sicherheitsdienst* badge. 'Take these people to Abwehr HQ immediately. Drive as quickly as possible.'

Catesby and his companion followed the soldier out of Limoges station on to the forecourt. The car, a requisitioned Citroën Traction Avant – the wheeled booty most prized by the German occupiers – was gleaming in the drizzle. The driver opened a rear door and gave a perfunctory heel click as Catesby and the female wireless operator, who was still angry and demanding, settled themselves on to the back seat.

The driver seemed to know his way around Limoges and headed off to where, Catesby assumed, the Abwehr HQ was located. He wondered what they were going to do next and knew that his companion was thinking the same thing. She leaned forward and tapped the driver on the shoulder.

'Can you turn left at the next street?'

'But, *gnädige Frau*, that isn't the way to the Abwehr.'

'The cryptologist we are meeting works directly for the *Sicherheitsdienst*. He is not a member of the Abwehr – I am sure you realise there are issues…'

'I have heard rumours.'

'Then keep those rumours to yourself – as well as the location to which you are taking us.'

The driver nodded and Catesby smiled. The rivalry and bad blood between the Abwehr intelligence service and the German security services were well known – and played upon by SOE and the Resistance.

Even though the woman hardly knew Limoges, she gave the impression of being a born native as she guided the driver through a bewildering haze of backstreets. They finally arrived at a cul de sac which stank of drains and rotting rubbish.

'We're here,' she said. 'Will you need any help backing out?'

'No.'

The woman leaned forward and put her left hand on the driver's shoulder. 'You've been magnificent. Thank you for your help – and remember this is our secret.'

The driver blushed. 'At your service, *gnädige Frau*.'

'You should call me *madame*. I am French.' The woman leaned further forward as if she were going to give the German soldier a collaborator's kiss. The soldier's blushing smile turned into an agonised grimace as the downward thrust of the knife cut deep through his chest into the aorta. As soon as Catesby saw what was happening, he put his hand over the driver's mouth to muffle his ear-splitting scream. They waited half a minute until the driver had stopped twitching.

'That might have been a mistake,' said the woman. 'And he looked like such an innocent boy.' She paused. 'Oh god! Our hands are covered in blood.'

The women pulled up her skirt. 'Here, wipe your hands on my slip.'

As Catesby wiped his hands on the thin white fabric and sensed her tense thighs beneath, he experienced a totally inappropriate frisson – and immediately felt ashamed. When the woman finished wiping her own hands, she pulled her skirt down again.

'I didn't want to ditch the radio,' she said. 'They are gold dust.'

'Then we need to get to a safe house quickly.'

The woman shook her head. 'I think our best chance of getting away with the transmitter is to use the car. Can you drive?'

'Yeah, but I think it's a bad idea.'

'We haven't time to argue,' said the woman. 'You worked with Guingouin's Maquis, so you know the countryside around here. Find us a hiding place.'

'Okay, I'll find a place to ditch the car and hide the radio. You go to a safe house and, if I succeed, we'll rendezvous later.'

'No, I'm staying with you.'

'Another bad idea.' Catesby got out of the car and began to push the body of the dead soldier into the footwell of the passenger seat.

'Let me help.'

'Help me get his tunic off. In fact, I'd better wear it.'

'Undressing dead bodies,' she said, 'is never easy.'

They finally got the tunic off and, although the sleeves were too long, it wasn't a bad fit. Catesby buttoned it up to the neck.'

'The bloodstain is awful.'

Catesby nodded at the dead man. 'If anyone asks, I'll say he vomited over me as we got him in the car. He's not dead, he's passed out drunk. You sit in the back and pretend you're an important guest of the *Sicherheitsdienst*. Shit, this is dangerous. Maybe we should run for it on foot.'

'It's too late.' The woman nodded at an urchin of ten who was staring at them from behind a dustbin.

Catesby got out of the car, went over to the boy and leaned down. 'Are you a brave lad?'

The boy nodded.

'Have you heard of the Resistance?'

'Yes.'

'We love France. Do you love France?'

'Yes – very much!'

'You are now a member of the Resistance too. You must swear that you will never tell anyone what you have just seen.'

'I swear.'

The boy saluted and Catesby saluted back, '*Adieu, mon brave partisan.*'

The boy held his salute as they drove away.

'I suppose,' said Catesby, 'you thought that was pretty corny.'

'I'm only thinking about what to do next. It won't be long before they discover they were tricked.'

'We need to get out of Limoges as quickly as possible and then keep off the main roads. The most dangerous bit will be crossing the Vienne.' Catesby leaned over the dead soldier's body.

'What are you doing?'

Catesby found a *Wehrmacht* half cap on the car floor and put it on his head. 'I need to look the part.'

Motor vehicles were rare on the roads of Limoges. Traffic consisted of bicycles, pedestrians, handcarts, horse drawn carriages and a few *gazogènes*, petrol vehicles converted to run on gas. Catesby was impressed by how many rude gestures he attracted in his *Wehrmacht* uniform – as well as a few shouts of *Ta soeur!* – the short version of 'your sister is a whore'. And once a teenage girl threw a stone at the rear window next to where Catesby's companion was seated. The girl shouted *putain*, whore, assuming the wireless operator was someone sleeping with a German officer, before disappearing behind a crowd queuing for rations. Opinion was turning against the occupiers, but, as the public mood changed, the crackdowns became more severe.

Catesby's original plan was to drive along the river looking for a bridge crossing that didn't have a checkpoint. He soon realised that was a stupid idea – and began to panic when he saw the barbed wire barricades which forced traffic back into the town centre. A pair of gendarmes gave him a hard stare as he drove past. Perhaps, he thought, it was the custom of the Germans to stop and have a chat.

'What's happening?'

'The bridges are too guarded. I think we need to follow the N141 towards Oradour-sur-Glane.'

Soon there were fewer and fewer buildings and they were in an open countryside of low hills. Catesby felt tenser than ever. He was going in the opposite direction from where the Maquis had a network of sympathetic villages and contacts.

'Fuck,' he said.

'What's wrong?'

'There's a checkpoint up ahead.'

Catesby put one hand on the wheel so that he could reach over to the dead soldier. He nearly lost control and went off the road.

'What are you doing?'

'I'm trying to get his gun.'

'Leave it – don't stop and keep driving.'

'Okay.'

As Catesby drove past, the gendarmes didn't even look up. They were checking a pair of bicycles with heavily packed trailers.

'It's a black-market road check,' said the woman.

'Bastards.' The gendarmes didn't arrest the black marketers, they fleeced them instead. If anything, the occupiers and the collabos encouraged rather than restrained black market. The occupation stank of corruption.

A few minutes of calm followed before Catesby looked in the car's rear-view mirror. They were being followed by a blue gendarmerie van.

'What's wrong now?'

'Look behind us.'

'Maybe it's just a coincidence.'

'We'll see.' Catesby abruptly turned the Citroën Avant off the main road. A moment later, the gendarmerie van followed.

'I wish,' said Catesby, 'that we had a couple of Sten guns.'

'This car's a lot faster than their TUB van. Step on it.'

The next ten minutes were as exhilarating as they were frightening. They finally shook off the van somewhere around Les Conces, but their cover was blown. Catesby drove as fast as he could. He wanted to get to a farm near Cussac where he hoped they could stash the car. He eventually found the rough track that rose steeply up a wooded ravine. He stopped to remove a pile of brush which concealed the track leading to the abandoned farm. The woman helped. As soon as the brush was back in position, Catesby laughed.

'What's so funny?'

'I'd better take this off. I don't want to be shot by a Maquisard.' Catesby removed the *Wehrmacht* tunic and draped it over the dead German.

They drove another four hundred yards to a ramshackle stone building which looked as if it had been long abandoned. Catesby got out of the car and walked over to the barn door. He tried the latch, but it wouldn't budge. The door was locked.

'Get a tool from the car,' said the woman, 'and break it open. Once we've hidden the car, we can find the Maquis on foot.'

Just then someone whistled from the wood line.

'They've followed us,' said Catesby. 'The gendarmes must have radioed for help.'

'Let's go.' The woman took off her shoes and started running across the damp grass. But it was too late. A figure in uniform carrying a submachine gun emerged from the trees – followed by another also carrying a gun.

Catesby realised they were well and truly fucked. But if they were lucky, the body of the dead German might provoke a summary execution without torture. As Catesby raised his hands he realised that the uniforms – leather jackets, green trousers and boots – were not those of any Vichy militia, but those of Georges Guingouin's Limousin Maquis. They were carrying British Stens.

'Don't move,' shouted the Maquisard in front, 'or you die.'

'I'm on your side,' said Catesby. 'I was with Lo Grand in Saint-Gilles-les-Forêts.'

There was a silence as the two Maquisards conferred in whispers.

'If you want more proof,' said Catesby, 'you can find a dead German in the car.'

The two fighters came forward. The lead one said, 'What's your name?'

Catesby answered with his codename, 'Jacques Dubois.'

The other Maquisard said to his mate, 'He's one of the Englishmen who parachuted in just before we blew up the viaduct.'

The first one glanced at the woman and turned to Catesby, 'And who's your friend?'

'I have my own tongue,' said the woman. 'My name is Marie and I am a wireless operator. You can find my radio in the car with a German soldier I killed earlier today.'

The second Maquisard went over to the car and opened the front passenger door. 'Look. They really have brought a dead *boche* with them.'

The other Maquis shouldered his Sten and said, 'There isn't any room in the barn to hide the car. It's packed with explosives and food. There have been a lot of parachute drops recently.'

The two Maquisards conferred in Lemosin dialect. Catesby only picked up a few words.

The first Maquisard shifted back into standard French. 'We'll take over now and my comrade will do the driving.'

Three of them crammed into the back seat. There was little conversation as they set off. The convention was to be tight-lipped, not out of unfriendliness, but for security reasons. They addressed each other by codenames and never provided clues about places or operations. If someone was captured and broke under torture, they could only provide codenames and nothing that would connect to other people or places. No one wanted to know Catesby's job or where the woman was from or how she ended up killing a German and stealing a *Sicherheitsdienst* car – but there was a body that needed to be disposed of. The car finally stopped near a steep gully. They dragged the young German out of the car and heaved him to his final resting place where he would be food for carrion, flies, beetles and mites. The Maquisards drove on and dropped Catesby and Marie off at a safe house in Sussac.

The safe house was a grocery shop. The owners were part of a vast army of *légaux*, legals. The *légaux* helped the Resistance, but lived openly in the community and didn't take a direct part in fighting or sabotage. Being a 'legal' could be more dangerous than being a guerrilla fighter. You hadn't a place to hide; you were out in the open waiting to be rounded up.

After a late supper of bread, cheese and wine, Catesby wrapped himself in a blanket and curled up in a storeroom amid tins of beans, tomatoes and fish paste as there was only one spare bed. Just as he began to doze off, he felt a hand on his thigh. Catesby would never know her exact age or much else about her. She normally kept herself a mystery, but there were no secrets about what she wanted in the bedroom. For decades afterwards Catesby would remember that evening as the most erotic experience he had ever had. The image of the woman's bloodstained slip – as she peeled it off and revealed her legs – haunted and excited him for the rest of his days.

Suffolk: November 2014

Catesby picked up the cat, who preferred lying on his keyboard to the softest and warmest cushion, and put him on the floor. The cat then jumped on to Catesby's lap. The purring translated as: *We're playing a game, aren't we? And isn't it fun?* The cat leapt back on to the keyboard, churning the opening paragraph of Catesby's war memoir into chaos. Fair enough. War was chaos.

Catesby didn't want to write about his war experiences. He was only trying to do so because his granddaughter, a history lecturer at a London university, had asked him to – but it was a story so full of contradictions, stupid risk-taking and unbelievable situations that no one would understand it. Except those who had been there – and only a few were left. Catesby was vain enough to be flattered by attention, but hated it when anyone called him a hero. He had known real heroes – and he wasn't one of them. The bravest, of course, had been the women. The faces of the dead ones had never withered and were still alive and young in his mind's eye. F Section SOE had sent thirty-nine women into occupied France. Fourteen of them had died. Twelve had been tortured and executed.

The cat finally tired of the keyboard game. He jumped on to the floor and a second later Catesby heard the noise of the cat flap. 'Leave the birds alone, you murdering bastard.' Catesby shoved the keyboard aside and picked up a copy of a French magazine that he had delivered once a week. After reading less than a page, he went back to his favourite daytime activity: drinking tea and staring out of the studio window at the garden. No birds, just dappled sunlight and mole hills, for the cat was walking hunch-shouldered across the lawn like an enforcer thug on the docks of Marseille. Then, suddenly, he took off running towards the hedge. Basic fieldcraft – like pigeons leaving their roosts or cows mooing – a stranger was approaching. And silently too, for lawns always muffle footfall. He heard the door opening and then her voice: 'Hello, Granddad.'

It was Leanna, the only daughter of his stepson Peter and his late African wife. Leanna was six feet tall and had given up a career as a professional athlete to become an academic. She had also turned down offers to be a model.

'The best thing,' said Catesby without turning around, 'was the ambush.'

'You began to mention it before, but then you stopped.'

'Killing them is always better than them killing us. Does that sound harsh?'

'Not at all.'

'It all happened so quickly. On reflection, we should have stayed in place and waited for the relief column – and then machine-gunned them too, and the survivors of the ambush who had crawled beneath their vehicles. We had just had a big supply drop of Brens to blast them with – so much more lethal than the Stens. Then we could have disappeared into the hills. If the Bushell girl had been with us, that's what she would have demanded.'

'Who was she?'

'Don't you know? Violette. She had been married to a Foreign Legionnaire named Szabo who got killed in North Africa. She was a fantastic shot, the best in SOE, but spoke French with a South London accent that stood out and…' Catesby stared out the window and went silent.

'Yes.'

'Nothing.' He turned to face his granddaughter and smiled. 'Why are you so good and so beautiful?'

'I'm pleased that you think so, but not everyone shares your opinion.'

'Where was I?' said Catesby. 'My mind is turning into a butterfly.'

'You were telling me about an ambush and Bren guns – and how you disappeared into the hills. You also mentioned Violette Szabo. I didn't realise that you had known her. She's famous. Haven't you seen the film?'

'I've never seen the film – or any film about the Resistance. And I've never read a book about it either.'

'I can understand why.'

'But there was passion, excitement and fun too. Nothing like the repetitive humdrum of ordinary life – and losing that exhilaration, losing it forever, is just as bad, maybe worse, than friends dying.' Catesby shook his head. 'I'm talking bullshit nonsense again. There was also boredom – long endless periods of soul-destroying boredom.'

'Perhaps, Granddad, it would be better if you just talked to me. I could record or take shorthand notes. Your brain is a repository of unrecorded history. We mustn't lose it.'

'The things I remember most vividly are the personal – the historical facts can go hang.'

'Can I make you another cup of tea?'

'Don't treat me like an invalid.'

'How about if I put some brandy in it?'

'You know how to twist my arm. Make sure it's not the good stuff, but the cooking brandy. And make one for yourself too.'

'You once told me that Henry Bone only used twenty-five-year-old VSOP.'

'You should have interviewed him. Henry knew where all the bodies were buried and put many of them there himself.'

Henry Bone was an enigma that no one ever solved. He was a typical English gentleman in looks and speech – but one who had been a close confidant of Blunt, Philby and the rest of the Moscow gang. No one would ever know the truth about Henry. Had he protected the traitors, or had he exposed them? Henry Bone wore his supercilious smile like a coat of armour.

'Did you ever meet him during the war?'

'Oddly enough, I did. The first time was at the Café Royal in 1942. Henry was with Anthony Blunt. They were sitting at a marble-topped table drinking absinthe – the Café Royal was the only place in London where you could get absinthe during the war. Absinthe is quite a palaver. I remember an elaborate silver device in the shape of a nude woman dripping ice-cold water through a block of French sugar on to a perforated absinthe spoon balanced over the glass of absinthe itself. Years later, Henry showed me his collection of absinthe spoons – an excellent birthday present for someone who has everything. The slow drip of ice water causes the absinthe to "bloom" thus releasing its aromas and flavours. The process is called "louching" – from where we get the word louche. As those who indulged in too much absinthe inevitably became.'

'I love your attention to detail.'

'It's part of the art of spycraft, my career, you know. Why are you looking at me in that tone of voice?'

'Granddad, how did you, a working-class boy from the docks of Lowestoft, end up in the Café Royal when you were barely out of your teens?'

'I was still in my teens – just. The war was the best thing for social mobility that ever happened to England. I was still in training with the Suffolk Regiment when I met a fellow soldier called Ewan Phillips. He was a few years older than me and had already made a name for himself in the art world as a curator. Ewan was extremely nice and generous – and curious to know how a rough kid from Lowestoft spoke French and had been to Cambridge. Two suggestions for social mobility: get in a war and have a Belgian mother. The Bushell girl, Violette, was another example. Her mother was a French seamstress. Ewan and I both had Christmas leave and he invited me to spend a few days at his family home in North London, Crediton Hill. It was a large flat full of art and antiques. They didn't have much money, but lots of style. There were bronze busts of Ewan's parents by Jacob Epstein. The family exuded civilised values. They were the sort of people the Nazis wanted to destroy – and, yes, I would have given my life to defeat that monstrosity. I digress. During the visit, Ewan took me to the Royal because, as he said, "You ought to see this place at least once." But he was pretty dismissive of it. He said it began to lose its magic in the mid-thirties and never recovered. But, I suppose, if you want to sip absinthe...'

'Thanks for that tip, Granddad. I must never go there again. Oh god, I've forgotten the tea!'

Catesby stared out the window. The sweet memories could be as painful as the horrible ones.

There was a clink of cups and saucers as Leanna came back into the studio.

'Oh dear, you've used the bone china, no problem – but I hope you didn't use the good brandy.'

'Nothing is too good for you, Granddad.'

'There are those who would argue that.'

As she put the tea down, his granddaughter noted something Catesby had written on the French magazine. She read it out. "*Et tout d'un coup...* And all at once, the memory appears before me." Are you getting back into Proust, Granddad?'

'How clever you are for recognising the quote. No, Proust is getting back into me.'

'Were you thinking of Violette Szabo?'

'No, I was thinking of another woman. Her face and everything about her suddenly appeared.'

'Did you love her?'

'That's a difficult question.' Catesby smiled. 'But don't worry Granny about her. She was a lot older than me and would no longer be alive. Time and memory are funny things. People die, but passion never dies.'

Cambridge: Michaelmas Term, 1941

It didn't feel right being a student at Cambridge University with a war going on and other young men dying. When Catesby told his mother that he was going to turn down the offer of a place and volunteer for military service, she flew into a rage. Which made him even more determined to volunteer. But somehow Mr Bennett, who had been his form tutor at Denes Grammar, got wind of the rumour that Catesby was considering turning down his Cambridge place. The teacher turned up, unannounced, at the family home on a warm summer's afternoon.

Catesby was surprised and embarrassed to see Mr Bennett standing in the doorway. It was unusual to see him not wearing his academic gown – which hid the fact that one of his arms was missing. Bennett had lost his arm at the end of the Great War – the same day, in fact, that Wilfred Owen was killed. Bennett joked that it was a lucky escape. The lost limb not only saved his life, but spared the world his own posthumous poetry.

'As it's so warm,' said Mr Bennett, 'I'm in shirtsleeve.'

Catesby gave a half-smile to Bennett's joke. Not all the students appreciated the teacher's sense of humour, but Catesby found it made his lessons memorable – or at least bearable.

'I was just passing this way for a walk. We still can't walk along the beach itself – even though the invasion danger's long gone – but we can now walk along the clifftops. I was hoping you would join me.'

Catesby's mother was busy in the kitchen. He called out, *'Ik ga wandelen met meneer Bennett. Ik ben zo terug.'*

'As I heard my name mentioned, could you grace me with a translation?'

'Nothing disrespectful, sir. I simply said, I'm going for a walk with Mr Bennett and I won't be long.'

'I thought you normally spoke French at home.'

'Not when Mother's cooking *Waterzooi*.'

The first part of the walk passed in silence. When they got to the Corton Cliffs, Mr Bennett turned to his former student. 'You are, William Catesby, one of the most remarkable students I have ever taught.'

'Thank you, Mr Bennett.'

'The most remarkable thing about you is that your absolutely incredible gift for languages – and not just the ones you speak at home – hides the fact that you are a complete idiot.'

'I'm sorry, sir, you think that.'

'Fortunately, the learned dons who interviewed you at Cambridge failed to recognise that lamentable facet of your character.'

Catesby smiled. 'I was, Mr Bennett, also a very good drama student.'

'No backchat, Catesby. To which particular example of idiocy do you think I am referring?'

'I don't think the RAF will have me, my eyes aren't quite good enough, so I'm going in the army.'

'Over what would be left of my dead body. No, Catesby. You are going to King's College Cambridge to read Modern Languages. Full. Stop.'

'I'm not going to bask in pampered privilege, Mr Bennett, while others are dying.'

Mr Bennett laughed. 'You were not, Catesby, a good drama student – and you have just proved it. Would you like to try that line again, with, perhaps, less emphasis on the too obvious *pampered privileged* alliteration? Ah, and now you are laughing.'

'Thank you, Mr Bennett, for making me laugh – and for, once again, making me see what a fool I am.'

'Idealism and self-sacrifice are not foolish. Forgive me, Catesby, for having been too hard on you.'

'There is, Mr Bennett, as we all know, method in your apologies.'

'Not everyone knows that, Catesby, only the brighter ones.'

'But I'm still determined to sign up.'

'Why so soon? The war isn't going to go away – and, as far as we're concerned, the next year or two may be pretty dull. All the action is going to be between Germany and Russia. If you want to see battle and die a valiant death, you ought to join the Soviet Army. They could use your help at Leningrad.'

Catesby looked out to sea. Two Royal Navy Patrol Service boats, converted trawlers manned largely by former trawler men, were heading out to sea. The losses among Lowestoft's fishermen since being absorbed into the Patrol Service were already horrendous. Catesby swallowed hard and felt a pang of guilt. They were his people and came from the same cramped terraces near the docks.

'I am not going to say, William, that I know how you feel.'

Catesby smiled. The sudden shift to first-name basis was another Bennett trick.

'Your mind belongs to you alone – and I would never trespass there. But may I suggest a compromise?'

'As you like, sir.'

'I contacted Cambridge University – not just about your case, but the wartime situation in general. They told me that's it's perfectly acceptable for a student to begin a course and then return to finish it after military service. You must do at least two terms, Michaelmas and Lent – and preferably Easter too. You could be in uniform no later than next June.'

Catesby remained silent.

'And if, Catesby, you want to be even more useful to your country, an extra year studying German would be very helpful.'

'Your logic, Mr Bennett, is faultless.'

'So you will accept your place at Cambridge?'

'I will, sir, think about it.'

'Good. And there is another reason, William, why this is so important.'

'Why, sir?'

'No one from your background, certainly not in Lowestoft and probably all of Suffolk, has ever got into Oxbridge before. You are breaking ground, solid class-privileged hard clay, that very badly needs breaking.'

Catesby looked at Mr Bennett with astonishment.

'No, Catesby, I am not a Bolshevik, but I am someone who knows that our country needs to change – and maybe this war will bring about that change. And you, William, if you don't get killed, are going to be part of it.'

Catesby watched as Mr Bennett strode off, a sprightly but slightly lopsided figure, through the clifftop heather.

When Catesby arrived at Cambridge, he soon found that he was no longer Catesby or William, but W.R. Catesby. One of his first friends was H.H. Strachan who came from what seemed a mad and eccentric Scottish family. He was also eager to get a year at Cambridge out of the way and enlist in the army.

'I'm going to join the Scots Greys,' said H.H. 'It's my family's regiment. The lads went a bit mad at Waterloo with kilted Highlanders hitching a ride on the stirrups of the Greys. They famously captured the Eagle of the French 45th Ligne. That turned them totally berserk and they kept charging. In the end, they were badly mauled and lost most of their horses.'

One of the things that most impressed Catesby about Strachan was the pair of ancient muskets that H.H. had mounted on the wall of his room above the fireplace. At first, Catesby thought they were duelling pistols, but Strachan soon put him right. 'No, they are proper weapons of war. I'm lucky to have these. They date from the seventeenth century. The Greys used to carry them when they were dragoons.'

What most bonded Catesby and Strachan, other than their eagerness to get into uniform, was night climbing. They both became members of a clandestine society known as The Night Climbers of Cambridge. The objective was not just to reach the top of numerous spires, ledges and gables, but to do so without being spotted by the police – nicknamed 'Roberts' by the students – or university porters, who had taken to hiding in the shadows hoping to ambush a night climber. The authorities were determined to stamp out the practice and punish the wrong-doers – which made the midnight conquest of a forbidden roof all the sweeter.

Catesby's first climb was the Old Library. It began with

traversing a barrier of cast-iron railings honed into black spears which pointed into the sky like the javelins of a Roman century. One misstep meant impaling. Having escaped the legionnaires, the next step was to get on to a ledge above an archway inscribed BIBLIOTECA. This required some nerve as you had to pull yourself up by inserting the tips of your fingers into the recesses between the stones so you could get a foot on the two-inch-wide outcropping. Once you got on to the ledge, you had to shuffle along with your face against the stone until you got past the Saintless Niche. The climb to the roof was now a question of The Sunken Drainpipe and The Old Library Chimney. Impossible if you were too short. You had to wedge your body into a space – the old chimney – between the library's two buildings and walk yourself up to the roof vertically. If you didn't keep the tension, using your feet to press your back against the wall, you fell down between the two buildings and fractured your spine. It wasn't, however, as difficult as Catesby thought it would be – but the final bit, grasping the roof parapet with both hands and pulling yourself on to the roof, was a bit disconcerting. Would your hands slip or the stone you were clinging to come loose?

After the climb, the roof itself was a midnight paradise with dark silhouettes of blacked-out Cambridge, a vista that could only be enjoyed by the secret cabal who took risks. It was, in a way, similar to the excitement that Catesby would later feel as an SIS intelligence officer. The EYES ONLY files provided a top secret view of the world and Britain that only the privileged few were allowed to see.

Once the roof was achieved, there was still one more climb: The Tottering Tower. The tower was about thirty feet high, but an easy climb because its elaborate ornamentation provided lots of hand and footholds – but, illusion or not, the tower seemed to wobble more and more the higher you got. Once he reached the cross on top of the tower, there was one more thing for Catesby to do. It was pointless to execute these high-risk climbs and not leave a mark. Catesby reached inside his jacket and pulled out his blue-and-white Ipswich Town football scarf. The tower seemed to sway as he tied the ITFC scarf to the top cross. Done.

The next morning, as the Ipswich Town scarf blew defiantly in the wind, the university authorities scratched their heads in confusion. 'Footer' was not a game popular among the undergraduates – particularly the sort who surreptitiously climbed towers. Their sports tended to be rowing, rugby, tennis and fencing. The fact that the scarf was that of a local East Anglian team pointed away from the assumption that all the climbers were undergraduates. One of the proctors shrugged. 'Well, I never,' he shook his head in disbelief. 'It looks like the townies have got involved.' Although Catesby didn't realise it at the time, the incident became his first successful deception operation.

Catesby's final climb was in the spring, just before he left Cambridge for the army. His objective was to reach the top of one of the spires of King's College Chapel. A few years before, the Night Climbers had celebrated the coming Christmas by decorating the tops of all four spires with party hats and tinsel. But neither Catesby nor the others had any intention of leaving a physical marker on this occasion. They had an audience instead – women from Homerton College who had come to bid farewell. Like Catesby, all four of the Night Climbers were leaving for the army. To serenade the Homerton women, the climbers had snatches of poetry they were going to proclaim from the pinnacles of King's Chapel.

As soon as it was Catesby's turn, he felt a bit awkward. All the other recitations had been light-hearted and in English – or Scots. The Homerton girls had given a special round of applause to Strachan's rendition of Burns:

> *He set his Jenny on his knee,*
> *All in his Highland dress;*
> *For brawly weel he kenned the way*
> *To please a bonnie lass.*

Catesby was next. He was sure his opening words made things worse. '*Je vous demande pardon*, this isn't going to be very interesting.' He then launched into the Rimbaud he had chosen because it seemed apt to recite when clinging to a King's Chapel spire at midnight: *'J'ai tendu des cordes de clocher à clocher; des guirlandes de fenêtre à fenêtre...'*

Catesby was interrupted by a refined and peremptory voice, surely a headmistress in the making. 'Don't be a showoff, give us the lines in English.'

'As you please, madam,' said Catesby. *'I stretched ropes from bell tower to bell tower; and garlands from window to window; then chains of gold from star to star, and now I dance.'*

After he had finished, there was one lonely set of hands clapping. He met her three times the following week.

'I'm not very good at French,' she said, 'but I still think it was rude that Constance interrupted you. I can, however, speak some Punjabi and a little Hindi.'

'Which I am sure are more difficult than any European language.'

'My ayah taught me. She was infinitely patient.'

They were walking along the Backs. It was a perfect spring day and there was a lot of punt traffic on the river. Striped blazers, boaters – and too-soon-donned summer dresses draped with scarves and cardigans for warmth.

'How,' said Catesby, 'did you end up in India?'

'My father's first regiment, a mounted one, was a bit too smart for his bank account – particularly with a family to look after. So, Daddy transferred to a regiment of foot, which meant going to India. And how did you end up speaking such marvellous French? I bet you lived there.'

'I've never been to France. Never been outside England. My mother's Belgian.'

'How incredibly interesting.'

Catesby inwardly squirmed, but kept smiling. He thought that she was patronising him as a ragamuffin from the Lowestoft docks. But then he realised that her comment was genuine. She knew so little about him. She really did think that he was one of *them* – and wasn't it curious that his family had *never* taken him abroad? For the first time, Catesby realised how much he had changed. At first, he had imitated the voices and manners of those around him because he didn't want to stand out. But it was no longer imitation, the changes had become a part of him.

'That French you recited. One of my clever friends said it was Baudelaire.'

Catesby's smile turned warm and sincere. 'It was Rimbaud. He was a bad boy.'

'Oh, I love bad boys. Are you one?'

'I'm willing to take lessons.'

A week later she led him across Clare Bridge just as dusk was falling. There was a field with cows. She climbed the gate first. Catesby's heart had already begun to pulse with desire as her body swayed in front of him. When they were out of sight of any passers-by in the lane, she turned to him, 'Has anyone ever told you how strange you are?'

'I...'

'Don't answer. Just kiss me.'

Her tongue rooted in his mouth like a demented serpent. He drew her close in a haze of desire. Then she broke off the embrace.

'We need to find a spot,' she said, 'where there are no cow droppings. I don't want my mac smeared with cow poo.'

'Are you always so romantic?'

'You can be romantic and practical at the same time.'

'I don't think the cows have been in this field long. The grass looks hardly cropped at all.'

'I was right. You are a bit of a country boy.'

They found a clear space where there were no cow pats or anthills. Catesby helped her out of her mac and spread it on the ground. She was only a year older than Catesby, but much more experienced. She took his virginity with loving care – and, after a brief rest, she rode him, her hips moving in syncopation like a well-oiled machine, into another round of lovemaking.

Catesby kept in touch with her all through GMT (General Military Training) and when he was in OCTU (Officer Cadet Training Unit). Writing and receiving letters wasn't a problem then – and even encouraged as a leisure activity that kept up spirits. But once he began training with the Special Operations

Executive, letters – and all other forms of outside contact – were, although not expressly forbidden, discouraged. The rules were strict:

> 1. All letters will be handed to the House Commandant in a stamped unsealed envelope for censoring. You must not mention or even suggest that your letters are censored. All of your letters will be posted from London regardless of your actual location – which must never be mentioned or hinted at.
> 2. Your address for receiving letters will be the Post Box address given to you on arrival. No other address is permitted.
> 3. Incoming letters. All letters addressed to you will be read and censored. If they are not suitable, they will either be returned to sender marked 'Addressee Unknown' or destroyed.

Catesby longed for the woman from Homerton, but the things he wanted to say to her were not ones he wanted to share with the House Commandant. He decided to stop writing. He tried to contact her after he returned from France, but, ironically, the letters were returned 'Addressee Unknown'. He knew that she couldn't have joined SOE for the war was almost over and they were no longer recruiting. He remembered that she had once said something about immigrating to Australia when she was finally established as a teacher. Catesby never found out what she did, but often lay awake remembering her thighs and hips grinding him into a heavenly powder.

Tracking down H.H. Strachan was easier. He burnt to death after his tank 'brewed up' during the battle for Caen. He survived a mere two weeks after arriving in Normandy.

Suffolk: July 1942

Catesby's earliest encounter with Ewan Maurice Godfrey van Zwanenberg Phillips was at Gibraltar Barracks, the Suffolk Regiment's depot near Bury St. Edmunds. At first, Catesby assumed that Ewan was an example of the levelling that the war had created. Although he bore the humble rank of private, Ewan's full name sounded pretty posh and had echoes of aristocratic European forebears. A fellow officer had whispered that Ewan was related to Queen Wilhelmina of the Netherlands who headed a government in exile in London – but the connection had to be hushed up to protect Ewan from the risk of kidnapping or assassination. Knowing the Dutch link, Catesby once started speaking to Ewan in Flemish. Ewan looked bemused, but didn't reply.

'I apologise,' said Catesby. 'I know that your Dutch connections should be kept secret.'

'There is nothing at all secret about my Dutch connections.'

'Then, if you don't mind my asking, how exactly are you related to Queen Wilhelmina?'

Ewan laughed. 'Not at all – but I suppose one of her family's cooks might have come into the shop to buy a rack of lamb.'

Catesby looked confused.

'My forebears from the Netherlands were Jewish tradesmen. They lived in a village near Amsterdam. My grandfather ran a butchery business which was very successful. He immigrated to London where he sent my father to Harrow. My father opened an art gallery in Duke Street, St. James's and specialised in the avant-garde.' Ewan smiled. 'So, thank god, we are not aristocracy, but honest tradesmen.'

Although his manner and voice were modest and self-deprecating, Ewan was clearly an establishment insider whose connections stretched far beyond artists and collectors. The colonel realised this and quickly lifted him from the ranks and put him on his staff.

Catesby wasn't surprised that he had been summoned to see the colonel and was prepared for a bollocking. A route march led by Catesby the previous day had gone badly wrong. He wasn't very good at barking parade ground commands. In fact, he thought the whole business was silly. Catesby's platoon had been approaching a T-junction. The route they were to follow went off to the left at a 45-degree angle, but Catesby couldn't remember the correct command. He began to shout, 'left wheel' – then remembered that was only for a 90-degree turn. Oh shit, it was on the tip of his tongue – but 'diagonal march, left incline' was still eluding him when the first rank of the platoon tumbled into the drainage ditch. The soldiers, not having been given a command to change direction, were right to continue forging ahead. Catesby closed his eyes in shame. It was the same lions-led-by-donkeys obedience that had led to the bloodbath of the Somme, but on this occasion there were no casualties – other than some scuffed and muddy kit. There was a lot of laughter. It was obvious that what had happened was more piss-take than mistake. Catesby knew that reprimanding his soldiers would only make things worse. Instead, he turned to the senior NCO and said, 'Manton.'

'Yes, sir.'

'Take over and march the men back to the barracks.'

The sergeant gave a snappy salute and turned to the platoon. 'Come on, you lot. Let's get sorted.'

Catesby strode ahead reciting *Die Lorelei* and thinking of the Homerton girl. If anyone suspected him of being an enemy spy, he would say that he was just practising his German.

Die schönste Jungfrau sitzet…
The most beautiful maiden sits
On the heights, a wondrous marvel
Draped in golden jewels sparkling

The colonel had an impeccably trimmed officer's moustache

which, Catesby thought, seemed to be issued as a standard item of kit. Catesby was still waiting for his. The colonel was sitting behind a desk sorting through neatly arranged files with the assistance of Ewan. 'Ah,' said the colonel, 'this is him. Suffolk born and bred, eh?'

'Yes, sir.'

Catesby stood rigidly at attention and braced himself for a reprimand while the colonel perused his file. From time to time the colonel stroked his moustache and said, 'Hmm.' He finally turned to Catesby. 'I see you are a board school lad who made it into Cambridge.' The expression 'board school' was, even in 1942, an old-fashioned one referring to state-funded schools established by the Education Act of 1870. 'You must, Catesby, be very clever indeed. I went straight from Repton to Sandhurst – never got beyond basic maths and simple sentence writing. How did you become fluent in all these languages being brought up in Lowestoft?'

'My mother, sir, is a Belgian who was brought up speaking both French and Flemish.'

'And why did she teach them to you?'

'She said the languages would be useful if we ever went into the export trade. She did some translating herself.' Catesby suspected that the real reason was that his mother loathed life in England and wanted to take her children back to Antwerp. But, in the circumstances, that was a family secret that must stay secret.

'But you went to Cambridge instead. What did you learn there?'

'I studied medieval French literature and German.'

'I am sure the latter will be more useful.' The colonel gestured towards Ewan. 'Phillips here is another clever dog – and speaks foreign languages too. Apparently, it helps in the art trade.'

Ewan hid his embarrassment with an ironic smile. 'It can, sir, be useful.'

The colonel looked at Catesby's file again. 'I think that your skills would be wasted in a line infantry unit. And, in any case, your OCTU report is somewhat mixed.' He read it: '"This officer cadet displays a high degree of physical fitness and endurance. His problem-solving skills and map-reading are above average. He is, however, slovenly and sometimes lacking in discipline and respect for his superiors."' The colonel paused and shook his head. 'Not good, Catesby, not good – and it gets worse: "I cannot recommend this cadet for a commission on the basis of his leadership skills. In a command position, Cadet Catesby is often impatient with and disrespectful to those he is leading, who in turn become resentful. On the other hand, Cadet Catesby is a risk-taker who displays little fear of danger. He could prove a useful member of an unconventional unit operating behind enemy lines. He also has the skills required of a staff officer: comprehension, analysis and administration. On balance, I recommend Cadet Catesby for a commission."' The colonel looked up. 'Sadly, Catesby, it sounds like your men would shoot you before the Germans had a chance. On the other hand, you have qualities which could be invaluable to the war effort. I have recently received a top secret request asking me to recommend officers and men for a hush-hush unit which officially doesn't exist. You seem to meet the bill. Would you like to volunteer?'

'Only, sir, if it means fighting the Germans and not sitting behind a desk.'

'You can be sure of that. There is, however, one proviso. Once you volunteer, there is no backing out. If you change your mind, fail the selection process or don't complete the training course, you will be kept in a secret internment camp for the rest of the war. No one must know that this unit even exists. What is your answer?'

'I will, sir, volunteer.'

'Good.' The colonel handed over a sealed envelope. 'You will find a travel voucher and further instructions in there. And, may I remind both of you, this meeting never happened.'

As Catesby saluted and left the office, he felt exhilarated by the adventure facing him. He also felt a glow of warmth for the soldiers he would be leaving behind. Catesby had gone into the colonel's office expecting a reprimand for the drainage ditch business, but it had never been mentioned. The men had covered up for him.

Whether by coincidence or design Catesby found himself sharing a train carriage with Ewan on the trip to London for his SOE interview. They were alone in the compartment. Ewan, dressed in civilian clothes, was reading a copy of an arts magazine called *Apollo*. Catesby put his kitbag on the overhead rack and took out a copy of the *East Anglian Daily Times*.

As he settled down with his newspaper Catesby whispered, 'We mustn't talk if anyone joins us. I don't think we're allowed to show that we know each other.'

'I'm not sure. I still haven't completed all my training.'

'Are you with SOE too?'

'Good god, no. I'm in the Intelligence Corps – which isn't nearly that hush-hush. We openly flaunt our IC cap badges and insignia.'

Catesby was a little ashamed that he hadn't noticed Ewan's different insignia in the colonel's office. 'So, you're not with the Suffolks?'

'I haven't been for quite a while. Six months ago, I saw a notice asking for people with a knowledge of languages to volunteer for the Intelligence Corps. I thought that would be more interesting than the infantry, so I applied. The colonel was annoyed at losing his dogsbody.'

Catesby looked puzzled. 'So if you're no longer with the Suffolks, why were you in the colonel's office when I was being interviewed?'

'Ah, that is hush-hush.' Ewan smiled. 'But, as a fellow Suffolk boy, I'll tell you anyway. As odd as it may sound, the arts and the army overlap a lot more than you would guess. When I volunteered for the Intelligence Corps I got in touch with a friend called Anthony Blunt. He used to be my tutor at the Courtauld. I thought Anthony could give me some useful tips as he had been in Military Intelligence himself. In fact, his own Field Security unit were the last to escape from Boulogne before it fell to the Germans. His escape is an interesting story – but I probably shouldn't tell you about it.'

'Go on, we're Suffolk boys.'

'It doesn't show Anthony in a very good light. The Second Panzer Division had already captured Boulogne. His section had been given an order to evacuate the port three days earlier, but Anthony didn't seem aware of it. In the end, the evacuate message got picked up by his batman who roused Anthony from his slumbers and told him he was under orders to get his section to the docks immediately. By now his soldiers were on the verge of mutiny and ready to shoot him and go to the docks on their own. They were, literally, the last British soldiers left in the port. They managed to persuade the captain of a small coaster to take them to Dover. They then had to wait four hours for high tide – fortifying themselves with the ship's rum. They left Boulogne harbour under fire using the hulk of a burning oil tanker for cover.' Ewan paused. 'In any case, he is now out of uniform and works in Room 055 at the War Office.'

'Very interesting,' said Catesby, 'but I don't see what this story has to do with me – and what's Room 055?'

'Oh dear,' said Ewan, 'me and my big mouth. I shouldn't be in the Intelligence Corps. Please forget I ever mentioned Room 055.'

'I promise. By the way, if it isn't top secret, what are your Suffolk connections?'

'Not secret at all. My family have a small farm near Halesworth. My wife and son were evacuated there during the Blitz.'

'I've got family near there who are farm workers.'

Ewan looked out the window with an embarrassed expression. 'I realise that I come from a privileged background.'

'It was tactless of me to play the working-class card.'

Ewan smiled. 'Don't apologise. It can be a useful card to play – or at least have on your CV.'

Catesby was beginning to enjoy the game and said, 'Room 055.'

'You got it. You were talent spotted and your file was passed on to Anthony Blunt in Room 055.'

Catesby felt a small shudder of alarm. 'Who spotted me?'

'I don't know – I guess it was someone at Cambridge.'

Catesby did a quick mental inventory of fellow students and dons, but couldn't find a face that fitted. He shrugged and said, 'I was a member of the Labour Club.'

'That would have helped. Anthony does prefer lefties. I'm a bit of one myself.' Ewan smiled. 'In fact, the Courtauld is full of them. We even have a bomb thrower.'

'Good god.'

'Well not very big bombs. A chap in the photography department worked out a way of turning lab chemicals into little bombs to throw at Mosley's Blackshirts.'

'I'd go along with that. The Blackshirts are scum.'

'You would have got on fine at the Institute. But you weren't talent spotted for the Courtauld, you were spotted for SOE – and maybe SIS.' Ewan paused. 'I shouldn't say this, but I have seen your file.'

Catesby leaned forward. 'Well, I wouldn't be human if I didn't want to know what was in it.'

Ewan gave a sly smile. 'To be honest there were many candidates who were far more impressive – and more experienced.'

'Thanks.'

'But you ticked all the criteria. You're a linguist. You're physically fit; your politics are sound for fighting the Nazis – and you can get lost in a crowd. If you don't mind my saying so, you are a bit mousy: medium height and brown hair. You could pass for a native of any European country other than Scandinavia. And the person who spotted you also thinks you are a good mimic who can imitate the voices and manners of others. When you arrived at Cambridge, he said you were obviously a grammar school boy from the sticks – but by the end of your first term, you could pass as a minor public schoolboy, not a very rich one, but one suitably louche and ironic.'

'It was Basil, the medieval French don, wasn't it?'

'I can't say. But Room 055 were impressed by your ability to adapt to your environment. And a grand bonus in recruiting you is that, underneath your self-applied camouflage, you are impeccably working class. It's important that SOE doesn't become a playground for toffs who like a bit of danger.'

Catesby looked out the train window. It was a dreary day. Part of him wanted to go back to the drudgery of the infantry. He didn't like being manipulated by puppet masters in the shadows. But like it or not, it would become his vocation.

'I hope, sir, I haven't said too much.'

'Please don't call me sir. It's absurd.'

'The army has its quaint customs, but the good thing about the Intelligence Corps in London is that you can live a quasi-civilised life. Our office is just around the corner from the National Gallery where Myra Hess gives her lunchtime piano concerts. I've also managed to resume some of my AIA activities – but I have to be discreet.'

'What is the AIA?'

'The Artists International Association – which also has a somewhat lefty reputation. All the better, in my view, to fight fascism – but not everyone agrees.' Ewan paused and lowered his voice. 'You ought to know about the vetting system because you will soon be going through it. It's a background check to verify people for sensitive posts. I'm surprised that I got through it.' Ewan laughed. 'Ironically, my own job is now in the recruiting section – and I've seen letters from MI5 rejecting people on very slender grounds, such as sympathy to the Republicans during the Spanish Civil War. But MI5 was bombed at the beginning of the Blitz and most of its records on suspect lefties were destroyed. In fact, the Luftwaffe might have helped me get my current job – and helped Anthony get his too. But he's so well connected, it probably wouldn't have mattered. Anthony is a cousin of the Queen.'

Catesby felt, and not for the last time, that he was passing through the Looking Glass.

'Anthony, as I mentioned, now works in Room 055 – the most hush of all hushes. It's located in the War Office, but is actually the London HQ of MI5. You won't, however, be going there, even though Five still does a lot of vetting.' Ewan betrayed a half-smile. 'Does the name Selwyn Jepson mean anything to you?'

'You mean the Selwyn Jepson who writes detective novels – *The Death Gong* and *Rabbit's Paw*?'

'That's the one. The books are entertaining, but not overly challenging. In any case, Major Jepson is now in charge of recruiting for SOE's French section. He'll begin by testing you with his own schoolboy French. Embarrassing, but try to keep a straight face.'

The requisitioned hotel had known better days. The War Office had turned the building's Victorian grandeur into a bleak functional desert of bare light bulbs, folding tables and chairs, and blackout curtains. There was only one other person in the waiting room, a woman. 'I'm here very early,' she said in a quiet voice, 'I am sure you will go first.'

Catesby tried to place her accent. It was more French than English, but had a hint of something else in it too. Although she was diminutive, there was something grand about her. A moment later, Catesby was summoned into the interview room – dead on time to the second. He looked at the woman who said, 'Good luck.' He never saw her again. When he finally discovered who she was, years later, Catesby realised that he had briefly brushed shoulders with the ultimate in lonely courage.

The only furniture in the interview office was two folding chairs and a green metal desk. A blackout screen was still drawn even though it was midday. A single naked light bulb flickered, making the man behind the desk look like a character in a badly spliced film. The light bulb stopped flickering and Catesby was surprised to see that his interviewer was wearing the uniform of a Royal Navy captain. Where, thought Catesby, was Major Jepson? The interviewer's first questions provided an answer. The language was French and grammatically correct, but the accent was pure English schoolboy – although certainly better than Churchill's. The other clue was a rough notebook on the side of the desk, set well away from the crisp official paperwork. A furtive glance revealed what might have been a scribbled title on the notebook cover: *Man Running*. The naval uniform was part of another fiction. Catesby began to feel a certain warmth for Major Jepson.

Once Jepson was assured that Catesby spoke fluent French, he shifted into English. 'I see, Mr Catesby, that you are a grammar school boy from, of all places, Lowestoft. Any connection with the fishing industry?'

'Quite a few of my father's family worked on trawlers and drifters, but few managed it for a lifetime.'

'Are you handy with boats?'

'Not bad. I've done a lot of long-lining with my uncles – and I've also crewed a few yachts.'

'Good. How an earth did you learn to speak such excellent French?'

Catesby knew perfectly well that Jepson had the answer in the file in front of him, but – as he later learned – good interrogators always like to hear the answer from the interviewee's own lips. It's a way of checking for cracks in what might be a cover story. 'My mother,' said Catesby, 'is Belgian. My father died in an accident at sea when my sister and I were very young. I think she wanted to turn us into little Belgians in case she ever decided to go home.'

'How interesting.'

Catesby bit his lip and cursed himself for having said too much, but Jepson was like a truth serum.

'Would you have liked to have gone back to Belgium?' asked Jepson.

'I've never been to Belgium – and I would have hated leaving England.'

'But if you get accepted for this job, you will certainly leave England.'

'I meant leaving England as child and being brought up by my mother's family.'

'That sounds a bit disloyal to your poor mother. Did you meet many of her Belgian family?'

'When I was about ten, my mother's brother and his Russian wife came to live with us for two years. It was all very mysterious. I'm not sure what they did during the day. My sister grew very fond of the wife and learned a bit of Russian from her – although she always spoke French or English to me.'

'This gets even more interesting. Tell me more.'

'Well, the Russian aunt by marriage was certainly not a Bolshevik. She claimed her family were aristocracy and they ended up in Paris either after the revolution or the civil war. The story kept changing. In any case, her brothers ended up driving taxis in Paris.'

Jepson smiled. 'That sounds typical. In the twenties, you couldn't find a taxi in Paris that wasn't driven by a Romanov prince. Didn't you find your aunt and uncle fascinating?'

'A little, but at that age I only wanted to be an English boy who was good at football and cricket. It was all too foreign. I could never bring friends to a home that was hung with Roman Catholic icons where the grown-ups spoke English with an accent.'

'I can understand the way you felt. But it could soon be your turn to pretend to be a European who can't tell a cricket bat from a fence post.'

'I am sure I could keep the English boy undercover. I had to do it with my mother's family.'

'Good. Tell me more about her and her family.'

'My mother worked as a bargirl in a tavern near the docks in Antwerp where she met my dad who was a merchant sailor. She told me her father owned the bar, which I'm sure was true. My uncle used to brag about having helped smuggle Belgian beer and spirits to bootleggers during the American prohibition – which ties in with a family already established in the booze business. In fact, I have the impression that many on my mother's side may have been crooks.'

Jepson broke into a broad smile. 'That's great. We love crooks in this business. Can't get enough of them. Any forgers? Belgians do excellent forgeries.'

'Not that I know of.'

'Could you contact your Belgian relatives if necessary?'

'It would be difficult. I know very little about them other than my mother's maiden name, Bastin, which is pretty common. I know that her own mother was Flemish – and that a marriage across the linguistic divide was very unusual. But I know nothing more. My mother is the most close-lipped and secretive person that I have ever met.'

'Any idea why?'

Catesby reddened. 'I think my mother has something in her past that she wants to hide.'

'I see.' Jepson looked at Catesby over a steeple of fingertips. 'Tell me more.'

'I honestly can't tell you more about the Bastins or my mother's past. She is now a very conservative and devout Roman Catholic – mass and communion three or four times a week. She hated my leaving Cambridge to enlist in the army. In fact, we once had a serious argument when she praised Marshal Pétain for signing the armistice. She said that Pétain was a hero for saving the present generation of French and Belgians from the slaughter of the Great War. I believe one of her brothers was killed in that war, but she never talked about it.'

Jepson nodded. 'Your mother's views are in no way unusual – and understanding and changing them is an important challenge for the Resistance. Most people want a quiet life; they don't want themselves or their families to get killed. What do you think?'

'It's a difficult point of view to argue against. I think the only way to change minds is to show them that the Nazis can be defeated.'

'Good. Would it be fair to say that your volunteering for such dangerous duties is a reaction against your mother?'

For a second Catesby was tempted to address Major Jepson as Dr Freud, but decided such sarcasm would wreck his chances of getting into SOE. On the other hand, maybe Jepson's interest in psychological motivation was why he was a successful crime writer. Catesby remained silent while Jepson stared, expressionless, at the blackout curtain and waited.

'I think, sir, that may be partly true. But another reason is that I love my country – I know that must sound young and naïve.' Catesby paused. 'But it's not just Britain, I don't want to see Europe crushed by barbarism.'

'Most of Europe is Roman Catholic. You seemed very dismissive of your mother going to mass several times a week. Are you a practising Catholic?'

'No, sir. I lost my faith when I discovered my brain.'

Jepson nodded. 'That's a very French Enlightenment answer.'

'Thank you, sir. I love eighteenth-century French literature.'

'And what about Zola?'

Catesby could see that Jepson was checking out the lefty rumours. He answered unabashed. 'I admire Zola's bravery in standing up against injustice.'

The interview ended after exactly forty-five minutes. Catesby was told that he would be called back in a few days if he passed further background checks. Jepson directed him to leave by a door opposite the one by which he had entered. They didn't want the interviewees to see each other. Catesby realised that his having briefly caught sight of the small young woman had been a mistake.

The second meeting was two days later in the same office, but the uniform had changed. Jepson had been demoted two grades and was wearing the uniform of a major in the Buffs. Jepson offered no explanation for the change of service and rank – and Catesby thought it unwise to ask. He suspected, however, that Jepson's wearing his own uniform signalled an end of prevarication. Likewise, the interview was more direct and frank. It was no longer a question of whether or not to accept Catesby into SOE, but how he could best be used – and whether or not he still wanted to volunteer. 'Your chances of surviving,' said Jepson, 'are one out of two.'

Catesby quickly calculated that his chances were about the same as a Battle of Britain pilot.

'My job,' said Jepson, 'is deciding whether or not I'm willing to risk your life – and I've decided that I am. Your job is now to decide whether or not you want to take that risk. Don't answer now. I want you to go away for a couple of days and think about it. This shouldn't be a rash decision.'

There was an awkward silence. The naked light bulb flickered and Catesby tried not to fidget – or smile at the major's on and off again face.

'One more thing,' said Jepson, 'and this is very important. You must not discuss any of this with anyone, no matter how close they are to you. The decision is yours and yours alone.'

The third interview, the next morning, was short and sweet. Catesby simply said, 'Yes, I'll volunteer – and I have no reservations about doing so.'

The first place Catesby was sent for training was a grand Tudor manor house with private parklands. Previous guests included Queen Victoria and Otto von Bismarck. Gladstone had sometimes held cabinet meetings there. Catesby finally understood the joke that SOE stood for 'Stately 'omes of England'. If it hadn't been for the war, Catesby and many others like him would never have set foot on such privileged grounds.

The head of the training school was a Cold Stream Guards officer in his sixties who led morning runs from the front. He was tall and slim with a black moustache slightly flecked with grey. His voice was soft and polite, even though the words were hard and stern: 'Leaving these grounds is forbidden unless you are accompanied and have written authorisation. Use of the telephone is forbidden. You will hand me all your identity documents. You will only be known by your codename and will not reveal any details of your past to your fellow trainees. You will also hand to me any notebooks or cameras in your possession as well as any valuables and money in excess of five pounds. If you can't take the rigours of this course, you will be reassigned.'

Catesby did well. A lot of the course covered what he had already learned in the infantry – map-reading, weapons, identification of enemy units and ranks – but the heart of the training was learning to be ruthless and cunning. Hand-to-hand combat was savage and utterly merciless. You had to overcome any feelings of compassion or revulsion. One highly recommended method of executing a sentry with a silent kill was a commando knife straight up the rectum: 'Ever try shouting when you're breathing in?' If you didn't have a knife, a pencil through the eye was a useful expedient. And, if you didn't even have a pencil, a finger in the mouth was very effective. As the instructor, who always wore black cords and a polo neck, pointed out, 'The human mouth is a very vulnerable organ even when it isn't screaming for help. The flesh tears surprisingly easily. Once you get a finger in the corner of a mouth, you can rip open the cheek all the way to the ear. They don't like that. Puts them off their stride. And then you kick them in the balls. Or, in the case of an officer, the testicles. Kicking, grabbing, twisting, ripping and tearing male sex organs is always effective. And pretending to offer fellatio can be a deadly trick if you've got sharp teeth.' One of the trainees gave a nervous twitch. 'We are not here,' said the instructor, 'to teach you to be proper ladies and gentlemen.'

One in five of those in Catesby's training group were women. They were also a mixed lot in terms of nationality and social background. He not only heard voices speaking cockney English, but voices speaking French with a cockney accent – not to mention every regional French accent from Flanders to Marseille. There were also a number of plummy voices – and ones that, Catesby suspected, were fake plummy. The trainees were not allowed to reveal their backgrounds, but Catesby was certain there were Spaniards, Poles, Italians and other nationalities. A diversity of trades and professions was also revealed by trainees who exposed expertise in fields such as railway engineering, telephones, medicine, forestry, forgery and burglary.

The training included a lot of surprises. One was that the bar was open all day. In fact, the recruits were encouraged to drink so that their behaviour could be observed when they had too much. There were also a lot of women around in the bar. Most of them were not trainees, but members of FANY, the First Aid Nursing Yeomanry. The FANY girls were mostly posh well-connected women who provided clerical support and administration for the training school. They were also fantastic drivers who hared around dark country lanes with only sidelights for illumination. The FANY women had another mission: flirting with SOE recruits in the bar to see if drink and the prospect of romance would loosen their tongues. Catesby never fell for it. As a young man with modest self-esteem, he was always suspicious of women who found him attractive. He usually thought they were taking the piss, but at the training school he correctly guessed the posh girl flirting was part of the course.

The instructors, many of whom had returned from missions

in France, were full of dire warnings about how carelessness could cost lives. A favourite cautionary tale was that of an SOE agent who was captured only days after being parachuted into France because he looked right instead of left when crossing a road. Catesby's recurrent blunder, which lasted decades after the war, was getting into the wrong side of a vehicle. But, as with his suspicions of the FANY women, sometimes his reactions were the correct ones. All the trainees were tested with a late-night visit between three and four in the morning. The visit began with a bright light shined into the face of the sleeping recruit. The initial test was to check the first words of the startled trainee. Would they be: *What the fuck!* (very bad) or *C'est quoi ce bordel?* (very good). For some reason, Catesby once explained to a non-French speaker, swearing often referred to prostitutes and brothels. Catesby, of course, passed with flying colours. Still half-asleep, he had reverted to childhood and, imagining that his younger sister had come for comfort, replied affectionately, *Ça va, ma puce? You all right, love?* Regardless of how they replied, the trainees were then dragged away for a brutal mock interrogation which involved ice-cold water, torture and psychological tricks. The manner in which the instructors had transformed into Gestapo thugs was chillingly convincing. So realistic that a few trainees thought the training school had somehow been taken over by the Germans and the rough interrogations were real.

Catesby found out he had successfully completed the course when he was summoned to the commandant's office and handed an envelope with a travel voucher to Scotland. 'The next stage,' said the Coldstream Guards major without a name, 'is paramilitary training in the Highlands. It lasts three weeks. Once again, don't give anything away. If you see anyone that you met here, pretend they are complete strangers. If they talk to you, politely give them the cold shoulder.' The major went to a filing cabinet and took out a cotton bag with a drawstring which he handed over. 'Here are your IDs and valuables. Please check they are all there, but I won't ask you to sign a receipt. Paper records are devils waiting to pounce.'

A FANY driver was summoned to take Catesby and three other trainees to the nearest railway station. She drove via a myriad of country lanes to disorientate her passengers so that they would be clueless as to the exact location of the stately home where they had trained. Catesby guessed it was somewhere in Surrey. The only conversation was the FANY saying how much she loved driving and that her dream car would be a Bugatti Type 35.

There were no FANY in the bleak countryside of the West Highlands training camp at a remote place called Arisaig. Many of the drivers and staff were civilians dressed in country gear, who Catesby guessed, were gamekeepers, ghillies and other workers seconded from the laird's estate. There was a lot of venison and salmon on the menu – and very good whisky in the bar. It was welcome after grinding slogs through bogs and over mountains. There was more close quarters combat training which concentrated on the commando knife, but always ended with '…and then kick him in the balls.' The training that Catesby enjoyed most was how to use a pistol. The instructor was a refined Scot with an effortlessly superior manner who was obsessed with natural history. On one occasion, he brought a bone into the bar and offered a double whisky to anyone who could identify it. The bone was about twenty inches long and two inches in diameter. The instructor passed it around. What interested Catesby was the fact that it didn't seem to have a knob or a hollow on either end that would form a joint with another bone. He guessed that it was the rib of a seal. He was wrong, but the instructor/naturalist gave him a hopeful nod. No one else came closer.

'Any other guesses for a double single malt?' said the instructor, rattling the shillings in his trouser pocket.

One of the trainees, who was a bit drunk, piped up, 'It's a human ulna from the forearm of an SOE recruit who failed the course.'

'Don't be silly,' said the instructor, 'we bury their bodies far out at sea.' He picked up the bone and flourished it. 'This, as any fool can see, is the penis bone of a sperm whale. They're called bacula – or baculum in the singular. The human being is one of the few mammals that doesn't have a baculum.'

The next day's pistol training contradicted everything Catesby had been taught as an infantry officer. The naturalist-turned-small-arms-instructor began by mocking the 'old-fashioned' practice of sighting the pistol by eye along the barrel. 'We are not training you to be a Victorian duellist defending the honour of an adulterous wife.' The instructor imitated the stiff stance of the wronged Victorian worthy. He held the pistol upwards and slowly levelled it at an 'unspeakable cad' that he was about to dispatch to perdition. 'That way of firing a pistol is as obsolete as the marriage in question. We're going to teach you the double tap.' The instructor sprang sideways in a predatory crouch with both hands on the pistol and fired two shots which hit the human silhouette target just below the waist.

Someone shouted, 'And now kick him in the balls.'

'Not very funny. I think you would best engage a second or third enemy instead.' The instructor sprang sideways, again firing two double taps that put four more holes into the body of the silhouette. 'It's not a question of aiming at a target with your eyes. You aim at the enemy by instinct with your whole body. If you fire from the waist, you hit at the waist. Always use a two-handed grip and always fire two shots in quick succession.'

The rest of the day was devoted to practising the technique in live fire exercises – and learning how to conceal a pistol so that it could be drawn quickly. The day ended with a hands-on familiarisation session with the various types of small arms that SOE agents were likely to come in contact with. They then had to choose a pistol and practise disassembling it and assembling it blindfolded.

Catesby met the instructor a couple of times in the bar. Their knowledge of natural history overlapped most when it came to birds and fish. Catesby feared that his fondness for estuary birds – redshank, curlew and oystercatchers – might give him away as an East Anglian. Clues to origin and identity were forbidden topics of conversation. But after the war, it was usually okay to tell all. Catesby wasn't surprised to discover that the instructor, who developed a lifelong love of otters, had become a famous author.

Catesby's finest hour came during the escape, evasion and survival part of the course. At midday on the last day, the instructors divided the group into teams of four and said, 'It's time for lunch.' Each team was given a live rabbit. The person in Catesby's team who had been given the rabbit was obviously a townie. He held the squirming animal up by its ears and said, 'What the fuck am I supposed to do with this thing?'

'You're hurting him,' said Catesby, 'give him to me.'

The fellow team member handed over the rabbit. Catesby held the animal close to his chest with his left hand, then pulled the rabbit's head hard with his right until the neck vertebrae popped. He twisted the head in a complete circle.'

'You said I was hurting him – and now you've killed the poor little bunny.'

'At least he's out of pain. You shouldn't hold them up by their ears. Why don't you chaps start a fire?'

The townie held out his Fairbairn-Sykes double-edged fighting knife.

'He's already dead,' said Catesby.

'Aren't you going to gut and skin him?'

'You don't need a knife to gut and skin a rabbit.' Catesby put a finger a little way into the rabbit's rectum, enough to begin tearing the furry layer of skin and then ripped it apart all the way to the neck. In less than thirty seconds, the rabbit's skin was only attached at the neck and four paws. Catesby then shoved his hand up through the vent into the body cavity and pulled out the guts.

The others looked on in awe.

'Well,' said Catesby, 'I suppose I could bite off the paws and head with my teeth – but I would save that for extremis.'

'You want to borrow the knife?'

'Yes, thank you.'

Within fifteen minutes the rabbit was spitted and roasting. They were the first team to have finished cooking their lunch.

The chief instructor passed them a hipflask of whisky as a reward.

The penultimate part of Catesby's training was the parachute course at Ringway Aerodrome near Manchester. The location wasn't secret. Ringway was the UK's main base for parachute training. Catesby loved every minute of it and treasured the parachutist wings sewn on to his uniform. The training began with jumping off platforms about four feet from the ground to practise PLFs, Parachute Landing Falls. Once the techniques were mastered, they jumped through metal holes suspended twelve feet over straw matting. You had to keep your knees together and develop the agility of a cat jumping from a window ledge. If you didn't get your PLF right and twisted a knee or ankle, you washed out. To execute a perfect PLF, you needed to land on the balls of your feet and cover your face with your forearms before doing a balletic turn to your left. The idea was that you cushioned the force of landing with the meaty part of your thigh and the muscles on the side of your back, what anatomy books call latissimus dorsi. It was a movement that required the grace of a Nijinsky – and Catesby was proud that he had mastered it. But on some occasions, his PLF was heels, buttocks and back of head.

The first jump with a parachute was from a balloon. Four trainee jumpers and a dispatcher sat facing each other on a circular bench suspended under the balloon while it rose to a thousand feet above the ground. When it was your turn, the dispatcher shouted 'Go' and you went. The first quick plunge, before the parachute opened, you felt like an emptied bucket of water sliding down a drain. Some found it sickening, Catesby found it thrilling. As the canopy billowed, exhilaration was replaced by heavenly peace. Catesby shouted, 'I'm an angel!' He wanted the descent to last forever. Sadly, the trees and figures on the ground were growing larger and larger. The landing wasn't as hard as Catesby thought it would be, but that might have been a trick of the adrenalin rush. It was a calm day, so he wasn't dragged along by the wind. There was no need to press the quick-release button, an emergency measure to separate jumper from the chute, so he slipped out of the harness and gathered up the canopy. He remembered the jokes of the WRAF girls in the packing shed when they picked up their parachutes, 'If it doesn't open, duck, bring it back and we'll give you a new one.'

The next jumps were from aging Whitley bombers, nicknamed the Flying Coffins. The Whitley made a hell of racket as it built up enough revs to take off and continued to shudder after it was airborne. The noise inside the obsolete bomber was deafening and the dispatcher had to shout and point to make himself understood. These jumps were designed specifically for SOE agents, who were parachuted from much lower heights than infantry and in much smaller numbers. A jump from five hundred feet meant that you hit the ground in less than twenty seconds and there was no time to correct a parachute malfunction. The most feared malfunction was the Roman Candle when, for some strange reason, the canopy silk fails to billow open and streams tightly into itself. There was even a song about it, *Beautiful Streamer*, sung to the tune of *Beautiful Dreamer*:

> *Beautiful streamer, why should you be?*
> *Blue skies above and no canopy.*
> *Billowing white silk is what I should see,*
> *Beautiful streamer, please open for me.*

The remaining four qualifying jumps were all at night and all at low altitude. Catesby still had no fear of jumping out of planes. He especially loved the magic transition from the deafening noise of the Whitley and the rough grip of the slipstream which flung you horizontal, to floating like a moth in the silence of the night. Sadly, it only lasted a few seconds before the earth gave you an unexpected rough kiss. The problem with night jumps was judging your height from the ground. You needed to know this to pull the toggle which released the equipment strapped to your legs – ideally at fifteen feet – and to prepare yourself for a PLF. On one jump, Catesby fixed his eyes on a large spreading chestnut tree in the middle of the landing ground. When he got level with the top of the tree, he would release the toggle. A second later, the chestnut tree turned into a lone patch of heather and he was lying next to it.

The final 'Stately 'ome of England' in Catesby's SOE training was a large estate in Hampshire replete with several manor houses. They weren't supposed to know it was Beaulieu, but everyone did. The estate was usually called 'The Finishing School'. There were no punishing route marches or commando training. The students were not being prepared for the physical rigours of leading a clandestine life in enemy occupied lands, but for the mental and emotional strains of double lives. A big part of the course was swotting up on the different types of police and intelligence services they would encounter. It was important to recognise different uniforms and different allegiances. Local gendarmes were not always dangerous and sometimes helpful, but the Vichy police reserves and the paramilitary were ultra violent.

In essence, the Finishing School was about security: plausible cover stories, secure communications and dealing with interrogations. Learning how to maintain a cover story under interrogation was the most difficult part of the course. It was about the art of staying calm while walking a tightrope over the chasm of torture and death. There are four questions that even the most plodding cop will ask:

1 Who are you?
2 Where are you from?
3 What identification papers are you carrying?
4 What are you doing here?

The best way to reply is in a voice that is slow, clear and firm. Try to convince that cop that you are the most boring and ordinary person on the planet. Avoid responses that lead to further questions. Each answer should be a dead end. In most cases, the cop will let you go. Taking someone in for questioning will mean extra work. But if he does take you in, the questions from a senior cop will be a lot more difficult:

1 How did you get here?
2 Where are you going?
3 Who is and where is the last person you spoke to?
4 Who knows your name and details?

If you don't get past that round, you may find yourself deeply in the shit. The next stage will be both physical and psychological torture – or they might just kill you. The important thing is to stick to your cover story and deny everything else – no matter what the price you have to pay.

Two entire days were devoted to exercises where students and staff interrogated each other. Things often got rough and bad tempered. There was a lot of self-discovery taking place. Catesby swore that he would never allow himself to be arrested. He would either fight, run or take the L pill. He confided as much to one of the instructors who replied, 'A lot of people feel that way, but try to do those things when five of them are lying on top of you.'

Some of the exercises were less gloomy. One was: 'How would you identify yourself as a member of SOE to another member of SOE if you were on the run and didn't know the current passwords?' Everyone came up with the same phrase to prove you had done SOE training: '… and then you kick him in the balls.' Another solution would be to identify yourself by translating London underground stations into French codenames. If someone said, *Je suis un ange*, the other SOE agent would prove their bona fides by answering, *J'habite rue Boulanger* or *Je m'appelle Marie le Bon*. There were some playful translations for Cockfosters and Shepherd's Bush, but the instructors agreed it would be a good idea. No Vichy collabo cop or Gestapo officer would ever guess the secret code.

The final test was an exercise that lasted five days. The trainees were divided into groups of three and given specific tasks: breaking into offices and photographing accounts and employee details; placing mock explosives on railway bridges or electricity substations; stealing cars and police uniforms. Catesby's group was given the most difficult task: springing an inmate from HMP Parkhurst on the Isle of Wight. The prisoner wasn't a real criminal, but an Intelligence Corps NCO posing as one. With the exception of the governor, none of the prison staff knew that he was a fake.

One of Catesby's team pretended to be the wife of the 'prisoner' and passed on two sets of details during a visiting day: one fake and one genuine. The fake one was discovered by the guards who were then on alert. The morning of the escape one of Catesby's team used a crossbow to catapult one end of a rope ladder over the prison wall during an exercise period. It was part of the fake escape plan intended to distract attention from the real one. Whistles immediately started blowing, but the accomplice had already ditched the crossbow and was on the run. Meanwhile, guards and police were sprinting to both sides of the wall. They nabbed one fleet prisoner who had actually managed to get over the top and hauled down two others who were climbing the rope ladder from the inside. Meanwhile, the prisoner to be sprung was hidden in a laundry basket. The normal checks were not carried out on the departing laundry van as so many staff were busy trying to prevent a mass escape. A few minutes later, Catesby, in a policeman's uniform, flagged down the laundry van, dragged out the hidden prisoner, handcuffed him and bundled him into a waiting car. The van driver was surprised that the car was unmarked, that there was only one cop and that the prisoner had gone without a struggle – but didn't ask questions.

The escape to the mainland was carried out undercover of darkness in a two-man folding canoe. Catesby and the escapee crossed the Solent and rode the tide up the Beaulieu River to Buckler's Hard where they disembarked. They were carrying the canoe up the bank when they were pounced on by an alert Home Guard unit. They were frogmarched to the yacht club which the Home Guard was using as an HQ. Catesby decided to wait for the police to arrive before he divulged the secret phone number which was the SOE get-out-of-jail-free card. Catesby and the escapee were given cups of tea while they waited. One of the Home Guards asked, '*Sprechen Sie Englisch?*' Catesby didn't respond.

In the end, Catesby didn't have to use the secret phone number – which was only to be divulged as a last resort. When the cops arrived, they were accompanied by staff from the Beaulieu training centre a few miles away. All hell seemed to have broken loose. A red-faced chief constable was shouting at the Beaulieu commandant who responded with an aloof diffidence that must have been maddening. It soon became apparent that the escapee wasn't the fake prisoner planted by SOE, but a real prisoner. At first, Catesby thought it must have been a massive cock-up, but he later realised there was method in the madness. For some time SOE had been trying to arrange the release of Midnight Slim, a skilled forger and safe-cracker, but the legal authorities had dug their heels in. Catesby's team had been unwitting pawns in an SOE ruse.

There were two weeks of final briefings and additional training before Catesby was deployed to France. The most enigmatic was a lecture in the St. Ermin's Hotel in which Catesby was an audience of one. In later years, Catesby would get to know the hotel and its louche bar, the Caxton, very well. It was a fifty-five-second stroll – he often timed it – from SIS HQ at Broadway Buildings to the Caxton Bar. The bar's atmosphere of intimate confidentiality combined with double G&Ts loosened tongues. Perhaps too much so. Catesby grew suspicious of fellow SIS officers who spent too much time there.

Even as a young man, Catesby's aesthetic sense had begun to discern the boundaries between refined good taste and nouveau riche vulgarity. He thought that St. Ermin's double-height foyer and its neo-baroque undulating balcony were the former, but the art nouveau plasterwork was the latter. Late in life, Catesby wished that he had become an artist or art historian instead of a spy – but all three professions relied on perception and judgement. And, for a spy, a mastery of *trompe-l'œil* was essential.

Catesby met Kim Philby in a committee room on the fourth floor of the hotel. At the time, Catesby hadn't a clue who Philby was, but Philby knew who Catesby was – and probably continued to do so long after he had received the Order of Lenin and his face appeared on a Soviet postage stamp. Catesby's first impression was that Kim Philby was a man who knew how to make others relax. The blackout curtains were drawn and sunlight filled the room. Philby was self-deprecating and he spoke with a slight stutter. But his manners were those of a born-to-power mandarin – and his half-smile always sardonic. It was impossible not to like him and trust him.

'Please sit down.' Philby looked at his watch. 'It's already half past twelve. I'm having a pre-prandial drink. Would you like one?'

'Yes, please.'

Philby looked in a low cabinet under the window and shook a bottle. 'No gin left. Anthony must have been here before us. So, it's either whisky or whisky.'

'Whisky would be fine.'

Philby poured two fingers in each glass. 'I see that you were at King's.'

'Yes, but only for one year.'

'Did you know Basil?'

'He was my tutor.' The question confirmed Catesby's suspicion that Basil, whose only interests appeared to be orchids, High Church Anglicanism and vintage port, had a double life as a talent spotter for SOE and SIS.

'Quite an eccentric. He was the only don who didn't mind being called by his first name. He had a crush on Anthony. But who didn't?'

Catesby nodded as he sipped his whisky and tried to look blasé. As if such secrets were everyday club chatter.

'I was,' said Philby, 'on the staff at Beaulieu until a few months ago. It was a temporary assignment – and demolitions aren't my strong point. But the FANY were accommodating. I'm now in charge of D Section.' Philby smiled. 'I don't know what the D stands for. I hope it's not demolitions. In any case, the Special

Operations Executive is growing fast – too fast for some people. And mistakes have been made. A couple of years ago, you, with your fluent Flemish, would have been earmarked for Section N – and you would now almost certainly be dead or rotting in a prison camp. Your Belgian-accented French suggested that Belgium or Northern France would be the perfect fit, but that isn't to be. You're going to be dropped into the Limoges area – about as *France profonde* as it gets. Have you ever been there?'

'I've never been to France – or any place foreign.' Catesby smiled. 'Except Scotland and Norfolk.' He wasn't sure Philby got the joke.

'In any case, the Resistance in the Limousin is growing faster than in any other part of France. Someone compared it to the Peasants' Revolt of 1381 – and its leader, Georges Guingouin, to Wat Tyler. But I hope Guingouin and his peasant army have a happier outcome. Unfortunately, you won't have time to become more knowledgeable about the Limousin before you are deployed.' Philby picked up a piece of paper. 'Here are your tasks. It's a big order and the priorities may change when you're on the ground. One: liaise with existing Resistance movements and arrange for airdrops of weapons and supplies. There are, apparently, five times as many *résistants* as there are guns for them to carry. Arming them is an urgent priority. Two: arrange training sessions for the *résistants* to learn how to use the weapons and explosives that we send them. How are you with the Sten?'

'I find it jams a lot.'

'But they're cheap and plentiful. Three: wireless transmitters.' Philby shook his head. 'There is a lamentable shortage of radios and trained W/T operators in this part of France. It is clearly the most dangerous job in SOE. There is a big push to train as many W/T operators as quickly as possible. I can't say how many we will send to you. But one of your jobs will be to meet them, look after them and place them where they are most needed. This means that you will have to travel outside the Limoges area. Your cover story and identity documents must be perfect.'

Catesby felt a chill run down his spine. It wasn't just going to be a matter of hiding in the woods in between blowing up railway lines and taking pot shots at German convoys.

'Task four: liaise with other réseaux in your area – and out of your area too. We reckon there are over three hundred resistance groups in France; some of whom have been rounded up and terminated, but they could spring to life again. The important thing is to bring all these réseaux together under one command – which looks like it's going to be de Gaulle. At the moment, control of the Resistance networks is mostly divided between BCRA and SOE F.' Philby paused. 'Excuse me, it looks like you have a question.'

'Excuse my ignorance, but who are BCRA?'

Philby frowned. 'It sounds like the Beaulieu staff are even more close-lipped than when I was there – and, in this case, it's a mistake. You can't leave agents to blunder in the dark. BCRA are the *Bureau Central de Renseignements et d'Action*. God, you should know that.'

Catesby felt a twinge of self-doubt. Had the acronym been lost in the alphabet soup that they had been bombarded with in various lectures?

Philby refilled their whisky glasses. 'You'll be arriving in France during a crucial time when the unified leadership of the Resistance is still in the balance. The most important figure is a leader codenamed Max. I'm not going to tell you who he is. So, if you are captured before you find out Max's real identity, the Gestapo will torture you in vain. Where was I?'

'I'm not sure.'

'BCRA and unifying the Resistance. A crucial task, otherwise the rivalries and backstabbing could lead to chaos. At some point, we want you to liaise with Max and report back to London the latest on the state of play. Although god only knows where he is at the moment.'

Catesby wondered if Philby was a little drunk. The Max business seemed like an impossible task and one far above his rank and status. But at the time, no one knew that Max would become a legend and an icon.

'I don't think I need to tell you about your other tasks.

Beaulieu would already have done that. Concentrate, of course, on cutting lines of transportation and communication. This will be particularly important when we get around to invading. And there's a rubber-making factory near Limoges that needs taking out. Sabotage would be better than the RAF – fewer civilian casualties. Any questions?'

'No.'

'Oh, and one last thing: security. You will almost certainly meet double agents – and even triple agents.'

At the time, Catesby was unaware of the irony. But in retrospect, hearing those words from Kim Philby himself was priceless.

'It's important not to let the agent in question know that you know he is doubled, but to report your knowledge or suspicions back to London. And sometimes double agents can be useful conduits for disinformation.'

Someone knocked on the door – and then peeped in without waiting for a reply.

'Hello, Henry. I was just finishing with Mr Catesby.'

'We're all waiting for you. It's lunch or die.'

The visitor was silky and smooth – and had all the characteristics of a Whitehall insider who preferred the shadows. It was the first time that Catesby was to see his future boss, Henry Bone.

Philby looked at Bone. 'What sort of state is Guy in?'

'Not blotto yet, but getting there.'

Philby held his hand out to Catesby and fixed him with a warm smile. 'Goodbye and good luck.'

As he was crossing the undulating rococo foyer of the hotel, Catesby felt a bit seasick. His existence seemed to be taking a turn as bizarre as it was dangerous. A voice from someone hurrying in the opposite direction roused him from his delirium.

'Have you just been to see the Head of the Iberian Section?' It was Ewan. He was in a uniform which now bore the three pips of a captain and was carrying a file under his arm.

'No, I've just had an interview with the Head of Section D.'

Ewan gave an enigmatic smile. 'Oh, he told you that, did he? He hasn't been in D for over a year.'

'Smoothed-down dark hair, side parting? Speaks with a slight stutter?'

'That's him,' said Ewan.

'He's gone to the bar with someone called Henry.'

'Thanks, I will divert to the Caxton. We must meet up soon. Sorry, I'm in a bit of rush.'

As Catesby walked into the cold late-winter air, his mind cleared. He began to perceive a secret world where job titles were temporary cover stories – and where the unknown would remain unknown.

England: February 1943

There wasn't time for a last visit home to Lowestoft, which in a way pleased Catesby. It would have been awkward and difficult. He wrote a letter to his mother in English, which was unusual, because he didn't want to arouse the censor.

> Dear Mum,
> It was great seeing you and Freddie at Christmas, but it doesn't look like another leave is in the offing. I won't bore you with details of my current army assignment which is an endless round of marching and boring training. I am, however, healthy and well fed (but I do miss your cooking) and get along fine with my fellow officers.
> Please don't worry about me. If I die of anything, it will be boredom. In fact, living in Lowestoft is probably a lot more dangerous than being here. Let me know if you ever want to change places. (That's a joke, Mum.)
> Sorry to hear that Ralph got arrested for netting by the water bailiffs, but Freddie says it's only a fine (this time). I used to love babbing for eels with him when I was a boy. Some of those eels were over two foot long! If Ralph's eels and pike are now off the menu, I'm sure a pheasant or two might 'just turn up' when I'm next home.
>
> Look forward to seeing you again.
>
> Your loving son,
>
> William

Catesby addressed and stamped the envelope, but left it unsealed as instructed. He hoped the censors were too busy to pass on information about potential poaching to the Suffolk police. Catesby was disappointed that he wouldn't get a chance to see his sister Freddie before being sent to France. Her London college, where she was a first-year student in Slavonic languages, had been evacuated to Oxford. He had tried to arrange a last rendezvous in London, but hadn't heard back from her. Maybe the censors had stopped her letters. Freddie had seemed to twig that her brother had volunteered for something dangerous and secret. One of her last letters had said, *Please, Will, with your brains you can get a nice desk job*, which might have set alarm bells ringing. As a big brother in a fatherless family, Catesby had always felt a strong responsibility to protect his sister. Otherwise, he would have loved her to be parachuting into France with him. They had always worked as a perfect team. But the thought of her coming to harm was his greatest fear.

Cut off from family or a lover, Catesby's final evening in England was spent in a pub in Fitzrovia – not far from the Wimpole Street flat where SOE agents waiting for deployment holed up. Catesby had been lying fully clothed on his bed staring at the ceiling with a Proust novel spread open and unread on his chest, when he was called to the phone. It was Ewan's voice. 'If you're not busy, I thought you might like to meet some interesting people before you leave.'

The pub was a bohemian gin joint where beards, smocks and eccentricity mixed effortlessly with men and women in uniform. A woman, who looked about sixty, made a beeline for Ewan. She quickly eyed up Catesby, turned back to Ewan and drawled, 'Good evening, darling. Give us a kiss.'

Ewan gave her a peck.

'Have you heard the latest?' said the woman.

'No, Nina, but I'm sure you have.'

'Don't be rude,' she said, giving Ewan a slap. 'It is so *drôle*, so absolutely *drôle*. What are we drinking?'

'We'd love to, Nina, but we're on our way to meet Hardy.'

She turned to Catesby. 'Then you'd better tidy yourself up, darling.' She pinched both sides of Catesby's tunic and shook her head. 'You must have this taken in. Uniforms shouldn't hang; they should cling and show a soldier's body. My father was in the army and he would never have gone out like this. But I shouldn't be rude. Perhaps you've had a long journey and had to sleep in your uniform.'

Catesby was more amused than offended. Meanwhile, the barman came over and placed an expensive-looking cocktail in front of Nina. 'Compliments, madam, of Major Amies.'

'Please,' she said, 'give him my warmest thanks.' She turned to Ewan. 'Hardy seems to have paid your ransom. For now, *au revoir, mon petit chou.* Be lovely to have a chat later.'

As they pushed their way through the bar throng, Catesby asked, 'Who was she?'

'Nina Hamnett, the Queen of Fitzrovia. She has seen better days.'

'You can certainly see the vestiges of beauty.'

'She posed for Gaudier-Brzeska, Sickert and Augustus John. When she lived in Paris, she knew everyone: Picasso, Cocteau, Pound, Modigliani, Diaghilev. With all her connections, she would be a great agent for SIS – except she would tell everyone in the pub what she was doing. Nina could have been a very good artist herself, but she now prefers drinking to painting.'

'Ah, finally.' The person greeting them was the most impeccably dressed officer that Catesby had ever seen. He looked like a model. His uniform fitted perfectly in every way.

'Thank you for rescuing us from Nina. She was trying to cadge drinks in exchange for telling us about Bunny and Angelica – *so absolutely drôle.*'

'Well,' said the major, 'I suppose marrying your father's lover is at least a little bit *drôle.* I do feel sorry for Nina – and I like indulging her taste for Old Fashions, which Albert mixes with flawless acumen.' The perfectly uniformed major looked at Catesby. 'In her younger days she was stunning. When she met Modigliani she was dancing naked on a table at the Rotonde.'

'Did it persuade Modigliani to buy her a drink?'

'And a lot more.' The major extended a hand. 'Good evening. My name's Hardy Amies.'

'Hello, I'm...' Catesby paused, wondering if he should give his codename or his real name.

'You're William Catesby. I've seen your file...' Amies looked towards the bar. 'Oh god, here she comes again. Poor thing. Wish I could do more. We'd better go to the private room. I've already booked it.'

The room was a panelled alcove without windows, but had a door that could be locked. As soon as they were ensconced, the barman turned up with a bottle of wine in a silver ice bucket and three glasses.

'Thank you, Albert,' said Amies. The barman closed the door behind him. Amies caressed the bottle. 'Not from the pub's cellar, of course, but Grand Cru Chablis spirited out of France by Lysander. And even better, the bottles came wrapped against breakages in Lucien Lelong dresses. And what do we send them in return? Sten guns and explosives.' Amies picked up the bottle and half-filled the glasses. 'Savour slowly.'

'I think,' said Ewan, 'we should drink a toast to William who, in a matter of hours, will be parachuting into the beautiful country that produced this wonderful wine.'

'Stand up, gentlemen,' intoned Amies. 'To the brave and reso-lute William Catesby, who will soon embark on a dangerous journey for freedom, human decency and civilisation.'

They clinked glasses and Catesby fought hard to hold back the tears. He realised that the bohemian pubs of Fitzrovia and the mould-breaking artists who drank, argued and loved in them would be high on any Nazi extermination list.

'We can sit down again,' said Amies. He turned to Catesby. 'I don't mind telling you, William, that I tried to poach you for T Section. Your Belgian-accented French and Flemish would have been perfect.'

Catesby stirred a little uneasily. The words were almost an exact echo of what Kim Philby, pretending to be the D Section boss, had said to him earlier.

'Perhaps,' said Amies, 'we can arrange a transfer later in the war.'

'I will,' said Catesby, 'serve wherever I can be most useful.'

Amies laughed. 'Well, what else could you say?' He turned to Ewan and his voice dropped to a whisper. 'I must say, I'm getting more and more worried about the slippery Kim Philby.'

'In what way?'

'I sometimes wonder who he's working for.'

'I know. SOE one moment, then D Section – and now SIS Iberian desk.'

'No. Something more sinister. Kim has been pestering me to pass on a secret – a very top secret – that has absolutely nothing to do with any of his jobs, past or present.'

Ewan gave, what Catesby considered, an inappropriate laugh.

'I don't know who he's working for or what he's up to,' whispered Amies as he stroked the fine cloth of his uniform tunic, 'but Philby wants to know the name of my tailor.'

The car sent to pick up Catesby and the two others was an open-topped Humber Super Snipe. The tall elegant FANY driver invited her passengers to 'hop into the hearse'. The long drive to the departure airfield, not far from the coast near Chichester, was cold and exposed – a foretaste of the Halifax bomber flight with its open 'Joe hole' that awaited Catesby and his W/T operator. The other SOE agent was a woman who said little, other than that she was going to the Loire by Lysander.

The long wait for nightfall was punctuated by briefings, final clothing checks – it was essential that none of their civilian gear had a hint of England – and issue of weapons. The final preparations took place in a large redbrick Tudor cottage overlooking the coast, hidden from the road by tall hedges. The interior of the cottage reeked of shabby genteel Englishness – oddly complemented by someone playing sentimental French songs on a phonograph. A favourite, *J'attendrai,* was a tale of a woman pledging to faithfully wait for her lover to return from the war. It was, however, played so often that the tune began to grate.

A blimpish voice eventually bellowed, 'Turn that bloody thing off!' and was met with a round of applause. 'No sense waiting, girl, he isn't going to come back.'

The bar was always open and the drinks were on the house, but no one got drunk. The danger and uncertainty facing the SOE agents awaiting their flights would have sobered up even the most confirmed dipso. The mood got darker when they were summoned to receive their drugs allowance and a briefing on how to use them. The green pills were Benzedrine.

'Never take more than one every twelve hours. That's more than enough to keep you going at full tilt without sleep for up to three days. If you exceed that dose, you might go loopy.' The medical officer's face turned serious as he spread some square white pills on the table before him. 'Taking one of these is entirely voluntary and a matter of conscience. If you are a Roman Catholic, I have been told to inform you that the Archbishop of Westminster has stated that taking such a pill would not be considered the mortal sin of suicide – provided that your reason for taking the pill was to avoid giving away information under torture that could endanger the lives of others. I have a copy of the Archbishop's statement of dispensation if you care to read it.'

There was a deathly hush. Catesby was sure that he wasn't the only one who wanted to get back to the free bar and its relaxing banter.

The medical officer continued. 'We call it the L pill because it contains a lethal dose of cyanide. It is square shaped with sharp corners so that you will not mistake the L pill for anything else – and can recognise it by feel alone. You could disguise it as a shirt button or sew it into your clothing – or hide it in a lipstick tube or the heel of a shoe. It works very quickly, about thirty seconds, and the death will be painless. But you must bite down hard on the pill to release the liquid cyanide, otherwise it would pass harmlessly through the body. Once again, carrying the L pill is your choice.'

The medical officer left the room. One by one the SOE agents shuffled forwards to pocket their cyanide pills – only two, one man and one woman, refused to take one.

The final pre-deployment meal was called The Last Supper, but the mood was buoyant. Excitement and wine had kicked out the gloom. They were all seated at a long trestle table in a converted outbuilding with whitewashed walls. Catesby had a chance to chat to his W/T operator who turned out to be another Suffolk person. Was there a plan to team up yokels? But Jimmy Fenn was a yokel turned Londoner. His voice was now more East End then East Suffolk.

Owing to SOE confidentiality, it was only towards the end of the war that Catesby discovered Jimmy's past. He was the youngest of eight siblings and had done a flit to London when he was thirteen to follow a much-admired older brother. He came from a family of farm workers who lived in a tied cottage in a corner of northeast Suffolk called The Saints. Jimmy's first job in London was working as a lookout for a fast-rising Whitechapel gangster called Jack the Spot. Jimmy had a piercing whistle that the villains could hear from a quarter of a mile away. And Jimmy was so fleet of foot he could outrun any policeman or rival villain. He progressed from lookout to delivery boy, passing on stuff that had been nicked to East End shopkeepers. Jack was a crook who put number one first, but there was an idealistic side too. He protected Jewish shopkeepers from the Blackshirts and other gangsters – but he did charge them ten pounds for the service.

A big part of Jack Spot's empire was gambling. He got Jimmy involved with the illegal side of greyhound racing and betting. Meanwhile, Jimmy had discovered girls – but preferred ones that weren't involved with the gangs. He knew that could be dangerous. He developed a taste for French au pairs who were often found perambulating their charges through Kensington Gardens. The au pairs were safe to chat up. No East End villain was going to be offended – and their protective brothers and fathers were far away. One au pair in particular attracted him. She required little courting. She was hungry for love, bored with au pairing and unhappy with the family who used her, not just to look after the kids, but as a general dogsbody. Jimmy and the unhappy au pair made passionate love in every nook and corner they could find. In retrospect, Jimmy realised she had wanted to get pregnant as an excuse to leave her job and go back to

France. Meanwhile, Jimmy was getting disillusioned with life as an apprentice villain. A fight in the Edgeware Road had turned nasty with slashed faces, smashed testicles and a couple of eyes knocked out. Jimmy decided it was time to start a new life. The au pair took him back to her family home in Nanteuil-le-Haudouin so she could have their baby – and where they duly got married in the local *mairie*. It turned out that the girl's father was an electrician who also ran a radio shop. He took Jimmy on as an apprentice, and he developed a flair for assembling radios from cheaply purchased components to be sold as *fabrication artisanale* sets. Jimmy loved his wife and son, but found life in the one-horse town twenty-five miles north of Paris dead boring. When war broke out, he volunteered for the Ambulance Service. He narrowly avoided capture as the Germans overran northern France and made it back to England via Dunkirk. Jimmy's knowledge of radios and French made him an ideal recruit for SOE.

It was after ten p.m. when they were driven to the waiting four-engined Halifax. The sky was clear, but the moon was waning. This was the last night in the current moon phase that they could do the drop. There had been a lot of hugs and kisses before they left to board the converted Halifax bomber – and many wishes to have a *bonne merde*, 'a good shit', the French equivalent of 'break a leg', which was a less fateful send-off to someone about to make a low-level parachute jump. There was one more ritual to be carried out before take-off. Catesby and Jimmy unbuttoned their flying overalls and peed on the tail wheel of the Halifax. It was an SOE tradition that even some of the women managed although it required unbuttoning a one-piece flight suit and rolling it down to the ankles.

The Germans had been defeated at Stalingrad and an allied victory now seemed almost assured, but being alive to celebrate that victory was far from certain. Catesby was twenty years old and vividly aware that an entire life stretched before him. Nonetheless, the adrenalin was also flowing. He was eager to fight and have adventures. But in the dark watches of the night he often lay awake and wondered how unlucky it would be if he ended up as one of the last British soldiers killed in the war – like Wilfred Owen in the previous one. It was a fear that Catesby regarded as weakness and once, while still in training, he mentioned it to an SOE officer who had been one of the first to be infiltrated into France. The officer, who ended the war as a highly decorated SOE legend, laughed and said, 'Don't worry. We all think that. At least, those of us who are sane…' He paused and shrugged, '…or remain sane.'

The flight time was under three hours – including a diversion for a supply drop. The interior of the Halifax bomber was a cramped metal haze of fuselage ribs and pipes. The only object from the human world was the Elsan toilet below the upper gunner. There were no curtains, so if you got caught short, your humiliation would be open to public view. There were no piss tubes, but the turret gunners usually brought along empty bottles as an alternative to the Elsan as they were not supposed to leave their posts. The sub-zero temperatures always created an urge to pee and there was also a huge empty fruit tin in front of the rear turret.

Catesby knew they were approaching the drop zone when the jumpmaster passed him a warm mug of brandy toddy. The warmth and kick of the brandy immediately made him feel braver. Catesby dangled his legs through the Joe hole, the section of bomb bay modified for aerial drops, the slipstream caught his legs and he gripped the sides of the Joe hole tight to avoid being sucked out. He glanced up to second guess the jumpmaster and make sure his static line was attached to the steel cable above the Joe hole. There were now two static lines clipped in place – the second belonged to Jimmy who was to follow him. Catesby looked back at his colleague as he was finishing his brandy toddy and gave him the thumbs-up. At that second, a red light flashed and the dispatcher shouted, 'Go.'

Catesby pushed and launched himself into the night as he shouted, 'One thousand, two thousand, three thousand, four thousand,' before uncurling and looking up to see if his parachute had deployed. There was nothing much he could do about it if it hadn't. They carried no reserve chutes for there wouldn't be time to use one on a six-hundred-foot jump. But the five seconds floating like a feather in the dark silence were delicious. The time seemed to expand. Catesby noticed treelines and hills in the light of the full moon. He tapped the pack against his chest to check that his Sten gun was still there. The pack also contained escape rations and two pills: a powerful Benzedrine amphetamine to keep him awake if he had to go on the run – and the notorious L pill.

'If you hear the reception committee speaking German, don't worry about burying your chute, just run like hell.' It was the last thing they told everyone before they were dropped into occupied France. Catesby didn't hear any German – but he did hear a lot of voices speaking a language that wasn't modern French. It was the first time that he had heard Occitan. In 1943, the ancient tongue was still the first language of many in the remotest areas of rural France. The version that greeted Catesby's ears was Lemosin, the dialect spoken in an area of the Massif Central, the most sparsely populated region of France. As soon as Catesby heard those voices, he realised that he had landed in a very different world for which no training could have prepared him. The German occupiers, most of whom had served on the Eastern Front, had nicknamed the area Little Russia.

A pair of hands grabbed him and a voice said, '*Bon ser.*' Someone else was gathering in his parachute and shouted what seemed to be a greeting, '*Cossíva?*' Another voice, older and with a note of authority, ordered, '*Despaiche-te.*' Catesby fell in love with the language as soon as he heard the first syllable. The ancient accents of Lemosin were to haunt him the rest of his life. It was as if, after lying hidden for thirty thousand years, the wonderful Stone Age painters of Lascaux had emerged from their caves to embrace him. It was time to rebel against the inhuman mechanical horror that had invaded their land. Time to regain the freedom to reflect and recreate the wonders of the world that fed and nourished them. That freedom was more precious than life itself.

Catesby felt the Sten gun strapped to his chest. It was still in one piece and more would follow in a supply drop. One other SOE agent had parachuted with him, but he couldn't see him or hear him. He turned to the first Frenchman who had greeted him and said, 'There was another one who parachuted after me. Have you seen him?'

The Frenchman jerked his head to the right, 'Over there.'

Catesby was relieved that his standard French was understood. 'Is he all right?'

The Frenchman shrugged. 'His parachute opened.'

Catesby looked towards the treeline and saw a figure who certainly looked like his wireless operator, Jimmy Fenn, walking towards him carrying the suitcase with his W/T set. Jimmy had insisted on parachuting with the heavy radio in a padded kitbag rather than entrusting it to container. It made for a hard, heavy landing.

Meanwhile, the engine noise of the Halifax filled the night as it returned for the supply drop. Catesby turned towards the older man who seemed to be in charge. 'Tell your team to watch closely in case some of the supply chutes don't open.'

'How many containers are there?'

'Ten.'

They were the new C-type containers, cylinders the size of a large man, and were packed with Sten guns, ammunition and explosives. Catesby watched the drop in the moon-bright night and was relieved to see all ten chutes deploy and descend in pendulum swings. He heard orders being shouted behind him in a combination of Lemosin and standard French – and the sound of a horse snorting. Catesby looked towards the nearest treeline and saw a procession of carts drawn by horses emerge on to the drop zone. The horses gleamed light grey in the full moon. His eyes were drawn irresistibly to the nearest cart which was pulled by a team of two harnessed nose to tail. Jimmy Fenn, who had now caught up with Catesby, was also staring at the cart horses.

'I wish my old man could see that,' said Jimmy. 'They look a tiny bit smaller than our Suffolk Punches – but not much, maybe half a hand.' Jimmy examined the harness. 'And look, they haven't got a swingletree, but are shafted directly to the cart.'

The containers were heavy and it took four men to lift them on to the horse carts which were rough-hewn and V-shaped, a good design for keeping the round containers from rolling off.

As they trudged through the darkness Catesby overheard Jimmy talking to a Maquisard. It was the first time he had heard Jimmy speaking French. Catesby winced and realised that it would be best for Jimmy to stay silent around possible informers or members of the *milice*, the French paramilitary police who collaborated with the Germans. Jimmy's French was fluent, but he spoke it with a strong Suffolk accent – which was odd, for his English had become cockneyfied. Catesby continued to eavesdrop. Jimmy was asking about the horses.

'All our horses are Poitevin,' said the Frenchman. 'They are calm and gentle, but slow to mature. They don't reach their full size until they are six or seven.'

'Our horses,' said Jimmy, his French sounding more Suffolk than ever, 'are Suffolk Punches. My granddad used to say they had the face of an angel and the backside of a farmer's daughter.'

'The Poitevin love humans, but can be stubborn when they are tired.'

'Who isn't?'

The late evening had turned into a surreal dream. Catesby wondered if he had been concussed and was imagining a conversation about draught horses between a Limousin peasant and the son of a Suffolk farm labourer.

The path from the drop zone was a rough farm track alongside thick woods. The only sounds were the creaking of the farm wagons, the plodding of hooves and soft whispers in Occitan. Catesby noticed that very few of the Maquis carried weapons, mostly ancient Lebel rifles, and made a mental note that unpacking the Sten guns and training the local Maquis to use them was an urgent priority.

They continued along the dirt track for half an hour before arriving at a single-lane tarmac road. The countryside was more open, and dark farm buildings began to appear. One of the wagons detached itself from the column and disappeared down a track. More and more people had materialised from the dark. The dozen or so who had formed the reception committee had swelled to forty or fifty. Catesby heard a number of voices speaking rapidly in dialect, but the only words he could make out were *Lo Grand*. He had been briefed on Georges Guingouin's Occitan nickname and now remembered it. The Great One had finally appeared.

No one could have mistaken the Maquis leader Guingouin for anything other than a combatant. He was wearing a military uniform with a hand grenade attached to his belt. It was pointless for him to go incognito, Lo Grand was too well known to be mistaken for an innocent civilian. Catesby listened to him as he greeted his fellow Maquisards in the Lemosin dialect. Catesby knew from his briefings that Guingouin had been born and brought up in the region – and admired the fact that he still spoke the language of peasants and workers.

Guingouin greeted Jimmy first and switched to standard French. 'We need to move quickly and hide the supplies. But first of all, we need more pencil timers urgently. Which containers are they in?'

'I don't know,' said Jimmy, 'I'm only the wireless operator. You'll have to ask the team leader.'

'That's me,' said Catesby. He could see that Guingouin didn't go in for introductions and small talk. 'The plastic explosives are in three containers marked with blue stripes. The time pencils are, for safety reasons, packed separately in a container marked in red – which also contains Sten guns.'

'Good. We need to get them out tonight. We might also need some plastic explosive as a backup.'

Catesby was impressed by how quickly things were moving along, but didn't like losing control. 'Wait a minute,' he said, 'there's a container marked W/T in large yellow lettering. We need to know where that one is.'

Guingouin turned away shouting instructions in dialect. There was some confusion before the W/T container, which contained a spare wireless set and personal belongings, was found.

'We must,' said Catesby, 'keep that one close to us.'

Lo Grand gave another order in Lemosin and disappeared into the night.

The Maquisard who had seemed in charge until Guingouin arrived put his hand on Catesby's back. 'You and the other Englishman have to come with me. I will take you to your safe house.'

The safe house overlooked a lake on the edge of a small village. They were greeted by a woman in her sixties – and two snarling dogs who reassured Catesby that no German patrol could get near them without loud warning barks. The woman held back the dogs as Catesby entered. 'Hush,' she said, 'otherwise I'll send you to Limoges as black-market meat.' The comment, spoken in French rather than Lemosin, was obviously intended for her visitors.

There was the smell of cooking from a great cast-iron stove. 'Your food,' she said, 'is ready now.'

One of the dogs was sniffing Catesby's hand. Jimmy said, 'Fee-fi-fo-fum, I smell the blood of an Englishman.'

The woman turned and pointed a spatula. 'You speak French in this house.'

'*Je suis vraiment désolé, madame,*' replied a chastened Jimmy.

'You will only be here one night,' said the woman. 'I have tried to make you comfortable. There are clean sheets – and I have cooked you *confit de canard*, a rare treat. And help yourself to wine.' There were two litre bottles of red on the table. 'There is no shortage of wine.'

There were roast potatoes and salad to go with the duck. After the woman had finished serving, she lifted an ancient shotgun out of the shadows next to the stove and flourished it. 'Enjoy your food. If *les boches* come I will see them off. As my husband used to write from Verdun, we only have two problems, *les boches* and the fleas.'

It was mid-morning. Catesby and Jimmy were sipping ersatz coffee made from acorns and chicory. It was awful and Catesby asked their hostess for mint so that he could brew his own infusion. She seemed impressed, 'You would make a good husband, but I will do it for you.'

Catesby turned to Jimmy. 'We have to contact London.'

'If it's okay with the old lady, I'll set up the antenna in the hayloft of the barn.'

On cue, the woman arrived with Catesby's mint tea. 'I told you we only speak French in my house.'

Catesby apologised and asked about using the hayloft. She said that all her property was for them to use as they pleased.

The antenna, which was seventeen feet long, was a problem for W/T operators. It could be looped back and forth, but still needed a lot of space. Once it was set up successfully in a secure place, a lot of operators were reluctant to move it, which was why they got caught. Catesby was determined that they were not going to get trapped by a Gestapo van with detector equipment which vectored in on suspected locations. He had been briefed that detector teams were more of a problem in towns than in the countryside, but he was new to occupied France and his level of paranoia was still high.

While Jimmy looped the antenna over ancient oak beams, Catesby composed and encrypted the message. It was short and sweet: ARRIVED SAFELY WIV NO PROBLEMS. The misspelling of 'with' as 'wiv' was an intentional mistake to signal that they hadn't been captured and turned. The other intentional misspellings included a Suffolk 'gorn' for 'gone' and omitting the final 'g' of any word ending in 'ing'. It was assumed that German intelligence officers would expect a captured wireless operator to transmit false messages in correct English. Catesby wasn't sure it made any difference. He thought it likely that at least one of the many captured SOE agents had revealed this trick under torture. He knew that they had been dropped into a twilight world where nothing and no one could be completely trusted.

Catesby looked on closely as Jimmy prepared the B2 for transmission. He attached the set to the six-volt battery and switched to DC power supply. Jimmy then inserted the quartz crystal and put on the earphones as he tuned the antenna. Catesby was determined to train himself to use the radio if need be. He had already learned Morse and watched with the fixed curiosity of a sorcerer's apprentice as Jimmy adjusted various dials. He felt a shiver run down his spine. The ladder had given a loud creak. A stranger was coming into the hayloft.

Catesby touched Jimmy and put his finger on his lips. He grabbed the Sten gun, rolled into the prone position and aimed at the top rung of the ladder. There was more creaking as the intruder continued up the ladder. A face finally appeared looking to left and right in the gloom. He mounted two more rungs. The visitor was wearing a jacket and tie and looked official. He peered around in exasperation and said, 'Hello. Is anyone here?'

Catesby lay quiet on the floorboards.

The visitor mounted another rung and continued to squint into the gloom. His eyes seemed to have spotted the strung antenna and he traced it to its source. 'Ah,' he said, 'there you are. Please don't shoot. Madam told me you were here.'

'Who are you?' said Catesby.

'My name is Jean. I am a doctor who sometimes helps Guingouin and his friends – but, if you pull the trigger, I will be of help to no one.'

'How are you supposed to help us?'

'Because I am a doctor, I am allowed to keep and run a car. I sometimes move supplies and people.'

Catesby passed the Sten gun to Jimmy and whispered, 'I believe this bloke, but we need to make sure. Follow me if you don't want to get trapped up here, but prepare to do a runner.'

Catesby descended the ladder and followed Dr Jean to where a black Citroën Traction Avant was gleaming in the farmyard. The upper range car was a contrast to the horse drawn carts of the drop zone – but the expensive motor with its distinctive twin-chevron grille triggered warning bells in Catesby's brain. SOE agents, particularly ones assigned to the Paris region, were warned to fear the car. The invading Germans quickly developed an insatiable appetite for motorised transport – and the Citroën Traction Avant became their chariot of choice. It was a spacious solid car that could take a lot of abuse. The Gestapo commandeered all the Tractions they could find and the sight of the black car became a harbinger of evil. Catesby wondered if 'Dr Jean' was feeding him a cover story. Meanwhile, Madam was calmly making her way towards them carrying a wicker basket. Surely, she wasn't part of the deception.

She handed the basket to the doctor and said, 'Eggs, cheese and potatoes – and also a bottle of André's plum brandy.'

'Thank you, Augustine. I am sure they will prove useful.' The doctor turned to Catesby. 'We've already loaded the dynamite, but I am sure there will be space for you and your colleague.'

The first part of the journey was open and brazen. The boot and back seat of the car were packed with dynamite and plastic explosive. Catesby sat in the front passenger seat cradling his Sten gun and looking out over the rolling and heavily wooded countryside. It was perfect guerrilla country. Jimmy sat squeezed in the back next to an armed Maquisard. The B2 radio was packed into what looked like an ordinary leather suitcase. The suitcase deception was, however, pointless when you were crammed between high explosives in the back seat of a car next to a *résistant* with a rifle between his knees. If they came upon a police or German roadblock, the plan was for Catesby and the Maquisard to pile out of the car and provide covering fire while Dr Jean executed a U-turn or reversed at speed. If they were lucky, they would escape and evade back to relative safety. Jimmy would stay in the car because trained wireless operators were less expendable than young officers. But would the car be safer? Catesby knew that the impact of bullets would have no effect on plastic explosive, but he wasn't sure what would happen if a bullet struck dynamite – and hoped he would never find out.

Catesby turned to the Maquisard in the back whose name, or cover name, was Marcel. 'Are there many Germans in the area?'

'They don't like coming here, but they often turn up after a parachute drop. You usually see them with the *milice* – who are growing in numbers.'

Catesby nodded. One of Catesby's tasks was reporting

back on the size and effectiveness of these collaborators. His pre-deployment briefings had also discussed the possibility of forging fake *milice* identity cards and obtaining uniforms to wreak havoc.

Most of the car journey was along one-track country lanes which ended up as dirt tracks and required crossing a field to reach another track. Catesby could see that they were deep in bandit country where checkpoints and roadblocks would be a pointless exercise. He was impressed that the Traction Avant, which translated as front wheel drive, was so able to cope with off-road conditions despite being low slung. They eventually came to a house and farm buildings on the edge of a wood. The buildings looked derelict. Dr Jean continued driving into the wood on an abandoned logging road. They stopped at a crude woodman's hut where they unloaded and hid the dynamite and plastic explosive. Jean managed to reverse the Traction Avant and drive back to the farm buildings which no longer seemed abandoned. Bicycles were leaning against the side of the stone house. Jean turned off the engine, rolled down the window and said, '*Salut*, Georges,' to an approaching bespectacled figure. This time Lo Grand was only partly in military gear: no helmet or pistol, but boots and military trousers.

'This was a bit risky,' said Guingouin leaning against the car, 'but we needed to get the stuff in place for next week.'

Catesby didn't know what Guingouin was talking about, but something about the words *next week* sounded artificial. If it was a week away, why the urgency? Later, Catesby realised that truth was too precious to be widely shared. If Jean was captured and broke under torture, *next week* would be false information.

Guingouin looked over Jean's shoulder at Catesby. 'I believe the procedure is to keep wireless operators and their team leaders in separate safe houses?'

'That is the current advice.'

'It makes sense,' said Guingouin, 'in a place like Paris, but I'm not sure it is always necessary here. The distances between you can create problems. But we will try it. Your comrade will be staying here.'

Catesby realised that, although Guingouin didn't know their real names, it was time to provide their cover aliases. Pointing to himself, Catesby said, 'I am Jacques Dubois and my colleague is Henri Martin.' They had various identity cards in these names. They had been selected because they were common French names – but Catesby felt that SOE had overdone it. Calling oneself Jacques Dubois was the alias equivalent of John Smith. He wished he could change it.

It felt odd saying goodbye to Jimmy in French and calling him Henri. Catesby had noticed that the *résistants* called each other *camarade*. He didn't know whether it was political – they were after all the Maquis Rouge – or common usage. Catesby decided to lay it on thick. He embraced Jimmy and kissed him on both cheeks. 'I hope, my good *camarade*, that we will meet again soon.'

Jimmy looked more amused than embarrassed. But Catesby was worried about being separated from his wireless operator. They were supposed to contact London at least twice a week. In case something happened to Jimmy, Catesby was taking the spare wireless set to his own safe house – even though he didn't have the codes or the skills to use it. If your wireless operator got killed or captured, you had to contact another SOE circuit and use their wireless man or woman to contact London. That meant making a dangerous trip across France – and a rendez-vous that could give both of them away.

As soon as Catesby began to open the passenger door of the car, the doctor stopped him. 'I don't think it would be safe for you to sit there.'

Something in Catesby's blood turned chill.

'I am visiting two hospitals in Limoges – on official business. Your next safe house is on the way. Unfortunately, part of our journey is along the main road to Limoges. There is a risk, a small risk, that there will be roadblocks and checkpoints. So it is best that you travel in the *coffre*.'

Coffre, the word for car boot, sounded uncomfortably like coffin. Catesby gave a bleak smile.

Despite being a large car, the boot of the Traction Avant was a crushed space for Catesby and all his gear – and still smelt of dynamite. As the car bounced over rough pasture, Catesby cradled his Sten gun close to his chest as if it were a much-loved teddy bear – except that he had never had a teddy bear. Maybe teddy bears weren't a Belgian tradition. If he didn't get killed, he would ask his mother. She was a strange woman. Catesby had noticed that she prayed in French, *Je vous salue, Marie pleine de grâce: Hail Mary, full of grace,* but swore in Flemish, *gie soepkieken.* But as someone who had worked as a barmaid in a pub on the Antwerp docks, Catesby was certain that his mother knew far worse swear words than *you soup chicken.*

They suddenly ground to a halt. Catesby tensed up and grabbed the Sten as he heard the door open and Dr Jean leave the car. *What the fuck.* A few seconds later Jean got back in the car, drove forward and stopped again and got out – and a moment later got back in and began to drive on. Catesby breathed easy again as he realised what had happened: *You stupid fuck, it was a gate!*

The Traction purred smoothly as it picked up speed. The bumps had stopped; they were now on a proper road, but there were a few potholes that bounced Catesby against the top of the boot. After five minutes or so the car slowed again and nearly came to a stop before turning. This time, Jean put his foot down and picked up speed. Catesby guessed they were going more than 40 mph. Were they on the dreaded *Route Nationale* into Limoges?

The claustrophobia of being locked in a boot began to grate on Catesby. Was it really necessary to separate team leaders from radio operators for security? The rules had been drummed in during his final training days at Beaulieu. Wireless operators were priceless and in short supply, but also the most likely agents to be captured. It was best that they worked in isolation so that their colleagues were not swept up with them in a raid. But now Catesby felt like the one in isolation – and deprived of control. Lo Grand and his band of Maquisards were calling all the shots. Being ordered about in French was like being a child again. Once more, the dark spectre of his mother returned to haunt Catesby. If she were now living in France, would she be a collaborator? Conservative Catholics, like her, were often the strongest supporters of Pétain's Vichy. They believed that many of France's ills were the result of jazz, nightclubs, short skirts and birth control. Vichy had replaced *liberté, égalité, fraternité* with *travail, famille, patrie*. His mother seldom talked about the brother she had lost in the Great War, but one of the few times she referred to him was in June 1940. Catesby was still at school and they were listening to the BBC news on the wireless. When it was announced that Pétain had signed an armistice with the Germans, his mother called out, 'Thank God for Maréchal Pétain. He has saved us from the slaughter of 1914 to 18. Never again.'

Catesby flushed with anger and embarrassment. *Was this woman still dressed in widow's mourning really his mother?* He wanted to run away from home and enlist immediately. He wanted to wear a British uniform and cleanse himself of shame. Catesby turned to his mother, struggling to contain his anger and contempt. 'You must never ever say those words again – especially not in front of English people.'

She returned his words with a stony stare.

The doctor seemed to be taking a long route to get to the safe house – or perhaps claustrophobic enclosure expanded time. The car was slowing down. Had they arrived? But odd that the safe house would be on a main road. The car came to a halt and there were voices – one of them speaking German. The end. Catesby blinked in the dark. At first, the anger was aimed at himself. Why had he allowed himself to get recruited into SOE? At any point he could have said no and been reassigned to a conventional army unit where, even as an infantry officer, the risk would have been halved. Or he probably could have got a cushy staff job owing to his language skills. Catesby watched the fifty, sixty or even seventy years of unlived life and love unfold. It was all now a dream. Then something clicked. All at once he felt alert and desperate like a trapped animal. The Sten gun was his claws. He listened to the voices. There were two French ones talking to the doctor about where he was going and what he was doing – and a German voice that seemed to be translating what was going on, presumably, to another German. Catesby pressed the selector stud on the Sten to choose automatic fire. He waited to hear footsteps coming to check the boot. For some reason, a Flemish curse in West-vlams dialect came into his mind, not one that he had picked up from his mother, but one that he had learned from a Belgian trainee on the unarmed combat course at Arisaig in the Scottish Highlands: *Kus men kloten, rukker* – Kiss my balls, tosser. It became their shared catchphrase. The Belgian had been assigned to N section and had been captured as soon as he landed. If he hadn't shouted *Kus men kloten* at the Gestapo, Catesby was now going to do it on his behalf. His heart was beating fast and he clenched his jaw – but there were no footsteps, just more talking.

The outside conversation had diminished into low confidential tones. Catesby struggled to make out the words. He wondered if the vehicle check was over and they were going to let Dr Jean continue on his way. But no. He suddenly heard the driver's door open and Jean get out. Was he being taken prisoner? Catesby tensed up again and hoped he would get off a burst as soon as the boot door opened. That would, perhaps, give him enough time to run to the nearest field. But what if one of his bullets hit Jean who, probably, would be the one unlocking the boot under duress. But that's war. Catesby now heard footsteps approaching the back of the car. This was it. A door opened. It seemed only inches from where he was lying. They were obviously inspecting the back seat of the car. He could hear someone breathing and then talking – so close to him. It was Dr Jean. 'I have promised some of these eggs to the hospital, but you're welcome to the potatoes and the butter. You might also want to try that plum brandy, but it's lethal.'

Catesby listened as the transaction was completed. Roadblocks were not just for catching Maquisards, but for collecting food as unofficial road tolls. War was not only about violence; it was corruption too. Farewells were exchanged. Dr Jean got back in the car and started the engine. They were on their way to the safe house. A few minutes later the car turned off the main road and on to a bumpy track – and, after what seemed only a few hundred yards, stopped. There were voices again, but this time speaking Limousin dialect. Even though it was a cloudy day, Catesby blinked at the light as the boot opened.

Dr Jean, as a doctor on his rounds, was neatly dressed in coat and tie with shined shoes. In contrast, the two *résistants* looked like farm labourers who had been slopping out. They reminded Catesby of the SOE training rules: *Dress to merge into the background and behave in the same way as those around you.*

Dr Jean closed the boot and turned to Catesby, 'We had some bad luck, but fortunately it was only gendarmes and a couple of ordinary German soldiers. They sometimes stop traffic going into Limoges – particularly on market days – to steal farm produce. It was unusual to see Germans with them.'

Catesby had been warned at Beaulieu that complacency could be a problem for an agent on the ground. In rural France you could go for weeks without seeing a German and let your security go lax – and suddenly you're in the bag. So maybe the scare had been a useful early warning.

'I'll now leave you with Louis and Paul,' said Jean. 'Goodbye and good luck.' He reversed the car and drove away.

The two Maquisards packed the spare radio and Catesby's gear into canvas sacks that they slung over their shoulders. They led the way: a timeless image of peasants trudging under heavy loads. Peasants never walked with empty hands; they were always carrying something. It was a lesson that an undercover agent had to learn.

The first part of the journey was following a path up a heavily wooded hillside. At the top of the hill was an open space – no larger than an English suburban garden – where a single cow was grazing. Catesby came to realise that the Limousin peasants were extremely thrifty. Not a patch of grass was wasted and they moved their cattle around as frequently as *résistants* changed hiding places.

After the tiny pasture, the path curved downwards and crossed a stream. There was the alarm call of a jay and the rustle of pigeons leaving their roosts. Birds were sentinels for both sides. Paul, the Maquisard who was leading the way, held up his hand. He put his sack on the ground and gestured for the other two to wait. Paul disappeared up a path to the right that ran parallel to the stream. Catesby looked up the stream and noticed an overgrown stone structure – which might have been an old mill. A few moments later, Paul returned and nodded an all-clear.

Louis turned towards Catesby and whispered, 'He was checking the cotton thread. I'm sure you know the procedure?'

Catesby nodded. In order to make sure paths hadn't been used by others, a piece of black cotton thread was stretched across the track about ten or twelve inches above the ground. If the cotton had been broken by a deer or other large animal, you would see their tracks.

A minute later they came to a rough stony track rutted by centuries of cartwheels that led to a stone building in fairly good condition and well concealed by trees and vines.

'We'll be staying here for a night or two,' said Louis. 'Don't normally expect such luxury. There's even a toilet.'

Catesby guessed that by the shape of the building and its proximity to the ruined mill it was an old malt house. As they unloaded their gear on the ground floor, more *résistants* appeared carrying food and other supplies. The building seemed to be a rendezvous point for a platoon-size unit. There were thirty or so Maquisards. One of them found a hook, opened up a trapdoor in the ceiling, pulled down a ladder and climbed into the roof space. Catesby heard his voice call down. 'This place is covered in rat and mouse shit. If we store any food here, it needs to be in vermin-proof containers.'

Two others responded in dialect. Catesby didn't understand a word.

Paul smiled and called out, '*Parlez français; soyez propres.*'

Catesby would later see the words, *Speak French; be clean*, inscribed on the wall of a schoolroom. He was amused that the instruction to speak standard French was linked to personal hygiene. It was as if there was a spiritual connection between speaking proper and soap.

Paul's schoolteacher intervention was met with howls of derision.

'Okay,' said Paul, 'but remember that our new comrade doesn't speak Lemosin.'

'I will try to learn your beautiful language,' said Catesby.

There was a smattering of applause.

Catesby spread his sleeping bag in the corner of a small back room which looked as if it might have been an office. There were two windows that could provide useful escape routes as they opened on to a wilderness of undergrowth. As Catesby was unpacking and checking his gear, Paul came into the room. 'We've got to kill someone. Would you like to come along?'

Catesby, unnerved by the fact that Paul was smiling, quietly asked, 'Who are you going to kill?'

'An old girl who has stopped milking.'

Catesby frowned. He was repulsed by Paul's tone. 'You mean a woman who has stopped giving you information?'

'No, I mean a cow who has stopped lactating. We passed her in a field on the way here. We need the food.'

Catesby knew that the Maquis had to be ruthless to survive, but was relieved he wasn't going to witness a human execution.

'It's a messy business,' said Paul. 'We have to cut the cow's throat and she'll thrash around. Shooting her would be too noisy and give our position away.'

'I've got a piece of kit that you might find useful.' Catesby took a metal tube out of a canvas bag.

'Is that a bicycle pump?'

'We like people to think that.' He slid a pistol grip into a slot on the metal tube. 'It's a Welrod Mark 2. It's fitted with a sup-pressor and doesn't make much noise – especially if you press the muzzle against your victim.'

Catesby later wished that he hadn't volunteered. The look in the cow's eye was of warmth and expectation. She associated humans with food and relieving the pain of her milk-swollen udders – although the latter hadn't been necessary for some time. Even though a town boy from the backstreets of Lowestoft, several of Catesby's father's extended family were farm workers in Suffolk. Catesby had worked with cattle during school holidays and had been taken by the gentleness of huge ruminants. But it was a deceptive gentleness. As one of his uncles used to say, 'The two most dangerous things on a farm are an unloaded shotgun and a tame bull.' Catesby reached out and stroked the doomed cow with his left hand. With his other hand he pushed the muzzle of the Welrod pistol behind the cow's left ear. He whispered, 'Sorry, my darling,' as he pulled the trigger.

It wasn't the placid crumpling death that Catesby had anticipated. The cow let out a deafening bellow and kicked out with both hind feet. The calibre of the bullet wasn't big enough to instantly kill such a huge beast. The cow stumbled sideways away from him and Catesby chambered another round. He approached carefully, not wanting to be taken out by a kick. He fired the next bullet in front of her ear. This time the cow went down on her front legs, but was still alive. It took two more shots before the cow was silent, but she was still breathing. A Maquisard farm worker said that it was only marginal breathing, but that they should wait a few minutes before they dragged her away for slaughtering. Catesby looked at the dead or dying beast. He was used to thumping fish or twisting the necks of rabbits or hens – but he had never killed something so massive. He wondered, not for the first time, what it would be like to kill a human and tried to harden himself to it.

It took six of them to drag the cow out of the clearing and into the forest. A Maquisard selected an oak tree and threw a rope over a thick branch. Another fighter bound one of the cow's hind legs with an end of the rope. It took eight of them – heaving like a tug of war team – to hoist the dead cow for slaughter. A Maquisard bearing a small gleaming knife told them to stop while the cow's head and forelegs were still lying on the ground. He cut around the hocks of the hind legs to begin skinning the cow. The most difficult skinning was around the udder, but after that the hide separated quickly from the carcass and eventually fell in one intact lump before it was separated from the neck and forelegs.

The next stage was gutting. It began slowly by cutting out

the anus bung and taking care not to rupture the bladder or pierce the intestines. The guts tumbled in a steaming mass on to a canvas sheet that had been spread below. The edible bits were quickly separated out. Catesby watched as a Maquisard frowned and squeezed excess blood out of the heart. 'We should,' he said, 'have bled her first.'

The fat and the offal were put into tubs and carried away to be buried along with the head and hooves. Meanwhile, the carcass was cut into half and then into quarters. Catesby was impressed by the speed and efficiency. It seemed likely that a few of the *résistants* had worked in an abattoir – or maybe slaughtering some of your own livestock was a way of life in the Limousin. They had reverted to speaking Lemosin. Catesby had begun to pick up a few words. He was sure that someone had said that the meat ought to hang for *un semano*, a week. Others disagreed because they were too busy fighting a war.

The meal that evening was late, but filling. A dozen fighters sat around the table at the safe house. The cooking had taken two hours to produce a thick stew of potatoes, carrots and beef. There was also a lot of stale bread that needed soaking in the stew – and plenty of wine. Catesby had begun to feel relaxed for only the second time since boarding the Halifax bomber at RAF Tempsford – the first time had been when his parachute opened. The Maquisard next to him was cutting a piece of meat with his clasp knife. Catesby had already noticed that all the peasants carried their own knives and used them as cutlery. They also had a handkerchief-sized cloth hanging out of their pocket for wiping the knife afterwards. Later, Catesby observed that they always washed these soiled cloths fresh and clean whenever they came across a stream or water source. And there were to be times when the cloths were thick with the blood of Germans or comrades.

The Maquisard called Paul pushed his way on to the bench next to Catesby and said, 'It's been moved forward to tomorrow – and Lo Grand wants you to come with us.'

Catesby didn't know what Paul was talking about and returned a blank stare. The Maquisard sitting next to him flourished his clasp knife in the air and turned to Catesby, 'They have been raiding houses all around Eymoutiers and gathering up conscripts. We kept telling the young fellows to take to the hills and join us, but so many won't listen. We should blow up the trains too.'

'No,' said Paul, 'Lo Grand doesn't want civilian casualties.'

'If,' said the Maquisard with the knife, 'you are silly enough to get caught in an STO trawl, you deserve to get blown up.'

'That isn't fair,' said another. 'There are three young men in La Varache, two farm workers and a wood cutter, who are only pretending to accept the summons, but will be helping us instead.'

Catesby's training had included briefings about the STO, the *Service du Travail Obligatoire*. It was a programme of worker conscription that the Germans had imposed on the Vichy government. All young Frenchmen born between 1920 and 1922 were liable to be deported to Germany as forced labour. The idea was to free up hundreds of thousands of German workers to serve on the Eastern Front. Those who dodged the STO were known as *réfractaires* and went into hiding. Part of SOE's job was to sabotage the STO, but Catesby was still in the dark about what was going on. He turned to Paul, 'What's happening?'

'You don't know?'

'No.'

'Good. It shows close security.'

'Can you tell me now?'

'It requires a lot of dynamite and a lot of bicycles.'

It was the first time that Catesby had been in action and the excitement was still blocking out the fear. He still hadn't seen someone killed. He still hadn't had a friend arrested and sent to a death camp. And it was a lovely night. There was a waxing gibbous moon which provided half the light of a full moon – but enough to cycle along the twisting country roads. Each bike was loaded with twenty kilos of dynamite or pipes. There were also a lot of guns. There was a brief break while a group of armed Maquisards did a recce of the route ahead. Meanwhile,

Guingouin had dismounted from his bike and was making his way along the column of cyclists whispering encouragement and instructions.

Guingouin stopped and sat next to Catesby. 'If this works, I hope you will tell London about it.'

'Is that why you want me along?'

'We also need the muscle,' Guingouin touched the Sten gun which was strapped to Catesby's chest, 'and someone who can shoot. This is the biggest operation we have ever attempted. It is not just a matter of blowing up tracks or blowing a hole in a viaduct arch. We want to destroy an entire pillar – something they will never be able to repair.'

Catesby knew that such a demolition would be a big job that required at least a ton of dynamite – far more than the loads of dynamite that were weighing down their bikes. The explosives would also need a lot of tamping down to direct the blast. During the demolitions part of his SOE course, a Royal Engineer sergeant suggested using the bodies of the bridge guards you had just killed to tamp down the explosives. No one had said whether or not they expected to find German sentries. What frightened him wasn't so much the gun battle, but what would happen afterwards. Getting the dynamite in place and fused could take over an hour – which should be more than long enough for a German relief column with armoured cars to turn up. He had the impression that the Limousin Maquis didn't go in much for contingency plans. Their philosophy seemed to be: just do it and clear off.

As they waited for the reconnaissance party to return, someone passed a bottle of wine around. Another Maquisard began to half whisper and half sing the words of *Le Temps des Cerises*, a song about forsaking love for the Resistance:

J'aimerai toujours le temps des cerises
Et le souvenir que je garde au cœur.

The words made Catesby unbearably wistful. Unlike the mostly older Frenchmen around him, he had never gathered cherries and had few sweet memories to keep in his heart. Part of him wished he hadn't stopped writing to the Homerton girl – but she belonged to a world in which Catesby had been an imposter. How could he have taken her to his home in Lowestoft? There was another memory that haunted him. Catesby had spent most of his teenage years in love, but it had never been consummated. The back windows of their terraced-house bedrooms in the cramped streets of Lowestoft had faced each other. It was a poor area and he and Dorothy were the only two kids from the neighbourhood who made it into the Grammar. She often failed to draw the curtain or turn off the light when she undressed for bed. Catesby wondered if the striptease, which never went further than knickers, was for his benefit. The memory sent a pang of unfulfilled desire running up his spine. The thought of dying without ever having known fulfilling love made Catesby curse himself once again for having volunteered for SOE.

The ghostly voice of a Maquisard hidden in the shadows continued the song:

Cerises d'amour aux robes pareilles
Tombant sous la feuille en gouttes de sang.

Was getting killed inevitable? Would the cherries of love always turn into drops of blood falling through the leaves? Would she ever think of him if he died? Catesby winced at his maudlin sentimentality. He should be thinking about blowing up the viaduct instead. He tried, but his thoughts kept drifting back to a life he had lost forever.

He and Dorothy had never shared a class at Denes Grammar. Her Higher School Certificate had concentrated on the sciences; whereas Catesby's had been arts and humanities. She had done Latin, but no French – so she wouldn't have understood the song about cherries. She was a practical and focused person. She wanted to be a doctor. But in the end, she didn't go to medical school. She got pregnant and married a painter and decorator – a very successful one – who was a lot older than her. So she would be comfortable.

The singing had stopped suddenly and a nervous hush ran

through the column. Everyone lay flat on the damp midnight ground. What the fuck was happening? Nothing. Once again there was only the mind-twisting silence of waiting in the dark. Catesby closed his eyes.

The last time he saw her was on his last leave home. It was the previous Christmas, but now seemed a different century. He had passed her in Lowestoft High Street – proudly resplendent in his uniform with officer's pips and parachute badge. She was pushing a pram and spoke first, 'Hello, William.'

'You're looking well,' said Catesby.

'Don't lie. I'm looking haggard and tired.'

'How's the baby?' Catesby knew it was an insensitive question, but couldn't swallow the words back.

She stared blankly into nothingness.

Catesby knew that her pregnancy had been dwarfed by a family tragedy. Her Aunt Millie, who lived around the corner, had been bombed out of her house. Millie escaped unscathed, but her six-month-old twins had been killed. And a few days later, Aunt Millie's husband, a trawlerman turned Royal Naval Patrol Service sailor, had been lost at sea. It wasn't an unusual story. Per head of population, Lowestoft had suffered higher civilian casualties than any town in the UK. As England's most easterly point, Lowestoft was the last chance for a returning Luftwaffe pilot to dump his unused bombs.

'I was sorry to hear about what happened to your Aunt Millie – and your cousins. It must be awful for her.'

She stared at the baby in her pram. 'The cousins would have been like big sisters to him. But don't worry about Aunt Millie.' Something in her face suddenly turned cold. She brushed a lock of her hair from her eyes and stared across a pile of rubble where a recent German bomb had opened up an unaccustomed view of the North Sea. 'Aunt Millie's fine. She's resilient.' Dorothy looked at Catesby with a face full of loathing. '*Resilient*, that's a clever word for one of us, isn't it, William? But I bet you learned a lot of posh words at Cambridge.'

Catesby touched her hand, which was gripping the push bar of the pram.

'You know something, William, I fancied you like mad – but you never picked up the signals.' Her eyes were glistening with tears. 'You shouldn't have left. You should have got a job on the boats – and maybe become a teacher.' She looked hard at Catesby. 'Remember how I used to take your sister out collecting on May Day – up and down the scores. She loved dressing up in my mum's old frocks. And the song we used to sing:

Climbing up the walls,
Knocking down the spiders,
Cabbages and turnips too,
Put them in your Hallelujah saucepan,
Then we'll have a rare old stew.'

'Well, William, look at yourself now. Even in those days, you were never a Bill or a Billy like everyone else – but always a William or a Will.' She glared at Catesby and gave a bitter laugh. 'You've gone and climbed that wall – and you'll never be one of us again.'

Before Catesby could say anything, she was on her way up the High Street with her back to him.

The memory was gone and Catesby was back in the Limousin lying on the damp ground – staring into nothingness. The people around him belonged to this place. If he didn't die in the next hour, thought Catesby, would he ever belong anywhere?

Something was happening. The reconnaissance party had returned and anxious voices were whispering in Lemosin. There seemed to be a dispute about whether or not to go on. Whatever had happened the argument was instantly settled by one word from Lo Grand, *Non.* They were going to the viaduct no matter what. Catesby picked up his Sten gun. The melancholy had dissipated and he suddenly had a sense of purpose. He thought of Dorothy and her aunt and whispered: *This, Millie, is for your twins and your husband.*

What happened next surprised Catesby. Instead of keeping to the high ground, they descended into a river valley pushing their bikes down a rough track. It didn't make sense. Surely, the idea was to lay the dynamite on the top of the viaduct to blow out an arch. He had never understood what Guingouin had meant by destroying an entire pillar.

It was now impossible to continue with the bikes. They had to remove the explosives and carry them by hand down a steep slippery slope. It was tough going. Catesby was clueless about what was going on. Suddenly, the column stopped and there was silence. The Maquisard behind Catesby touched his shoulder and pointed to the left. The viaduct silhouetted against the moon-bright sky was enormous. Catesby shook his head and tried not to laugh. Blowing up such an enormous piece of civil engineering with a few hundred pounds of dynamite was an impossible task. You would need to call in RAF Lancasters armed with eight-thousand-pound blockbuster bombs. Why was Guingouin leading them on a fool's errand? And wasting their time and risking their lives. It became apparent why they had stopped. Catesby looked up at the viaduct. Two figures with rifles on their shoulders were walking along the tracks towards each other. They stopped in the middle and seemed to be having a conversation. Had they heard or spotted the Maquisards on this pointless sabotage trip? After about a minute or two, the sentries turned and went back in the direction from which they had come. The Maquisards remained motionless and silent for what seemed a long time. It was a still night and noises travelled. Finally, a signal was given and they moved forwards.

They came to the bottom of the valley which the viaduct had been built to span. The ground was marshy and it was difficult to walk so heavily burdened. Someone fell with a splash. There was muffled laughter and the sound of running water. The Maquisard behind Catesby whispered, 'Has he decided to go for a swim in La Vienne?' It was the river from which the Haute Vienne department took its name.

A soaking Gaston was pulled back up the bank and they continued along the river towards the viaduct, now in the shadow of the nearest pillar – which was their target. The front of the column reached the enormous brick edifice and started to unload the dynamite and pipe – there was a clanging of metal against metal, followed by laughter and a loud *shhh*. Catesby was certain they had all gone mad and wondered if the guards would hear them. He continued to the base of the pillar and joined the others. Someone helped divest him of his sack of dynamite and began to unload the sticks of explosive into sections of pipe. A moment later, Catesby realised that a work of demolition genius was taking place. It wasn't madness after all.

Guingouin was standing beside him and pointed to a black hole about five feet from the base of the pillar. 'That's a drain that goes through the centre of the pillar. It channels rainwater from the track bed – but also provides a perfect place for dynamite.'

Catesby watched as section after section of dynamite-filled pipe was shoved upwards into the drain, a fatal penetration of seemingly impenetrable brickwork. Explosives are most effective when they are compacted into a narrow space. Dynamite laid on top of a bridge will do little damage. Eighty per cent of the explosive force will disappear into thin air. On the other hand, close packing explosive charges into a drainage duct is a demolitionist's dream. The pent-up force will explode through anything to achieve its release. Timed detonators were slid into place, followed by more dynamite pipes. The Maquisard who seemed to be in charge of the technical side of things, said in a voice that seemed too loud: 'Check your watches, comrades, we've got fourteen minutes.' Catesby heard, or thought he heard, a German voice from the tracks far above. The only word he made out was *Waß*. It was time to leave.

The withdrawal was quick and seemed disorganised. The Maquisards divided into groups of two or three and retreated into the dark pine-scented loneliness of the Limousin. The job was done. Catesby followed close behind Guingouin. They were halfway up the side of the valley when the explosion rocked the ground around them. Catesby stopped and looked back towards the viaduct, but the view was blocked by the trees. The moon had also gone down, making everything darker. The operation had been timed so that they had the final hour of moonlight to carry out the demolition, followed by total darkness to escape and evade.

'We might,' said Guingouin, 'be able to see what happened when we get to the road. But we can't hang around. It's too risky to go back to a safe house. Most of us are going to be lying low around Saint-Gilles-les-Forêts.'

'Where should I go?'

'That's for you to decide.'

There was something in Guingouin's tone that Catesby found grating – and affirmed the gossip he had heard about him from the Free French Gaullists before his deployment. The Free French were die-hard patriots. They distrusted any Resistance move-ment that owed allegiance to London, Moscow – or any other outside power. They mocked Guingouin as *le bolchevik illuminé* and his arrogance in signing notices as *le préfet du Maquis*. There was no love lost between the followers of de Gaulle and the followers of Guingouin. On the other hand, Catesby's offi-cial and secret SOE briefings had described Guingouin as an excellent organiser and leader, but one inclined to stubbornness. An additional problem was that Guingouin, in common with the Free French, was suspicious of the British and didn't like their interfering. Catesby had been advised that he had to be as much diplomat as guerrilla warrior – not something for which his temperament was suited.

They reached the track where they had hidden the bicycles. It was possible to look over the tops of the fir trees. Guingouin pointed towards the viaduct. There was enough starlight to see that the third pillar was totally missing. The huge gap between the intact parts of the viaduct was spanned by two strings of sagging rails.

'Tomorrow's STO convoy will be cancelled,' said Guin-guoin, 'and I'm sure the young conscripts will know whom to thank.'

Catesby was surprised by the pride and satisfaction in Lo Grand's voice. The vanity made him more human. 'Do you think it will be repaired?' said Catesby.

'Certainly not. But I must be going. It's a long trek – about twenty kilometres.'

'Shall I come with you?'

'If you like. I am sure we can find a spare haystack or hole to put you in. There are no luxuries at Saint Gilles.'

It was a difficult journey. Lo Grand had decided that cycling along roads was too dangerous. The bikes had been hidden in various barns. Consequently, the return from the Bussy-Varache viaduct had been a difficult slog through forests, undergrowth and across sodden fields. Guingouin disdained following well-trodden paths. There was something about him that was self-flagellating and puritanical. It had taken more than seven hours to cover a distance of twelve miles to reach their forest hideout. Guingouin had spoken little during the dark trek, but one conversation had marked a turning point. During a brief break, Lo Grand had turned to Catesby and said, 'I believe that you went to Eton and Oxford?'

Catesby tried not to laugh. 'I went to neither.'

'Then I must have been misinformed.'

'Who told you that I went to Eton?'

'I can't reveal my sources, but our intelligence network supplies very accurate information.'

Catesby suspected that the information had been passed on from a Free French Gaullist who was pretending, or not pretending, to play both sides of the divide between themselves and Guingouin's FTP, the *Franc-Tireurs et Partisans*. The Free French, who dominated the scene in London, knew a lot about SOE and the people in it. Describing Catesby as public school and Oxbridge could have been a ploy to sow discord with the communist Guingouin.

'Your intelligence,' said Catesby, 'wasn't accurate in this instance.'

'Then what is your background?'

'My family are poor. I was brought up in a fishing port called Lowestoft.' Catesby hesitated as he began to speak. SOE training forbade sharing biographical information, but bonding with Guingouin was critically strategic – and also more important than having someone think he was an Etonian.

'Then how did you learn to speak French?'

'My mother is Belgian.'

'Ah,' said Guingouin, 'that explains your accent. You should try to hide it – and learn Lemosin.'

'Thanks.'

'But there is something about you that doesn't ring true. You don't have the manners of a worker.'

'No one would have said that at Cambridge.'

'What is this Cambridge?'

Catesby wished he had kept his mouth shut. The actual truth of his background would have made a bad cover story. 'Cambridge University. I was there as a student.'

Guingouin gave a sly smile. 'Your story about fishing-port poverty is falling apart. You went to an elite university where a select few of the British ruling class are trained to oppress and rule.'

'I was lucky and it's a complicated story.'

'I can understand why you want to keep it private.'

'Why do you think that?'

Guingouin gave a weary sigh. 'Sometimes a very rich man has a mistress who is poor and needy. The mistress becomes pregnant and the rich man feels a sense of obligation – and, perhaps, that is how you ended up at Cambridge University and became an officer instead of a common soldier. It happens in France too.'

Catesby laughed. 'I bet it does. But it isn't my story. My father was an ordinary sailor who met my mother in a bar in Antwerp. He was killed in an accident at sea when I was two years old.'

'Then we have something in common. I was eighteen months old when my father was killed at Bapaume.'

As Guingouin had warned, there weren't any luxuries at Saint-Gilles-les-Forêts. The sun was already high in the morning sky when they arrived. They were greeted by bowls of hot soup, but what Catesby craved most was sleep. He looked for a place. The only shelters above ground were a few camouflaged lean-tos which were already occupied by exhausted Maquisards. Catesby guessed the lean-tos were temporary accommodation. He could see that underground hiding places were still being dug and fitted out. A smell of woodsmoke filled the air, but there were no fires. They had been doused as soon as it turned light. Ribbons of smoke could have given the camp away. Meanwhile, everyone was busy and even a little jolly. On the edge of the camp two Maquisards, who introduced themselves as *les fonctionnaires sanitaires*, were digging a slit-trench latrine. Catesby felt like a loose end amid all the activity. He decided to drink his soup while it was still warm. A second later he was stretched out beside his empty bowl with the early spring sun on his face. He fell into blissful sleep – but it didn't last long.

Catesby didn't know what had woken him up, but a mournful bell was tolling in the distance. Other than this the camp had fallen silent. Guingouin made a sign for everyone to lie flat. He himself disappeared into the trees. There was a long tense wait before a message arrived and spread via whispers. A patrol of gendarmes had arrived in Sussac. 'We must disappear,' said the Maquisard nearest Catesby.

The forest undergrowth was almost impenetrable and had sheltered deer and wild boar for centuries. Everyone who had a gun was carrying it. There were no paths or clear spaces, only thick thorny undergrowth – the French word for such scrubland was *maquis* and, in this case, the *résistants* of Saint-Gilles-les-Forêts were living up to their name. Catesby tried to hollow a space where he could lie down, but was told to stay still and keep quiet. 'Don't worry,' whispered another Maquisard, 'the gendarmes will never come in here. The real danger is the *boches* who would use flamethrowers and machine guns.'

They remained in hiding until nightfall and then filtered back into the camp. The mood relaxed and fires were lit. Potatoes were passed around and roasted on sticks. Catesby heard the voice of Guingouin next to him, 'The patrol was to be expected – and I'm sure there will be more. We can't take any chances. But the good news is that the STO train was cancelled – and many of the conscripts have decided to go into hiding.'

Catesby found Guingouin's voice didactic, which wasn't surprising as teaching had been Lo Grand's profession before the war.

'You will, of course, report the destruction of the viaduct to London.'

'I can't unless I'm in contact with my wireless operator.'

'You will see him soon – but not now. There is too much police activity. Our sabotage has struck a raw nerve.'

Catesby was beginning to chafe at his lack of freedom of movement. He felt like a captive.

'You are welcome to use my underground hiding place,' said Guingouin. 'It's fairly comfortable and well hidden – and I won't always be there.'

'Good,' said Catesby with a wry smile.

The next few days in the forest hideout were an education and a revelation for Catesby. Any remaining doubts and cynicism that he had about Lo Grand and the Maquis Rouge quickly disappeared. He became aware that he was part of a resistance movement that was disciplined, organised and growing. But it wasn't just about resistance, it was about revolution too.

Everyone had a job and each Maquisard carried out his task with enthusiasm and without complaining. The most pressing assignment was building underground bunkers. Guingouin's own lair was the model. The walls were built from stout chestnut branches the thickness of a person's arm. The ceiling was constructed of thicker logs that could withstand any bombardment except a direct hit. The top of the hideout was covered by a tarpaulin hidden under a layer of earth which was strewn with dead leaves and branches. It was so well disguised that Catesby often had difficulty finding it, especially at night. The only furnishings were two low benches woven from birch twigs which served as beds, a table and a set of shelves for weapons, cutlery and books. Guingouin mourned the lack of books. Catesby was surprised to see that Lo Grand's sparse library contained several English and American books in French translation: *Treasure Island*, *The Adventures of Huckleberry Finn*, *Robinson Crusoe* and, somewhat ironically, *The Last of the Mohicans*. Catesby decided it would be tactless to mention that the book's hero,

Hawkeye, was a British colonialist fighting French colonialists and their Indian allies. There were also the usual French classics: *Les trois mousquetaires* and *Les Misérables*. If somehow, thought Catesby, they could escape from between their covers, Gavroche and Huck Finn would end up best mates.

'You are welcome to borrow them,' said Guingouin gesturing towards the books. 'Sadly, I've read them all – several times. They are books from my childhood. My mother was a schoolteacher and taught us to love reading. I'm sure that I must have damaged my eyes as a child reading by candlelight long into the night.'

'It looks as if you liked books about adventure.'

Guingouin smiled. 'Yes – and I think they left their mark. What about you?'

'I loved books about the sea and ships. I was probably trying to discover a dead father that I never knew. My favourite author became Joseph Conrad. When I read *Lord Jim*, I was only twelve. I imagined it was about my own dad – and that the hero's valiant death was why he was no longer with us. Silly.'

'I never fantasised about my own father.' Guingouin took a bottle from the shelf. 'I think some wine would be good.' He extracted a loose cork from a litre bottle and poured wine into a pair of tin cups. 'There's not much bread and very little meat, but no shortage of wine. In moderation, it's good for morale.'

Catesby raised his cup. 'To our fathers.'

'I would rather drink to my mother,' said Guingouin. 'She is a much braver person than my father ever was.'

'Even though he was killed in the war?'

'The twenty-eighth of August 1914. It was a stupid pointless death – like so many others. They were told to fix bayonets and attack across a recently harvested field of stubble. They ended up part of the harvest. The Germans had hidden their machine guns in bales of straw. Someone who was there told me that my father had spotted one of the machine guns and was rushing towards it when he was shot in the chest.'

'That sounds very brave.'

Guingouin shrugged. 'But pointless. There were two

thousand killed in the attack – six hundred of whom had been recruited here in Limousin, many by my own father who was a career soldier. My parents lived in married NCO quarters in the infantry garrison at Magnac-Laval. My mother was a teacher in the village. And after my father's death she continued teaching, but dressed in mourning. She will be in widow's clothes until the day she dies.'

'My mother is the same. Always dressed in black and mass every Sunday and many weekdays too.'

'My mother is an atheist – but no one can attack her for that, as anti-clerical republicanism was a foundation stone of the 1789 revolution and state schools are religion-free zones.'

Catesby looked closely at Guingouin. Many of his mysteries were beginning to unravel. Lo Grand's thick glasses – he was very short-sighted – disguised an inherited soldier's face of stern discipline and duty. The glasses turned him into an intellectual and reinforced the image of the schoolteacher that he had been.

'The general who ordered the stupid attack that killed my father was cashiered and sent back here. It was the beginning of the expression, *Limogé*. Sacked incompetent officers were sent to the Limoges region, far from the frontline where they could do little damage.' Guingouin smiled. 'But the Germans have given us another name. They call the Limousin *la petite Russie*. They say being here reminds them of service on the Eastern Front. I hope we live up to the compliment.'

'Your men show remarkable discipline and motivation,' said Catesby.

'Until now the comrades have been handpicked. I used to interview all of them. I wanted ones who were big, strong and aggressive – and ideologically committed. But recently we have had a flood of recruits – mostly young men who want to hide from STO conscription. It is a dilemma. We need a bigger force, but we haven't the food to feed them or the weapons to arm them.'

'We can help you with the weapons.'

'You already have – and you must begin to give lessons on the Sten gun. Not to everyone, but to a cadre who will become instructors.' Guingouin lowered his voice. 'What does London want?'

'I don't know. I'm only a small cog.'

'Guess.'

'I think that London wants a Resistance that will tie down large numbers of German troops when we open up a second front.'

'Why haven't you done that already?' said Guingouin. 'The Russians are doing all of the fighting.'

'Not all of the fighting. We've nearly kicked the Germans out of North Africa.'

'A sideshow – and one that is going slowly. Churchill is dragging his feet in order to bleed the Soviet Union.'

'What are your war aims?' said Catesby.

Guingouin put on a stony face. After a pause, he said, 'Have you ever been a member of the Communist Party?'

'No.'

'Why not? You come from a working-class background. Have you no sense of class solidarity?'

'On the contrary, I was a member of the Cambridge University Labour Club.'

'Why not the Communist Party? We are the only party that doesn't make compromises with capitalism.'

'One reason was because the Molotov-Ribbentrop Pact left a bad taste in my mouth.' There were other reasons, but Catesby was reluctant to tell Guingouin that most of the Communist Party members at Cambridge had come from public schools – and that he didn't want to join and be patronised as their token prole.

Guingouin smiled and nodded. 'On Molotov-Ribbentrop, we agree. But, in terms of tactics, the non-aggression pact did give the Soviet Union time to re-arm. Otherwise, the victory at Stalingrad may never have happened.'

'But I believe,' said Catesby, 'that you didn't follow the Party line?'

'It was a balancing act. My first act of defiance was an underground newspaper, *A Call to Action*.' Guingouin laughed. 'Well, it was hardly a newspaper. We didn't have any stencils, so we had

to type out each of the twenty copies. I wrote that I would refuse
to follow the French Communist Party line that told us not to
attack the German occupation or to take sides in an imperialist
war. I rejected that policy and denounced the German occupation. It was no longer a question of telling the workers to remain
neutral in a war between imperialists.' Guingouin hammered
the table with his fist. 'Our country had been invaded and we
needed to fight a war of national independence. I wrote that in
September 1940 – nine months before the Party line changed
when Hitler invaded Russia.'

Catesby felt an unease that was to dog him throughout his
career as an intelligence officer. A big part of the job was reporting on other people – being a snitch. Catesby had already made
notes for a coded report to London on Guingouin. One of his
tasks was to let London know about Lo Grand's relationship
with the French Communist Party. They also wanted to know
whether Guingouin was a Titoist or a Stalinist or a Trotskyite
– and what would be his role after the war. And would the Resistance turn from a war of liberation into a workers' revolution?

'The problem with Maurice,' said Guingouin, 'is that he
doesn't understand local conditions – and we had the same
problem with Gabriel before he was arrested.'

Catesby nodded knowingly – even though he hadn't a clue
about either person Guingouin was talking about. He suspected that Lo Grand was playing a game to test how much he
knew. The first name did, however, ring a bell that he should
have heard immediately. Maurice was Maurice Thorez, head of
the PCF, the French Communist Party. Catesby remembered
that 'the leader's letter' in *Humanité Clandestine*, the PCF's
underground newspaper, was always signed: 'Maurice Thorez.
Somewhere in France.' Sometime later he came to realise that
Gabriel was Gabriel Péri, a communist journalist who was executed in 1941 and who was famous for singing while he was
being tortured. Péri didn't live long enough to join those who
fought from the shadows, but his heroic death inspired those
who did.

'Why,' said Catesby, confident at least about the identity of the other man, 'doesn't Maurice understand local conditions. Hasn't he been to the Limousin?'

Guingouin laughed. 'Maurice Thorez hasn't been anywhere in France since the beginning of the war. He deserted from the army rather than fight the Germans. The Party line still supported the Molotov-Ribbentrop non-aggression pact and he fled to the Soviet Union. He's been safely tucked away in Moscow ever since, but pretending to lead the resistance struggle from within France itself.' Guingouin paused. 'But please keep what I have told you secret. One must never appear cynical in front of the comrades. The struggle requires complete discipline – even when one puts common sense before the Party line.'

'You can trust me,' said Catesby. He was still young and inexperienced enough to mean the words, but one day he would learn that 'trust me' was spytrade slang for 'fuck you'.

'You must get used to sleeping during the day,' said Guingouin. 'We are nightshift workers – but at least the day is less cold than the night and you get used to sleeping with the sun in your face. The light doesn't matter, it feels good. The winter is terrible. Once you have survived a winter in the woods, you are a true Maquisard.'

Catesby looked again at Guingouin's meagre pile of books. 'Have you read any Shakespeare?'

'No, they only studied Shakespeare at the *lycée* – which was at Châteauroux, over a hundred kilometres away. I would have needed lodgings – and my mother hadn't the means for that. The only Shakespeare I know is "To be or not to be".' Guingouin beamed behind his thick glasses. 'And all of us here have answered that question.'

'We were lucky,' said Catesby. 'Our equivalent of a *lycée*, Denes Grammar, was a five-minute walk from our house. Many of our teachers had survived the trenches – and were completely mad or half-mad. Our English master, Mr Bennett, wasn't particularly mad, but only had one arm. We never knew how much of the blasted-off arm was missing for the stump was hidden beneath his academic gown – which he flourished like a wizard's cape.'

Guingouin was glowing. 'There is no calling more sacred

than that of teacher. What a coincidence that we both had inspirational one-armed teachers. Mine was René Timbal, who not only lost an arm but had respiratory problems from mustard gas. He was forever quoting Victor Hugo and gave me a copy of *Le Feu* by Henri Barbusse – a part of Timbal was pacifist, but another part was revolutionary. I'm not sure he ever reconciled the two.'

Catesby decided not to comment. None of his own parts reconciled. A side of him was proud of his working-class Lowestoft background, but when he arrived at Cambridge he had wanted to breathe in the new world of refined privilege around him. On one occasion he had been invited by a classmate for a weekend at a stately home: the paintings were museum pieces, the wine and manners were faultless. And the voices were quiet and understated. When you have power, there is no need to shout. In contrast, he remembered how ill at ease he felt during his Christmas visit home after his first semester at Cambridge. When he went to the pub to meet his boyhood friends – many of whom were in uniform as ordinary soldiers and sailors – he tried too hard to talk in a Lowestoft accent. He noticed a coldness from those around him. One of his uncles, a fitter in the shipyard, leaned over and whispered, 'What you trying to do, boy? I think it's time you went back to Cambridge.' The words still rankled.

The day before he was supposed to catch a train back to Cambridge, a hit-and-run bomber swept in from the North Sea and dropped its load in the town centre. It was midday and people were out shopping. Waller's department store was flattened. Sixty-three people were killed – including three of Catesby's school friends, who had been having tea in a café. That evening Catesby joined in with volunteers who were helping to clear the site and to look for victims. He felt useless among workers with calloused hands who were used to shifting heavy loads. When he returned to Cambridge, he decided it was time to join up.

'You look very tired,' said Guingouin.

'Sorry, I drifted into a different world. Mr Bennett used to comment upon it too. He knew me better than my mother.'

'Weren't you close to your mother?'

Catesby laughed. 'Perhaps not, Dr Freud.'

Guingouin looked blank. Either he didn't get the joke or, thought Catesby, he hadn't heard of Freud.

'I was an English boy who loved the sea, long cycling trips, football and visiting my English cousins who lived in the countryside. My mother was a foreigner who said the rosary every night and hated speaking English. It was embarrassing when my friends came to our house.'

'I had students like that: refugees from Spain and Jewish children who didn't want to talk about where they came from. Your friends should have welcomed your being different – and you should have loved your mother more.'

'You are treating me like one of your students.'

'If I am, I make no apology for that.'

'I've noticed you expect a lot of people – you are demanding of your Maquisards.'

'I make no apology for that either. Since the age of thirteen, my life has had only one purpose – and for that I must thank my teacher, René Timbal.'

There was something in Guingouin's voice of almost religious awe. It reminded Catesby of some of the mad monks he had met during his Roman Catholic childhood. The severe sincerity of their voices had at first frightened Catesby and, as he reached his teens, made him laugh and turned him into an atheist.

'Timbal,' continued Guingouin in hushed tones, 'had known my father and survived the same attack in which he was killed. One winter's evening after classes he summoned me into his office. He made sure that we were the only ones left in the school and locked the door behind us in case we weren't.'

Catesby's eyes grew round. It was turning into a good story.

'At first,' said Guingouin, 'it seemed that Timbal wanted to tell me about the battle in which my father had fallen. He began by talking about how they had departed for the front full of high spirits and bloodlust – *On to Berlin; Bury the Kaiser; Let's have at them* – and how that bravado had turned into tragedy and farce. It was, of course, a story that I already knew well. My mother hadn't spared me the details. Bayonets against machine guns – and the men of Limousin soon screaming and dying in heaps on the harvest stubble. What Timbal most wanted to say was conveyed in two words that he repeated several times: *horror* and *absurdity*. His voice, owing to the mustard-gas lung damage, was often a whistling hiss. Even at that young age, I thought he was a damaged person and, not having a family of his own, needed to talk about what had happened. But I was wrong. Timbal had no self-pity – only a passion to put things right. What happened next surprised me and I will never forget the moment.'

Once again, Catesby thought of Mr Bennett – a different one-armed man from Monsieur Timbal. Bennett always warned how too much emotion could turn a story from pathos to bathos – and that *King Lear* skirted the boundary but never crossed it. Catesby wondered where Guingouin's story was going.

'René Timbal opened a desk drawer and took something out. He looked hard at me and shook his head. For a second, I thought he had changed his mind about whatever was about to happen. Finally, he said, "You must never tell anyone about this. Not a word, a single word, to any of your classmates." I, of course, promised that I wouldn't say a word. He then handed me something that was more a pamphlet than a book. I opened it – and I felt my life change as soon as I read the first words.'

Catesby had already guessed what was coming. It wouldn't be the first time he had heard the words recited aloud and with passion.

Guingouin began with the opening words of the Communist Manifesto: 'A spectre is haunting Europe.' His voice rose in volume and intensity as he recited the final lines: 'Let the ruling classes tremble at a communist revolution. The proletarians have nothing to lose but their chains. They have a world to win.'

Catesby wondered if Mr Bennett would have agreed.

'But,' said Guingouin, 'the path isn't always clear to everyone. Look at Trotsky, the Mensheviks, the anarchists.'

Once again, Catesby decided to bite his tongue and listen to Lo Grand.

'There are problems and disagreements with where we are now and what we should do.'

Catesby wanted to know more for his report. There were rumours that Guingouin was considered a renegade by the Moscow-orientated leadership of the PCF. But, as he waited for Lo Grand to say more, he realised that the Maquis leader was stretched out on his rough bed, eyes closed, but glasses still on.

The next day Catesby gave his first lesson on the use and care of the Sten gun. The classroom was an outbuilding of an abandoned farm near Sussac. It appeared to have been a workshop for there was a table with a rusty vice attached. Catesby laid out a Sten on the table. There was a larger farm building a few paces away where another lesson was taking place. Catesby could hear Guingouin giving a lecture on Marxist-Leninist theory.

'The important thing about the Sten,' said Catesby, 'is its simplicity. You can teach anyone to use it in a matter of minutes – but there are precautions you must emphasise.' He lifted a rectangular cylinder that was about ten inches long. 'First of all, do not overload the magazine. It holds thirty-two rounds, but if you fully load it, it is likely the gun will jam. Don't put more than twenty-nine rounds in the magazine.' Through the walls, he could hear Guingouin lecturing about class struggle. Catesby lifted the Sten gun. 'This is a worker's weapon built by workers. The Sten is being produced in the millions to free the people of Europe.'

None of the Maquisards responded.

Catesby shifted to English. 'Well, that went down like a fucking lead balloon.'

A Maquisard, who always seemed to wear a smug smile, turned to the comrade next to him and said, *'Il a dit quelque chose à propos d'un putain de ballon.'*

'You obviously,' said Catesby, 'speak fluent English.'

'Un peu,' replied the smug Maquisard.

Catesby realised that the teaching profession was not for him, but carried on. He lifted the Sten gun and returned to speaking French. 'This is not a high-quality weapon produced at great expense. The cost of labour and material to turn out each one comes to fifteen shillings, a sum that would buy a worker fifteen pints of British beer – or, in French terms, four bottles of drinkable table wine.'

'You've made the point,' said one of the Maquisards.

'Thanks. On fully automatic, the Sten fires nearly five hundred rounds a minute – which means you could empty the magazine in less than four seconds. Try instead to fire in two- to three-round bursts – or you can easily shift to semi-automatic,' Catesby showed them, 'by pushing this button with your thumb.'

'We need extra magazines,' said one of the older men. 'There was only one magazine per gun in the supply drop.'

'That was a failing and I will send a message to London about it.' If, thought Catesby, he was ever reunited with his radio operator. Keeping them separate was a security precaution too far.

'And speaking of magazines, tell your people not to use the magazine as a grip when firing. I know, because the magazine sticks out horizontally, it's in exactly the right place for a comfortable fore-grip – but using it like that will damage the lips attaching it to the gun.' Yet another design problem thought Catesby.

'Where is the safety mechanism?'

Catesby looked woefully at the Maquisard. 'There isn't one. The best you can do is slide the bolt into this slot,' he showed them how, 'which, as long as it stays in the slot, prevents the gun from firing. But,' Catesby frowned, 'if you bump the Sten or drop it, the bolt may come out of the slot and slam forward causing the gun to fire uncontrollably on fully automatic. On the other hand, the Sten is easy to disassemble,' Catesby rapidly dismantled the gun, 'and, if you take it completely apart, it is totally safe.'

'Bravo,' said one of his audience, clapping.

Catesby knew that the Sten had two annoying habits. One was jamming and the other was firing like mad when you didn't want it to. A year before an SOE team had been dropped into Czechoslovakia to assassinate Reinhard Heydrich, the 'Butcher of Prague'. After ambushing Heydrich's car, a Czech agent aimed his Sten at the top Nazi – but the gun jammed as soon as he pulled the trigger. Meanwhile, another agent managed to fling a grenade at the car and Heydrich died of his wounds a week later. One lesson from the assassination was the unreliability of the Sten, but a more important lesson was the danger of reprisals. The SS reacted to Heydrich's assassination by levelling villages and murdering thousands of civilians.

Catesby snapped the Sten back together in a few seconds and flourished the submachine gun like a gangster. Normally, he hated showing off, but he wanted to make a point. 'Despite its faults, I love the Sten – and you and your fellow fighters will learn to love it too. In the next few months we are going to parachute in tens of thousands of these weapons. The Sten does not have the range or reliability of your Lebel.' Catesby was referring to the First World War rifle that many of the Maquisards still carried. 'Sure, if you want to pick off a *boche* at five hundred metres, use a Lebel. But if you want a weapon that is easy to conceal and lethal at close range, this is the one.'

One of the Maquisards said, 'You can easily hide one under your coat; you can't do that with a Lebel.'

'And very easy if you detach the stock. It's now time for you to get to know these guns.' As Catesby handed over the Sten to the Maquisards, part of him hoped he himself would soon have a chance to use it. That chance came sooner than expected.

The next few days were devoted to the usual chores of building shelters, resupplying, training and shifting and hiding stores. Catesby was agitated because he needed to send reports to London and there was no sign of reuniting him with his wireless operator. He also needed to do a reconnaissance of future drop zones for London. Catesby demanded a meeting with Guingouin. It occurred after midnight in an abandoned farmhouse near Châteauneuf-la-Forêt. The farmhouse was grander than any dwelling Catesby had seen so far in the Limousin. He had been led there on foot by the tall Maquisard called Paul.

'Nice place,' said Catesby looking at the furniture and paintings.

'And an excellent wine cellar.'

'Any chance of a tasting?'

Paul seemed distracted. He was staring at what looked like an early Renaissance painting of the Virgin and child. A slim-waisted Mary had bared a plump breast. The sensuality was striking. 'I doubt,' said Paul, 'if it's a genuine Fouquet – most likely an homage by a student. In any case, we should put it in safekeeping.'

'Is looting a problem?'

'Not with us. We have strict rules and accountability. Lo Grand would execute any *résistant* who stole for personal gain. But the higher-ranking German officers have no such scruples. The brighter ones realise they are on the losing side and might soon need to buy and negotiate their way into a different life. They particularly like works of art – and fine wines. We don't want this collection to attract attention.'

'Who owns this place?' said Catesby

'A Roman Catholic royalist.'

'It sounds like he's more of a marquis than a Maquis.'

'He is, in fact, a baron.'

'But he's still part of the Resistance?'

'Ah, that's an interesting question. We're not sure that he has made a decision.'

'In that case, I will try to be on my best behaviour.'

'You won't need to be. The baron isn't here: he's in North Africa.'

For the first time, Catesby noticed that Paul spoke French in a manner that was more refined and urbane than that of his comrades. Catesby was about to say something, but Paul had gone across the room where he had both hands on the frame of the Virgin and child painting and was trying to lift it off the wall. 'Can you give me a hand,' he said, 'the wire is twisted around the hook.'

Catesby reached behind the canvas and managed to undo the wire.

Paul placed the painting on the floor leaning against the wall. 'I hope no one puts their foot through it. We'll deal with it later.'

Catesby was struck by the eroticism of the painting, but refrained from making a crude barracks' room remark. Instead he said, 'The Madonna doesn't look particularly pious.'

'She wasn't intended to be. The model for the Fouquet original would have been Agnès Sorel, the king's mistress. She was a fascinating woman. Her early death might have been part of a coup attempt.'

'Lo Grand,' said Catesby, 'doesn't like having women around. Is he afraid of a coup?'

'He regards love affairs and mistresses as security risks.'

Catesby was still too inexperienced to comment, but in his later career he discovered that the honey trap was an intelligence officer's best weapon for turning an agent.

'Don't think,' said Paul, 'that Lo Grand is a warrior monk. He has a fiancée, but keeps her existence secret to protect her from reprisals. Protecting those we love is a problem for many of us.'

Catesby nodded at the portrait of the Madonna, who might have been Agnès Sorel, now on the floor and leaning forlornly against the wall. 'The king didn't do a very good job of protecting her.'

Paul smiled. 'We love more truly.'

There was suddenly shouting from an adjoining room. 'That sounds like a lovers' tiff.'

'I would call it a dialectical discussion between comrades,' said Paul.

Catesby strained to hear. The louder of the voices, not Lo Grand's, was shouting something about 'Party policy' and the need to 'make common cause with the proletariat in the towns – and to stop hiding in the woods'.

Paul frowned. 'Have you got your Sten gun?'

'It's with my pack in the corner.'

'I was only joking – but there are those in the Party who are calling for Lo Grand's liquidation.'

The shouting got louder. There was now a second voice which seemed to be screaming at Lo Grand.

'Actually, it might be a good idea if you did get your Sten.'

Catesby picked up the gun and followed Paul to a pair of

ornate double doors of dark oak. There was more shouting from within. Paul hammered on the door. There was a sudden silence; then a voice, Guingouin's, said, 'Come in.'

Paul opened the doors into a room which was a vast library. Guingouin, in battle dress, was seated at a table with two men in suits – who looked surprisingly bourgeois for Communist Party apparatchiks. The older of the two men had long flowing moustaches and nodded towards Catesby, 'Put your gun down. We're not here to play games.'

Catesby noticed that the younger man had drawn a pistol and was aiming it at him. His immediate reaction was not the safest option. Catesby pretended to un-sling the Sten but swung it towards the older comrade and put his finger on the trigger. The older man, unfazed, shook his head and turned towards Guingouin. 'Silly theatrics, Comrade Georges.'

Decades later Catesby learned that such a situation was called a 'Mexican stand-off'. Once, after too much wine, he bragged to his teenage grandchildren that he had actually been in one. They were impressed. Much more impressed than his stepchildren – or his wife – were ever about anything from his past. The oddest thing about the incident was that Catesby, not the bravest of people, had felt no fear at the time. As he looked at the gun pointed at him – and at the other faces in the room – he felt that he was a character in a gangster film. The guns weren't real and the room was a film set.

Guingouin looked at Catesby and said in English, 'Stop.' Catesby didn't get what *stop* meant. Guingouin made a gesture indicating that he should put his gun down. Catesby complied – as did the Party official with the pistol.

Guingouin shifted into French. 'Our comrade is British. He doesn't fully understand the situation. But if you kill me – and him – there will be no further supplies. The weapons and explosives we need will stop.'

The comrade with the pistol sneered. 'We don't need help from de Gaulle and the Free French.'

'The help,' said Guingouin, 'does not come from the Free French. It comes from the British. No, comrade, let me finish.

We will not, at least not in the near future, ever receive guns and ammunition from Moscow. If you can't give us guns, you shouldn't dictate tactics.'

The apparatchik with the long flowing moustaches shook his head. 'I have never heard a more stupid argument – nor one that is more in contempt of Communist Party leadership. You are not, Comrade Guingouin, merely a useful dupe of the bourgeoisie; you are a *useless* one as well. No wonder they call you "the madman of the woods".'

Catesby felt that he had a front seat on the making of European history. He wished that his fellow members of the Cambridge University Labour Club could see him now.

The moustached apparatchik gave Catesby a brief glance that registered contempt. He fixed Guingouin with a hard stare. 'You will be hearing from us again.'

Guingouin sat in silence as the two visiting Party members put on their trilbies and left. The silence continued until the outside door slammed. Guingouin gave a bleak smile, 'At least they didn't accuse me of being a Trotskyite; that would have made orders for my liquidation irrevocable.'

'I think,' said Paul, 'that the comrade who made the disparaging remark about the Free French isn't up to date on Party policy. Cooperation with them, and de Gaulle too, is now advocated.'

'This visit,' said Guingouin, 'was a warning. Maurice is worried about losing control. He is afraid of my popularity and influence.'

Catesby suspected that Lo Grand wasn't so much bragging, as stating a fact.

'In any case,' said Guingouin, 'the madman must be getting back to his woods.'

As Guingouin got up to leave, Paul gave a snappy salute. Catesby awkwardly followed with one of his own. He wasn't sure what the protocol was for British officers, but he held the salute until Lo Grand had left the room.

'Thank you,' said Paul. 'He needs respect and support.'

'One of the first things that Lo Grand told me was that he was a committed communist, but one who doesn't always follow the

Party line. Which line hasn't he been following now?' As soon as he said the words, Catesby wondered if he had probed too far.

Paul looked away. When he spoke, he seemed to be choosing his words carefully. 'The older of our two visitors is the Inter-Regional Commander – and someone who always acts on the instructions of the Central Committee. The Party line is that resistance to the occupation must come from the urban prole-tariat. They believe that we should be fighting in the towns and not the countryside.' For a second, Paul's face seemed etched with pain. 'And I've seen what happens when we…'

Catesby broke the silence that had fallen. 'Your accent sug-gests that you aren't from around here.'

'A lot of us aren't. I'm sure you've heard Spanish accents – and ones from Marseilles as well as the north. I'm a Parisian – and I saw what happened during the student protests in the summer of 1941. My nephew was one of those who were arrested and executed. But it didn't end there. An underground communist group, *les Bataillons de la Jeunesse*, decided to extract revenge and killed a German officer at the Barbès-Rochechouart métro station. In the following weeks, more assassinations were carried out. In the end, a dozen or so German soldiers and officers were killed. But at what price? At least eight hundred hostages were executed and thirteen thousand people thought to be commu-nists were arrested.' Paul shook his head. 'Maybe you shouldn't listen to me. Their tactics might have been crude and the price high, but these young people were the first in France to fight the Nazis.'

'Will Lo Grand ever fight in the towns?'

'Of course he will. But only when the time comes.' Paul paused. 'The problem with towns is that they have too many eyes and ears – and too many people you can't trust.'

Catesby looked longingly at the comfortable surroundings of the house.

Paul smiled. 'I know what you're thinking. We all get fed up with the woods.'

'Any news of when I'm going to be reunited with my wireless operator?'

Paul reached into his pocket and handed over a piece of paper which was in code.

Jimmy Fenn's message was written in the Playfair Cipher. The cipher was a simple one based on a keyword or phrase that had to contain at least eight different letters including two of the last six letters of the alphabet. While on a training exercise in the Scottish Highlands, Catesby and his partner had chosen the word SUPPLEMENTARY, but his partner kept misspelling it and they never succeeded in decoding each other's messages. There was a lot of frustration and cursing as their frostbitten fingers scribbled nonsense from the decoding squares. Jimmy Fenn, however, came up with a more memorable key which was also easier to spell: YOU WANKERS. An additional benefit was that if a Gestapo or Abwehr decrypter managed to discover their secret key, the Nazi would get a clear British message. If, however, an enemy decrypter had broken the code, they would have been none the wiser. Catesby admired Jimmy's accurate map-reading as much as his sense of security:

RV LOCATION – MIDDLE OF FUCKING NOWHERE
TIME OF RV – WHENEVER YOU GET HERE

It was still dark when Catesby set off for 'fucking nowhere'. He was led on bicycle by a relay of two guides. It was a gruelling journey of more than twenty miles which required much off-road pushing along rough tracks. The safe house was an abandoned farmstead, but there was a pasture with two grazing heifers – which gave a peasant courier an excuse to visit and pass on messages and warnings.

The last part of the trip involved pushing the bikes up a muddy lane that ended at a gate. The guide motioned for Catesby to stay hidden and went towards the house himself. Catesby felt ashamed that, if the safe house had been betrayed, the guide was willing to give his own life to protect his. Watching from the shadows of scrub oak and pine, Catesby saw a woman open the door – or was it Jimmy in disguise? The guide beckoned Catesby to come forward and then disappeared into the house.

A battered door, hanging precariously off rusty hinges, led directly into a kitchen. There was a hearth with a smouldering fire and a pot hanging from a hook with the woman bending over it. She was wearing a headscarf, a long skirt and boots. The only part of her that was uncovered were strong-looking forearms. It looked like one of the women from Millet's painting, *The Gleaners*, had popped in to do some cooking.

The inside of the house was dark and smoky. The guide whispered something to the woman and then took his leave. There was the sound of footsteps coming down a creaking loft ladder. Then a laugh. It was Jimmy's laugh. 'Great to see you, Mr Catesby. Thought you were coming, so I've strung up the antenna. London's been going off their nut over the lack of communication.'

Catesby nodded towards the woman.

'That's my wife Hélène. She decided to join us. Her parents are going to look after the kid for the duration.'

Catesby was appalled that nothing had been cleared with Guingouin or London, but Jimmy was a law unto himself.

'By the way, Hélène had already been doing jobs for the Resistance before she came here. She's strong as an ox and brave as a tiger.'

Hélène pointed a dripping ladle at Jimmy.

'And she understands English. Would you like some ersatz coffee, wine or plum brandy?'

'Plum brandy.' Catesby warmed his hands at the fire. 'You seem to be living at the Ritz compared to the rest of us.'

'But it's a long way to the pub.' Jimmy handed over a chipped glass with the homemade brandy.

'Where was yours?'

'The Rumburgh Buck. My dad is an expert at biking back from there on a winter's evening without lights and pissed as a newt. He'd be a great Maquisard.'

Catesby nodded. Endless wet cold bike journeys at night along winding country lanes were the essence of life in the

Resistance. 'Let's go outside,' said Catesby, 'and have a chat.' He didn't want to burden Jimmy's wife with more secrets than she already had. Jimmy understood and followed him.

'Is the radio in the loft?'

'No, I've buried it in a metal case in the woods – and I've hidden the one-time pads separately. But London prefers using the WOK. Maybe they've misplaced their one-time pads.'

Catesby frowned. The one-time pad was a more secure system, unbreakable – unless you had a copy of the pad. The WOK, Worked-Out Keys, was a code system printed on what looked like a silk handkerchief. Silk, unlike paper, doesn't rustle during a body search and was easily concealed in the lining of clothing. Each time an operator used a particular key, he cut that piece off the handkerchief. The system meant that operators didn't have to memorise a code. If he or she was captured, they couldn't be tortured into remembering the discarded code – and the Germans would be unable to decipher the encoded messages they had copied. Catesby's own silk WOK was in the lining of his woollen scarf, something he could easily throw away if in danger of capture.

'I've got copies of London's latest messages,' said Jimmy, 'but I haven't yet decoded them.'

It was after dark when Catesby began the decoding under the light of a flickering candle. He unstitched his silk WOK from his scarf as he sat next to the fire. If the Germans burst in, the codes would quickly go up in smoke. Catesby put his Sten on the table next to him. He would take a few of them with him. He put his hand in his trouser pocket to make sure the L pill was still there. The plum brandy had fuelled Catesby's bravado and also his tendency to melodrama. In fact, there was little chance of complete surprise. In a town, yes. But not in the deepest countryside thick with Maquisards and peasant sympathisers.

The first message, as Catesby suspected, was a telling-off.

1 Essential REPEAT essential that you maintain more regular wireless contact. Inform of any difficulties preventing this.

2 Begin planning for 3 airdrops which will take place during next moon. Explosives, detonators, weapons, Sten ammunition, 9000-volt transformers, bicycle tubes and tyres with French manufacture marking. Inform of any additional requirements. Personnel may accompany air drops.

No need to save a copy, the details were easy to remember. He balled up the decoding and tossed it on the fire. The second message was both intriguing and annoying.

1 NEW CONTACT: GILBERT. Air Operations Specialist and Organiser.
2 GILBERT will arrive in Limoges before next moon.
Contact at Boulangerie des Frères between 9 and 10 am.
Password procedure as follows:
'How is Mathilde's poor mother?'
'Yes, she's getting better.' (Means GILBERT has NOT yet arrived.)
'Sadly, she has taken a turn for the worst.' (Means GILBERT HAS arrived.)
'The poor dear. I must go see her.' (Confirms that you will rendezvous on the rue de la Boucherie at 12:05. GILBERT will be walking southwest and carrying a book in his left hand. Your passwords to GILBERT: 'Is the library open?' His reply: 'I'm going there now.'

Catesby memorised the procedure and consigned the decoding to the fire. He had no intention of making risky trips to Limoges every day to check if GILBERT had arrived. Nor was he going to assign the job to a courier. The whole thing sounded unnecessary – and a bit fishy. No, thought Catesby, he wasn't going to discuss it with Guingouin. The suggested method for making contact with GILBERT – risking an agent on a daily basis to see if he had arrived – defied every rule of security. Catesby began to write a reply – one that London wouldn't like.

1 Your Para 1. No need of Air Operations Specialist
in this circuit. Local Maquis organise air drops with
professionalism and concerns for security. They have
EXCELLENT knowledge of countryside. Outside advice
would not be appreciated or productive.
2 Your Para 2. GILBERT RV Limoges. Unacceptable
security risk. Compared to rural Limousin, Limoges is
swarming with Germans and collabos. Cannot REPEAT
cannot risk agent making visits as suggested to RV site to
contact GILBERT. It is best that local Maquis arrange RVs
and security checks.

Catesby spent four days with Jimmy and Hélène before they
moved on to new locations. The most important task was renew-
ing radio communications with London – which was safer in the
remote countryside than in a town where the Germans had per-
manent monitoring stations. Nonetheless, the Germans often
made forays into rural Limousin with *Funkpeilwagen*, vans with
direction-finding antennae. Years later Catesby always warned
his stepchildren to pay their TV licences because the BBC *Funk-
peilwagens* would track them down. Catesby's stepdaughter, who
seemed to know everything, tired of the nagging and informed
him that the BBC vans used a different technology based on
fluctuating light signals – and that you could avoid detection by
hanging heavy dark curtains in the room where you watched
TV. It didn't work and his stepdaughter was fined. Afterwards,
Catesby's wife warned him not to put on his I-told-you-so face
because 'it always makes things worse'.

SOE W/T operators were trained to limit their transmissions
to less than five minutes, but many of Jimmy's exceeded that.
He reckoned that frequently changing locations minimised the
risk. 'In any case,' he said, 'Hélène is dying for a chance to shoot
up a *Funkpeilwagen*. She's handy with a Sten.'

Catesby came to admire Hélène. She looked like a woman who
was used to a lot of hard physical labour, but also one who could
let her hair down and become disarmingly seductive. She was not
only strong and fearless, but quickly mastered Morse code and

could flawlessly copy messages from London. Jimmy wanted to fully train her to be a W/T operator in case he was killed or captured, but feared that if London found out that Hélène was W/T proficient, they would send her a radio and dispatch her to another circuit. There was a desperate need for wireless operators.

'The Resistance,' confided Jimmy when Hélène was out of earshot, 'saved our marriage.'

'How did you find out she was in the Resistance?'

'It happened when I was still on the wireless course. I got friendly with a guy from Paris codenamed Gustav, who had been exfiltrated by Lysander to do W/T training. Neither of us was very good about keeping mum about our backgrounds. When I told him about Hélène and her dad's radio business, Gustav said, "Bad luck for him. All those shops have been shut down and the radios confiscated." Not surprising, I thought – but I was a bit concerned and showed it. A few days later, Gustav came to me and whispered, "A woman who sounds like your wife is working for Prosper." He didn't tell me how he got the information and I didn't ask. I hoped it was her and I was relieved. For a long time, I was jealous and wondered if Hélène had gone off with someone else.'

'So how did you get in contact again?'

'I got a friendly lady in a safe house to make phone calls for me. She got in contact with Hélène's dad – who knew how to talk in codes – and after a few more phone calls, including a tall tale about a job in Limoges, my wife boarded a train at Gare d'Austerlitz with false identity papers and a cover yarn as a nursery nurse. Hélène, by the way, was glad to get away from the Prosper network. She thinks a lot of them are pretty careless.'

'Why?'

'She hears some of them chatter away in English in big restaurants. There's something about Paris that loosens tongues – which is bad when all the expensive eateries and cafés have at least one informer taking notes.'

'We should message London about it.'

'Do you think it would do any good? Look at that stupid rendezvous plan with the GILBERT geezer.'

'Any chance we can get Hélène to do a recce of the boulangerie?'

'She'd love to.'

The next morning Jimmy's wife was on her bike. Women attracted less suspicion than men and could move around more easily. It made them invaluable as couriers and spies. But operating in the open exposed women to more danger. Jimmy and Catesby felt uneasy as they waved her off. Hélène looked the part: a raw-boned country girl cycling into town with a shopping bag. Someone of no interest to Germans and collabo cops.

Meanwhile, Jimmy retrieved the wireless from its latest hiding place and strung out the antenna to receive the scheduled transmission from London. Catesby placed himself in a well-hidden position from where he could observe anyone approaching. He knew they were unlikely to be disturbed, so he put aside his Sten and took out a novel by Stendhal, *The Red and the Black*, that he had nicked from the safe house where Guingouin had a run-in with the Party bigwigs. Catesby found the novel disturbing and wished he had chosen something else. There were too many parallels between the low-born Julien Sorel and himself – except that Julien had a more interesting sex life. He put the book aside and thought about Jimmy with envy. He had found contentment with Hélène. Was it because they came from similar social backgrounds? Or because they were both sex mad? On the first night Catesby had shared the kitchen floor with them as a place to sleep. He was woken up just before midnight. Catesby pretended to sleep through the session – and, to relieve any embarrassment on their part, faked a few snores when they finally finished. Catesby had barely fallen back asleep when they began again. He was woken twice more, the last time when dawn had already broken. Catesby rolled over and stared into the darkness. He wished he had a woman.

It was early afternoon when Hélène returned from Limoges. The bike's panniers contained a greyish-looking baguette, a tin of cooking oil and cloth – the sort of things a countrywoman would plausibly fetch from the town.

'Is the baguette,' said Jimmy, 'from the Boulangerie des Frères?'

'It is – and required two ration tickets.'

'Did you ask about Mathilde's mother?'

'No. There was a queue and I didn't want to attract attention. But I did visit the linen shop next door before I went to the bakery.' She held up a piece of grey patterned cloth, 'This is the best they had. It's an old curtain. We chatted and I said I was new to Limoges and asked if their neighbours were good bakers. They said the boulangerie had been vacant for months and that the couple now running it had only arrived recently – from Paris, they thought. They also said if I wanted good white bread I would have to buy it on the black market or go to the countryside.'

'The fact that the bakers are strangers makes the rendezvous procedure more toxic,' said Catesby.

'You think,' said Jimmy, 'that they can't be trusted?'

Catesby tried to keep the raging fires of paranoia at bay. 'I don't know. But we can't send someone to the bakery every day to check if GILBERT's turned up. It's not just a matter of getting spotted by an informer and picking up a tail – but of running out of ration tickets. I'm glad we told London it's a no-go. Can't wait to hear what they say.'

The reply came the next morning and was not what Catesby had expected.

1 GILBERT's imminent arrival in Limoges cancelled REPEAT cancelled. Cease all rendezvous procedures immediately.
2 Agent JACQUES DUBOIS to make contact with FARRIER on 02/05/43 at 1330 hours local time to arrange temporary return to England to report on progress.
3 Immediate FARRIER Contact and RV: CLAIRE at the tomb of Agnès Sorel in the church of Sainte-Ours Loches. CLAIRE will be wearing an open-necked blue blouse with white stripes.
Passwords:
JACQUES DUBOIS: What a beautiful lady she was.

CLAIRE: Her love saved the king.
CONTINGENCY: If there are others in the tomb, JACQUES
will exit and wait for CLAIRE at church entrance.
4 JACQUES will temporarily hand over his sector
organising role to GILBERT who will pass on contact
details by courier.
5 Prepare to receive new W/T operators, organisers and
couriers.

It took Catesby a second to twig that Jacques Dubois was himself.
He wasn't used to seeing his cover name written down – and he
was usually just called *le camarade* or *monsieur*. He had mixed
feelings about his recall to London. He didn't want to miss out
on the action, but a break from the discomfort of Lo Grand's
strict regime in the woods would be welcome.

He looked again at the message. It was all very strange. Why
had the Limoges rendezvous with GILBERT been cancelled?
Had it anything to do with the objections Catesby had sent? If
so, how odd that the chiefs in London had so quickly taken the
advice of someone as junior as himself? But despite the Limoges
change of plan, GILBERT was still coming to the Limousin to
take over his duties. Catesby picked up a pencil and scribbled
a caricature of GILBERT on the message. He was hopeless at
drawing and the best he could do was a stick figure with horns
coming out of a round head. He had never seen the man, but
Catesby had already begun to perceive GILBERT as the type of
shapeshifter that you found in children's books.

Then there was the Agnès Sorel connection. The fact that the
owner of the château safe house had a rare portrait of a king's
mistress, at whose tomb Catesby was soon to meet a contact,
seemed more design than coincidence. Catesby had a premo-
nition of shadowy figures, with sophisticated senses of irony,
pulling strings as much for amusement as for power.

It was Catesby's final evening with Jimmy and Hélène before
they moved on – and there was a big question that needed
answering. The meal was rabbit – a tame one, the local peasants
bred them – and potatoes.

'Do you think you will be coming back here?' said Jimmy.

'Probably. What do you think?'

'I have the impression that a lot of organisers hop back and forth.'

'How did you get that impression?'

'When I was in training I ran into a lot of radio operators who talked too much – probably because it's such a lonely job. The Lysanders are used like flying commuter trains – but Limousin is beyond their reach.'

Catesby looked at Hélène. 'How would you feel if I booked a place for you on a Lysander?'

'Why?'

'To train as an SOE W/T operator.'

Jimmy's eyes flared in the candlelight. 'Thank you, sir, for trying to ruin my fucking marriage.'

'A lot of people have been separated by this war. Look at Guingouin and his fiancée.'

'Guingouin is a communist monk. I don't think he's ever got laid – or wants to.'

Hélène turned to Jimmy, 'Please, Bijou, let me talk.'

Catesby laughed. It was the first time he had heard Jimmy's marital nickname. He repeated it in English, 'Okay, Jewel, let's hear what Hélène has to say.'

'Personally, I would love to go to England and be properly trained as a radio operator. But my husband does not want that.' She turned and faced Jimmy. 'You don't want to be separated from me – but how do you think I feel about being separated from our son? It doesn't seem to bother you, but it hurts me deeply. You don't see the tears on my face, but there are tears inside me and they are etched on my heart.'

There was a heavy silence. Each of the three stared into space. Finally, Jimmy spoke. 'I have been selfish.' He took both of Hélène's hands in his own. 'One day Victor will be so proud that you are his mother. He will brag about you to his schoolmates. Please, Hélène, do what you think is best.'

She smiled. 'I think it's best we finish the rabbit stew.'

Catesby refilled his glass with wine. 'I'm going for a walk.'

The night was clear and still bright with the last half of a waning moon. He heard the sound of aircraft engines and looked into the sky. He could see the silhouettes of two Hali-faxes heading east. He assumed it was a drop for the Stationer circuit in the Auvergne – and it reminded Catesby that he would soon be meeting HECTOR, the SOE officer in charge of organ-ising Stationer, the largest circuit in France which ran from Châteauroux to the Pyrenees. Catesby realised he was a minnow compared to HECTOR.

When Catesby returned to the farmhouse, the candles had sputtered out. Jimmy and Hélène were lying curled together in a dark corner talking to each other in soft voices.

Catesby was surprised that the meeting with HECTOR took place in the same grand house where the near fatal confron-tation between Guingouin and the Communist Party officials had occurred – and where the bare-breasted portrait of Agnès Sorel had graced the walls. After a long cycle ride, Catesby was greeted by Paul.

'HECTOR is already here,' said Paul. 'He arrived by car.'

'Dangerous?'

'At times speed is more important than security.'

'Is Lo Grand here as well?'

'He won't be attending this meeting.'

There was, Catesby noted, something distant in Paul's voice and manner. It was also odd that everyone kept referring to Paul as 'Colonel Charles'. Catesby guessed that something was afoot. As they entered the house, Paul took Catesby aside and whis-pered, 'Lo Grand wants me to pretend I'm in charge. He's afraid that the British and Free French wouldn't want to drop supplies to a group led by a communist.'

'That's ridiculous. They will supply anyone who is effective.'

'Perhaps, but we have to play along with Guingouin's plan.'

HECTOR turned out to be a career RAF officer who looked like he was in his early thirties. Catesby was a bit cowed by him: HECTOR had 'leader of men' stamped all over him. The first item on the agenda was the sabotage of a rubber factory in Clermont-Ferrand and a tyre factory on the outskirts of Limoges. HECTOR asked Catesby about his experience in sabotage operations.

'I took part in the destruction of the rail viaduct near Eyemoutiers.'

'Wasn't that carried out by the communist-led FTP?'

'I believe,' said Catesby, diluting the truth, 'that they were part of it.'

'The destruction of the viaduct was an extremely impressive operation. Especially, considering the fact that the FTP used industrial dynamite and primitive fuses.'

'Indeed,' said Paul/Colonel Charles winking at Catesby.

'The FTP,' continued HECTOR, 'are to be congratulated. I am sure that the supply of plastic explosives, primer and time-pencil detonators will vastly improve their ability to carry out sabotage.'

Catesby wished that Guingouin could hear those words of support and praise. But he could also understand Lo Grand's dilemma. Guingouin had to walk a tightrope between the Moscow-controlled leadership of the PCF and those on the right of French politics. A tightrope that eventually would be powerfully jolted from both sides throwing Guingouin into the abyss.

After discussing the factory sabotages, the meeting moved to air drops and the shortage of W/T operators which was hampering operations.

'Have you heard,' said Catesby, 'of an air operations officer codenamed GILBERT?'

'He has an excellent reputation,' said HECTOR. 'He's organised dozens of secret landing operations that have gone without a hitch. He was a test pilot before the war – so GILBERT understands aircraft and pilots and appreciates their limitations. He spends, I believe, most of his time with Prosper, but I would love to have him here to advise on landing zones for heavy drops.'

'I received a message from London saying that GILBERT was coming to Limoges – but the following transmission said his visit had been cancelled.'

'I am sure that GILBERT's skills are very much in demand.'

Not for the last time, Catesby began to question his own judgement. But in the end, he would learn to trust his judgement – even when no one else did.

'Speaking of skills in demand,' said Catesby, 'we have a courier who would make an excellent W/T operator. Any advice on how to get her to England?'

'We'll link her up with Josette.'

Catesby looked blank.

'Josette is my W/T operator and she arranges exfiltrations.'

Catesby felt a chill run down his spine. This was what Hélène wanted, but he wished that he wasn't one of those arranging it.

The Wattelez tyre factory was located in Le Palais-sur-Vienne, a few kilometres up the river from Limoges. Guingouin, who always led from the front, was going to lay the charges himself under the factory's main boiler. Catesby's role was showing Lo Grand how to use a time-pencil detonator.

'How do you set the time delay?' said Guingouin, staring at the time pencil on the table in front of him.

'You can't set the time delay, you have to—'

'But I was led to believe that these devices could be set to detonate at any interval from a few minutes to several hours.' Guingouin's voice carried a note of irritation. He was in a hurry.

Catesby picked up a tin box, the size of a container for small cigars, and spilled out six time pencils on the table. 'You don't set a time delay. You choose a time pencil that is already set for the delay you want.' He pointed to a black metal band that went through one of the detonators. 'That's the safety strip. They're all colour coded. Black means a time delay of ten minutes.' Catesby picked up another time pencil. 'The ones with blue strips give you a time delay of twenty-four hours – but it could be a few hours longer if the weather is cold.'

'So which colour gives a time delay of one hour?'

'There are no one-hour time pencils. You have to choose between red, thirty minutes, and white, two hours.'

'I was hoping for one hour.'

'In that case, you could start a two-hour time pencil an hour before you get to your target – but, if you get delayed, that could be dangerous. And you risk getting debris in the safety-strip hole which would impede the striker – and then it wouldn't go off at all.'

'I think we will go with the two-hour delay.'

'That would be safest.'

'How does the timer work?'

'You crush the copper-coloured end with a pair of pliers or your boot. That breaks an ampoule of corrosive liquid that dissolves the wire that holds back the striker spring.'

'And the concentration level of the corrosive liquid determines the length of delay?'

'Exactly.'

'I admire the simplicity. Weapons that can be used with little training are what we need for a people's war.'

The words reminded Catesby of the Sten – easy to use, but prone to jamming. 'By the way, it's a good idea to use two detonators from different batches as a backstop.'

There would be plenty to spare. During the next eighteen months hundreds of thousands of time-pencil detonators would rain from the skies of France – in addition to weapons and plastic explosives. The bomb that nearly killed Hitler in the 20th of July plot was detonated by a captured British time pencil.

The attack on the Wattelez factory involved a lot of late-night cycling without lights and with rucksacks heavy with explosives. They had decided to place bombs under two boilers which, to avoid casualties, would be set to go off a couple of hours before the morning shift arrived. Catesby wasn't to be part of the operation. When he objected, Guingouin replied, 'You are too valuable to risk losing.'

'You are a lot more valuable than I will ever be.'

'But I need to set an example.'

What Guingouin wanted, Catesby suspected, was independence of action for himself and the Maquisards he led. Lo Grand didn't want interference from Moscow or London.

The first part of the operation went like clockwork. Guingouin and his team cycled unnoticed throughout the night to a safe house at Rilhac-Ranson, about three miles from the factory. They slept through the day to be fresh for the late-night sabotage and pre-dawn scamper to Châteauneuf-la-Forêt. Lo Grand placed the charges himself, which meant crawling under the noses of the guards. After the explosives were in place, they crawled back to their bicycles. It was too late to make it back to Châteauneuf before dawn. They spent the daylight hours sleeping in a remote safe house which was just over halfway. The next night's bike journey was going to be a problem. The explosion had stirred up a hornet's nest of normally lethargic local police. There was now a price on Guingouin's head and the few *flics* who were still committed Vichyistes wanted it. Returning safely meant avoiding roadblocks and cops in hiding. They were doing well until they reached a crossroads where a voice shouted from the darkness, '*Halte! Gendarmerie de la Haute-Vienne.*' The Maquisards didn't stop, but cycled fast into the night followed by a flurry of shots. Ten minutes later, Guingouin halted and listened. There was no more gunfire. He hoped that his comrades would stay dispersed for safety, and work their way back to Châteauneuf-la-Forêt singly or in pairs. He was about to remount when he heard the sound of a bike coming up the lane behind. The bike didn't have a light, so Guingouin assumed it was one of his group. As soon as Guingouin saw the silhouette of the gendarme's kepi, he reached for his pistol and was a second quicker on the draw than the *flic*. Two bullets hit the gendarme in the chest and he tumbled sideways still astride his bike. Guingouin put one more bullet into his head while the back wheel of the bike was still spinning.

The reverberations from the gendarme's death were worse than those of blowing up the rubber factory. The Maquisards had to quickly remove themselves from the safe houses and abandoned farmsteads to the deepest darkest countryside as raids were launched into the surrounding villages and people taken in for questioning. Fortunately, Paul had an informer high up in the *Préfecture de la Haute-Vienne* who kept him up to date with developments. Paul was aware that the informer wanted to have a foot in both camps and couldn't be completely trusted, but his information about police movements and raids was accurate. On the other hand, Paul's informant bragged to his Vichyiste colleagues that he knew someone who was in contact with Guingouin. After the German defeat at Stalingrad, the more perceptive Vichyiste officials and police realised they may one day have to prepare to jump from a sinking ship by establishing bona fides with the Resistance – but it was still too dangerous to do so overtly. They needed to keep both sides sweet. After several days of intense police activity, the informer passed on a message that the heat was off, but only temporarily. He warned that the GMR, *Gardes Mobiles de Réserve*, were moving into the area as the local gendarmes seemed unable to cope with Guingouin's Maquis. The GMR were ruthless and had no local ties. The rules were changing because Vichy die-hards were beginning to panic with a rapidly deteriorating situation. Civil courts were being replaced by military tribunals. Anyone found guilty of supporting the Resistance would be executed. As the possibility of defeat began to loom, repression became more brutal.

Catesby took advantage of the temporary lull to cycle to the railway station in Limoges, the first stage of his exfiltration back to London. He was dressed in a suit and carrying a smart leather bag with his overnight gear: wash bag, change of clothes and some innocuous documents that supported his cover story of being a commercial translator fluent in German and Dutch. He also had a forged medical document stating that he had suffered from tuberculosis and was exempt from STO conscription. A history of TB, real or feigned, was also useful for making interrogators keep their distance. Catesby was nervous about his first rail journey in occupied France, but was assured that the trains were always too crowded for detailed ID and luggage checks. Hélène once told Catesby she had spent a train journey with a shopping bag full of hand grenades while crushed against a German officer – who tried to make jokes about the over-crowding in poor French.

Catesby's train was indeed packed, but he was relieved he didn't see anyone in uniform. Most of the passengers were middle-aged women carrying food parcels to relatives in towns north of Limoges. He had to change trains at Tours for a short hop to Loches. It was at Tours that he saw uniformed Germans for the first time – six of whom got on the Loches train. He didn't want to attract attention by too obviously avoiding them, so he got in the same carriage. The Germans behaved more like tourists than members of an occupying army.

Loches was picturesque and Catesby felt like a tourist himself. The town was dominated by a huge medieval castle that Charles VII had given to Agnés Sorel as a present. The turrets and keep wall of the castle looked more like a prison than a house of pleasure. He felt a chill. He was on his own until the next day's rendezvous. No safe house or hotel had been recommended in any of the communications – which was just as well. The worst nightmare was an instruction that had been intercepted and decrypted.

Catesby chose a hotel near the town centre. There was one room left and it was a room without an escape route. The window overlooked the main road and there was no window in the bathroom – or hot water. And there was no way into the roof space. He lay on the bed without taking his shoes off and tried to piece together what was happening. Part of the problem was success. The Resistance was growing so rapidly that control was becoming difficult – and that meant confusion and security lapses. The greater number of recruits meant more chance of penetration by double agents. He heard someone knocking on the door. Catesby wondered if he should pretend he wasn't there. The knocking came again followed by a young woman's voice, 'Monsieur.'

They knew he was there. Catesby looked out the window. The drop was too far. He would break both legs. He turned to the door. 'What is it?'

'I have, monsieur, brought you some hot water.'

He opened the door. An enormous jug of steaming water was held in the hands of a slight girl, who looked no more than sixteen.

'How kind of you,' said Catesby. 'Shall I take it from you?'

'No, monsieur, I need to return the jug – we don't have enough of them. Where would you like me to pour it?'

'I suppose the sink would be best.'

The girl came in. Her eyes seemed to dart around the room taking in all the details. She went into the bathroom and poured the water into the sink. '*Voila!*'

'Thank you.'

'I am sorry that there is no hot water from the taps. That must be annoying. Have you come far?'

'Not particularly.'

'And you will be staying only one night?'

'I'm not sure.'

'I can recommend a good restaurant, monsieur.'

'I am sure I will find one.'

'Please, monsieur, let me know if you need more hot water – or anything else.'

'I will, mademoiselle.'

The girl gave him a flirtatious smile, turned on her heel and left.

Catesby sat on the bed. The demons of paranoia were leaping and heckling in every corner of his brain. He wondered who the girl was reporting to – whoever it was, they hadn't trained her very well. What next? He wasn't going to stay in the hotel. The problem was his briefcase and belongings. If one of the hotel staff saw him leaving with his leather overnight bag, they would know he was on the run. People didn't take their bags when they were going out to dinner. Catesby rescued his toothbrush, but everything else would have to be left behind – casualties of war. He regretted losing his bag. It was the smartest piece of luggage he had ever carried.

The town's biggest restaurant was pulsating with gaiety. The customers seemed oblivious of the war – even the German soldiers who were tucking into beef steaks. Catesby was tempted to get lost in its crowd, but spotted the girl from the hotel drinking an aperitif at a table with two older men who looked more like black-market spivs than undercover police. He decided to move on. He found a small rough-looking restaurant where he had gratin dauphinois with a piece of ham. Most of the other customers were workers with stained hands from the local tannery. Catesby felt safe among them and was directed to an elderly woman who took in lodgers. No one asked any questions – nor did the elderly woman who provided him a room. She spent over an hour sharing red wine with Catesby and telling him about her marriages and love life, beginning with her youth as a farmer's daughter in the 1880s. She confided, with a knowing laugh, that having a lover was like being a member of the Resistance. It didn't matter to Catesby if his cover was blown, he trusted the old woman and slept well.

The next morning Catesby tried to look inconspicuous while exploring the town. If something went wrong, he wanted to know where to run. The deep welcoming River Indre was the dominant feature of the town, but as there were only two easily blocked bridges, it cut off an escape route to the east. The rendezvous point, the tenth-century church of Saint-Ours, was in the middle of the historic town. Catesby cursed whoever had planned the meeting. The rendezvous was a cul de sac.

The tomb of Agnès Sorel was in a crypt deep below the floor of the church. Catesby swallowed as he began to descend the spiral staircase. The ancient stone walls reflected dimly in the candlelight from the crypt below. He heard muffled voices, men's voices, but couldn't make out the words. He thought of turning and fleeing, but running had dangers of its own – and he had to know what was going on. Catesby continued downwards. The narrow corkscrew spiral of the case meant that you couldn't see into the crypt until you were almost at the bottom. The first thing that Catesby saw in the crypt wasn't the white marble of the tomb, but the broad uniformed backs of two German officers. One of the Germans, only three feet away, turned to see who had arrived. Catesby said, '*Bonjour.*' The German nodded what seemed a reluctant welcome. Catesby knew it was too late to bolt and joined them. He was relieved to see a woman on the side of the tomb opposite the Germans. She looked older than most people in the Resistance, late forties perhaps, but was wearing the blue blouse with white stripes as specified in the contact instructions. Catesby passed behind the German officers to stand beside the woman, whom he assumed was Agent Claire.

Despite the tension of the situation, Catesby found it difficult not to laugh. The recumbent effigy of Agnès Sorel, carved in white marble, was utterly overblown. It wasn't so much her flawless beauty, but her accessories, that made the effigy ridiculous. Two lushly winged angels fluttered protectively around her face while a pair of affectionate sheep cuddled to keep her feet warm. Catesby faked a moment of rapt contemplation before he uttered his half of the password sequence, 'What a beautiful lady she was.'

Before Claire could respond, one of the German officers broke in. His words were neither in French nor German: '*Requiescat in pace et in amore.*' Catesby remembered enough Latin: '*Rest in peace and in love.*' Lucky her.

Catesby glanced at the German and saw that he was wearing the insignia of a chaplain. The devil, he thought, wears many disguises. Catesby felt the German returning his glance. He averted his eyes to the sublime face of Agnès Sorel and made the sign of the cross.

This time the other German intervened before Agent Claire could confirm her identity passwords. His French was heavily accented, but good. 'There are rumours that Agnès Sorel was murdered while the king was fighting the English in Normandy.'

When you're undercover, the word 'English' spoken in any context by a German officer sends a shiver down the spine. Catesby repressed a shudder and asked, 'How was she murdered?'

'She may have been poisoned by arsenic when she was six months' pregnant causing her to die of dysentery. She probably died in agony.'

Catesby noticed that the German was wearing the vertical caduceus insignia of the *Wehrmacht* medical corps. They were an apt pair: the priest and the doctor; harbingers of the end; morphine and last rites.

'I have suggested to the French authorities,' said the German doctor, 'that her body be exhumed for a post-mortem. I would carry it out myself. But so far, the French have said nothing.'

'That would solve the mystery,' said Catesby. He hoped that the German wouldn't ask for his help.

The woman finally spoke the words confirming that she was Claire: 'Her love saved the king.'

The doctor wanted more. 'In what way did her love save the king?'

'He had been very unhappy, perhaps clinically depressed, until he met her.'

'Ah, that is an interesting question.'

The priest glanced at his watch and said, 'We must go now, Hans, otherwise we will be late for lunch.'

The Germans made formal, but polite, farewells and ascended the staircase. Catesby breathed a sigh of relief when he heard their jackboots echoing across the church floor towards the door.

'That was unexpected. They arrived while I was waiting for you,' said Claire.

'An unusual choice for a rendezvous point.'

'But not an obvious one. This is the last place you would expect to find members of the Resistance. Our colleagues are not known for paying homage to royal mistresses.'

Catesby could see that she had taken umbrage and decided not to press the point.

'Our safe house isn't far from here. It looks like we're going to be crowded tonight.'

Catesby didn't like having such a conversation in the crypt. He had visions of a priest with soft shoes listening, crouched in the staircase. He began to mount the stairs.

The safe house was a tall stone building on the edge of the town with a walled garden. Unlike the crypt of Agnès Sorel, it was well suited for undercover activities. There were wine cellars with mysterious passages heading god knows where. The house seemed to have been a gentleman's residence. There was a billiard room, long corridors hung with antlered deer heads and a well-stocked library of unread books – many of the bindings hadn't been cut. The wine and the beef bourguignon were superb. Catesby was disappointed that he would soon be leaving. Not only because he was enjoying the luxury, but because he wanted to know more about Claire and her entourage.

The table was set for four, but there were three of them when the meal began. Claire explained, 'Henri will be late, but it's all right to begin without him.' The other person at the table was a man, a few years younger than Claire. Catesby guessed that he was her husband or lover. She referred to him as 'Jean' and he called her 'Juju'. Jean was smartly, but not ostentatiously, dressed and appeared to be a man of substance and authority. At one point he leaned towards Catesby and whispered, 'We only do this as a diversion. We have businesses in Paris.'

'And what is your business?' said Catesby, emboldened by vintage Burgundy.

'I'm in the legal profession. I have over four hundred clients. I don't, by the way, do criminal law, only business law which is largely about contracts and compliance with regulations. My client base is very useful for finding safe houses – which is Juju's job. In fact, this house belongs to a client.'

'The best safe house,' said Claire, 'is one owned by a wealthy merchant who regularly dines with the *préfet de police*.'

'And with a portrait of the *maréchal* in a place of honour,' said Jean, pointing to a painting over the fireplace.

Catesby looked at the painting. Pétain's eyes were flinty and his look anything but avuncular. He could imagine the *maréchal* signing Agnès Sorel's death warrant – even though he had been a womaniser with numerous mistresses.

'I hope you don't mind eating black-market beef,' said Claire.

Catesby glanced at his plate. 'Sorry, I'm a slow eater.' He tried to smile. Light conversation wasn't a strong point of his. 'And what, may I ask, is your business?'

'I'm in the film industry.' Something in her voice suggested she had been dying to say that.

'Do you make films?'

'We make them, commission them and distribute them.

I started the business with my ex-husband who's now in Hollywood.'

Catesby swallowed a huge morsel of the beef and sipped the fine wine. Life in the Farrier and Prosper réseaux seemed a world away from the cold wet forest lairs of Guingouin's Maquis.

There was suddenly a loud knocking at the front door. Catesby instinctively grabbed for a Sten that was over a hundred miles away.

'That must be Henri,' said Claire. She dabbed her mouth with a linen napkin and got up to answer the door.

Jean swirled his wine and held it up to the light. 'The last bottle was a little oxidised, but this one is fine. I fear the cellar also has an issue with cork taint.'

There was coquettish laughter from the hallway and a gentle slap, but the man who entered the room was not a well-groomed playboy. He was a tramp with muddy trousers and a face covered in stubble.

Jean smiled at Catesby and stood up. 'I would like to introduce the remarkable and talented GILBERT. You look, Henri, like you need a drink.'

Catesby was slightly abashed that his host had so casually given away GILBERT's real name. They seemed very blasé about security.

'I need a wash-up and a change,' said GILBERT/Henri.

'We love you the way you are,' said Claire.

'What happened, old boy?' said Jean.

'I thought it best to return from Poitiers incognito. I did most of it by bicycle – which was good. I need to lose a few kilos.'

'We got a garbled message from André,' said Claire. 'He can be a bit useless.'

GILBERT gave Catesby a warm smile and extended a hand. 'You must be Jacques from Stationer.'

'Yes,' said Catesby who found GILBERT's hand warm and soft. He was a pilot, not a manual worker or a hard-living resistant like Guingouin's guerillas.

'We'll be getting you out tomorrow night,' said GILBERT. 'I don't know whether Juju and Jean have told you, but I organise secret aircraft landing operations in the Loire – and sometimes further afield.'

'We had been expecting you in Limoges,' said Catesby.

GILBERT gave a frown. 'I don't know what went amiss.'

'I bet it was André again,' said Claire.

It was clear to Catesby that the local réseaux could be bitchy.

'That looks like very fine wine,' said GILBERT.

Jean poured him a glass which GILBERT raised: 'To Jacques and his timely and safe arrival in England.'

Three more England-bound agents turned up the next day, two were women – one of whom was Hélène. There was little chance to talk because GILBERT was organising everything. At midday, they set off separately on bicycles to a farmhouse rendezvous. The idea was to follow the person in front of them without appearing to be together. If there was a sign of danger, they were to leave the road and hide themselves and their bikes – and there were plenty of places to hide because the land, though flat, was heavily wooded. Catesby guessed that the countryside they were cycling through had once been a playground where kings and aristocrats had hunted deer and wild boar. It was more a managed wilderness than an area for farming. The royals had, unwittingly, created an ideal environment for undercover operations. The area was too remote and unpopulated to be easily controlled.

The rendezvous turned up more quickly than Catesby had expected. He doubted they had cycled more than three miles before they turned off up a dirt track to a well-hidden farmhouse – but they were still a long way from the landing site.

There were six others at the farmhouse – and a large quantity of weapons, grenades and torches. There were also two full mailbags labelled *pour Londres*. This was the place where cover stories ended. They had a late lunch of bread, cheese and red wine and laid low until nightfall. Catesby found time to have a word with Hélène.

'How do you feel?' he said.

'What do you mean, how do I feel? I feel fine.'

'Sorry.'

Hélène smiled and shifted to English. 'Sorry I bite your head off.'

'You need not apologise.'

She shifted back to French. 'This is important for me. It means I can be closer to my son. I am sure that when I come back I will be assigned to Prosper. It makes sense. I know the region and I speak with the accent.'

Catesby remembered the pair's passionate lovemaking on the farmhouse floor. 'How will you feel about being apart from Jimmy?'

'Jimmy has had his turn with me.'

'He will miss you.'

Hélène laughed. 'Our last night together he sang *J'attendrai*. His voice is awful! At least, I know he will never seduce another woman with his singing.' She grabbed Catesby's arm. 'Please tell me we are winning.'

'We are winning.'

'When will the English come back to France? Someone told me the invasion will be this summer.'

'I don't know.'

'I sometimes think that I would like a normal life.'

'What do you think the other times?'

'That I would hate it. I went to London as an au pair to escape Nanteuil-le-Haudouin – and I hated the drudgery of being an au pair, so I flirted with Englishmen in Kensington Gardens.' She looked at Catesby. 'I am a woman who is easily bored. I like excitement and adventures. Does that sound awful?'

'No, it's something to be admired.'

'It is a side of me that Jimmy does not always fully understand.' Hélène smiled. 'Do you think they will teach me to parachute?'

Before Catesby could answer, GILBERT came over and interrupted their conversation.

'The women,' said GILBERT, 'will go together in the first Lysander. As the ladies are smaller, there will be room for the mailbags.'

Catesby felt a pang of disappointment. He had looked forward to a long chat with Hélène discovering the mysteries of women.

The final part of the journey to the landing zone was in a heavily laden Traction Avant. The Citroën bumped over fields and heavily rutted lanes in the dark. A lesser car would have suffered a snapped suspension. They passed a number of lakes that glistened ghostly in the moonlight. The land seemed marshy.

They unloaded the car when they reached a long corridor of cleared ground with forest on both sides. Catesby imagined the thundering of hooves as the king and his retinue chased deer or simply raced along the open strip. GILBERT busied himself with directing others where to put the landing lights. They waited tensely, speaking in low murmurs. Everyone had their own vision of a nightmare outcome. Planes would arrive, but spewing gunfire followed by German paratroopers. Or more likely, the landing site had been compromised by an informer and surrounded by *Feldpolizei* while a Teutonic voice bellowed from the cover of the trees: *Put your hands up and surrender or we will open fire.*

The ones with the sharpest ears gave whispered shouts, 'They're coming.' The dim distant noise of the aircraft engines grew louder. GILBERT gave a shout and the landing lights came on in the shape of an inverted letter L. What followed was quicker than Catesby could have imagined. The Lysander was suddenly on the ground and executing a U-turn. The cockpit canopy was slid back, the new arrivals and a number of bags were out, the two England-bound women and the mailbags were in; there was an engine roar and the Lysander was airborne. Catesby reckoned the operation had taken less than three minutes. And now the second Lysander was touching down. The procedure was practised clockwork precision. Any doubts that Catesby had harboured about GILBERT began to disappear. It was impossible not to admire the stubby Lysander and her fat landing wheels which looked like a clown's oversize shoes.

The aircraft's engines made a harsh grinding sound as the pilot began to turn the plane around for take-off. The Lysander shuddered halfway into the U-turn. There was more engine noise and shuddering. The plane tilted at an awkward angle; it was well and truly stuck in the soft damp earth. The cockpit canopy slid back and a litany of fucks rent the night air. Catesby heard the pilot shouting to his passengers. 'Can you two get the fuck out? That might help.'

The new arrivals threw their bags to the ground and slid out of the plane. One of the bags started shooting. A Sten had un-jammed itself. The pilot's fucks grew louder. 'Can you fucking check to see if any of those fucking rounds hit the fucking plane? That's all we fucking need.'

Volunteers ran forwards to help the two new arrivals with a fingertip search of the Lysander for bullet holes. The scene was turning into a Hieronymus Bosch hellscape. Catesby, checking the landing wheels for bullet damage, saw that one of the wheels was buried more than halfway into the soft earth. Meanwhile, GILBERT had grabbed the two new arrivals and was shepherd-ing them towards the Traction Avant. 'No sense in you two staying here. Let's get going.' GILBERT then shouted to the pilot. 'I'm going to get some help.' A moment later, the Traction was bumping across the field. The pilot shouted after it. 'You could have used the fucking car to pull me out of that fucking hole.'

Catesby's fellow passenger was sitting on the ground next to his bag. His face looked more bemused than worried in the moonlight. 'I am a victim of the curse of the House of Prosper,' he said in unaccented English.

It looked like Catesby and the other two Brits had been left alone with the crippled Lysander in the middle of occupied France. He heard voices. Two Frenchmen were leaning against the plane and talking in whispers. Catesby went over to them.

'Thank you for staying with us.'

One of the Frenchmen shrugged. 'Henri told us to. If the Germans turn up first, we're supposed to take you to a safe house.'

Catesby frowned. GILBERT didn't use a codename with the locals.

'It might be an idea,' said the other Frenchman, 'to get a head start. If *les boches* find us, we won't have a chance.'

'Then what are we waiting for?' said Catesby.

'We've sent for help. We hope there is a local farmer who can pull the plane out with horses or bullocks.' The Frenchman spread his hands. 'But I wouldn't hold your breath.'

Catesby turned to the pilot who was leaning against the fuse-lage and didn't look happy.

'What did the froggies say?' said the pilot.

'They said they've sent for help, but it may be a good idea to leave the plane and hide out in a safe house.'

'No way, mate, am I leaving my fucking plane.'

It was a long wait. The only sounds were hooting owls from the woods who seemed to be mocking them. The first indication that something was happening was when one of the Frenchmen said, 'Shhhh. Quiet. Not a sound.'

'Germans?' said Catesby.

'Not unless they've taken to wearing bells around their necks.'

The sight of the four bullocks swaying towards them in the moonlight would become one of Catesby's most cherished memories. Decades later he tried, unsuccessfully, to render it as a watercolour. The animals were too noble and too beautiful to reproduce. The peasant farmer who was leading them knew his business. The bullocks were harnessed horizontally so that the trace chains would exert the maximum pulling power. The peasant didn't need the pilot's help to know where was best to attach the trace chains to the Lysander. It was as if pulling stuck aircraft out of boggy ruts was all part of a peasant's daily grind. The bullocks surged forward with gentle strength and the Lysander emerged on to firmer ground.

As the pilot restarted the engines, Catesby took out his wallet. It only contained a few hundred francs, but he pressed them into the hands of the peasant – who accepted the money without a quibble. 'I will wait,' said the peasant, 'to make sure you do not get stuck again.' As the Lysander took to the sky, Catesby looked back to the landing site and saw the peasant and his bullocks still patiently waiting.

Suffolk: 15 March 2015

Catesby's granddaughter was annoyed to see him digging the garden so soon after a bad cold. 'Granddad,' she said, 'if you won't pay for a gardener, I will.'

Catesby leaned on his spade. 'This keeps me alive – and in touch with my peasant ancestors.'

'Who lived to be about forty.'

'But if they made it to thirty, they would probably make it into their fifties. Go into the churchyard and have a look – and you'll see one who made it to ninety-two.'

'I know – and her tombstone describes her as a "gentle-woman". I don't think she dug her own veg patch.'

'Good point. The iniquity of inequality. A kid born in Kensington London will live twenty years longer than one born in Kensington Liverpool.'

'You should have gone into politics instead of spying, Granddad.'

'I tried, but the voters rejected me.' Catesby was referring to his unsuccessful attempt to take a safe Tory seat in the 1945 election. He had campaigned while still in uniform, but despite the Labour landslide nationally he had been roundly defeated.

'You should have tried again. I bet the party would have given you a safe seat.'

Catesby looked at the soil. 'Maybe, Leanna, I should have spent my life in France,' he said in a low voice.

His granddaughter looked mildly shocked. 'Are you serious, Granddad?'

'I don't want to talk about it.'

'But I want you to talk about it. You owe it to me.'

'Why? You're only my step-granddaughter.' Catesby saw he had hurt her and tried to smile. 'If you had any of my blood you wouldn't be so beautiful.'

Catesby felt her arms around his neck and her tears dampening his cheek.

'Please let me make you a cup of tea,' he said.

She pulled back and smiled. 'One of the reasons I love you, Granddad, is because you are so awful.'

'And I love you because you are the only one in the family who tries to understand me.' Catesby laughed. 'And you don't know half of it.'

'Tell me.'

'The last words she said to me were, "You are my Rosenkavalier." Catesby paused and smiled. 'Well, her exact words were, "*Tu seras toujours mon Rosenkavalier.*"'

'So, who was this Frenchwoman who admired both you and Richard Strauss's opera?'

'I don't think she admired either me or the opera. I suspect that her words were meant as a joke – and it is considered a comic opera.'

'But one that makes people cry, particularly older women.' Leanna gave Catesby a searching look. 'Was she an older woman?'

'You're probing too far. The war was a strange place.' He looked at her. 'It created your very own father – and your Aunt Geraldine.' Catesby laughed. Thinking of his eccentric stepdaughter as *Aunt Geraldine* was funny. 'Your granny had the right idea. Have twins and get it over with fast. The war, despite all its heartbreak and horror, was our Swinging Sixties. When you didn't know whether or not tomorrow was going to dawn, you took your pleasures where you found them. The years afterwards were an attempt to sort out the wreckage.'

'Did you admire this woman?'

'Admire is a good word for some of my feelings about her.' Catesby smiled. 'But there were other feelings too. I'm dying for a cup of tea.'

'I'll make the tea, Granddad.'

Airborne Near Angers: May 1943

'On your right,' said the Lysander pilot over the intercom in the voice of a tour guide, 'you will see the River Loire. Correction. Because you're facing backwards, it's on your left and my right. But we are now crossing the Loire and heading due north. Are you chaps all right?'

'A lot better than we were fifteen minutes ago,' said Catesby's fellow passenger.

'There are empty milk bottles with corks somewhere back there if you're desperate for a piss or want to have a wank.'

'We'll manage.'

'Wasn't that a fucking fuck-up?' said the pilot. 'I'm never going in there again.'

'Don't blame you.'

'By the way, keep your eyes peeled for any enemy aircraft. But the bigger problem will be flak when we get to the coast. I'm signing off now until we get to the English coast, but if you want to report something press the transmit button.'

Catesby and his companion took off their earphone mics.

'Which circuit were you in?' said the companion.

'Stationer, near Limoges. And you?'

'I was a W/T operator with Prosper, right in the fucking middle of Paris. But I won't be going back there again. My cover was well and truly blown. I was lucky. I was having a shit in the safe house loo when the Gestapo broke the door down. I escaped, dirty bum and all. I managed to go through the loo window, over a roof and into a neighbour's mansard window. Luckily, they didn't search the whole block of flats. The people were nice. They gave me a clean set of underwear and trousers too.'

'Was the safe house one of those arranged by Agent Claire?'

'You mean Juju, Henri Dericourt's ex-mistress?'

'I didn't know about that connection. She now seems to be with a lawyer called Jean.'

The blown W/T operator gave a bitter laugh. 'I don't want to talk about that lot – and if you do say anything, no one will believe you.'

The rest of the flight passed in silence. When they reached the coast near Caen there was a spectacular display of anti-aircraft fire, but the flak was aimed at other planes. If, thought Catesby, you are not one of those in the line of fire, war can be an exhilarating spectator sport.

Catesby felt guilty about being treated like a returning hero after they landed at Tangmere. He felt that he had done nothing to merit the champagne breakfast that greeted them in the mess hall. Afterwards, a FANY drove Catesby to London. Their destination was the same Wimpole Street flat where he had spent the night before deployment.

'You look like you're travelling light,' said the FANY driver.

'I did manage to bring my toothbrush.'

'Don't worry. They'll sort you out with some new kit. A lot of them turn up like you did.' She glanced at Catesby. 'But that looks like a smart suit.'

'It needs to go to the cleaners.'

'They'll arrange that too.'

Catesby was surprised and pleased to see that his uniforms, civvy clothes and other personal belongings had been kept in storage while he was in France. Nonetheless, a FANY girl arrived to measure him for a new uniform and brought a supply of toiletries. It was like being a guest in a top hotel, but what Catesby wanted most was a chance to sleep – and he wasn't going to get that soon. He had been in his digs for less than an hour when a FANY knocked on the door. Even though it was less than a five-minute walk, he was driven to SOE HQ at 64 Baker Street. When he mentioned as much to the FANY driver, she replied, 'They don't want you to escape. But I think they will let you walk back.'

At Baker Street Catesby was required to write a report

describing everything he had done in France. There were cups of tea, but no further mollycoddling. He was half asleep and asked if he could have a Benzedrine tablet. A FANY from the clerical staff raised an eyebrow, then went off in search of the pill and came back fifteen minutes later with the Benzedrine on a silver salver. Catesby popped the pill and a few minutes later was writing the report like a demon possessed.

An hour after he had finished, Catesby was called for interview. It wasn't until the end of the war that Catesby discovered the identity of the major who interviewed him. They spoke French at the beginning of the session – and, to Catesby's ear, the person sounded like a native speaker. The accent was educated and refined and suggested a Parisian background. Afterwards, Catesby reflected that the purpose of the conversation in French had been to impress, to let him know that he wasn't dealing with a Colonel Blimp type. But it also sowed a seed of suspicion. There was something about the major that was ostentatiously clever and tricky. He wasn't someone Catesby would want to follow into battle.

The major looked at Catesby's report for a few minutes before launching into English. The voice was public school, but not as refined as his French one. 'Would you say,' said the major, 'that Georges Guingouin is obsessed with security?'

'He has to be. The Germans and the Vichyistes are baying for his blood. He has a price on his head. And the leadership of the French Communist Party would like to have him executed for not carrying out Party policy.'

'One can, however,' said the major, 'appreciate the PCF criticising Guingouin for not operating in towns and cities.'

Catesby tried to keep a blank face. He was pleased that he hadn't mentioned in his report that he had personally intervened with his Sten gun during Guingouin's showdown with Party officials. Nonetheless, Catesby was conscious that the major was giving him a penetrating stare.

'What do you think?' said the major.

'I had only been operating in the Stationer réseau for a few months and tended to defer to local judgement and experience.'

'Up to a point, but only to a point, that is a reasonable course of action – but going along with the locals isn't the purpose of SOE F Section. Our role is coordination, direction, intelligence gathering – and subterfuge.'

If someone other than the major had said those words, Catesby would have accepted the statement of mission without a quibble. But there was something about the major's attitude that seemed too smug and self-assured. He had the tone of an intellectual telling an experienced bricklayer a better way of laying bricks.

'The problem,' continued the major, 'with a Maquis based in the countryside is that you don't get to know the enemy close up. On the other hand, by operating in towns, you begin to perceive changes in personnel and morale – and procedures. You meet informers, double agents and possible double agents. You become a player in the fog of war – and you have a chance to pass on false information.'

Catesby knew that the major was describing a game that the peasants of Limousin could never play. Years later, he was to discover that it was a game that few highly trained and experienced professional intelligence officers could play either. Espionage and counter-espionage were games where the opponents egged each other on to take more risks.

'We will,' said the major, 'be sending you back before the end of this moon. You will be accompanied by a W/T operator who will establish a communications base and letter boxes in Limoges. Our aim is to establish a web of interconnecting réseaux from Bordeaux to the Alps. The most important part of that web will be Lyon. Have you ever met Germaine?'

'No, sir.'

'She has several other codenames, including Marie of Lyon, but is best known as *la dame qui boite*.'

Catesby smiled. 'The limping lady' was an odd choice of alias. 'Is the limp part of her cover story?'

'No, it's part of her real-life story. She accidentally shot herself in the leg. The wound became gangrenous and the lower part of the leg had to be amputated.'

'I hope she wasn't a victim of the Sten gun – a dropped Sten went off and nearly shot up our Lysander.'

The major frowned. 'People have to be trained to use the Sten with care. No, Germaine's amputated leg had nothing to do with the war. It was the result of a hunting accident – crawling under a fence with a shotgun. She is a very sporty lady.'

Catesby nodded. She sounded like one of the hearty outdoor types he had known in Suffolk. He didn't relish meeting her; that sort could be frightening.

'Before fleeing from Lyon, Germaine established a network of safe houses, letter boxes and escape routes for downed pilots. Lyon is now a hotbed of resistance that needs more radios and supplies. Part of your job when you get back will be to help build up those networks and contacts.' The major gave Catesby a sideways look. 'Have you heard of Max?'

'No, I haven't.' Catesby kept a straight face as he lied. He had been told about Max at his SIS pre-deployment briefing at the St. Ermin Hotel, but something in Catesby intuitively knew that the briefing had contained secrets he shouldn't share with the major. Later in his career, Catesby discovered there were more walls of secrecy between organisations than there were between the intelligence services and the enemy.

'Then,' said the major, 'either your ear hasn't been very close to the ground or Max's security is better than we supposed. In any case, Max is a key figure in bringing together all the Resistance movements under a unified leadership. We believe there is going to be an important meeting in Lyon this summer led by Max. We want you to attend that meeting and report back to us.'

Catesby blinked in disbelief. He doubted that he had the rank and status to carry out such an assignment.

Seeming to read his mind, the major added, 'In order to get to that meeting, if it does occur, you will find your new radio operator an asset. Normally, it is essential for agents to work separately and anonymously from the leadership for security reasons. But the Lyon meeting is an exception. Have you any questions?'

Catesby tried not to laugh. There were hundreds. 'Will I still be working with Guingouin?'

'Yes, but as I've just tried to explain, you will be branching out into pastures new. In the next few months the skies will be raining supplies on Guingouin's Maquis. Their most important mission will be to interdict German troop movements from the south of France to the invasion beaches in the north.'

Catesby felt he had just received an electric shock. Was it really happening?

'I can't tell you the exact day or week,' said the major, 'because I don't know it myself, but the invasion will certainly take place between June and late August this year – we can no longer put it off to 1944 – and the main landing beaches will be in the Pas-de-Calais. That, of course, is top secret information. Do not reveal it to anyone else – and, if you are in danger of capture, I would advise that you take the L pill. It would be catastrophic if anyone leaked that information under torture. The Maquis, of course, as they are showered with more and more weapons and explosives, might come to the conclusion that an invasion is in the offing, but be guileful and say nothing that confirms that suspicion.'

There was something about the major and his words that didn't seem right. It was like biting into a piece of cheese that tasted like fish. Catesby longed for fresh air.

After leaving the building, Catesby looked both ways on Baker Street. The FANY driver had told him he could make his own way back to Wimpole Street, but he wanted to make sure there hadn't been a change of plan. He was about to start walking when he heard a voice behind him, 'Have you already been?'

Catesby turned. It was the W/T operator that he had shared the Lysander with. He was now dressed in the uniform of a Signal Corps NCO.

'Yes,' said Catesby, 'but I'm none the wiser.'

'They don't listen.' The radio man laughed. 'It's my mother's fault. She ran off with a Frenchman and took me and my younger sister with her. Otherwise, I wouldn't have ended up in this mess.'

'That's how you learned French?'

'Yeah – and how not to trust anyone. I should have stayed in formation when they asked French speakers to step forward.' The radio man looked at his watch. 'I've got to go.'

'Just one thing, what do you think of GILBERT?'

'Call the double-dealing shit by his proper name, Henri Déricourt.' The radio man nodded towards the upper stories of the Baker Street building. 'But that lot think sunshine streams out of his buttocks. I'll tell you something. If Déricourt doesn't have an identical twin, then I would like to know who gets lifts around Paris in the head of Gestapo's Traction Avant. Cheers.'

Catesby watched the radio man square his shoulders and walk defiantly into the Baker Street HQ. He didn't know how much of his words he should take seriously. Disgruntled and bitter NCOs were a normal feature of army life – and Catesby had become sceptical of the lions-led-by-donkeys cliché. If Déricourt was a pal of the Gestapo, how did they manage to escape in the Lysander despite the long delay after being stuck in the mud? They had been sitting ducks.

The initial buzz of the Benzedrine tablet had begun to wear off and Catesby remembered that he was dead tired. He put his hands in his pockets and strolled down the street singing *J'attendrai*. His reverie was halted by an elderly man clicking his tongue. He realised how unmilitary he must look. Catesby straightened up and strode off smartly towards his digs in Wimpole Street. Now, almost wide awake, he began to go over his interview with the major. In retrospect, one thing stood out as shocking. Why had the major trusted him with a highly sensitive military secret to which only the Prime Minister and a few generals would be privy? And how did the major himself know? The fact that D-Day was going to take place that very summer in the Pas-de-Calais surprised Catesby. He was only a humble cog in the vast machine of war, but nothing seemed ready for such an enormous invasion.

As Catesby set off south on Baker Street he felt a buzz of excitement in the spring air. Two middle-aged men in suits and trilbies were steering an embarrassed and young-looking RAF airman towards a pub. When he got to the corner with Porter

Street a newsagent was bellowing from a kiosk, 'Latest on dam bombings. Ruhr valley flooded. Devastation spreading.'

Catesby reached into his pocket for a penny and bought a paper. He thought it was odd that no one at Baker Street had mentioned the RAF raid on the Ruhr dams that had wreaked havoc. Apparently, whole German industrial towns were under water and thousands were fleeing for their lives. He wondered if the dam-busting raids would shorten the war. It was good news, but it brought into perspective what SOE was accomplishing. What was blowing up a railway line or a boiler in a rubber factory compared to flooding the industrial heartland of Germany? No wonder no one at Baker Street had mentioned the Ruhr raids. But maybe, thought Catesby, SOE was about more than sabotage. The meeting with the major began to haunt him. What were they doing?

In normal circumstances, it would have been a pleasant walk seeing London burst into green. But to Catesby's mind, there was something sinister about the spring weather. The sun itself was behaving like a nervous secret agent: in the open one moment, undercover the next. Catesby paused as he passed through Paddington Street Gardens. A large part of the green space had been turned into Digging for Victory vegetable gardens. An elderly man in shirtsleeves, braces and flat cap was earthing up rows of potatoes. Catesby caught his eye. 'Have you put in any earlies?'

The man looked at Catesby with disdain. 'Not when there's a war on – or in peacetime either. These are all main crop Duke of York – and that bed over there are King Edward. And I cut all the seed potatoes in half to make them go further.'

'I can't argue with that.' Catesby walked on and wondered if a couple of terms at Cambridge had turned him into a decadent Champagne Charlie. He cast a parting glimpse at the old man who was walking to the next bed with a pronounced limp. Probably a wound from the previous war – or an accident on a building site. Working-class people were prone to injury. Missing fingers were a common sign that you were in a factory town.

Was all of London limping? A woman about twenty yards ahead of him was striding forward purposefully, but she seemed impeded by a hobble to the left. Otherwise, she looked strong, tall and fit with glistening dark hair. Catesby would have had to break into a run if he wanted to overtake her. When she got to the T-junction with Marylebone High Street, the limping woman turned right. It was now obvious to Catesby that she was heading in the same direction that he was. She wasn't, however, taking counter-surveillance precautions. She hadn't plunged into a crowd or a large building with more than one exit. Maybe she assumed that London was safer than Lyon – but she did seem to know Marylebone well because she was taking the quickest route to Wimpole Street.

Number 32 Wimpole Street was, like most SOE locations, a prestigious address. Four stories high plus a mansard and a basement flat; separated from the street by black iron railings with an arched entrance porch and heavy oak doors. Catesby was twenty paces behind when *la dame qui boite* disappeared into the building.

Catesby's room was on the third floor and he was lying on his bed fully clothed. The grand staircase that led off the entrance hall ended on the floor below. He suspected that his room, accessible by narrow stairs, had been servants' accommodation. As he decided to undress for a needed nap, he heard someone thumping their way up the uncarpeted stairs. 'Why the fuck,' said Catesby, 'can't they leave me alone?' A second later there was a knock on the door. 'Just a minute,' he shouted.

The woman facing him as he opened the door was not beautiful in a conventional way – or even in an unconventional way – but she was striking. She looked like a games teacher who wouldn't stand for any nonsense. 'Are you Jacques?' she said.

Catesby was surprised to hear an American accent, but it sounded refined and cosmopolitan. He later found out that she came from a prominent Baltimore family and had worked in the US Embassy in Warsaw. 'That's my cover name,' said Catesby. 'Are you Germaine?'

'Germaine is no more. I've been rechristened Diane. Can we have a little talk?'

'Please come in.'

The woman entered and Catesby shut the door behind her.

'Do you mind,' she said, 'if I sit down?'

'Please do.'

There was a chair, but the woman chose the bed instead. 'I need,' she said, 'to give Cuthbert a rest. Otherwise, he can be troublesome.'

Catesby was confused. He didn't realise that the female agent was working with someone else. 'Is he staying here?'

'Cuthbert never leaves me. In fact...' the American's voice dropped to a husky whisper. 'In fact, Cuthbert is an intimate part of me. I don't know what I would do without him – even though I seldom sleep with him. But sometimes, when travelling by train for example, I have to. Do you mind if I...?'

Catesby didn't know what she wanted to do, but said, 'No problem. As you like.'

'Thank you.'

He half-expected her to take out a packet of cigarettes, but instead she lay back on the bed and pulled her skirt up. Catesby wasn't particularly shocked. SOE attracted unconventional types. But when he realised what was happening, he was a little more disappointed than relieved.

'May I introduce you to Cuthbert?' said the woman as she began to undo the leather straps that held the artificial leg in place. She then placed the flesh-coloured wooden prosthetic on the bed beside her. 'I mustn't let the stump get too dry,' she said. She took a small jar out of her handbag and began to rub ointment into the end of her amputated leg which extended about seven or eight inches below her knee. 'When we were escaping over the Pyrenees, Cuthbert got very angry and rubbed my stump raw – but I mustn't blame him. It was December and the weather was freezing and awful. And then after we crossed the border we got arrested by the Spanish police.'

Catesby began to realise that *la dame qui boite* was worth ten of most agents with both legs.

'But I'm not here to talk about me,' said the woman. 'I'm here to brief you about Lyon. It is the heart of the Resistance, but it is also a city full of informers, gangsters and German sympathisers. You have to be careful – and always have an escape plan in mind, which is why I managed to get back here. But you have to take risks too. My best contact was Madame Guérin – who was a madame in both senses of the word. By the way, if you get to Lyon, I would love to know what's happened to her. She was a lovely lady who ran a brothel frequented by German soldiers – whom she plied with drugs and alcohol to find out information. Madame Guérin also had a doctor friend who supplied the girls with health certificates that, frankly, they may not have deserved. I suspect the doctor also supplied the drugs that Madame Guérin mixed into the wine and brandy that she served the German soldiers. Sadly, both of them have now been arrested.' The woman hammered the bed with her fist causing Cuthbert to jump up. 'It's so unfair!'

'What is?'

'That they won't let me go back to Lyon. I've already been practising with disguises. I can be a very convincing old woman. But Baker Street is against it – which is why I'm briefing those of you who are being sent. Can you turn away, please? We Americans do have some modesty.'

Catesby faced the wall, waited a few seconds – and then panicked. Was she a German agent using an underwear adjustment as a ploy to stab him in the back? He turned around in time to see her buttoning up her blouse.

'I told you not to look.'

'Sorry.'

'Naughty boy.' She handed over a piece of paper. 'This is a list of safe houses and contacts in Lyon. If you take this list with you into France – or even an encoded copy of it – I will personally track you down and get Cuthbert to kick you to death. Try, as best you can, to memorise it. The only other person with a copy of this is Vera at Baker Street – whom I totally trust. If you forget anything on the list and have access to a W/T, you will be able to get the addresses and names – and also an update on any safe houses or contacts that have been compromised.'

Catesby looked at the list which smelled faintly of lavender. 'Some of the places rhyme; I'll try to turn it into a poem.'

'Good. As you undoubtedly know, if you are on the run and without a radio your memory is your best friend.'

Catesby nodded.

'I think it's time,' said the American, 'that Cuthbert and I got back together.' She began to reattach the wooden leg. 'There are three people in Lyon that I must warn you about. The first one is obvious: the head of the Gestapo, Klaus Barbie. He is a sadist who takes pleasure in torturing people. He has been known to skin prisoners alive. But Barbie is also an effective administrator and counterintelligence officer. He is a dangerous and ruthless enemy. He is also slippery and always one step ahead.'

It was the first time that Catesby had heard Barbie's name, but the evil legend was to haunt him for his entire career as an intelligence officer.

'The other two?' The woman looked out the window as if trying to conjure faces. 'I'm not sure what their real names are or who they are – but they are both dangerous and subtle. One duped me out of a hundred thousand francs. He said he needed the money to pay for intelligence from informers and to set up a Resistance network. Much of the intelligence proved true, but useless – and I suspect most of his Resistance recruits have been betrayed.'

'How do I recognise him?'

'He is a Roman Catholic priest from Luxembourg – and, despite keeping mistresses, looks very priestly. He is fair-haired and looks about forty, but maybe a bit younger. I think his name, or one of his names, might be Robert. He comes across as learned and sincerely intellectual.'

'Are you certain that he is a collaborator?'

'In this business we can never be certain about anyone – least of all the third person. I've never met him, but he has approached several members of the Resistance.' The woman looked at Catesby. 'Nick told me you were Belgian, but you sound awfully English.'

Catesby wondered who 'Nick' was. Could it be the major who had interviewed him earlier? Catesby stared out the window. The sun was still playing hide and seek.

'I can understand,' said the woman sounding more American than ever, 'if you don't want to answer.'

'No, it's not a problem. Nick got it partly right. My mother is Belgian, but I'm British.'

'Good. Then if you ever meet Félix you might know whether or not he really is Belgian.'

'Who is Félix?'

'He's this guy who keeps trying to join the Resistance in Lyon. He wears glasses and a beret. Félix says he's from Belgium which is why he speaks heavily accented French.'

'The accent isn't that heavy – especially if you are a Walloon.'

'I thought that might be so. In any case, Félix spends a lot of time in cafés trying to find out what people think about the Germans and dropping hints about the Resistance. He says that he had to flee Belgium because the Germans suspected that he was trying to set up a resistance group.'

'How does he support himself in Lyon? Has he got a job?'

The American smiled. 'He never says what he does – but there is a rumour that Félix admitted to someone that he is an Abwehr agent, but one that hates the Nazis and who wants to come over to our side.'

'Sounds like he could be an agent provocateur.'

'Exactly.' The woman got up from the bed and smoothed her skirt. 'I've got to go.' She extended a hand. Her grip was firm and dry. 'Good luck – or *bonne merde* as the French say. Fortunately, I've always had good bowels.'

'You're lucky,' said Catesby as she headed for the door. As she reached for the door handle, he said, 'By the way, what do you think of Nick?' He was now pretty certain that the major and Nick were the same person.

'He's great. Nick was the one who got me into SOE. His wife's an American who loves the arts. Sometimes we all have dinner together.'

Catesby watched her through the door and listened to Cuthbert thumping down the stairs.

The Wimpole Street FANYs collected all the personal post that had been sent to SOE agents at their anonymous London cover address. Catesby was disappointed that he had received so few letters. Most of them were from his mother or sister, but there were two from Strachan, Catesby's night-climbing friend from Cambridge, who reported that the Scots Greys had been withdrawn from Africa to be refitted with Sherman tanks. Strachan had complained to his senior officers that they should have attacked the German artillery on horses while waiting for their new tanks. Catesby was envious.

The longest letters were from Catesby's sister, Frederieke. Her university had been evacuated from London to Oxford during the Blitz – and she was in love. There was a telephone number in Oxford where she could be contacted, and Catesby rang it.

The dinner at the Ritz was hastily organised and Freddie's new boyfriend, Tomasz, was one of the most glamorous characters that Catesby had ever met. Strikingly handsome, Tomasz was a Polish pilot who had fled his country after its defeat in 1939 and enlisted in the French air force. After the fall of France, he had escaped to Britain where he became part of 303 Squadron in Kent. Tomasz quickly mastered the differences between miles per hour and kilometres per hour – and the fact that you pushed the throttle forward to accelerate and not backwards. He became a Battle of Britain hero – on one occasion bringing down a Messerschmitt by crashing his damaged and out-of-ammunition Hurricane into the German fighter before parachuting out.

'I feel badly about that,' confided Tomasz to Catesby over the Ritz's champagne. 'I wish that I had enough money to buy you another Hurricane.'

And yet money did not seem to be a problem as Tomasz splashed out freely and lavishly. When Tomasz was out of earshot, Freddie told Catesby that Tomasz's family were Polish *szlachta*, aristocracy, and had money salted away all over the place. The question that Catesby wanted to ask his somewhat mousy sister, but didn't, was how she had managed to win such an attractive man. There must have been a lot of competition. It was a mystery that would taunt Catesby for years. When he finally thought he had uncovered the answer, it didn't add up. The secret intelligence that Tomasz was trying to get from Freddie in 1953 didn't exist in 1943. Could it have been love, after all?

The most embarrassing thing about that evening at the Ritz was the way Tomasz kept winking at Catesby whenever he gave evasive answers about his duties in the army. The Pole seemed to have inside information and wasn't buying Catesby's cover stories. On one occasion Tomasz warned Freddie: 'Ask your brother no questions and he'll tell you no lies.'

There were times when Catesby wanted to punch Tomasz in his too-handsome face – and other times when he was completely won over by his charm. He loved the Pole's irreverent sense of humour and his natural grace. There was a niggle about Tomasz that still bothered Catesby: a vague similarity between the Pole and Henri Déricourt. They were both daredevil pilots and both loved the good life.

Catesby slept late at Wimpole Street, but the good thing about champagne is that it doesn't give a hangover. He was in reasonably good shape when one of the FANY staff roused him from his slumber. Catesby was in a dressing gown when he answered the door. 'Sorry, I was having a lie-in.'

'You had a telephone call from Baker Street. They want you to ring back immediately.'

'I'll get dressed now.'

'No, they want you to ring back immediately.'

Catesby felt silly traipsing through the Wimpole Street house in dressing gown and bare feet behind a contemptuous-looking FANY in uniform. He felt like a brothel user who had been arrested in a police raid. The phone call, however, was straightforward: he had an appointment to see 'Vera' in just over an hour. At least he would have time to dress.

Vera was the sharpest person that Catesby had ever met at Baker Street. She had jet black hair and, at five foot ten, was taller than most of the men at SOE HQ. She was wearing a well-tailored dresssuit that looked like a uniform – and was chain-smoking Senior Service. Vera gave the impression of being in charge – although she referred to her job as 'housekeeping'.

'You will,' said Vera, 'be leaving for France in two days' time. I hope all goes smoothly because it's the last night of the moon.' She paused to light another Senior Service.

'Will I be returning by Halifax and parachute?'

'No, you will be leaving by Lysander from Tangmere – with a new W/T operator/courier. She's excellent. I will be at Tangmere on the night to carry out last-minute security checks on your clothing and papers before seeing you off. We're trying to tighten up.'

Catesby would have liked to ask why, but held his tongue.

Vera gave Catesby a look so piercing that he felt it exiting through the back of his head. 'There's another reason why I wanted to see you. I am going to ask you a question that is highly sensitive and confidential. Answer honestly and frankly – and I promise that what you say will never be traced back to you.'

Catesby nodded.

'What do you think of Henri Déricourt?'

Catesby told her.

Catesby's final evening in London before deployment ended in drunken decadence. It began with Ewan who took Catesby to the summer exhibition at the Royal Academy. As most of the gallery space had been destroyed in the Blitz, it was a small and cramped exhibition and there were no refreshments as the Refreshments Room had been bomb-damaged and was closed for the duration. Catesby could see that artists were trying to extend the boundaries of realism into abstraction. The most striking work was by Richard Eurich, an official war artist, who had been tasked with painting the ill-fated Dieppe Raid of the previous summer. The raid was a disaster with sixty per cent of the troops killed, captured or wounded. The painting was a chaos of smoke, waterspouts, broken machinery and sunlight in which it was difficult to perceive human figures. Once again, Catesby felt he wasn't part of the war.

Ewan steered Catesby to the Courtauld where there was a party and lots of refreshments. That's when things began to get out of order. The first woman who grabbed Catesby said she was a photographer from Vienna. At some point, they became part of a group – largely composed of European expats – who decided to go to a pub. Catesby searched for Ewan who shouted that he would 'catch up later' – and that 'she', presumably the Viennese photographer, 'is very interesting'. On the way to the pub, Catesby began to practise his German on the Viennese woman. He found her Austrian accent difficult to understand, but gathered that she was a committed *Kommunist* and that was one of the reasons she had to leave Vienna. 'It is important,' she said, 'that my photography does not exist in a vacuum, but reflects my political beliefs.'

As they walked, Catesby became aware that they were attracting curious stares. A British Army officer with parachutist's wings speaking German to a diminutive Austrian was odd even for Fitzrovia. Catesby felt a cold chill run down his spine. Was he still being talent spotted? And, if so, by whom?

When they got to the pub, the photographer detached herself and began speaking Austrian German with another woman of about the same age. Catesby eavesdropped and picked up that the other woman's name was Litzi and that they were both from Vienna. They briefly spoke about a man who was Litzi's estranged husband. They were still on good terms and the husband had an important job in the British government. It was years before Catesby put together all the pieces and all the people.

At closing time, the crowd of cosmopolitan bohemians moved on to a party. The only other people in uniform were two black American GIs and a British officer in a kilt with a ludicrously upper-class accent who was braying about his friendship with Ivor Novello. Catesby became entangled with a woman in black who was either an artist or an artist's model or both. They ended up at her digs at three o'clock in the morning – only a few hours before Catesby was due to catch 'the Hearse' which would take him from Wimpole Street to Tangmere.

'You seem a bit worse for wear,' said Vera when she saw Catesby, 'but I can't blame you.'

'For a Suffolk boy like me London can be a wicked place.'

'London can be a wicked place for anyone.'

Paranoia again gripped Catesby. What had Vera found out? He looked at her. Something about Vera was strange and discordant too. There was the slightest hint of a foreign accent that he hadn't noticed before – and her thick black hair was coiffed and cut in a manner that was more continental than British.

'Your uniforms and personal belongings have been stored in a packing case at Orchard Court. If you don't come back, they will be sent to your next-of-kin. Is your mother's address in Lowestoft still current?'

'Yes.'

'I only ask because there has been so much bombing there.'

'Thank you.'

'Are you comfortable with your French clothes?'

'They are a perfect fit.'

'They're not French. They are made by a tailor in the East End, but he has attached labels linking them to French designers. I suggest you memorise the names of those designers in case anyone compliments you on the fine cut of your coat. Now, turn out your pockets.'

Catesby did so.

'Good. No British coins or Swan Vesta matches.'

'I don't smoke.'

'You should. Everyone in France smokes.' Vera reached into her bag and took out a silver cigarette case. 'Here, this is a going-away present. Fill it with Gauloises when you get to France.'

'I'm most grateful.'

'And one more thing, let's have a look at your trouser turn-ups. It's amazing what we find there: dropped coins, theatre tickets, baked beans.'

Catesby turned out his turn-ups and they were empty.

'Good. I think you're as clean as we can make you.' Vera sniffed. 'Your girlfriend was wearing very cheap scent.' She took a small bottle out of her bag and dripped a few drops of liquid on her fingers and dabbed the liquid on Catesby's neck. 'That will make you smell as if you have been with a proper Frenchwoman – perhaps the wife of a *préfet*.'

Catesby was momentarily in heaven. The unexpected intimacy from such an elegant woman had sent a shiver of pleasure through his body.

The remaining hour before the flight was spent in the redbrick Tudor house that overlooked the channel. The bar, as always, was open and once again *J'attendrai* was playing on the phonograph. A young nervous-looking agent, most likely one being deployed for the first time, was sitting alone in a corner talking to himself in French – probably practising his cover story.

The free bar beckoned. Catesby ordered a double brandy. While he was cradling his farewell drink, Catesby noticed two women having a conversation – one was Jimmy's wife, Hélène. The other woman was tall, fair and wore glasses. Hélène gave Catesby a look of recognition and he went over to join them. The tall bespectacled woman was the first to speak. 'Hello, my name is Marie. We will be leaving together on the first Lysander.'

Catesby shook hands with Marie and kissed Hélène on both cheeks. 'I'm still Jacques.'

'It's a pity,' said Marie looking at Catesby, 'that they didn't give us a chance to meet before this evening as we will be working closely together.'

The woman was older than most of the agents, perhaps in her late thirties. She had the assured air of someone who had been running a successful business – and had been landed with a new member of staff that she hadn't had a chance to interview.

'It's a quick turnaround,' said Catesby. 'I've only been in England four days.'

She glanced over Catesby's shoulder. 'You had better finish your drink, we've been called.'

They were driven to the waiting Lysander in a large open-topped Ford in camouflage paint. It was an enormous car and Catesby guessed, by its left-hand drive, that it was a present from the USA. They needed a large car because they had been loaded down with a number of bags and boxes.

'I believe,' said Marie, 'that most of that stuff is for the reception committee. We must make sure that the radio case doesn't get mixed up with it. There is a small revolver with the radio – and some chocolate too. Would you like to carry it?'

'Only the chocolate.'

'Good. The gun is just as incriminating as the W/T so we might as well leave it where it is. I see you've got a case with your personal belongings.'

'Only a toothbrush and other toilet things.' Catesby didn't add that there was also a pill packet in which aspirins were innocently resting beside amphetamines and cyanide.

'I suggest you put your personal things in my bag. It will look more natural since we'll be travelling as a couple – and it will also make it easier for you to deal with that heavy radio.'

Catesby thought it best not to mention their age difference, but said instead, 'But our identity cards are in different names.'

The woman smiled. 'It often happens in France.'

The Lysander looked like a fat black cat waiting to pounce in the light of the half moon. Marie climbed the boarding ladder first and Catesby handed up the luggage. They were both dressed in bulky flying suits that they would abandon in France. Catesby, brought up in a home of working-class thrift, hoped the padded suits would be passed on to returning agents. The big Bristol Mercury engine began to roar like an angry cat as Marie slid the Perspex canopy forward.

'My name is Bunny,' said the pilot, 'and I believe that you've both flown in a Lizzie before. She's a fine girl, my Lizzie – and my wife says that if I don't stop spending so many nights with her, she might go off with that Yank officer who keeps giving her fancy underwear. Enough about me, let's get airborne.'

The rear-facing seats gave them a view of the moon-bathed English coast fading in the distance. Catesby wiped a tear away. 'I love you,' he whispered.

The woman leaned over. It was the first time she spoke English. 'I hope you love France too.'

Catesby laughed and switched to French, 'You weren't meant to hear that. I'm a sentimental fool.'

'All heroes are sentimental.'

The pilot's voice crackled over the intercom. 'Our cruising speed is a hundred and seventy miles per hour. We'll be on the French coast before the ref blows the half-time whistle. We're going to execute a tricky feint westwards to avoid the search-lights and flak at Cherbourg. Enjoy the ride but let me know if you see a night fighter.'

'Will do,' said Catesby.

As the pilot signed off, the woman said, 'Did they tell you they bought our train tickets in advance?'

'No.'

'I've got them in my pocket. Tickets paid for and dated in advance are always a good ruse. If they know there was a Lysander landing nearby, it means you can't be one of the agents who just arrived.'

Catesby was impressed by Marie's professionalism.

'And what about the money?' she said.

'I've got a million francs.'

'And where is it?'

'In my jacket pocket.'

'You need to hide it before we get to the railway station.'

'I know and I will.' Catesby was a bit annoyed. He didn't like being treated like a child. A million francs was an average yearly French salary. Luckily for the British taxpayer, the money they carried was counterfeited by SOE. After the fall of France, a French treasury official had escaped to Britain with a full set of currency printing plates.

'I know we're not supposed to ask other agents about their past histories,' said Catesby.

'But you want to?'

'I bet you were in business.'

'I don't know what you were,' said the woman, 'but I suspect that one of your parents was from Belgium or somewhere around Lille. But for a job? You look too young to have had a career, but I could imagine that you were training to be a bank clerk or teacher before you joined the army – a career where you could use your knowledge of French.'

'You're wrong. I learned French when I had a job dancing in

top hat, tails and spats before lines of semi-naked ladies at the Folies Bergères.'

'Of course, I remember you well. I was the one who did peek-a-boos clad only in ostrich feathers. All the girls adored you.'

Catesby laughed. 'What an odd conversation to be having in the circumstances.'

'It helps to be light-hearted – but please don't use the Folies Bergères as a cover story.'

'You're right. I was too young to have begun a career. If I survive the war, I don't know what I will become.'

'And you were right about me too. I was in the wine trade.'

'It sounds like a dream job.'

'It isn't now.'

Catesby noted a hint of bitterness in Marie's voice – and suspected there were secrets that wouldn't be revealed. He suddenly felt very tired and closed his eyes. The banter and human contact had relaxed him. When he woke up they were over Brittany.

'I hope you had a good sleep,' said Marie.

'Fine, thanks. Where are we?'

'Almost there. The Loire is always a beautiful silver thread in the moonlight – as refreshing as a chilled Muscadet with oysters.'

'Thanks for the wine advice.'

'It's now time to be serious. I know the region – and several places where we can find refuge among growers and *commerçants* if things go wrong.'

'Safe houses?'

'No, I wouldn't trust safe houses near a compromised landing zone.' Marie smiled. 'Are you a good runner?'

'Cross-country was my best sport at school.'

'Good – and that's why I'm wearing flat shoes.'

'Why are you so suspicious?'

'There are secrets that I can't tell you.'

'Why?'

'Because if you were captured, they might torture them out of you – which isn't to say that you are not strong and brave.'

Then why, thought Catesby, had 'Major Nick' told him about the impending invasion in the Pas-de-Calais?

'Look,' said Marie, 'you can see her!'

'Who?'

'*La Loire.*'

The river was a wide glittering band of silver as she flowed towards Nantes and the sea.

Catesby began rummaging among the bags.

'What are you doing?'

'I'm going to get the pistol out of the radio case.'

'Leave it there. We don't want an accidental discharge when we're about to land.'

'Don't treat me like a child.' Catesby then remembered the dropped Sten which had nearly shot up the Lysander on the trip out to England. 'Sorry.'

'If something does go wrong, you can try to grab it before we start running – but it would only be useful against a stupid *flic*, not a pair of German military policemen with submachine guns.'

The Lysander began to lose height and for the first time Catesby noticed that another aircraft, hopefully the second insertion Lysander, was following in their wake. He could also see the L-shaped landing lights as Bunny completed his landing circle. A moment later there was a blinding flash, but no noise. For a second Catesby thought he was dead, but the Lysander was in one piece and was bumping on a rough pasture with the brakes howling.

Bunny was smiling as they unloaded the aircraft. 'High tension lines,' he shouted. 'Lizzie's okay, but they fried her radio. Good luck, chaps.'

The unloading and loading took less than three minutes. The only person in the reception team that Catesby recognised was Déricourt, aka GILBERT. There was the shadow of a Traction Avant in the treeline. 'We can give you bicycles or a lift in the Traction,' said Déricourt.

'Where are the bicycles?' said Marie as she stepped out of her flying suit.

'We'll get them for you.'

A few minutes later their bags were lashed to the bikes and they were pushing them along a rough moon-dappled track. There were shots in the near distance. At first neither Catesby nor Marie spoke. There was another shot. 'It isn't that far,' said Marie, 'about fifteen kilometres. I suggest we ditch the bikes and go on foot.'

'Why?'

'Because they'll be expecting us on bikes.'

Catesby followed her into the woods well off the path. She finally laid her bike on its side and sat on a tree trunk. She clasped her arms across her body and shivered. 'I'm cold.'

'Maybe we should burn a few thousand francs.'

'Don't try to be funny. Just stay quiet and wait.'

A few minutes later there was the sound of bikes on the track and whispered voices. Then the sound of the Traction Avant, then more bikes. The landing zone was clear, but the night was pierced by the sound of dogs howling. Catesby knew that things had gone tits-up – and the sound of more gunshots seemed to prove it. Except that there was something odd about the shooting. There were no automatic weapons firing. It wasn't a battle. It was more like a hunting-down with dogs followed by swift executions.

The moon was gone and predawn twilight was creeping in the eastern sky when they set off. The first road they came to was the Route Nationale that stretched along the Loire, but at that hour it was still abandoned. 'It's obvious,' said Marie, 'that we had to set off early to get to Angers for the first train. If anyone asks where we spent the night, I will give them the name of a Saumur grower who produces Chenin Blanc.'

There were numerous farm tracks leading off the road. They eventually saw one up ahead where several vehicles were parked. They could hear loud laughter and animated conversation. They continued walking. Catesby could make out a circle of figures huddled around a flat-back van – and dogs too. The voices were now clearer – and some of them were speaking German.

'Keep walking,' said Marie.

The clink of wine glasses joined the voices and laughter. They were celebrating. As they approached the van Catesby avoided eye contact, but he gave a quick glance at the three bodies lying on the van's flat bed. The wild boar were beautiful tusked creatures trussed to staves. Catesby found a German captain staring into his face. He obviously needed to say something. '*Guten Essen*,' said Catesby. He hoped speaking the conqueror's language made him sound suitably compliant.

The captain smiled and said, '*Danke*.'

They continued walking. When they were out of earshot, Marie said, 'They were playing, not working.'

'Our Lysander landed less than a kilometre away from where the Germans were having a wild boar hunt – and no one blinked. Something isn't right.'

'How are you doing with the radio?'

'It is one heavy fucker,' said Catesby shifting the case from one hand to the other. 'I tried not to show it when we walked by *les boches* even though it was pulling my shoulder out.'

'Can I take over for a while?'

Catesby swallowed his pride and handed the radio over. They kept swapping for the rest of the way to Gare d'Angers-Saint-Laud – a railway station, Catesby suspected, that would be doomed for RAF destruction as soon as the invasion was on the cards. He hoped the bombs wouldn't rain down while they were waiting for the first morning train.

The journey to Limoges required one change, at Vierzon, a small station in the middle of deepest France. The trains were crowded, but there were no Germans and few police. Catesby could see how members of the Resistance and SOE agents could be lulled into a deceptive sense of security. At times, occupied France could seem so boringly normal. The conversations that flowed around them were about food, clothes, families, travel problems and illnesses. The only indications that a war was going on were mentions of ration cards – and one of a son who had been conscripted into STO and was working in Germany. There was no indication that a descent into hell would be waiting for them at Gare de Limoges-Bénédictins. A hell only averted by Marie's quick thinking and fluent German.

Suffolk: April 2015

Although Catesby was an old man he often thought about sex and mating. In fact, it was impossible not to with the view from his office over the garden in April. His favourite couple were Monsieur et Madame Turdus Philomelos. The song thrush pair had a carefully delineated patch of grass which they almost gardened. Catesby deduced that they were not just feeding themselves, but picking up beakfuls of mud to line the bottom of the nest they were building. Thrushes were the most house proud of birds. Woodpigeons were at the other end of the spectrum. They made sloppy ramshackle nests that often came down in the wind bringing eggs and nestlings to a sorry end – but there was no short supply of woodpigeons because their rampant sex lives provided chicks all year round. And they had no shame. The back of a falling-to-pieces garden bench was their favourite playground. They would spend hours necking, but it was always the hen bird who initiated the serious sex stuff. The hens would flaunt their backsides and push themselves at the cock pigeons – and sometimes pursue the male birds across the garden. The collar doves behaved in a more seemly fashion – perhaps because they were foreign.

Catesby was watching a goldfinch hop across the grass when he heard someone at the door. He knew it was his granddaughter by the polite tentative knocking. 'Come in, my dear.'

She entered carrying a thick folder of A4 paper and gave Catesby a hug and kiss.

'What's that?' said Catesby, nodding at the folder even though he already knew.

'I've printed out what I have of your memoir so far, but I've interpolated it with historical context – and, dare I say, my own interpretations. It's fifty-seven thousand words – so I would say we are halfway there.'

'Are you pleased?'

'Your recollections are clear and detailed, but what pleases me most is your emotional honesty.'

'Oh god, can you cut those pieces out? It's because you got me drunk.'

'History is as much about what people felt at the time as what they did.'

'My dearest darling, what I felt at the time should go to the grave with me.'

'If that's what you want, Granddad, I will respect your wishes – but please let me keep your thoughts and feelings.'

'Fine, if you restrict it to my fears about death, my suspicions of treachery and my hatred of the Nazis – but I can't see what the love life of a foolish young man has to do with history.'

'History is about inner lives too.'

Catesby began to laugh.

'What's so funny, Granddad?'

Catesby looked at his granddaughter. He knew that others found her stunningly beautiful as well. 'I was just thinking about your inner life – which has always been a mystery to me as well as others in the family.'

'My ex was too clingy.'

The cat flap suddenly opened and slammed shut. A black cat miaowed and jumped on to Catesby's lap. 'Speaking of clingy. But this one's only hungry.' Catesby opened a tin and dropped two dollops into a bowl. 'I thought that relationship ended four years ago.'

Leanna stirred uneasily.

'Apologies,' said Catesby, 'I shouldn't pry.'

'It isn't prying – at least, Granddad, not when you ask questions. From you it's a sign of love and concern.'

'And I would never tell anyone else.'

She smiled. 'I bet you used to say that to all the agents you were running.'

'But in your case it's true.'

Leanna laughed. 'And I wouldn't want you to use me as a honey trap.'

'Good god. Where is this going?'

'I have an awful confession to make, Granddad, and you are not going to like it.'

'I would never disapprove of anything you did. If you robbed a bank, I would call it a necessary redistribution of wealth – even if you kept a large chunk for yourself.' Catesby began to sing, '*The people's flag is deepest red...* Why are you laughing? Am I that badly out of tune?'

'I'm not laughing, Granddad, I'm crying.'

'What's wrong? You do look upset. Have I said something wrong?'

Leanna looked away. 'You will never forgive me.'

Catesby kept quiet and waited.

'I am having an affair with a Tory MP. But don't worry, we're not going to get married. He already has a wife and has no intention of leaving her.'

Catesby got up and put his arms around his granddaughter. 'That doesn't make one bit of difference.'

'Now why are you crying, Granddad?'

'Not because you're having an affair with a Tory! But because I love you and want you to be happy.'

'Thank you, thank you. You are the only, only person I can trust. I can always say anything to you and that means so much to me.'

Catesby smiled. 'Good. Now tell me more about this piece of Tory scum you're sleeping with.'

'Granddad!'

'Sorry.'

'He says he's a one-nation Tory, but I take that with a grain of salt. He can be witty and charming. I would love you to meet him.' Leanna smiled. 'Maybe you could convert him?'

'If he met me, he would probably join the right-wing of his party.'

'I doubt it. He says he hates them.' She raised an eyebrow. 'Would you like some insider info?'

'I promised I wouldn't use you as a honey trap.'

'I am a willing agent acting on my own volition.'

'Okay then.'

'Cameron is going to promise a referendum on EU membership. He says that Cameron wants to use a remain win to boot the awkward squad who hate the EU into the long grass – and the PM is sure it will happen. My lover, who likes a glass or three of wine, was a bit tipsy one night and dropped a bombshell. He says if there is a referendum, he's going to stab Cameron in the back and campaign to leave. He can be charming and warm, but I'm beginning to think he has a nasty side.'

Massif Central: May 1943

At first, the narrow escape at Limoges railway station and its immediate aftermath had left Catesby exhilarated. But the adrenalin rush was soon replaced by weariness and caution. The Gestapo wanted revenge and they had given orders to hunt down Marie and Catesby at all costs. They both knew it would be unwise to continue to lie low with Guingouin's Maquis in the woods of Limousin. They radioed what had happened to London and Baker Street agreed. Their mission to establish a communications base in Limoges was now scrubbed; Catesby and Marie were instructed to leave the area immediately. Their new priority was to contact and liaise with members of the Resistance in Lyon who were lacking in radio communication facilities – and, by any means necessary, to report on the important Resistance leadership meeting with the mysterious Max.

There was no time for fond farewells from Guingouin and his former comrades, but they did pass on messages from Maquis intelligence sources reporting that French rail staff at Limoges station were being replaced by ones from Germany. It seemed to Catesby that the Germans, anticipating that they may soon be moving troops north to face an invasion, were taking precautions against insider sabotage of the rail lines. He forwarded the intelligence to London – the big one was imminent.

Their first task before setting off on the trek to Lyon was to change their appearance. It was easier for Marie than Catesby. She dyed her hair brown and stopped wearing her glasses. 'Does it make me look younger?' she said.

'Yes,' said Catesby, 'but it also makes you look less distinguished and less intellectual.'

'Good,' she said with a hint of a miaow. 'I will look mousy like you. Maybe I can pass as your aunt.'

Catesby's disguise consisted of growing a moustache and wearing glasses. As clear glass would have given the game away, he wore genuine prescription glasses which distorted the world around him and made him stumble on stairs. 'Maybe,' said Marie, 'I could pass as a nurse looking after the village idiot.'

Catesby no longer responded. He had realised, since she killed the young German driver in Limoges, that Marie had a cruel streak and that answering back only hardened her. Maybe that cruel streak was also part of her sexual magnetism. She never dug her fingernails in or hurt Catesby when they were in bed together, but the threat of a deep scratch or something worse was always there. She didn't take charge, but showed Catesby what to do and performed unexpected things on him. And sometimes she got extremely excited and lost control as she climaxed. Once, she screamed and woke up the safe house and its neighbours – one of whom pounded on the wall. Fortunately, it wasn't the sort of sound that attracted the suspicions of the Vichy police or the Germans – even if it did attract their envy. Screaming orgasms weren't what you expected of members of the Resistance working undercover. And she did say some odd things. She sometimes suggested threesomes – including one with her younger sister. But the strangest was: 'There are times I'd like to kill a man as he begins to come. A knife to the heart as he spurts inside me.'

They were passed from safe house to safe house during their cross-county trip to Lyon. Much of the travelling was by bicycle and on foot across the blossoming countryside. The radio was often sent on separately via couriers to the next rendezvous point. It was a matter of sharing the risk – and, in cold stark calculation, losing a young courier and a radio was less of a price to pay than losing a radio plus its highly trained W/T operator and an organiser.

As they travelled eastwards, Catesby was impressed by the numbers of active *résistants* as well as the large network of *légaux* willing to help with food, accommodation and transport. But he could also see that this growing edifice of resistance was a fragile structure that could be easily crushed by tanks and heavy guns – and that there were many who wanted to keep their heads down.

The first part of the journey was on foot across the Plateau de Millevaches where Guingouin's territory overlapped with GILBERT's part of the Stationer réseau. They were guided by Maquisards sometimes dressed as local peasants or openly wearing paramilitary uniforms. The countryside was a beautiful wilderness of ancient forests, pastures, lakes, streams and peat bogs – an ideal place for guerrilla operations.

They spent a night at an isolated village called Saint-Merdles-Oussines where there were Roman ruins and dark lakes. It felt like being on a walking holiday. Around midnight Jimmy turned up unexpectedly. Jimmy was now working primarily as the W/T operator for HECTOR, the senior SOE officer in charge of the vast and expanding Stationer network.

'Any news about Hélène?' said Jimmy. His voice sounded irritable.

'She followed us in the second Lysander, but we didn't have a chance to talk before we were off.'

'No problems on the LZ?'

'None.' Catesby wasn't telling the whole truth, but he could see the state that Jimmy was in and didn't want to make things worse.

'I wish she had stayed in Nanteuil with our son. Why the fuck did she have to leave the kid and get involved in this mess?'

Catesby could see that Marie had understood the English and was about to say something. He gave her a look to tell her to keep quiet, but she ignored him.

'There are many women,' she said, 'who have made the choice to put country before family.'

'I've heard that before,' said Jimmy, '...about a thousand times.'

'We're not just fighting this war to free France; we're fighting to free women too.'

Jimmy laughed and continued speaking English. 'You sound like a bloody suffragette.'

Marie turned to Catesby. 'Suffragette?'

Catesby translated, 'It's a woman who fights for the right of women to vote.'

Marie turned on Jimmy. 'Then why don't you change sides and fight with the Vichyistes?' She went through her bag. She found a coin and hurled it at Jimmy. 'That's a Vichy franc. Turn it over and look what they've done to us.'

Jimmy, chastised, read Vichy's new motto for France in silence.

'They've turned our beautiful words, *Liberté, Égalité, Fraternité* into,' she spat out the Vichy motto, '*Travail, Famille, Patrie.*'

Jimmy looked about six inches tall and Catesby felt sorry for him.

'Your wife, Hélène, is a wonderful and brave woman. You should be proud that she took you on. Pétain and the Vichy puppets believe that women are either virgins or whores. One of them said in a broadcast that women should not be allowed access to higher education because it would turn them into prostitutes.'

'I understand and agree with what you've said,' replied Jimmy, 'and apologise for being an ignoramus.'

Marie put her arms around Jimmy. 'You are a wonderful and brave man – and I apologise for being a dragon.'

Catesby had begun to realise that the Resistance wasn't just about fighting the Germans, it was also a war of ideas.

The next morning, they set off on bicycles for the village of Ussel, a small industrial town with a population of about eight thousand. The plan was to stay in a safe house which was the home of a foreman at the sawmill. It was early evening when they arrived, too early to go to the safe house. They stopped in a square in the centre of the town and rested their bikes against an ancient stone fountain. A few minutes later there was a roar as *Wehrmacht* motorcycles with sidecars poured into the square. One of the German motorcyclists came over to the fountain and put his hands, which were stained with black grease, into the water and tried to scrub them clean. Catesby assumed there had been a mechanical difficulty en route which the soldier had dealt with. The town filled with more *Wehrmacht* vehicles: armoured cars, self-propelled artillery and trucks carrying troops. Catesby eavesdropped on conversations and it became apparent that the German unit would be spending the night in Ussel.

Without saying a word, they wheeled their bikes a couple of hundred yards to a wall overlooking a fast-flowing river. Catesby stared into the water and thought he could see small young trout. How wonderful to be a fish or a bird or any sort of wild creature that could move from place to place without identity papers.

'The problem with Ussel,' said Marie, 'is that it's on the main route between Bordeaux and Lyon.'

'And we've had the bad luck to run into a convoy.'

'It looks as if they are heading, like us, towards Lyon.'

'Shall we still go to the safe house?'

'I think it's best I go to see what's happening. You can wait for me in a café,' said Marie.

The Café de la Place had a tiny terrace – and there was only room for Catesby, an elderly couple and the four German soldiers who arrived a minute after he had settled down to a red wine. The elderly couple had whispered a warning to Catesby that the ersatz coffee was nearly undrinkable. The Germans, all ordinary soldiers, ordered the coffee and didn't complain. One of the soldiers, wearing glasses and looking totally out of place in uniform, sat apart from the others reading. Catesby glanced at the book's title: it was Rilke's *Duino Elegies*. What a strange world. The elegies had remained incomplete for years owing to Rilke's severe depression brought on by the First World War and his being conscripted into the army. Catesby tried not to stare at the German soldier. How could civilised people end up doing barbaric things? The soldiers were suddenly summoned out of the café by a shouting NCO. The bespectacled one gave Catesby a brief look. It was as if the German had read Catesby's thoughts and the answer to his question was, *I don't know either*.

The click of a bicycle sprocket announced Marie's return. 'Finish your wine and let's go,' she said.

'Can I pay first?'

'Sure.'

Catesby thought the proprietor looked at his hundred-franc note with suspicion. Was it paranoia or had the café owner been dealt SOE counterfeit currency before? The change he handed over was in genuine Vichy francs.

'What's the situation?' said Catesby as they pushed their bikes away.

'Michel is sure his house won't be requisitioned for *Wehrmacht* accommodation – it's too much of mess.'

The house was indeed a mess – and so was Michel. It was part of his cover story. Michel was in his fifties and had lost his wife the year before. He had been grief-stricken, but he exaggerated his grief and the amount he drank. He cultivated an image of a hopeless drunk and eccentric who only kept his job in the sawmill because the owner felt sorry for him. The police ignored him because they considered him a wreck incapable of hiding ammunition and explosives and providing courier services and a safe house.

As was the custom, Michel didn't ask his visitors from where they were coming or where they were going. He provided a simple evening meal of cheese, bread and wine.

'Is there usually this amount of military traffic?' said Catesby.

'No, and it looks bad for our comrades around Clermont-Ferrand.'

'Is that where they're heading?'

'It's likely. We have passed on intelligence reports from informers in the *préfecture*.'

Catesby exchanged a glance with Marie. What rotten fucking luck. Clermont-Ferrand was their next stop.

It was ninety kilometres from Ussel to Clermont. Not an enormous distance by bike, but they set off at first light. The countryside was gently hilly with pastures interspersed by woodlands. The traffic was sparse: mostly other cyclists, walkers and horse-drawn farm carts. There was a smattering of gas converted cars, but the tiny number of petrol-driven vehicles seemed to be government cars and vans. The few privately owned cars still travelling French roads tended to belong to rich people who had the foresight to hoard petrol when they saw defeat looming in 1940 – and later had worked out a deal with the authorities to prevent their cars from being requisitioned by the Germans. One of the things that puzzled Catesby about Déricourt was how he managed to have access to so many petrol vehicles and drive them openly around the countryside.

As it got close to midday, the sun shone and it grew pleasantly warm. Marie took off her pullover and put it in the bike's front basket. Leaning forwards on the handlebars emphasised her cleavage. When Catesby teased her about it, she said, 'You like my body?'

A short time later as they freewheeled down a hill she began to sing *J'attendrai*. Marie braked to a halt at the bottom and stopped singing. She was staring into a beech forest to the right. '*Regardes les jacinthes des bois.*'

'The French name is so much more beautiful than the English.'

'What is their English name?'

'Bluebells.'

'Blue balls?'

'No,' laughed Catesby, 'they are something else. Blue*bells* – the things that go ding-dong.'

'Ah, I see! It is because they are shaped like tiny bells.'

'I assume so.'

'I think the English name is more poetic – and do you know something?'

'What?'

'I have always dreamed of making love on a forest floor covered in *bluebells*.' She smiled. 'Shall we see if they make me chime?'

Marie was on top and grinding both of them into paradise when the clanking noises began. They were too far into the woods to be seen by the passing German military convoy – but the nearness of death and danger intensified their pleasure. Catesby gripped her buttocks hard as she began to scream – and hoped that if a sharp-eared German heard her shout of pleasure, he would mistake it for the warning call of a woodland bird.

The safe house in Clermont-Ferrand belonged to a university professor, an Egyptologist who specialised in the Ptolemaic Kingdom. Catesby was ashamed that he had never heard of the Ptolemaic Kingdom.

'Too many people haven't,' smiled the professor, 'and that is one of the reasons why higher education is so important. I would say that the period began with Alexander's conquest of Egypt in 332 BC. The Egyptians offered little resistance and welcomed Alexander as a deliverer from Persian rule. The name, of course, comes from Ptolemy the First who succeeded Alexander after his death in 323 BC. The kingdom continued until Cleopatra's death and the Roman conquest in 30 BC. Little, however, changed. The Romans continued the Ptolemaic system, Greek remained the language of government and Greeks continued to staff most government positions. And the Romans, like the Greeks before them, respected and protected Egyptian religion and customs.' The professor smiled again. 'But, as I warn my students, modern comparisons with ancient history are never valid. Each generation must make their own decisions – which is why I, though a man of nearly sixty, have joined the Resistance.'

'There was a lot of German military activity on the road between Ussel and here,' said Catesby.

'I know. Our situation is difficult. We are still in effect the University of Strasbourg. We were evacuated to Clermont-Ferrand early in the war when Alsace-Lorraine became a military zone. Most of our students are Alsatians who, after the annexation of the region, are now deemed to be German citizens. This means that it's not for them just a question of being conscripted into the STO, but into the military itself. As manpower becomes more critical for Germany, there are more frequent sweeps through the university and Clermont-Ferrand aimed at gathering up Alsatians to send to the Russian front. We try to protect our students by hiding them or giving them altered IDs showing that they were born in non-annexed parts of France. It's difficult and risky.'

Catesby sensed the situation of the professor and his colleagues was more than desperate, it was hopeless. At the end of the war Catesby discovered that the professor had been shot and killed in a corridor at the university while chatting to a colleague. During a sweep searching for students, the head of the Gestapo in Clermont-Ferrand had ordered the two professors to put their hands up. The Egyptologist hadn't raised his hands quickly enough to satisfy the Gestapo chief, so he shot him in the stomach. The professor died in agony a few hours later.

Marie and Catesby were restless that night and slept badly. 'I feel that we are walking into disaster,' said Catesby.

'Why?'

'Because I sense the Germans know what we are doing and are closing in.'

'They've been doing that since the beginning – but as the Resistance grows it is beyond their resources to control. They become more desperate, so they lash out more viciously.'

'If there are too many Maquisards to sweep up, you concentrate on the leadership. You kill the commanders,' said Catesby.

Marie stirred uneasily.

'You think that too?'

'It's only logical,' she said.

'What are we supposed to do in Lyon?'

'You know. Attend the meeting with Max and report back to London on the outcome.'

'Why have they chosen us?'

Marie brushed her hair from her eyes. 'I don't know. I think the whole thing is a mistake and a security nightmare. I am sure that Max has the ability to inform London of what happens without our help. It's as if someone wants us to spy on Max and the leadership.'

'Who is Max?'

'I can't tell you.'

'But he is important?'

'He is the most important person in the Resistance and the only one who can unify the factions under de Gaulle.'

'Do you like de Gaulle as leader?'

'What I think is unimportant – but General and Madame de Gaulle are loving parents. Their youngest daughter has Down syndrome and they love her more than words can say. No matter how busy he is, the general walks with her every day, caresses her and quietly talks to her – sometimes for hours. She's the sort of person that the Nazis would exterminate – which is why fighting them is so important.'

Catesby was struck by the passion in Marie's voice and embraced her.

On the advice of the professor, they completed the final part of the trip to Lyon by train. His students had informed him that there was an increasing number of checks on the roads out of Clermont-Ferrand. The influx of Gestapo into the town resulted in many young people and students fleeing to the countryside. The increase in road checks meant fewer police were available to oversee rail passengers. This was, perhaps, one of the reasons the train to Lyon was so packed. The weather had turned warm and humid and the train carriage reeked of sweat. Catesby leaned towards Marie, 'Are you all right?'

'I'm fine.'

'I need to pee.'

'Good luck.' Marie meant that he was unlikely to find a toilet cubicle that was unoccupied.

'It would be nice to have a walk too.'

Predictably, the first two toilet cubicles that Catesby came to were in use. He continued to move down the crowded train murmuring *Excusez-moi* like a litany as he stumbled over bags and stepped on feet. He suddenly came upon a carriage that was almost empty. There were only three men in it. Catesby wondered if it was some sort of first-class accommodation reserved for the rich or high-level officials. The three men must be in the same party because they were seated close together. Catesby suddenly realised that the man in middle was in handcuffs and had a very bruised face. Poor bastard. The man made eye contact with Catesby – and he immediately recognised the face beneath the bruises. It was Michel, the sawmill foreman who had provided them a safe house two nights before in Ussel.

Catesby guessed it would look less suspicious if he continued down the train. As he passed through the carriage, Catesby made an excuse to the Vichy policeman about needing *un pipi*.

There was no further sign of recognition between him and Michel. The next toilet cubicle was unoccupied. As Catesby made his way back through the carriage he noticed that Michel's face had hardened into despair. For a second, Catesby was tempted to try to overcome the police with some of the unarmed combat stuff he had learned in SOE training – *and then you kick him in the balls* – but thought it best to discuss the plan with Marie.

When he got back to their carriage, he whispered the situation to Marie who replied, 'I need a pee too.' She left to recce the carriage.

A few minutes later she returned. 'We are not going to do it. It's impossible. There is now a third guard and they've got guns.'

Afterwards, Catesby wondered if Marie's report was truthful – or was it a way of saying that avoiding an incident that could endanger the success of their mission in Lyon was more important than Michel's life.

The ID and luggage checks at Gare de Lyon-Perrache were cursory. It was a grand old station built in the classical style to impress nineteenth-century travellers. Catesby tried not to think about what was going to happen to Michel. He wanted to linger in the station café over a Pernod, forget the horror of war and watch the world go by. He liked the ambience of Lyon and didn't care if it was a dangerous place brimming with eager *résistants* who were being hunted down by equally eager Gestapo and Abwehr who wanted to use the Resistance-riddled city to make a name for themselves. Catesby loved the way that two rivers flowed through Lyon and longed for a stroll along the quays, but soon found Marie tugging at his coat sleeve and guiding him towards a waiting bus. Their first safe house wasn't in the city, but in a small town called Trévous, north of Lyon on the banks of the Saône.

As the bus was packed to overflowing, Catesby and Marie had to wedge themselves into places on the roof which bowed under piles of luggage, bags and chattering women returning to the countryside. It was a holiday atmosphere with a lot of laughter. The countryside was beautiful and the river, seldom out of view, gleamed invitingly beside them. The kilometres went by too quickly and Catesby didn't want the bus trip to end.

The safe house was the home of a small family. The daughter looked about twenty and the boy was fifteen. There was a large garden planted with potatoes, onions and lettuces – and a view of the Saône from the bedroom window. Catesby felt guilty putting such domestic bliss and the family who enjoyed it in danger. He wanted to leave and to tell the parents to cut their ties with the Resistance and to keep their heads down until the war was over – but they were fervent patriots who would do anything to rescue France. The daughter, who had trained as a secretary and was an excellent typist, was eager to help.

'Is there anything I can do?' she said. 'I spent hours typing lists for Monsieur Max and I know how they must be set out.'

Catesby was alarmed that someone as important as Max had stayed with the family. 'When was he here?'

'He left two days ago.'

The news worried Catesby. It was bad security for a safe house to be used so frequently.

'Monsieur Max is a charming and cultivated man. He said that he grew up wanting to be an artist, but became an administrator instead because his family was poor. Let me show you the paintings he did while he was here.' She got up and returned with two watercolours. One was a painting of the house and the garden bursting with spring flowers and light. The other was a portrait of the girl working at her typewriter. It captured her rapt concentration, her subtle beauty and the grace of her arms and long fingers. Catesby stared in awe at the paintings. Max was indeed a talented artist, but the watercolours did reveal a flicker of vanity. Max had signed them with his real name: Jean Moulin.

'They are beautiful,' said Catesby, 'but you must keep them hidden – and show them to no one else.'

The young woman looked distraught, but said, 'I understand.' She glanced at the watercolour of herself. 'In any case, I think this one flatters me out of all recognition.'

Catesby was about to disagree, but Marie was in the room

and he didn't want to get caught flirting – particularly as Marie could not have failed to notice that the girl was about the same age as Catesby. Later he realised that jealousy was not part of Marie's nature.

'The typing,' said the girl, 'was extremely boring – and Max constantly apologised. There were no words, just random groups of letters dictated in groups of four.'

Catesby didn't need to tell her that the lists were encoded messages waiting transmission.

'Can you please hand them to me?' said Marie.

'I believe that was Max's wish,' she said with a smile.

'Has our heavy friend arrived?' said Catesby referring to the radio.

'She has just been delivered with a cartload of well-rotted manure.'

'I can wash it for you,' said the daughter.

'That would be kind.'

That evening, as there wasn't a loft, the W/T was set up in the bedroom. Marie sat on a low chair under a spider's web of antenna tapping away at the Morse key, totally unaware of the meanings of the letter groups that she was transmitting. Being a W/T operator required the ability to do boring tasks with skill and accuracy. And, if London didn't have the decryption code, it would be a pointless task too. It was the first time that Catesby had seen Marie transmit and was amazed by her speed and sureness of touch. The task done, sooner than expected, Marie put on her headphones and waited for a reply from London. There was a receipt acknowledgment followed by a message to stand by to receive a transmission. Marie sat with a pencil and pad. She looked at Catesby, 'This could take hours.' More boredom.

Catesby smiled and slipped his hand inside her blouse. 'Your nipples are firm and erect.'

Marie touched his crotch. 'And so are you.'

Catesby was tempted to undo his flies, but the transmitter had sprung into life. Marie copied down the message and handed it to Catesby for decoding. Before he had finished the first letter groups, he realised that it was bad news. Very bad.

```
1 WARNING. PROSPER CIRCUIT ARRESTS. Awaiting
final confirmation, but it appears that Prosper has been
totally penetrated and blown. VIDAL and GARIN are now
in GESTAPO custody...
```

Catesby stopped decoding and looked at Marie. 'Who are they?'

'This is terrible news. VIDAL is Charles Delestraint, a retired lieutenant general and head of the *Armée secrète*. He is de Gaulle's man in France. GARIN is Joseph Gastaldo, Delestraint's chief of staff.'

Catesby wondered how Marie knew such things, but wasn't going to ask. He returned to the decoding.

```
BAKER, BUTCHER, PHYSICIAN, CINEMA, DONKEYMAN,
CHESTNUT, PRIEST, GLAZIER, ORATOR and ALICE have
been reported arrested. All information possessed by any
of these agents should be considered compromised. This
particularly applies to codes, codenames, safe houses and
letter boxes.
```

Marie sighed and touched her forehead. 'They've got Hélène too. She was CHESTNUT – what a wonderful strong woman.'

Catesby was certain that Jimmy would receive the same transmission and couldn't imagine his hurt and his bitterness.

'All of those codenames are English ones, they only refer to SOE agents who were captured – but for every one of them, there will have been ten, maybe fifty, *résistants* and *légaux* caught up in the sweep. I can hear their screams inside my head.'

Catesby put his hand on her arm and she quickly withdrew it. 'Don't touch me.'

'I have never seen you so emotional.'

'You don't know anything about me.'

'Will you ever tell me?'

'Not now – maybe never. There are more important things to do – like decoding the rest of the message.'

Catesby picked up the pencil. He wondered if he was writing out their death sentence.

2 URGENT: AVOID ALL OF AGENT DIANE'S SAFE
HOUSES IN LYON. All are compromised or under
surveillance.
3 REMAIN at your location to await following message:
DIDOT VOUS ATTEND. Proceed to Lyon for rendezvous
the next day. Meet DIDOT at PLACE DE LA COMÉDIE.
Carry a copy of LA VOIX NATIONALE under your arm.
Await contact with DIDOT next to fountain at 1235.
4 PROCEED ALONE WITHOUT AGENT MARIE. AGENT
MARIE awaits further instructions.
5 END OF TRANSMISSION.

Catesby looked at Marie. 'Would you like a French translation?'

She frowned. 'You could translate it in one word. *Merde.*'

'It doesn't sound like London fully knows what's going on. I think Prosper being blown has left them in a panic.'

Marie gave a bleak smile. 'I thought the British never panicked.'

'They do all the time, but don't show it.'

'I don't like the sound of DIDOT. I hope he isn't who I think he is.'

'Who do you think he is?'

'I can't tell you.'

'Just give me a hint.'

'You're a man who looks taller than you are; he's a man who looks smaller than he is. He is desperate for people to think that he is attractive and important – and he has a mistress who is too beautiful for someone like him.'

'Have you expressed these suspicions to anyone else?'

'Yes – but only to those who share my suspicions about him.' She gave an enigmatic smile. 'Otherwise, I could be making myself a target.'

'Traitors?'

'Treason isn't a fact. Treason is a point of view.'

Catesby stared into space. He had often been teased about having the same surname as England's greatest traitor – the accusation of treason was one that the infamous Robert Catesby threw back at his killers as he lay dying of a gunshot wound while clutching a portrait of the Virgin Mary.

'What's wrong?' said Marie.

'I want to know what's right – and then do what's right.'

'The first part is more difficult than the second.'

'I can see that.' Catesby paused. 'Why do you think they want me to go to Lyon and meet DIDOT without you?'

'Maybe they don't want to lose both of us if things go wrong.'

'Thanks.'

'And you will be less conspicuous without an older woman.'

'Do you really think that?'

'No. I was thinking of the way you must feel having me around all the time.'

Catesby leaned forward to kiss her, but she pushed him away.

'I am not,' said Marie, 'going to stay here awaiting further instructions. It is too dangerous for the family. I will go to Lyon with you.' Marie reread the message. 'The worst thing is telling you to buy a copy of the *Voix Nationale* as a rendezvous prop. It's a terrible pro-Vichy rag – but it may be good as camouflage. Most people sympathetic to the Resistance wouldn't be caught dead with it.'

'Or maybe it's the sort of newspaper that DIDOT agrees with?'

'You don't know him so you can't make that assumption.' Marie smiled. 'Even if it turned out to be correct.'

'Why is such a person part of the Resistance?'

'Because we need to be as broad a movement as possible.' Marie laughed. 'As you worked with Guingouin's Maquis Rouge, you might have come to the conclusion that the Resistance is basically a communist affair?'

'And I can assure you that there are even deep divisions within the PCF.'

'I'm not surprised. Almost every Resistance movement is divided within itself – and every movement is in conflict with other groups that don't share their politics. They all have different ideas of a post-war France.' Marie looked at Catesby. 'What did you think of things in London?'

'Are you pressing me for classified information?'

'It may be classified, but everyone knows what's happening. All the Resistance groups are competing for help and supplies from the British and the Americans and are willing to cut throats to get what they want. The most right-wing Resistance group is *Combat*, the one that DIDOT supports. On the left are the *Franc-Tireurs et Partisans*, who follow the communist leadership. In the middle are the Free French and the Gaullists – and on the fringes are various royalist and Catholic networks. They all want the occupation to end, but they want to bring about its end in their own ways – which may include...' She paused.

'What?'

'A certain amount of treachery and collaboration.' She glanced at Catesby. 'Why are you looking at me in that way?'

'Because I'm now suspicious.'

'About what?'

'About you.'

'Why?' said Marie.

'Because it sounds like you might be manipulating me to report someone of treason.'

'That's good.' There was a sarcastic tone in Marie's voice. 'Being suspicious of everyone and everything is a good way for a *résistant* to survive – of course, you won't accomplish anything or even see the light of day.'

'What makes me suspicious is how you can know all these things.'

Marie smiled. 'You seem to have forgotten something about me. I was in the wine trade. Have you never heard the phrase, *In vino veritas*?'

'And you travelled a lot?'

'How do you think I learned German?'

Catesby remembered the ruse at the railway station. 'You sounded fluent – and fooled the goons from the *Sicherheitsdienst*.'

'Another lesson for you. The Germans are not easy to fool – try selling wine to them.'

'Is DIDOT selling something to them?'

'We're still not sure who DIDOT is.'

'Can you draw me a picture of the person you think he is?'

Marie sighed and reached for a pencil. 'I'm not very good at this.'

Five minutes later Catesby examined a rough sketch that showed a man with a triangle-shaped face, hollow cheeks and a frail nervous expression.

'He has pale blue eyes and narrow shoulders. He doesn't look robust or healthy. Max would have done a better job. He's an excellent artist – and a great cartoonist too. He could have done it for a living.'

'But instead Max chose to be a…?'

'A government official. At one time he was the youngest prefect in France. His management skills are superb. Max is the only person who can bring together all the strands of the Resistance under a unified leadership – which is why the meeting you are supposed to attend is so important.'

Catesby had heard those words before. They echoed what the major had told him during his last briefing in London. He wondered if the major had given Marie the same briefing – or if she knew about Max and the meeting from other sources. There was something about the whole business that made Catesby uneasy. There were too many people in the know.

'It's a mess,' said Marie.

'You were reading my thoughts.'

'Let's go to bed. You need comforting.'

The next day was tense and worrying. Not just for Catesby and Marie, but for the family too. The daughter had left the house early with her bicycle, ration tickets and bags for a round of shopping. When she returned, the bike panniers were less than half full, her face was pale and her voice breathless.

'You look as if you've seen a ghost?' said her mother.

'I don't know who he was.'

'Sit down, Andrée,' said her father. 'You need something to drink.'

'Water, please.'

He poured her a glass and she drank it with a trembling hand. 'What happened?' said her mother.

'A man approached me as I came out of the boulangerie and asked if my name was Andrée Martin. I was about to lie, but then I thought, what if he is a policeman and asks for my ID? So I said, "Yes," and waited for him to say what he wanted. He stared at me for a long time and I began to feel uneasy. I didn't recognise him, but finally I said, "Were you one of the teachers at the *lycée*?" He laughed and said, "No, I follow a much holier vocation."'

Marie finally spoke, 'Was he dressed as a priest?'

'No, he wasn't wearing a collar – but a dark shirt and suit, no tie.'

'What did he look like?'

'About forty, maybe older. Medium height, brown swept-back hair. An average-looking man.'

Marie glanced at Catesby with a worried frown and pursed lips.

'Was that the end of it?' said her father.

The girl shook her head and swallowed more water. 'No, he reached into his coat pocket and took out a sealed envelope. He handed it to me and said, "This is for your guest."'

'Did you read what was in it?' said Marie.

'No, of course not; it was for our guest.' She took an envelope out of the shopping bag and handed it to Marie.

'Thank you. But I think it might be intended for your other guest.' She passed the sealed envelope to Catesby who opened it with his thumbnail while Marie looked on. The message was short, sweet and predictable: *DIDOT vous attend.*

Marie looked at the girl. 'Did the man say or do anything after he gave you the envelope?'

'He stared at me for a few seconds – in a way that made me feel uncomfortable.'

'Sexual?'

'I think so. He walked away without saying another word. As soon as he was gone, I began to cycle back here.' She paused. 'A minute or two later, a car overtook me – a big shiny car, the sort the Germans often use.'

'It sounds like a Traction Avant,' said her father.

Catesby nodded. 'Were they in uniform?'

'No, but they looked official. I couldn't see their faces, but the back and side of the head of the one in the front passenger seat looked like it could have been the man who gave me the envelope.' She shrugged. 'But it could have been anyone. When you're frightened your mind makes things up.'

'I know the feeling,' said Catesby.

'But that doesn't mean you're wrong,' added Marie. She turned to the parents. 'Thank you for looking after us. You have been very brave – and have done more than enough. We are going to go now, within the next hour.'

'You must take some food with you,' said the mother.

'That would be kind,' said Marie, 'but I don't think you should stay here either.'

The father looked taken aback.

'Have you family or friends in the countryside with whom you could stay?'

'Yes,' said the mother, 'my...'

'Don't tell us who they are.'

'I want to come with you,' said the girl looking at Marie.

'No,' said the father.

'You cannot forbid me.' The girl nodded towards Marie and Catesby. 'Even if they will not let me come with them, I will not spend the rest of the war buried in the countryside. I have lost friends – and I cannot dishonour their memory by giving up the fight after having done so little.'

They argued for half an hour. Marie pleaded Andrée's case. She was too valuable as an experienced courier to remain in hiding – and she might again prove useful as a trusted typist for Max. Catesby could see it was difficult telling parents that their dearly loved child must be allowed to risk her life for a cause.

'But,' said the mother pulling at a handkerchief wet with tears, 'there are others who can do it.'

Marie put her arms around the mother. 'If everyone said that, no one would do it, and the nightmare we are fighting would win.'

The parents held their daughter as they said a tearful fare-well. Catesby and Marie were also in tears. Marie took Catesby's hand in both of hers, looked into his eyes and whispered, 'To the end, *mon camarade*.'

For the first time Catesby felt a rod of iron stiffen his spine. 'To the end, *ma camarade*.'

They caught the last morning bus to Lyon. Again they perched on the roof, but this time they looked like a genuine family. Catesby could see the addition of young Andrée provided good cover. She could easily pass as Marie's daughter. Catesby wasn't sure whether he fitted in as a loutish brother or a boyfriend. They were taking the radio with them in its scuffed and realistic-looking suitcase. An inspection was less likely if they appeared to be a normal family visiting relatives. If they did get inspected, thought Catesby, their IDs would give the game away. But Marie had worked that out. 'If we get checked, I'm Andrée's aunt and you're a boyfriend,' she said.

'Your boyfriend or hers?'

'Don't be silly. Hold hands with Andrée if you see a suspicious *flic*.'

Another advantage of having Andrée with them was her knowledge of Lyon. She had been to the *lycée* there and had a young person's appreciation of the city's haunts and dangers. She knew safe houses, cafés and meeting places which hadn't been busted or put under surveillance by the Vichy police or the Gestapo. Her Resistance contacts were new, and fresh networks were springing up. Catesby suspected that one of the reasons Prosper had been penetrated was that the circuit had been in action too long.

The safe house that Andrée led them to was located among the *traboules* in the Croix Rousse quarter of ancient Lyon. The *traboules* were narrow hidden passageways dating back to the fourth century. They enabled silk workers to move their fin-ished products from their workshops to the merchant houses along the river without the delicate silks being exposed to the weather. The passage of goods was also quicker as there were few streets which ran perpendicular to the river. The *traboules* were a spider's web of over three hundred hidden and interconnecting passageways. Many tunnelled through buildings and the silk workers could hear voices from sitting rooms or bedrooms as they trundled their produce to the river.

The safe house was the most secure that Catesby had ever seen. Andrée had met a friend who had led them down a *traboule* to an abandoned workshop where long-derelict silk looms lay covered in cobwebs. The friend was quietly singing *Le Chant des Partisans* as he led them along. When they got to the workshop he repeated the line, *Ohé, saboteur, attention à ton fardeau: dynamite.* He laughed and pointed to some boxes stacked under a tarpaulin in the workshop. 'We really need to hide them better than that.'

'I'll help you,' said Andrée, her voice full of eagerness.

'We'll need to do it tonight.'

The friend searched the wall with his fingertips looking for a crack. When he found what he was looking for, he tapped on the wall with a metal spike which gave a metallic echo. He waited a few seconds. Someone answered by playing notes on a piano. Catesby recognised it as the opening verse of *Le temps des cerises*. The young partisan again tapped the wall with the iron spike. Catesby was late to realise it was a Morse message, but saw that Marie had picked it up.

'What was it?'

'An homage to the workers who used to live here: *Les canuts de 1831*. I'll explain later.'

The section of wall had turned into a doorway. As soon as they stepped through, the hidden door shut behind them and resumed its cover as a built-in bookcase. The room looked like a professor's study: a baby grand piano, paintings of nineteenth-century Lyon, mostly river scenes – and books and papers scattered everywhere. Among them was a journal entitled *Obstétrique, gynécologie, santé de la reproduction*, which indicated that someone in the safe house was a doctor with faith in the future. Their host was a young man who looked in his teens, definitely not the doctor. Catesby guessed that either his mother or father was the medical one, but in these situations the etiquette was not to ask questions. The Resistance must remain a shadowy world. The young man showed them hiding places and another hidden escape door leading into the labyrinth of *traboules*.

'The *flics* and the Gestapo,' said the young host, 'have so far steered clear of searching the *traboules*. They know that many of the tunnels are rigged to explode if they try to search them. This part of Lyon has always been a dangerous place for the authorities.' He smiled. 'You must get Andrée to tell you the story of her ancestors.'

The young woman flushed more with pride than embarrassment. 'My parents used to bring me here as a child to show me the *traboules* and the places where the *canuts* fought the battles.'

Catesby looked puzzled. 'I don't know the word. Who were the *canuts*?'

'It is a word unique to this region. A *canut* is a silk weaver. My family were silk weavers here, in the Croix Rousse. My great-great grandparents and their comrades always demanded fair wages for the skilled work they did in awful conditions. In 1831, the economy went bad and silk prices dropped – so the wealthy merchants cut the wages of the workers. The *canuts* refused to accept such treatment. They captured the police barracks and raided the arsenal. They distributed the weapons, defeated the local militia and took control of Lyon. Louis Philippe sent the army to take back control of Lyon. It took twenty thousand soldiers and a hundred and fifty cannon to do so. In the end, they fought to a stand-off – and no workers were arrested or punished. There were two more *canut* revolts in 1834 and 1848. Their saying was "Live Free or Die Fighting" – and that is what we will do today.'

There was silence in the room. No more words were necessary; the determined faces said it all. The solemnity was broken by Andrée's laughter. 'I propose,' she said, 'we honour the brave silk workers by eating their brains. The dish is called *cervelle de canut*.' She looked at the host. 'I'll need a slab of *fromage blanc*, also some *fromage à la crème*, shallots, any fresh herbs you can find, seasoning, vinegar and olive oil.'

The dish, which they ate with bread and wine, did indeed look like someone's brain – but more because of the way Andrée artfully shaped the cheese to resemble a human cortex. Catesby wondered if living in danger had given her a macabre sense of humour. Years after the war, he realised that macabre turns were not uncommon to those, including himself, who had survived horrific experiences.

That night Marie and Catesby spoke in whispers. 'Are you worried about tomorrow?' she said.

'Yes.'

'Good. You should be. I'm going to follow you, but I will keep undercover so that neither you nor DIDOT will see me. Don't look around to find me.'

'I'm not stupid.'

'Then you're in the minority. People often get arrested because they are stupid, not because the Germans are clever. I've heard SOE agents speaking loud English in Paris cafés – as if they were in a London bar.'

'I know the type.'

'I will be carrying a gun – and I think you should too,' said Marie.

'What is the logic?'

'In the current situation, I don't think either of us could bluff our way through an ID check and search. We stand a better chance of surviving a shootout – and there are many places in Lyon to run and hide.'

'Do you think we might have to shoot DIDOT?'

'That isn't what we are supposed to do – even if it's a good idea. But we need to keep him alive to find out the time and place of Max's big meeting.'

'Isn't there any way to find out other than DIDOT?'

'I wish there was. I fear that he, or others in *Combat*, have tricked someone in London into manipulating you.'

'Who do you think that "someone" in London might be?'

'I would rather not – as a Frenchwoman – make judgements upon one of your British colleagues. You must decide yourself.'

Catesby stirred uneasily. It was something that had been haunting him ever since his briefings in London.

The rendezvous location in the Place de la Comédie was a fifteen-minute walk from the safe house. The weather was wet and gave Catesby an excuse to wear a borrowed overcoat in which the .32 revolver was less conspicuous. The rendezvous spot was sandwiched between the town hall and the opera house – and there were a number of police around. Catesby remembered that he needed to buy a copy of the hated *La Voix Nationale* as a prop to signal who he was. He went into a *tabac* on the edge of the square and picked up a copy of the paper. As he handed over the franc coins, the proprietor gave him a look of disgust. Catesby knew that the shop had to stock the Vichyiste rag to avoid suspicion. He wanted to tell the proprietor that he only bought it to see the latest lies that the Vichy *putains* were spreading, but didn't want to risk blowing his cover. Catesby pocketed the change and gave a bleak smile. As soon as he left the shop, he saw a familiar face. It was Paul, Guingouin's trusted lieutenant.

'Greetings, comrade,' said Catesby.

Paul nodded at the copy of *La Voix Nationale* under Catesby's arm. 'Can I share your copy?'

'No problem. It looks like we may be here for the same reason.'

Paul glanced at his watch. 'We're ten minutes early.'

'What do you know about DIDOT?'

'His real name is René Hardy – and I don't trust him. That's why I persuaded Lo Grand to let me come in his place.'

Catesby tapped the sagging pocket of his overcoat. 'Let's shoot the bastard.'

'We need to find out where the meeting is first – and it is an important meeting.'

'Have you met Hardy?'

'Yes, but I don't think he remembers me. He's a member of *Combat* – and they are getting a lot of money from the Americans.'

Catesby looked across the square and saw a slim figure with fair hair striding towards them. 'Is that him?'

'That's him.'

The figure approached Catesby first and looked at his copy of *La Voix Nationale*. 'Sorry to bother you,' said the figure, 'but I was supposed to meet a certain Monsieur Jacques Dubois.'

'That's me,' said Catesby.

The figure extended a fine thin hand. 'Hello, I'm DIDOT.' He looked at Paul. 'And I believe your friend is a visitor from the Limousin?'

Paul gave a curt nod.

'I believe that we were supposed to meet by the fountain?' said Hardy.

'We're still five minutes early,' said Paul.

Hardy glanced at the town hall belfry clock. 'Ah, so you are.'

Catesby found the town hall an imposing building. It was protected from the public by spiked gilded railings. It was suffused with the pomposity of the Second Empire and two huge pavilions stood like guard towers looking down on the square. Catesby imagined Vichyiste officials studying them with binoculars from its upper windows.

'The meeting,' said Hardy, 'is scheduled for next Monday, the twenty-first of June.'

'What time and where?' said Paul.

'It will be in the early afternoon. The location, for security reasons, will not be decided until the very day.'

'How then,' said Catesby, 'do we find our way there?'

'You haven't let me finish, Monsieur Jacques. I will meet you at the lower terminus of the Croix-Paquet funicular at half past one and lead you there.'

'What should we do if you don't turn up?' said Paul.

'Can you give me the address of your safe house?'

'No,' said Paul.

'Why are you so suspicious?'

'I'm not suspicious. Not sharing safe house details is a standard security procedure.'

Hardy shrugged. 'It is a pity that Colonel Guingouin will not be attending this meeting. We were looking forward to congratulating him on his valiant work. I hope he is not ill or injured.'

'No,' said Paul. 'Lo Grand is fine.'

'Is there any reason why he has chosen not to come and to send a delegate instead?'

'I cannot answer for the *préfet du Maquis*.'

'Is that what Guingouin calls himself?'

'No, it is what we call him.'

Hardy turned his eyes away. 'I look forward to meeting you at the Croix-Paquet funicular on the twenty-first.'

As Catesby watched Hardy stride away, he remembered that the meeting was scheduled for the longest day. The twenty-first of June had always been Catesby's favourite day of the year ever since he had caught a six-pound sea bass from an uncle's boat on the River Ore as the late evening sun was touching the horizon. He was thirteen at the time and had stroked the beautiful fish for an hour afterwards. Served with samphire it had provided a feast for a family of eight. A chill ran down his spine. Was Jean Moulin another prize catch for the longest day?

Catesby and Paul walked in silence towards the Rhône. As they reached the river, they heard the click-click of a woman in heels running behind them. Catesby turned to see a flushed Marie catching up with them. She seemed so beautiful and desirable at that moment.

'It's him,' she breathed, 'definitely him. DIDOT is René Hardy.' She caught her breath and looked at Paul.

'Don't worry,' said Catesby, 'he's a comrade from Guingouin's Maquis. He'll be attending the meeting too.' Catesby felt a flicker of jealousy as Marie's eyes lingered on Paul.

'What did he tell you?' said Marie turning to Catesby.

Catesby recounted the bare details that Hardy had given them.

'Meeting him will be dangerous,' said Marie. 'I am sure that his mistress, who must despise him, is a Gestapo informer.'

'How do you know her?' said Catesby.

'My husband was seduced by her too.'

Catesby thought it best not to say what he was thinking.

Marie seemed to have read his thoughts. 'Do not think that

I am saying these things about her out of jealousy. My husband and I were estranged long before the affair.'

'What evidence is there linking her to the Germans?' said Paul.

'The wine trade was full of it.'

'So your husband was also in the wine business?' said Catesby.

'I didn't marry into it if that's what you're thinking. My family were growers; his family were merchants.' She turned from Catesby and answered Paul. 'At first, she was used by a German to try to trick my husband into a wine deal – and later to become a collaborator.' She paused. 'Which he did with unseemly alacrity.'

'It's a difficult situation,' said Paul. 'We don't know for certain what game Hardy is playing. But if we refused to deal with every *résistant* who had contact with a German or a Vichyiste – or who had been called in for questioning and released – we would be a very small movement.'

'We need to find out where this meeting is without the help of Hardy,' said Marie.

'If we can't,' said Paul, 'I will meet him at the rendezvous and go with him myself.'

'I'll follow you with a gun,' said Marie.

Catesby felt that all three of them were blundering in the shadows.

They made their separate ways back to the safe house, each following anti-surveillance procedures. Catesby decided to check out the Croix-Paquet funicular terminus that Hardy had given them as the rendezvous point for taking them to the Monday meeting. It was located on a leafy square on which several streets intersected. There were a number of shops and cafés – and tall buildings overlooked the square. It felt like being in the centre of a stage. It occurred to Catesby that it would be easy to spot Hardy and to follow him. The problem was the funicular. If Hardy got on it, it would be impossible to trail him unobserved. Catesby decided to take a ride to see what it was like. He bought a ticket in the newsagent which was part of the funicular terminus – and went back into the square. There was a broad set of steps leading up the steep hill to Croix-Rousse for those who preferred a vigorous walk to the ease of the funicular. There weren't many people choosing that option. The stairs were a perfect counter-surveillance choke point, a way of checking to see if you had grown a tail. Catesby decided to mount the stairs. The action would, of course, alert any tail that he was doing such a check. Why would he buy a funicular ticket and then make the arduous trip on foot?

Catesby continued up the stone stairs which twisted backwards and forwards. It was a steep climb, but a pleasant walk that afforded excellent views of Lyon and the Rhône. After he had gone three hundred yards, Catesby stopped and leaned on the stone wall – pretending that he was enjoying the vista of city and river. It was a lovely view and Catesby found himself singing the song that played so relentlessly on the phonograph in the bar at RAF Tangmere while they waited to be flown to France. *J'attendrai* was sentimental drivel, but now seemed apt.

A moment later he heard the sound of footsteps and someone panting. If he had grown a tail, it wasn't a very fit one. He continued singing as a somewhat fleshy woman rounded the corner echoing the words of the song in a seductive voice.

She looked about thirty and exuded a hint of decadent sensuality. Her eyes opened wide when she saw Catesby.

'I apologise,' said Catesby, 'for not being a very good singer.'

The woman looked surprised and embarrassed, but then she trained her face into a smile that was meant to be coquettish. 'Were you, monsieur, waiting for me?'

'I don't know who I was waiting for.'

The woman reached out, touched Catesby and continued the song in a throaty voice.

'Where do you live?' said Catesby.

The woman slid her hand from his elbow to his crotch. 'We would have to go to a hotel.'

'Why are you doing this?'

'Because you are a handsome man with a kind face – and I

have two children to feed. But I want to give you a good time as well.'

Catesby knew the woman wasn't a prostitute, but that she would go to a hotel rather than blow her cover story for having followed him. Part of him was tempted in revenge for Marie having flirted with Paul. Catesby began to see the wisdom of Guingouin's camps being places of monkish celibacy.

'Do you ever sleep with Germans?'

'That is a terrible thing to say. I would never do such a thing – I love my country.'

'*Woher weißt du, dass ich kein Deutscher bin?*' Catesby studied the woman's face as he switched languages and could see that she understood each word.

'I don't understand,' she lied, 'what you are saying – why are you speaking German?'

'I'm a terrible tease.'

'It's not funny – and it's cruel.'

'And sleeping with you would be a cruel betrayal of my wife.' Catesby didn't want the woman to know that her cover was blown. He reached into his pocket and gave her a thousand-franc note. 'Here, this is for your children.'

She took the money, but didn't seem to know what to do with it. She slipped it into her handbag. The woman then stared at Catesby as if she had something to say.

'What is it?' he said.

She stuttered, 'There's… there's…'

'There's what?' said Catesby.

'Nothing, nothing at all.' She put a hand to her forehead, closed her eyes and seemed to be talking to herself. 'I just don't know…'

'What do you want to tell me?'

Her voice was suddenly firm. 'Nothing.'

'Please.'

She shook her head, turned away and began to rapidly descend the stairs. Catesby started to follow her. She looked back at him, 'If you follow me, I will scream that you were trying to rape me.'

Catesby stopped and called after her. 'If you love France, you can trust me.'

The woman quickened her pace. She said something, but Catesby didn't catch the words. It sounded like, *I don't know who I love.* But he could have been mistaken. He heard footsteps and the voices of people coming down the stairs. It was an elderly couple talking about where to get food. Catesby remembered the figure, fleshy as well as sensuous, of the woman. She obviously had her sources in a hungry France. Catesby felt the funicular ticket in his pocket. He decided to keep it for another day and to continue up the stairs to the Croix-Rousse terminal.

The top of the steep hill was a plateau. The funicular terminus was next to a tram stop. Catesby wondered if Hardy had been lying about not knowing the location of the Monday meeting. The public transport links suggested a definite and planned route. Catesby walked east on a straight road called the Boulevard de la Croix-Rousse. There were green spaces, but it wasn't a picturesque neighbourhood. It was a functional part of the city where the workers lived – and where the Resistance thrived. The end of the boulevard was also the end of the plateau. The slope was a pattern of red roofs descending to the lower city. The sinuous Rhône looked like a blue-green cat stretched in the sun. On the other side of the river was a large park with a gleaming lake in the middle. Catesby longed to visit it and wondered if he could use a secret rendezvous as an excuse to do so. The Resistance had chosen a beautiful place for their main urban battlefield – and where the Germans were more than willing to lock horns.

Catesby was about to head back to the safe house when he spotted a café with a splendid view over the city. Why not? He would look less suspicious if he had a glass of wine and read a newspaper. He chose a table near the window and took out the copy of *La Voix Nationale* which he still had in his coat pocket – the same pocket where he had his revolver. He wished that he could get rid of both of them. The waiter frowned when he came to take his order. Catesby flicked the hated newspaper with his finger as he said, 'I found this on a park bench. I'm only reading it to discover their latest lies.'

'What would you like, monsieur?'

'A glass of red.'

'Any red in particular? We have a good cellar.'

'Any Burgundy would be fine.'

The waiter gave an expressionless nod and brought the wine, as well as a plate of bread cubes that had been dipped in a cheese fondue. It was a fine place – and the war seemed a million miles away. Always a dangerous feeling.

A smartly dressed customer came into the café. He was wearing spectacles and a dark blue beret. He had a slightly bohemian air. Not an artist, too neat and tidy, but maybe someone running a private gallery. But there was something about him that didn't fit in with the Croix-Rousse. And when he spoke to the waiter, the sense of estrangement increased. His French was heavily accented. Catesby avoided eye contact, but continued to eavesdrop as he sipped his Burgundy.

The customer didn't take off his beret as he ordered lunch. The café began to fill. It was obviously the best place to eat in the quarter. Catesby strained to hear the man over the other voices as he spoke to the proprietor. The man in the blue beret excused his accented French by saying that he was from Belgium – a patently false claim. They were talking about wine. The fake Belgian said that he had been in the wine trade and was fond of the Pinot Gris from Alsace. Well, thought Catesby, you've annexed the province, you might as well help yourself to the wine. A chill ran down Catesby's spine. Was the fake Belgian an Abwehr agent who had been trailing him? Catesby left his wine unfinished and headed for the toilet. He didn't need a pee, but he needed to find a back way out of the café. The loo was occupied, but there was a passageway by the kitchen which led to an open door. A young woman in the kitchen took no notice as Catesby made his exit through the 'staff only' part of the café. It led to a dark alleyway where two lean and scruffy cats screeched at Catesby.

'Sorry, lads, nothing to give.'

Catesby turned left towards where the alley joined what he assumed was the Boulevard de la Croix-Rousse. He didn't know the quarter well, but his plan was to stay off the busy boulevard and follow quiet streets to where he hoped to find the safe house. Just as he got to the end of the alley he found a figure blocking his way. There was a Traction Avant parked behind the silhouetted figure with the beret. Catesby reached into his pocket to touch the .32 revolver.

'You might manage to get a shot or two into me,' said the man in the beret, 'but my men in the Traction will cut you down like a stray dog. If you are still alive, they will take you to Gestapo headquarters where Captain Barbie will skin you alive.'

Catesby tightened his grip on the pistol. It was the end. If he was quick enough, he could put a bullet into his own head after he dispatched the pig in front of him.

'I need your help,' said the man in the beret.

Catesby slowly continued to draw the revolver. He didn't want to alert the thugs in the Traction.

'I hate Hitler and the Nazis and I want your help getting to London.'

One voice in Catesby's head was shouting, *He's lying. Do it!* Another was saying, *Maybe he is telling the truth – and you don't have to die.*

The man in the blue beret continued, 'I am an Abwehr officer – and I'm sure you know that many of us in the Abwehr hate the Gestapo. But I've gone further. I hate the Nazi regime and want to help England win.'

'I'm not English,' said Catesby.

The man in the beret smiled. 'You are, Mr Catesby, entitled to keep your cover story.'

Catesby tightened his grip on the pistol.

'I will, however, give you some morsels to prove my good faith.' The German paused. 'And what I am going to tell you will save the lives of many brave members of the Resistance.'

Catesby remained expressionless.

'The *Combat* member, René Hardy, who goes under the codename DIDOT, turned traitor after being arrested by the Gestapo. His sometimes mistress, who despises him, is also the mistress of a Gestapo officer who paid her to seduce Hardy with diamonds and gems stolen from deported Jews. Another traitor to your cause is the air control officer, Henri Déricourt, who passed on information to the chief of Gestapo in Paris that resulted in several recent arrests.' The German gave a sly smile. 'Another person you should not trust is Léontine – who, I believe, is your radio operator-turned-mistress. I knew Léontine when I was a wine merchant before the war. And doesn't she have beautiful legs – all the way to the top. Léontine has worked for both sides.'

Catesby felt sick.

'But there is one more thing that I must tell you – and it is important. The Gestapo know that the leading members of the Resistance are meeting on Monday afternoon. Captain Barbie will lead a raid on that meeting. Barbie is obsessed with capturing Max, the leader of the Resistance.'

'I will help you get to London if you tell me the exact location of the meeting,' said Catesby.

'I would tell you if I knew. For security reasons, the Resistance are keeping the location secret until the last minute.' He paused. 'And one last thing – the meeting was not initially betrayed by René Hardy, but by the communists. They do not want to be part of a united front under de Gaulle. Have you any questions?'

'No,' said Catesby.

'I look forward to meeting again. I often have lunch at the café – and they have a fine cellar.' The German turned and made a signal to the Traction Avant. The driver started the engine and the Abwehr officer got in the back seat next to another man in civilian clothes. Catesby saw they were both laughing as the car drove off.

The evening in the safe house was tense. What the German officer had said about Marie concerned Catesby deeply, but his words did more to incite sexual jealousy than to make him suspect her of being a double agent. Catesby didn't hold anything back as he huddled in conversation with Marie and Paul. He began with the woman he confronted on the steps up to Croix-Rousse and then went on to his strange encounter with the Abwehr officer. He looked closely at Marie when he recounted the German's accusations that she couldn't be trusted and 'worked for both sides'. Catesby added with a face that betrayed hurt, 'And there was a suggestion that he knew you before the war.'

Marie had turned pale, but she spoke calmly. 'His name is Otto Bömers. He comes from a well-educated prominent family in the north of Germany – and yes, we were briefly lovers. It was a mistake on my part for I was unhappy and vulnerable at the time.'

'Should we,' said Catesby, 'believe his story about hating the Nazis and wanting to change sides?'

'He may well hate the Nazis; Otto is too cultivated and intelligent a man to believe their party line – but he would never change sides. I am sure he enjoys being an Abwehr officer. Otto gets pleasure from manipulating people and deceiving them. It makes him feel superior.' Marie paused. 'Otto is an intellectual who has a bedroom full of books. It impresses some women. He may not be a Nazi, but he is a Nietzschean who loves Wagner.'

'You seem to know a lot about him from a brief affair.'

Marie gave Catesby a look of condescension that withered him to the core. 'Thanks to Otto we can drop cover names. I have, William, made a study of men. Both men and wine give me pleasure – but not to excess and only on my terms. Otto was like a new wine that pleases at first with its zingy citrus flavours, but then becomes one-dimensional and tiresome.'

Catesby gave a half-smile.

'Pillow talk, vile pillow talk. It wasn't the sex with Otto that disgusted me; it was the talking afterwards. He thought that adolescent Nietzsche stuff about living without fault and beyond truth was somehow romantic.'

Catesby looked at Paul. The Frenchman was looking at Marie with both admiration and amusement. He wondered if Paul was on Marie's tasting list. 'When did you discover that Otto was an Abwehr officer in France?' said Paul.

'He tried to contact me via my collaborator husband. It was in the spring of 1941. Otto wanted a rendezvous in Paris.' Marie shrugged. 'Whether for sex or to recruit me as a collaborator – or both – I do not know. I ignored his summons.'

'Could Otto have any evidence that you ever worked for both sides?' said Catesby.

Marie's eyes flashed with anger. 'Of course not. He was trying to make you distrust me – and seems to have succeeded.'

'No, he hasn't succeeded,' said Catesby. As soon as Catesby said the words he knew that he was lying. Bömers had convinced Catesby to suspect that Marie would never be a faithful bed partner, but whether sexual betrayal turned into treason was another question.

Marie sighed. 'France is an occupied country full of informers and collaborators. What would you do if you were arrested and taken to Gestapo headquarters and they offered you a deal: turn informer or we arrest your family? Will they be tortured and murdered? Or sent to a camp in Germany from which they will never return? The games they play are cruel – the difference between a collaborator and a loyal *résistant* is not always clear.' Marie raised her voice. 'But I have never informed or collaborated! I may have flirted and teased to keep my freedom, but that is all.'

Catesby looked closely at Marie and tried to see who she really was.

'The problem with Otto is that I dented his self-image as a superman when I ditched him. He pestered me, but I wouldn't see him again. I was briefly reconciled with my husband – who, despite being selfish and weak, has a sense of humour.' Marie paused. 'But what is disturbing is that Otto has found out where I am and followed me here. We must—'

Before Marie could finish there was an urgent knocking on the bedroom door. Paul opened it and found the young *résistant* who had shown them in when they first arrived.

'What is it?' said Paul.

'My mother would like to have a word with you.'

Paul looked for affirmation from the others and then said, 'Invite her in.'

A tired-looking woman with greying hair arrived. She gave

them a warm smile. 'I try,' she said, 'to stay out of the way.' She paused. 'But something has happened and it is very worrying.'

'Do you want us to leave?' said Marie.

'That's not my choice. My home will always be a welcome refuge for members of the Resistance. But I am not an active *résistant*, I am a hospital doctor. Nonetheless, many know where my sympathies lie – which is why my friend came to see me. He is head of the Red Cross in Lyon. He is in a difficult position. He has to appear to remain neutral so that the Red Cross can carry out their humanitarian work. But today he broke that neutrality...'

'We will protect his identity,' said Marie.

'I know you will. This morning, as soon as the Red Cross offices opened, a woman came in and demanded to see him urgently. My friend was perplexed. The woman looked confused. He feared for her mental health, but when she began to speak she seemed sane and focused. She confessed that she was having an affair with a German intelligence officer. The one secret that she kept from her lover was that she had a good knowledge of German. He often said rude and obscene things to her in German, but she pretended not to understand. She said that the previous evening two colleagues of her German lover had come to the house for a drinking session. They ignored her presence and spoke in German of intelligence matters that were secret. She picked up that the Germans were bragging about a raid they were going to carry out on a top-level Resistance meeting. She knows that the raid is scheduled for Monday.'

'The day after tomorrow,' said Catesby with a frown.

'Unfortunately,' continued the doctor, 'she was unable to tell my friend where and when. He tried to find out more, but when pressed the woman became agitated, almost demented, and left the office. It occurred to him that the woman could have been an agent provocateur who was trying to compromise the neutrality of the Red Cross – but she could have genuine mental-health problems. My friend visited me at the hospital to share his story. On reflection, he thought that the woman was telling the truth about the Resistance meeting being raided – and she wanted to send out a warning – but that she was lying about her relationship with the German.'

'In other words...' said Catesby.

'He thinks the woman is a collaborator with a guilty conscience.'

'Where are the Red Cross offices located?' said Catesby.

'Near the Croix-Paquet funicular terminus.'

The final piece of the jigsaw slotted into place.

As soon as the doctor left the room, Marie turned to the group. 'We need to send an urgent message to London.'

It was decided to set up the radio away from the safe house to avoid it being raided if the transmission signal was picked up by one of the many detector vans that were now prowling the streets of Lyon. Andrée arrived later that night and reported that the mood among the Lyonnais *résistants* was tense. She also said that she could guide them to a safer place in the *traboules* to set up the transmitter. She led Catesby and Marie through a labyrinth of passageways until they came to a courtyard surrounded by abandoned workshops. In the middle of the courtyard was a pink tower almost hidden by the shadows of the taller buildings surrounding it.

'The police have told the Germans that there is nothing here,' said Andrée. 'It isn't true, there are caches and *résistants* in every corner, but the *flics* are too frightened to lead the Gestapo here.'

Catesby looked at the tower with suspicion. It was almost too ideal, and hence too obvious, a place to hang antenna for a radio transmission. 'Let's do it quickly,' he said, 'and get out of here.'

He and Marie mounted the tower. Andrée stood guard below. If she noted anything suspicious, Catesby said she should warn them with what the SOE training staff used to call an ST ONE. It baffled new recruits until they realised that an ST ONE was nothing other than a *stone*, the simplest and most effective danger signal ever devised.

They quickly strung up the antenna and began to send the encoded message. The only sound in the late-night air was someone singing *La Marseillaise* in a drunken voice. The singer could have been two or three hundred yards away, but his voice carried:

> *Aux armes, citoyens,*
> *Formez vos bataillons…*

It was as if the singer was invoking them personally. The Morse message that Marie was tapping was almost an echo of the verses, but would London listen and respond to their desperation? Would Baker Street be able to warn Jean Moulin and the Resistance leaders that they were stumbling into a trap?

The route back to the safe house was a short walk along a public road. The last thing they wanted was to be caught after curfew carrying a radio. Andrée found a hiding place in a *traboule* where they stashed the radio. Having managed to get an after-curfew *Ausweis*, she scouted the return route for Marie and Catesby. When they arrived at the safe house, Andrée seemed troubled.

'You look concerned,' said Catesby.

'It's a feeling – I've had it before.'

'What is it?'

'I get a sort of tingling sensation when someone's staring at my back. I had that feeling a few times this evening, when we were going along the road and also in the *traboules*.'

The next day they put on their best clothes and pretended to be a family going to Sunday mass at Saint-Bernard's, but disappeared into the *traboules* instead. They needed to recover the radio to receive a transmission from London. It was crucial to find out how Baker Street had responded to their warning about the meeting. The radio was hidden in a dark and dank section of the *traboule*. They removed the masonry and rubble covering the transmitter, but it had been disturbed. The radio was gone.

'Are you sure we've come to the right place?' said Catesby.

'Totally sure – we were being followed.'

'Let's get out of here,' said Marie. 'We need to disappear.'

The next two days were nervous, excruciating – and ultimately hopeless. They were still in the same safe house in the *traboule* and feeling increasingly anxious about it. That evening they had a council of war with Paul and a few trusted Lyon *résistants*. Everyone agreed that the meeting had to be cancelled, but no one knew how to contact any of those attending. One of the *résistants* said, 'This is an example of how too much personal security can be your undoing – but we will try to make contact with them.'

When Paul, Marie and Catesby were alone they discussed the information passed on by the Abwehr officer pretending to want to help the Resistance. Catesby looked at Marie, 'Your former friend, Otto, didn't tell me anything about the meeting that we didn't already know.'

'It's the way Otto works. He pretends to be a close confidante by telling you secrets that you would have discovered without his help. He knew that the woman who followed you on to the Croix-Paquet stairs and went to the Red Cross had already alerted the Resistance that the meeting had been compromised, so Otto had nothing to lose by passing on the same information.'

'But was Otto lying when he said he didn't know the location of the meeting?' said Paul.

'I'm not sure,' said Marie. 'He might be trying to find out the location – and was hoping he could trade what seemed a genuine warning for more information. No one should trust him.'

'My guess,' said Catesby, 'is that he will put someone on Hardy's tail to follow him to the meeting.'

'Unless Hardy has already told him,' said Paul. 'On the other hand, I don't think the other Resistance leaders trust Hardy enough to let him know the location.'

'All our covers, everything,' said Marie, 'are blown. There's nothing we can do other than disperse and hide.'

'That's unlike you,' said Catesby.

'What is?'

'Giving up in despair.'

Marie raised her voice. 'I'm not giving up. It's pointless to sacrifice ourselves for nothing.'

'Then I will sacrifice myself,' said Paul. 'I will meet Hardy at the Croix-Paquet funicular rendezvous tomorrow as he instructed.'

'And then what?' said Marie.

'As soon as I get to the meeting, I will tell them that they've been betrayed and the Gestapo are about to arrive. With a bit of luck, we might be able to escape before the Germans pounce.'

'A suicide mission,' said Marie. 'The Gestapo will have surrounded the meeting place and will shoot down or capture anyone who flees.'

'But if you get to the meeting,' said Catesby, 'it might be a good idea to take out Hardy so he can't give any more help to the Germans.'

'Except,' said Paul giving Marie a searching look, 'we can't be a hundred per cent certain that Hardy is an informer.'

'Is it not curious,' said Marie staring at Catesby, 'that London has ordered us to attend the meeting? Is there someone there who wants us to be gathered up in the same Gestapo swoop?'

Catesby could see that the fires of paranoia were raging. Marie had posed a troubling question, but he wasn't going to answer it. Instead he said, 'Even if Hardy has informed the Germans about the meeting, he might not know its exact location. If he did, we could abduct him and torture the fuck out of him until he spilled the beans.'

'A silly idea,' said Marie. 'The best solution is for all of us to follow Hardy so that we don't lose him, maybe in disguise. If he doesn't know where the meeting is going to be, he will be with someone who does.'

'He could prove too slippery,' said Paul.

'And we might not be the only ones following him,' said Catesby, thinking of the troubled woman he had met on the stairs to Croix-Rousse.

Paul folded his hands. His face was determined. 'I'm the senior one here. It's my decision. Too many of us would give the game away. I'm going to follow Hardy on my own.'

The rendezvous with Hardy at the Croix-Paquet funicular was scheduled for one-thirty, but all three arrived early. Catesby looked at his watch and then at Paul, 'You've got twenty minutes to change your mind.'

Paul shook his head. 'No, I've got to warn them.'

'Then I'm coming with you,' said Catesby feeling the revolver in his pocket.

'No, I'm going alone.'

'You're both being stupid,' said Marie, 'and falling into Hardy's trap.'

'We're both armed,' said Catesby. 'If there's a gunfight, we and some of the others might escape.'

'None of you will,' said Marie. 'The Gestapo are going to turn up heavily armed and you will be outnumbered. They will surround the place; no one will escape. It won't be a gun battle with a couple of *flics*. You will be facing a German military operation.'

Catesby shrugged. 'You're being too pessimistic. I am sure the Resistance leaders have chosen a meeting place with multiple escape routes – and hidden Maquisards keeping watch.'

'Then they've changed their tactics. Look what happened to Delestraint and Gastaldo,' said Marie.

Catesby looked away. He didn't know it at the time, but the tragedy unfolding was one that would haunt him and France for decades to come. Could it have been avoided?

'Shh,' said Marie, 'don't stare, but Hardy has arrived.'

Catesby glanced quickly towards the funicular terminus and turned away. 'He's not alone; he's with someone else.'

'I recognise him,' said Paul, 'he's another member of *Combat* – but high up. I'm going to join them.'

'Wait,' said Catesby. 'Look. There's a guy on a bicycle talking to Hardy.' Catesby turned to Paul. 'Stay here, this looks bad. The fellow on the bike looks angry. He might be an undercover *flic*.'

'Oh my god,' said Marie putting her hand over her mouth, 'he's not a policeman. The man on the bike is André Lassagne.'

'Who's he?' said Catesby.

'Lassagne is someone who can be completely trusted. I met him when I first joined the Resistance.'

'He seems to be having a hell of an argument with Hardy and the other chap,' said Catesby.

Fragments of Lassagne's shouting drifted across the square, but they couldn't make out the words.

'Stay here,' said Marie. 'I trust André. I'm going to tell him what's happening.'

'From all that shouting, it sounds like he already knows. What are you doing?'

The plan for Paul to do it alone quickly fell apart. It all happened in less than a minute, but in retrospect those seconds played back as interminable. Marie shouted to André and headed towards the three men, but Lassagne had already ridden away. Marie continued running after Lassagne as he cycled up the steep hill towards Croix-Rousse. Paul walked swiftly and determinedly towards Hardy and the other man. When they turned into the funicular entrance, Paul started running. Catesby began running after Paul, but was diverted when he saw a fleshy woman emerging from behind a kiosk from where she had been watching Hardy. Catesby ran towards her and shouted, 'Stop!' But she also was running towards the funicular entrance.

They were seconds too late. Hardy and the other man were already in the carriage and the doors were shut. Paul gave the funicular car door a slap as it pulled up the slope, but the driver ignored him. 'Shit,' said Paul, 'they decided not to wait for us.' He looked at his watch. 'They left ten minutes before the rendezvous.'

'Where's the woman?' said Catesby.

Paul ignored the question. He hadn't seen her. 'We need to get the next funicular,' he said.

They travelled in silence up to the single stop at Croix-Rousse. The car was too packed to have a conversation. When they emerged from the funicular terminus, there was no one to be seen, but a tram was pulling away.

'I suppose the meeting could be somewhere around here – but it would be like looking for a needle in a haystack,' said Paul.

'Or they hopped on the tram to go someplace else. I think we're stuffed.'

'Look, there's Marie.'

She came towards them. She was hot, sweaty and out of breath.

'Did you catch up with your friend?' said Catesby.

She shook her head. 'He either didn't hear me – or didn't know who I was. But I'm sure he will be going to the meeting – Lassagne used to be second to Gastaldo, so he's probably taken over his position in the *Armée secrète*.'

'What do you think he was arguing about?'

'I think he was angry that Hardy was going to the meeting.' Marie smiled and pointed north. 'André was pedalling that way, so the rendezvous must be in that direction. What happened to Hardy?'

'He and his friend jumped on the funicular just before the doors closed – a good way to lose a tail.'

'You lost them?'

'Hardy changed the game plan. He must know that we're on to him and that our being taken isn't worth the risk that we will warn the others.'

Marie looked at the sign next to the tram stop. 'There's only one more stop north on this line, Caluire – and that's the way Lassagne was heading.'

The Number 33 tram creaked and rumbled through run-down neighbourhoods and abandoned building sites. Although only one stop had been noted on the sign, the driver drew up wherever he was hailed or whenever a passenger wanted to get off. Catesby shook his head with frustration. If Hardy and the other man had taken the tram, they could have descended anywhere.

When they got off at the Caluire terminus, Catesby turned to Marie. 'We're probably wasting our time, but it's worth having a look around.'

'It's a big place,' said Paul, 'more a town than a village.'

There was a road next to the tram stop which went up a steep hill. A stream of people, mostly women with bags, was filing down the hill and heading for the waiting tram.

Marie looked around. 'Most of the shops are closed. It looks like you've got to go to Lyon for shopping.'

'Let's start with a walk up the hill,' said Paul.

They had gone about forty yards when, for some reason, Catesby turned and looked back at the still stationary tram. Afterwards, he wondered if there was some validity in Andrée's claim that she could feel eyes staring at her back. Otherwise, he wouldn't have noticed. The woman had taken some trouble to change her appearance. She looked older and more poorly dressed than she had at Croix-Paquet. She had donned an untidy headscarf to hide her features, but it was definitely her. Catesby started running – and, once again, a public transport carriage pulled away before he could get to it. He realised her escape wasn't an accident. She had been trained to make getaways – but they hadn't warned her about staring at someone's back.

Catesby returned to the others. 'At least we know we're in the right place. At that moment, the question still hadn't arisen in Catesby's mind: *Had the woman already discovered the meeting's location and was she returning to report it to her Gestapo lover?*

They continued to the top of the hill to a leafy square called Place Castellane. The square, lined by plane trees which provided welcome shade, sloped down to the river. The three decided to disperse and look separately for signs of the doomed Resistance meeting. They agreed to rendezvous an hour later in a café they had passed on the way.

The hindsight telescope is a cruel instrument – and Catesby never managed to stop staring through it. Feeling guilty and being at fault are not always related – but the bicycle at the GP's surgery haunted Catesby for decades. But had he actually seen a bicycle leaning against the wall at 6 Place Castellane? The years played havoc with memory. And even if he had, how could he be certain it was the same bicycle that André Lassagne had ridden after the confrontation with René Hardy at the Croix-Paquet funicular? In 1943, most French bicycles looked the same. Catesby had indeed walked past Dr Dugoujon's surgery, but had no idea that Hardy and four Resistance leaders were in a dining room on the first floor – directly above Dugoujon's consulting room – waiting for Jean Moulin and two others to arrive. If a guardian angel had descended and pointed at the window, could Catesby have saved the day? Or some of it? Jean Moulin and the two other latecomers might not have had time to decamp and avoid the closing Gestapo net. But the 'what ifs' were something that Catesby would never get out of his mind.

Catesby arrived at the rendezvous café before the others. He chose a seat inside and ordered a red wine. As he sipped the wine he heard a woman's voice from the kitchen singing:

Le temps des cerises:
Cerises d'amour aux robes pareilles
Tombant sous la feuille en gouttes de sang

Catesby fought hard to hold back his tears. He hoped that the beautiful lives of Jean Moulin and the others would not be the falling cherries turning into 'drops of blood'.

Marie arrived. 'Such a beautiful song,' she said. She looked at Catesby. 'You're almost crying, aren't you?'

Catesby nodded.

'It's nearly three o'clock,' said Marie. 'If the Gestapo were going to raid the meeting, they would have done it by now.'

'You think they might have been lucky?'

'I hope so.'

Paul turned up. He ordered an ersatz coffee.

'We shouldn't stay here long,' said Paul. 'I may have done something very stupid.'

'What?' said Catesby.

'I've been spreading the word that an important Resistance meeting taking place somewhere in Caluire is going to be raided and, if they know anyone involved, they should be warned. I know it was taking a big risk, but the situation is desperate. If I accidentally told an informer, we could be in big trouble. You can't always judge people by their faces.'

'I've been doing the same,' said Marie, 'so we had better drink up and disappear.'

Catesby felt ashamed that he hadn't done likewise. 'Let me pay,' he said.

Just as Catesby was walking to the bar, shots rang out. The

woman in the kitchen fell silent. The *patron* froze, a half-polished glass still in his hand, and stared out the window. 'Keep your heads down.'

There were no more shots, but they heard shouting in French and German.

'Stay seated,' said Marie. 'There's nothing we can do.'

Catesby sat staring out the window. He no longer felt guilty about not warning strangers that a Resistance meeting was about to be busted. He silently cursed Marie and Paul for revealing that they were members of the Resistance. In the road, two German soldiers were dragging a thin middle-aged man who was shouting at them in fluent German.

'That's the baker,' said the *patron*. 'He came here from Alsace.'

The woman from the kitchen appeared. She looked at Marie and said, 'You and your friends, come with me. I think it's best.'

They followed her – and, for the next few hours, they were passed from safe house to safe house. They had escaped the Gestapo, but Jean Moulin and the others hadn't.

Jean Moulin was tortured to death because he refused to betray others. He died seventeen days after he was captured. He finally succumbed to his horrific wounds while being sent by train from Paris to Berlin. The Germans returned his body to Paris where it was immediately incinerated. A box, numbered 10137, containing an urn labelled 'ashes of an unknown, incinerated 09-07-43', was sent to Père Lachaise Cemetery. In a ceremony at the Panthéon in 1964, writer and Resistance hero André Malraux referred to the man embodied in those ashes as 'the face of France'.

The day after he was taken prisoner, Klaus Barbie, the Gestapo chief in Lyon, submitted Jean Moulin to more than an hour of severe beating before he had him thrown into a chair in front of his desk. Barbie handed Moulin sheets of paper and a pencil and told him to write down the names and addresses of Resistance members and everyone helping them.

Moulin smiled at Barbie and began to scribble on the top sheet of paper. A few minutes later, the Gestapo chief got up from behind his desk to see what his prisoner had written.

There were no names on the paper, but a caricature of Barbie's own face. Barbie exploded with rage and began to beat and kick his victim more violently than before. The few witnesses who glimpsed Moulin in the days before he was sent to Paris described him as semi-conscious and covered in bruises. His head lolled on his shoulders and he could only stumble along with two German soldiers holding him under his arms.

The remaining days of Jean Moulin's life were unspeakable torture. The last Resistance prisoner, who had been summoned to Paris to confirm 'Max's' identity, described Moulin as having his head swathed in bandages and his face a sickly yellow. Jean Moulin may have been scarcely breathing – but his eyes were still alive and defiant. It was, as Malraux said, 'the face of France'.

Suffolk: June 2016

'Thanks for writing this all down, Granddad.'

'I haven't finished yet. I wanted to record the bare facts while I can still remember them.'

'We'd love you to give a talk at the university.'

'I'm still bound by the terms of the Official Secrets Act – and I'm not impressed by the wine cellar and conjugal facilities at Wormwood Scrubs.'

'There are a lot of other retired SIS officers who give talks.'

'They're more careful than I am; they know when to shut up.' Catesby paused. 'That's why writing history is so difficult. Those in power drip-feed the past – and edit what they pass on. In the eyes of the Secret State, the worst criminals aren't traitors – treason is part of the game – but those who expose the lies of those in power. That's why Daniel Ellsberg nearly got a prison sentence of 115 years for releasing the Pentagon Papers which told the truth about the Vietnam War; why Clive Ponting was prosecuted for telling a member of Parliament that the government had falsified information about the *Belgrano*'s sinking, and why Washington is baying for the blood of Julian Assange.'

'And you, Granddad, have never done anything like that?'

Catesby gave a sly smile. 'Forty years in the Secret Intelligence Service does endow one with a degree of cunning.'

'But I could always see through you. One of my earliest memories is you playing peek-a-boo with me. You would put your hands over your face and say, "Where's Granddad?" But I always knew you were there.'

'You ought to have been in counterintelligence. Burgess, Maclean and Philby played peek-a-boo with SIS all the time and never got caught.'

'Do you regret your career choice?'

'Enormously. I wish I had become a doctor or a teacher and

done something good for the world. But I also loved literature and the arts.' Catesby smiled.

'I could imagine you teaching Proust at the university.'

'I hope you're not being ironic. Proust is a delightful writer – and one with a dry and wicked sense of humour.'

Leanna laughed. 'We seem to have come a long way from Jean Moulin and the Resistance.'

'Not really. Jean Moulin was a refined man who ran an art gallery as part of his cover story. In fact, he was an excellent artist who would have preferred a career as a painter to that of a civil servant.' Catesby pointed to a watercolour on the wall of his office. 'I'm surprised you never asked me about that. Did you think it was something I picked up at an auction in Halesworth?'

'Oh god, I feel so…'

'Don't feel ashamed; I shouldn't have said anything.'

'I've always admired it, but I thought it was something that Grandmother had given you.'

'Oh dear,' said Catesby, 'the curse of marrying above oneself. Every time anyone saw something nice or interesting in our house, they always assumed it came from Frances or her family – and not from a ragamuffin from the Lowestoft docks.'

'Granny's family do have some nice things,' Leanna looked again at Moulin's painting, 'but nothing with as much warmth and colour.'

Catesby laughed. 'What about the Duncan Grant nude that Henry Bone thought was a self-portrait?'

'It was a bit embarrassing for us as children.'

'But Frances's family didn't just collect works of art. They collected people too – and I was one of them. They gave love and acceptance and wanted nothing in return.' Catesby had met his wife when he went back to Cambridge to finish his degree. She came from a left-wing family and had toddlers from a wartime liaison with a Canadian air force officer who pissed off back to Canada.

Leanna reached out her hand and took Catesby's. 'And you are the most wonderful person in the family – and I'm not the only one who thinks so.'

Catesby wanted to make a flippant reply, but the sudden lump in his throat made it impossible to speak. After a minute or two, he said, 'Thank you.' He gestured again to Moulin's watercolour. 'I was lucky to get that at an auction in the 1950s. The light and countryside suggest Provence – probably not far from *La Lèque* where Moulin had bought a dilapidated farmhouse. He also revelled in the louche low life of bohemian Paris – and he drew wonderful caricatures – but he loved the simplicity of country life too. His tastes embraced all of France. When the Gestapo killed Jean Moulin, they killed the best of France.'

'What is the best of Britain?'

'For me, taking you for your first sea swim at Walberswick. You loved playing in the breaking waves and I can still hear your shouts of delight.' Catesby looked out the window at the sun-dappled garden alive with wrens, blackbirds and goldfinches. 'Moulin had Provence and I have Suffolk. Had they executed me, my last mental picture would have been the deserted beach at Covehithe. Deserted except for lovers. Speaking of which, how is your Tory MP?'

'I ended it. The whole thing was a mistake. At first I was taken in by his boyish charm. I thought he tried to be funny all the time because he was shy and insecure. But then I realised that he was totally selfish – and a lying piece of shit. I'm deeply ashamed that I ever had anything to do with him – and so are a lot of other women.'

'I can understand. Whitehall and Westminster are places where even the ugliest and most unpleasant people can seduce. Power is an aphrodisiac.'

'I've learnt my lesson.'

'Then you're brighter than most.'

Leanna gave a nervous smile. 'On a less embarrassing note, who betrayed Jean Moulin?'

'I don't know – and I'm not sure that anyone will ever know. Some believe that Moulin's betrayal was part of a power struggle about who would rule France after the war. There were some frightening characters on both sides. Pierre Bénouville, the number three man in *Combat*, had been a member of *Cagoule*, an extreme right-wing group that stormed the National Assembly in 1934 in an attempt to remove the left-alliance Popular Front government by force. And by the middle of 1943 a lot of the Vichy collaborators could see the tide had turned and it was time to jump ship and join the Resistance. They regarded Jean Moulin – and even de Gaulle – as too far to the left. Not everyone wept over Moulin's fate. On the other hand, Moulin's capture could have been the result of pure incompetence and bad security. There was no back door or escape route from the doctor's surgery in Caluire and too many people knew about the meeting.'

'What do you think?'

'My guess is that Moulin's betrayal was mostly the work of René Hardy, an unattractive and lonely man. Hardy was seduced and turned by the ultimate *femme fatale*, a Frenchwoman named Lydie Bastien – an intellectual oddball who was a fan of Nietzsche and the occult. She liked hanging around with writers and artists. As a Nietzschean, Bastien thought she was beyond good and evil. As such, she became the mistress of Harry Stengritt, a Gestapo officer, who showered her with priceless jewellery and gems that had been confiscated from Jews.'

Leanna looked at her notes. 'Hang on, this doesn't sound like the frumpy woman you met in Lyon and who followed Hardy to Caluire.'

'No, no, no!' Catesby laughed. 'The confusing thing about history is that there are too many people with too many lovers. The frumpy one was Edmée Delétraz. More about her later. Lydie Bastien was completely different – and almost open about her collaboration with the enemy.'

'Was she never prosecuted?'

'Sadly not. It was a disgrace. On the one hand, Lydie Bastien was a brazen liar who was skilful at burying the past. On the other hand, I think the French prosecutors were intimidated by her – and by her connections in high places.' Catesby paused and laughed. 'I met her once. It was at an art exhibition in Nice when I was operating under dip cover as a junior cultural attaché. The curator, thinking I was the real thing, introduced me to a surrealist writer – who, I later found out, was quite well known. The writer, who was a bit drunk, pointed to a woman in black who was surrounded by a gaggle of admirers. He described them as "moths attracted to her *luciférienne* flame". It turned out that the writer was one of the many lovers she had ditched – and he was still tortured by the experience.'

'Were you attracted to her?'

'No. She wasn't as attractive as I thought she would be. She was, except for her eyes, a very ordinary woman.'

'And the eyes?'

'Pure demoniacal. She was Satan – and it must have attracted men. One of her last lovers was a fabulously wealthy maharajah. She was friends, if not lovers, with Aldous Huxley and Jean-Paul Sartre. She wrote books on yoga and hypnosis – and ran a bar in Paris famous for hosting post-punk bands.' The cat flap sounded. 'Thomas must have heard us talking about Satan.'

The cat ignored the granddaughter and jumped purring on to Catesby's lap.

'Hunger and cuddles make whores of us all.'

'But Thomas is a cat.'

'Exactly.' Catesby took a half-empty tin of cat food out of the small office fridge and put it in a bowl. 'There you go, boy. Thomas's loyalties are transferrable. He would love anyone with a tin opener – but René Hardy was a pathetic human being with emotional as well as physical needs. He was also a bit stupid. Whenever attractive women flirted with me, I knew they were honey traps – but Hardy believed that Bastien fancied him. She found Hardy repulsive, but seduced him at the behest of her Gestapo lover.' The cat flap banged shut as Thomas headed into the garden. 'So much for that seduction. I wonder if Harry Stengritt got some perverse pleasure at compelling his mistress to bed a man she despised. There were rumours that Stengritt sometimes secretly watched their couplings. But that aside, Hardy was one of the most valuable informers that the Gestapo ever recruited. He not only betrayed Jean Moulin, but was responsible for the arrests of Delestraint and Gastaldo a couple of weeks before.'

'How was Hardy recruited?'

'Oh dear, my butterfly brain was jumping ahead. Hardy was in Paris and his affair with Lydie Bastien had already begun. She bought him a train ticket for Lyon – where her parents lived – and promised to join him later. Bastien then told her lover which train Hardy was travelling on and he was arrested at Chalon-sur-Saône and taken to Gestapo HQ in Lyon. Harry Stengritt then sent his mistress to see Hardy in his prison cell. Bastien begged Hardy to agree to work for the Germans. Otherwise, they would arrest her and her parents. Hardy, I imagine, was terrified about his own fate – and too obsessed with Bastien to realise he was being duped. But, to be fair, I think that many who were braver than Hardy would have made the same decision.'

'What would you have done, Granddad?'

'I hope my suicide pill would have been close at hand because I don't think I could have endured torture without talking. The unforgiveable thing about Hardy is that, after being released, he never told the Resistance what had happened. They would have understood and sent him into hiding – or used him as a triple agent to pass on false information to the Germans – but Hardy's infatuation with Bastien was too strong and he feared losing her. I think he probably detested himself for betraying Moulin – and maybe hoped that the meeting would be cancelled.' Catesby stared out the window. 'There is one question that has always troubled me.'

'Which is?'

'Did Hardy know the location of the meeting? I am sure he would have told the Gestapo if he had known – anything to keep Bastien coming to his bed – but maybe he didn't know. What bothers me is that the meeting was scheduled for two in the afternoon, and Hardy would have told them that, but Jean Moulin and two other Resistance leaders didn't arrive until forty-five minutes later. If the Gestapo had pounced at two, or even half an hour later, Moulin wouldn't have been captured. But they didn't raid the surgery until minutes after Moulin arrived. So how did the Gestapo know that he and the others were running late?'

The granddaughter looked at her notes. 'What about the frumpy woman, Edmée Delétraz, who followed Hardy to the meeting place in Caluire?'

'Well listened, Leanna. Defenders of Hardy blame Delétraz for the betrayal and defenders of Delétraz blame Hardy – but I came to the conclusion, and it took me years, that Delétraz was a reluctant triple agent and innocent. She was caught up in what Angleton used to call "a wilderness of mirrors".'

'You mean James Jesus Angleton, the CIA head of counterin-surgency, whom you despised?'

'I gave up despising Jim years ago. He was mentally ill – a victim of paranoia, a health hazard common to those in our business. In any case, Edmée Delétraz began as a brave Resist-ance fighter – and then was betrayed and arrested by the Gestapo. Fearing for her life, she agreed to work for them and was released – but, unlike Hardy, she reported to the head of her réseau what had happened. The réseau chief, who was safely based in Switzerland, decided to use Delétraz as a pawn in a dangerous game. He told her to pretend to be a willing German agent – and she even became the mistress of the man who was running her. As a triple agent, Delétraz's job was to pass on to her réseau boss in Switzerland what the Gestapo wanted from her. In theory, this would reveal how much the Germans knew and what networks had been betrayed. But the Gestapo were too cunning and careful to reveal anything useful to an agent like Delétraz. They were ruthless professionals and trying to outwit them was a stupid game. I need a cup of tea.'

'You are becoming a bit like your cat. Here, there's some left in the pot.'

'Thank you. Edmée Delétraz certainly followed Hardy and the others to Caluire. She said that she was following them on the instructions of her lover – who, by the way, was a French-man working for the Gestapo – and she had to do so otherwise she would have blown her cover as a triple agent. Delétraz had already taken enormous risks. As soon as she found out that an important Resistance meeting had been betrayed, she tried desperately to pass the information on to the Resistance all over

Lyon. I assume that she was unable to contact her réseau chief in Switzerland – whose role I still find a bit of a mystery.' Catesby sipped his tea and looked reflective.

'Something troubling you, Granddad?'

'I'm lost again in a wilderness of mirrors. There are dozens of witnesses who testified that Delétraz warned the Lyon Resistance that the meeting had been betrayed. After the war, we found out that the Resistance tried, but were unable, to pass her warnings to those attending the meeting.'

'So, surely she was innocent?'

Catesby shrugged. 'But why, after she had followed the traitor Hardy to the surgery in Caluire, did she not go inside and warn them? Delétraz testified that she didn't need to. She assumed that the Resistance leaders already knew that the meeting had been betrayed. But why were Hardy and the two others still heading for the meeting? Her account gets even more complicated. She said she went back to Croix-Rousse to meet the Gestapo, as agreed with her lover, and show them the way to the meeting place. As she led them to Caluire, she claims that she stalled for time and pretended to have lost her way – which explains why the Gestapo raid was so delayed.'

'She sounds like a woman who was very frightened and uncertain.'

'I should have thought of that.' Catesby looked closely at his granddaughter. 'Maybe there's something in me which is too hard and unsympathetic. Your grandmother used to tell me that I had little empathy, I couldn't think like a woman.'

'You are harder on yourself than other people. Why are you smiling?'

'You've caught me out. Once a Catholic, always a Catholic. I was brought up to feel guilty and self-critical – and you expect the same of others. Part of my European inheritance. Can you remember anything of my mother?'

'I was only eight when she died. I did find her austere and a bit frightening – and always dressed in black. In retrospect, she looked more Mediterranean or Eastern European than Belgian.'

'I often thought that myself. She was an enigma.'

'But she had marvellous thick black hair. She once let it down and asked me to help comb it – not a fleck of grey.'

'She didn't dye it. And she didn't like Britain – which made me love my country more.'

'Even now?'

'We're heading towards the abyss, that fucking referendum, and it breaks my heart. If the leavers win, it will betray the memory of every one of us who fought in France. I can almost hear my mother say, *Tu vois… You see, I told you so.* How did we end up talking about her?'

'You were telling me about Edmée Delétraz.'

'Poor woman. I shouldn't judge – and perhaps I shouldn't judge René Hardy either. Hardy was tried twice for treason: once in 1947 and again in 1950 when proof emerged that he had lied during his first trial. And here is a secret that I've never told anyone: I was called as a witness for the second trial.' Catesby smiled. 'As a member of the Secret Intelligence Service, this was indeed irregular. The DG called me into his office to say I would have to go to Paris to give evidence – but it would be *in camera*. The DG didn't like it but said that he had been put under pressure from "higher up". I thought someone in Whitehall was trying to help the French prosecutor nail Hardy – but when I arrived in Paris, I realised the truth was otherwise. Whoever sent me wanted my testimony to cast doubt on Edmée Delétraz and to exonerate Hardy. I tried not to do so, but I was given a right royal grilling by Hardy's lawyer, Maurice Garçon – what a wily professional! How Hardy came to be defended by France's most skilful and famous lawyer is another mystery. Somehow Garçon had discovered that I was one of those who had seen Delétraz trailing Hardy – and put pressure in the right places to force me to come to Paris. Garçon had all his facts in order and there was nothing I could deny. When I pointed out that Delétraz had tried desperately to warn the Resistance, Garçon grilled me with silence and a supercilious smile – then hinted that I might be part of a conspiracy. I did regain some ground when questioned by the prosecutor, but he was nowhere near as good at twisting facts as his opposite. In any case, Garçon

– great *avocat* and showman that he was – failed to convince the tribunal. Four of the seven judges found Hardy guilty.'

'So the prosecution *was* successful!'

'No,' Catesby laughed. 'A guilty verdict requires a majority of two votes. A majority of one isn't enough; so Hardy, though guilty as hell, walked free. The second trial had taken place because records emerged – from the French railways and the Germans – that Hardy had lied at his first trial when he denied having been arrested by the Gestapo. Hardy now admitted that he had agreed to work for the Gestapo in order to protect Lydie Bastien and her parents – but it didn't matter because he had never told the Germans about the Caluire meeting or anything else important. After being freed, Hardy became a novelist. One of his books was turned into a film starring Richard Burton.'

'Wasn't Hardy arrested when the Gestapo raided the meeting?'

'Oh yeah, but they ran out of handcuffs when they got to him. They bound his hands with leather thongs instead and as they led the prisoners outside, Hardy freed himself and did a runner. I didn't see it, but I heard the shots being fired at him. I only counted three, a paltry number of shots as the Germans had automatic weapons, and witnesses said that no one ran after him. Afterwards, Hardy shot himself in the arm and sought shelter in the house of a friend. A day later, the French police turned up and took Hardy into custody. Seeing he had a minor gunshot wound, the police delivered him to a German military hospital – where, despite having his arm in a cast, Hardy escaped by jumping out of a window. The whole business was staged. The fake escape and gunshot wound were intended to hide the fact that Hardy was a traitor.' Catesby paused and shook his head. 'Maybe it's best that you forget everything I've told you and destroy all my notes.'

'Why?'

'Passing on judgements of comrades to those who weren't there isn't fair to those who were.'

'But you were there.'

'And I should keep my mouth shut – and my emotions locked

away. My experiences in occupied France warped and twisted me. I came back a damaged and bitter person full of hate. The worst that happened I still haven't told you about – and those images have never left my mind.'

'Your emotions are also part of history.'

'But the reputations of others should not be smeared. Do you know, only one per cent of the French population were active in the Resistance? And one in four of them died.' Catesby got up, pulled out a filing cabinet and removed a slip of paper. 'Sadly, I don't have the French original. This is my translation of Camus's article.'

'Albert Camus?'

'That's the one. I never met him, but I roughly copied down what he wrote about René Hardy. Camus's article appeared after Hardy was acquitted by the minority decision in 1950. This is the important bit: "Had he stayed home, like so many others, had he not chosen the hard and dangerous road, he would be an honoured man today. We cannot judge this man. He must be left to judge himself."' Catesby smiled. 'Obviously, Albert Camus was a more generous-spirited person than I have ever been.'

'Do you still want me to destroy your notes and everything you've told me.'

'No, keep them. I don't want to compete with a Nobel Prize winner for generosity of spirit. But I shouldn't be flippant. I loved his writing. When my sister phoned to tell me that Mother had died, the first words I said were the opening lines of *L'Étranger*: "*Aujourd'hui maman est morte… Mother died today. Or maybe it was yesterday, I don't know.*" But I do know which day, it was Christmas Eve. I hope it didn't affect your Christmas?'

'I can't remember – and I can't remember when my mother died either.'

'How insensitive of me.'

'The circumstances were difficult.'

'She was a brave woman.' Catesby didn't know what else to say. Leanna's African mother was a human rights activist who died in mysterious circumstances. As an intelligence officer

Catesby had tried to find out the facts, but the Africa desk told him nothing – either through ignorance or design.

'As you well know, Granddad, history is much less painful when viewed from a distance – and doesn't involve those you love.'

Le Massif Central: Summer 1943

When your cover is blown, you have to lie low. As Catesby and Marie were passed from safe house to safe house, their primary concern was survival. They still didn't know the full impact of the Gestapo raid in Caluire – they didn't know if Jean Moulin had been one of those arrested – but they did know that the Resistance had been heavily penetrated by double agents and they could trust no one. Their paranoia began to ease as they got further into the countryside and closer to Guingouin's safe areas in the Limousin. The biggest help to *résistants* on the run was the vastness of the French countryside and the inborn defiance and stealth of the peasantry.

Catesby and Marie paid back the farmers who sheltered them by helping with farm work and domestic chores – and there were many other *résistants* who did the same. The farms of Little Russia were a rural commune where peasants and fighters laboured side by side. Catesby loved sweating in the summer sun. At times, the war seemed a bad dream.

There was a need for physical labour as much farm machinery had been confiscated by the Germans – and a shortage of petrol meant that tractors stood idle. But the big problem at harvest time was a lack of *batteuses*, threshing machines. A *batteuse* was too expensive for most farmers so they were dependent on wealthy landowners or they pitched in with groups of farmers to buy threshing machines which were used communally. At the behest of the German occupiers, the Vichy government ordered the confiscation of all threshing machines. The machines were then installed at railway stations. This made it easy for the Vichy to enforce the farm produce levy demanded by the Germans. A peasant farmer taking his wheat harvest for threshing at the local railway station would find a large percentage of his crop levied at a knockdown price for export to Germany. The

Resistance responded by dynamiting the threshing machines. Consequently, the farmers had to go back to old-fashioned methods of threshing by hand with flails. As one farmer joked to a group of sweating threshers stripped to the waist, 'If you're discovering muscles that you forgot you had, you can thank the Maquis.' The Maquisards also provided security by bringing their weapons into the fields and setting up lookout posts to provide early warning in case the Germans or the Vichy police tried to do a sweep. The Vichy authorities, however, kept a low profile. They knew that pushing past Maquis ambushes would require armour and troops.

Catesby felt like he was a character in a medieval painting. It took a while to learn the rhythm of flailing, but once you acquired it you were part of the land and reconnected with your ancestors. The flails were two pieces of wood attached to each other by leather thongs. The handle was about five feet long and an inch and a half in diameter. The *battant*, the rectangular piece of wood that beat the sheaves of grain, was just over three feet long and swung freely and lethally from the leather loops connecting it to the handle. The flail wasn't just a farm tool, but a deadly weapon that peasants had for centuries wielded against enemies.

The key to threshing, as a university lecturer turned peasant warrior explained to Catesby, was to achieve *un rythme parfaitement cadencé*. Otherwise, your flail would knock out the brains of your threshing partner instead of the grain from the sheaves. The pairs of threshers became sweat-oiled machines in the Limousin sun. The sound of the flails echoing on the wooden threshing floor was the timeless music of harvest.

The threshing was a communal chore involving the whole village. Children winnowed the flailed sheaves and carried them away. The women, dressed in black and Marie among them, were armed with brooms and swept the grain from the floor on to a canvas sheet which they gathered up to funnel the grain into large jute sacks. Others brought in fresh sheaves and spread them over the threshing floor. Every twenty minutes or so, the men wielding the flails were replaced by fresh arms and shoulders. The flailers then took on the lighter task of unloading more sheaves as the horse-drawn wagons arrived from the fields.

Communal lunches were served in the open air on improvised tables of rough planks on trestles. The meals began with *charcuterie*, bread and salad and progressed to duck with heaps of green beans. There was crumbly homemade cheese at the end. Everything was washed down with huge quantities of light red wine served in litre bottles. It was the best food that Catesby had eaten in occupied France – a rare moment of plenty and everyone knew it. In a few weeks, the Maquisards would once again be in deep hiding subsisting on root vegetables, apples and crusts of stale bread.

That night Catesby lay next to Marie in a hayloft, kept awake, not just by a cacophony of snores, but by a troubling thought. He knew that being near her body would, like the harvest lunches, soon be a lost and forbidden pleasure. But there was something else that troubled him. When was it going to happen? It was late August 1943 – and there was still no sign of it. It would be the beginning of the end and they all longed for it. At the time, he was surprised that he had been trusted with such an important secret. But why? The final pre-deployment briefing by the strange major at Baker Street kept replaying in his head like a record stuck in a groove. *I can't tell you the exact day or week, but the invasion will certainly take place between June and late August and the main landing beaches will be in the Pas-de-Calais. That, of course, is top secret information. Do not reveal it to anyone – and, if you are in danger of capture, I would advise that you take the L pill. It would be catastrophic if anyone leaked that information under torture.*

If they land now, thought Catesby, there won't be time to break out of the Pas-de-Calais and race towards the Rhine before the weather turns. They are leaving it late. Catesby sighed and tossed uncomfortably. He woke up Marie.

'What's wrong, *chéri*?'

Her calling him *chéri* had become more ironic as the months wore on, but he ignored her tone.

'I'm worried about something.'

'At last, *chéri*, you understand our situation! I thought you would never get there.'

'Stop patronising me. I'm not a child.'

'But you are young. Sorry, I'm worried about the future too.'

'I trust you – and I've never been closer to anyone than you.'

'That is very sad.'

'I'm not talking about me or our relationship.'

Marie touched his cheek. 'One is doomed and the other is in danger.'

Catesby felt Marie put her hand between his legs and grab his penis which had grown erect. 'You always know how to change the subject.'

'What is the subject?'

'Not now. You are the answer to nothingness and death,' said Catesby. 'Let's make love first.'

Afterwards, Catesby held her close. 'I hope the others didn't hear.'

'It wouldn't matter; they are French. Are you going to tell me what you are worried about?'

'It is something top secret – and I was told to kill myself if in danger of revealing it.'

'Then you shouldn't tell me.'

'But I now think that secret was a lie.'

'Then tell me.'

'During my final briefing I was told that an allied invasion of France was going to take place at the Pas-de-Calais between June and late August 1943.'

Marie smiled. 'And I was told the same thing. I think we all were.'

'Maybe it isn't a lie. We all know that a large number of arms and supplies have been parachuted in for the past few months. It looked like they were getting us ready to harass the Germans when they headed north. Perhaps the invasion has been delayed for operational reasons.' Catesby paused. 'Why are you smiling and shaking your head?'

'Why would they have told us, ordinary members of the

Resistance, such a vitally important secret? Why did we need to know? And what use was our knowing?'

'None.'

'You're wrong. It was very useful. Supposing, *chéri*, the Gestapo had captured you before you managed to swallow your suicide pill. You are a brave man and would have refused to talk for the first few torture sessions. But then they stripped you and led you into a room with a chopping block on the table and a meat cleaver lying next to it. And a corporal wearing surgical gloves – these types can be very hygienic – reached out and,' Marie touched Catesby's now spent and flaccid penis, 'and put our dear Monsieur Zizi on the chopping board. And the Gestapo officer asks for the final time, "When and where are the allies going to invade France?" What would you have answered?'

'I hope they would have believed me.'

'They wouldn't have believed you alone. But if they had already tortured ten or fifteen of us and always got the same answer, they would have believed you. And they would have kept several divisions on alert in the Pas-de-Calais instead of fighting in Russia.'

'You think Baker Street, knowing that many of us would be captured and tortured, fed us lies so that, in extremis, we would repeat those lies to the Germans?'

'Yes – and I think many of us were betrayed to the Germans for that very reason.'

Catesby propped himself on his elbow. 'Something's wrong with you; you must be mad. No one, at least no one on the British side, could be so cynical and manipulative.'

'Then why did he tell us that?'

'He was showing off. I doubt if he knew himself. He was being stupid.'

'You really think that?'

'No, but your truth has poisoned my mind.'

'War poisons everything. If we live to see the victory, we will soon taste a bitter lingering poison after the cheers have died down and the flags have stopped waving. Why are you laughing?'

'Because you are such a ray of sunshine.'

'You're beautiful when you laugh, you should do it more often. Ah, but one more thing – and it isn't funny.'

'What is it?'

'They are out to get Guingouin and they might not wait until the end of the war.'

Trois-Chevaux: Autumn, 1943

There is no place named Trois-Chevaux in the Limousin. In fact, there is no village, hamlet or town of that name in all of France. The Abwehr and the Gestapo were not fools. After systematically poring over maps of the region and finding no trace of a Trois-Chevaux, they finally realised that it was a codename for Guingouin's forest HQ. When they found the real Trois-Chevaux, they would find Lo Grand. Trois-Chevaux became their Holy Grail. The Gestapo knew that it lay somewhere between Limoges to the west and the Millevaches plateau to the east – and between Guéret to the north and Tulle to the south. It was an enormous rectangle of woods, hills and sparsely populated farmland. It was ideal terrain for hiding thousands of guerrillas who could strike and suddenly disappear. But what the Gestapo did not realise was that Trois-Chevaux was not the codename for a fixed location, but the name of a moveable place. There wasn't one Trois-Chevaux, there were dozens of them. It made the Gestapo doubt the authenticity of informers who reported locations in different places. In general, however, the Trois-Chevaux rotated around the heavily wooded hills and isolated villages south of Châteauneuf-la-Fôret. There was, Catesby noted, a sameness to the countryside which made map-reading difficult. It was a navigation nightmare for anyone who hadn't been born and brought up in the region. As Jimmy said, it reminded him of the remote farms and villages of the Saints in his native Suffolk – a place of inaccurate road signs and hopeful lanes that then petered out into fields or farmyards. Both Catesby and Jimmy had Suffolk kinsmen in the Home Guard who had been trained to fade into the countryside as an East Anglian Maquis if there had been a German invasion. And both men knew, like their French counterparts, who could be trusted and who couldn't.

When summer turned into autumn, Catesby found himself again entrenched with Guingouin's Maquisards. His job was largely as a liaison between the Limousin Resistance groups and London. A bounty of supplies, weapons and explosives continued to rain from the skies, even though it was obvious that a 1943 invasion had been cancelled – or had never been on the cards. There were also more SOE teams and British personnel on the ground. Radios and their operators were no longer a rarity, but were still kept stashed away from the main Maquis concentrations for fear of detection. Catesby seldom saw Marie, who was living undercover with a farming family pretending to be a relative helping with childcare. She found looking after an eighteen-month-old and his three-year-old sister exhausting, but rewarding. When Catesby asked her if she had children of her own, she gave him a blank look that chilled him to the marrow.

The *période clandestine* was over. Catesby no longer pretended to be undercover, but wore a British uniform and beret. Likewise, Guingouin and his men usually wore ersatz paramilitary uniforms that were gradually becoming more similar. The most prized possession was a leather Sam Browne belt – especially one with a pistol and holster attached. Catesby could see that the uniforms were good for morale and a sense of unified purpose. The younger *résistants* no longer doubted themselves as a rabble hiding in the woods to avoid deportation to Germany, but as a trained and serious military force. There was even close-order drill and saluting. The uniforms also made those who were not members of the Limousin Maquis stand out when they visited Little Russia. One of those was Henri Déricourt who turned up unannounced in Domps, a firmly Maquis village, wanting a meeting with Catesby. Déricourt had a Traction Avant with a full tank of petrol. He was accompanied by a Brit and an American, neither of whom was introduced with names or codenames, and was sitting in the kitchen of an elderly widow who sometimes provided accommodation for the Resistance. She was sharp as a needle, but pretended to be batty whenever the police or other Vichy officials turned up. They left her alone.

Déricourt addressed Catesby by his codename. 'Thank you,

Jacques, for coming to meet us. The Guingouin Maquis are rightly suspicious of strangers and refused to take us further.'

'Lo Grand keeps tight security,' said Catesby.

The Brit broke in, speaking English. 'That's good – and we are pleased to see that so many of them are armed with Sten guns.'

'The airdrops have been useful,' said Catesby, 'but we still have more Maquisards than guns. My preference, shared by Guingouin, would be Bren light machine guns, three-inch mortars and US Army bazookas.'

The American gave a warm smile. 'It sounds like you guys are getting ready to take on Panzers. By the way, let me introduce myself, I'm Hank Vaseline.' The American paused. 'It's obviously a codename – and, as I can see from your expression, a pretty odd one. I get a lot of teasing about it from your fellow Brits at Milton Hall who say that the Hank should begin with a W.'

The British officer gave Hank what seemed a warning look.

'Oops,' said the American, 'me and my big mouth. I shouldn't have mentioned that place that doesn't exist.'

'Hank,' broke in the Brit, 'is part of Operation Jedburgh and the reason we have brought Hank here is to familiarise him with what the Jedburgh teams can expect when they are parachuted into France. The Jeds are going to be three-man teams consisting of one American or British officer, one French officer and one radio operator.'

'When are they going to start arriving?'

The Brit looked a bit cagey. 'No sooner than the spring. You will be informed in advance.'

'Can I tell him,' said the American, 'about our crazy codenames?'

Catesby had already had enough. He gave a half nod towards Déricourt. 'I'm not sure we should be having this conversation in these circumstances.'

Déricourt smiled and said in accented, but clear English, 'What circumstances? You think the old woman can hear us and that she understands English?'

'GILBERT,' said the British officer, calling Déricourt by his codename, 'is one of our most trusted agents and has a top secret clearance.'

Catesby looked closely at his fellow Brit. He wanted to say, 'And who the fuck are you?' but decided to be two-faced instead. Catesby looked at Déricourt and addressed him by his real name, 'Forgive me, Henri, I apologise for any rude mistrust. Living in the woods with Lo Grand makes us all a bit paranoid.'

'There is, my friend, no need to apologise.' Déricourt reached over to Catesby and they shook hands.

Catesby was beginning to enjoy being a two-faced shit and promised himself to do more of it in the future.

The still nameless British officer fixed Catesby with the bleakest of smiles and said, 'I am pleased that you and GILBERT, I mean Henri, are on such good terms as you will be working closely together to organise air ops.'

'Well, sadly,' said Déricourt switching to French and turning to Catesby, 'not that closely. I will only be arranging airdrops in Haute-Vienne while you, my brave friend, will be taking over all the air ops in Creuse and Corrèze.'

Catesby watched the face of the American and saw that he was struggling to understand Déricourt's rapid French.

The Brit broke in, also speaking French, but more slowly for the American's dubious benefit. He looked at Catesby. 'I know it's not a question of taking over Creuse and Corrèze, for you have been handling air ops for all three departments. But during the next few months the pace and number of airdrops will increase enormously and you would not be able to coordinate them on your own.'

It was still unsaid, but obvious to Catesby. They were stocking up for the invasion. Fingers crossed, it would be in May 1944. It wasn't fair that the Russians were still bearing the brunt of the fighting. There were grumbles among the more political of the Maquisards. They said, in covert whispers, that Churchill wanted to bleed Russia dry. At first, they would cease such discussions if they noticed Catesby in earshot. But more and more these overheard grumbles seemed intended for his ears.

'Would anyone else,' said Déricourt, 'like a glass of wine?'

'I'd love one,' said Catesby.

'I'll go and find Madame.'

Two minutes later, the old woman appeared bearing a carafe of red and a bottle of her own homemade plum brandy. She was laughing at something that Déricourt had whispered to her. It was obvious that she was charmed by him. He had a way with people – and he would need it. The wine was coarse and honest, but the brandy, like Déricourt, was smooth and lethal.

As soon as the widow disappeared, the British officer looked at Catesby, 'Before we were sidetracked, we were discussing Jedburgh's use of codenames. There is more method than madness in the system. The first half of a codename is a first name; the second half, the name of medicine or medical supply. The idea is to confuse German listening stations as to whether intercepted transmissions are about supply requests or Jedburghs. Try to weave fake or genuine references to medicines in your messages: "Detonators and novocaine still awaited."'

Catesby suppressed a frown. The whole thing would be an unnecessary pain in the arse for radio operators hard pressed to do quick and clandestine transmits.

The American sipped the plum brandy. 'These people sure know how to make some first-class moonshine. Does Georges Guingouin have his own still?'

'No,' said Catesby. 'Life in the camps is austere and puritanical.'

'But,' said Déricourt slapping the table, 'there are lectures on Marx and Lenin to cheer things up.'

Catesby struggled to keep a blank face and hide his annoyance at Déricourt's attitude.

'Is it true,' said Déricourt, 'that even the Communist Party call Guingouin "the madman in the woods"?'

Catesby could see that Déricourt was trying to provoke him, but he didn't rise to the bait. 'Why don't you ask him yourself, comrade?'

Déricourt slapped the table again and laughed. There was something in his laugh that was warm and infectious. It may have been false and contrived but it dissolved conflict and bitterness. It was one of his most useful weapons.

The American broke in. 'I certainly hope that we are going to meet Georges Guingouin. I've heard he is a legend.'

'I will try to arrange it, but you may have to agree to security measures.' Catesby knew that the escorting Maquisards insisted that visitors be blindfolded on their way to the hideaways and the indignity often caused arguments.

Events passed more smoothly than Catesby had feared. The next morning Déricourt agreed to be blindfolded, and the other two followed suit. A Maquisard drove the Traction Avant through a maze of country lanes. Catesby kept on eye on the three in the back seat to make sure their blindfolds remained in place. Déricourt kept whispering, 'Nobody peep!' After about twenty minutes the Traction ground to a halt next to a small clearing where a single tethered cow was grazing. The blindfolds were removed and they continued to Guingouin's HQ on foot.

The visit proved a valuable one for the American and he passed the lessons learned on to his fellow countrymen preparing to parachute in with the Jeds. In the end, the first Jedburgh teams did not arrive until just before D-Day. It was a long lonely wait as Catesby and the others prepared for a hard winter of hiding in the dark hills of Limousin. There were occasional hit-and-run raids to keep up morale and relieve the boredom, but the main tasks of the Maquis were surviving and stacking supplies until D-Day.

Déricourt's job as air operations officer for Haute-Vienne lasted less than six weeks. Catesby assumed that his early departure had been the result of his own secret campaign to undermine Déricourt, but the truth was otherwise. Déricourt was someone who liked good food, fine wine, warm beds and the company of beautiful well-dressed women. None of those were available in Guingouin's camps. Nor did his ready smile charm the hardened Maquisards with whom he had to share food and rough log hideouts dripping with damp. Déricourt wasn't trusted and was kept under close scrutiny. If he wanted to compromise the location of an airdrop, he would have found it impossible to pass on the information. No one, however, could complain about the operations he organised. There was even some grudging admiration for his professionalism. Déricourt used Marie as his W/T operator to contact London. She had the radio hidden in a hayloft. The second time they went into the loft he tried to seduce her. She was lonely and frustrated and almost gave in, but when he roughly put his hand up her dress she pushed him off. He wasn't happy about it and complained that she had 'got him all excited' and it wasn't fair to stop – which made her despise him more. Her refusal had repercussions.

The raids began a week after Déricourt had left the Limousin. The first victim was the old widow in Domps. The raid took place at three in the morning and caught the Maquis off guard. She was taken by the Gestapo who were accompanied by Vichy *milice*. It was carried out quickly and professionally. The Germans knew they were in the middle of Little Russia and had to get back to Limoges as soon and as surreptitiously as possible.

When the woman's family found out what had happened, they went to the *préfecture de police* and also to the *Feldkommandantur* for the Limoges region to try to obtain her release. The Vichy police and the Germans provided the same answer. The old woman had been bullied and threatened by 'Guingouin's terrorists' into providing food and accommodation for 'other terrorists and criminals'. They described her as a vulnerable victim and, when she could take no more, she contacted the authorities to ask for help. She was taken into protective custody, but sadly her health deteriorated and she had to be hospitalised. The *Feldkommandantur* oozed sympathy and offered a car to take the family to the hospital. They said they would prefer to make their own way. When they visited her there were no signs that she had been beaten or tortured, but she was unconscious. The doctor whispered guardedly that he suspected she had been injected. She was a woman of tough peasant stock and lingered four days before she died. The lies were never believed by anyone. A memorial plaque in Limoges inscribed with the words *Aux morts pour la France* includes her name.

If, thought Catesby, Déricourt had been sent to the Limousin as a German spy, the logic and timing were perfect. The

Wehrmacht high command knew that an allied landing was planned for the spring or summer, but they didn't know where. In preparation they needed to clear and eradicate Guingouin's Maquis from their strategically important position in the centre of France. Lo Grand's fighters were ideally placed to harass and delay German units en route to reinforce the Atlantic Wall – or an attack from the Mediterranean. In preparation for a large-scale operation to clear the Maquis from the hills of Limousin, the Gestapo supported by the *milice* and the GMR, *Gardes Mobiles de Réserve*, began to raid the villages around Guingouin's hidden encampments and to send probes into the countryside. The GMR were Vichy's paramilitary police and it was the first time that they had appeared in the Limousin. Unlike the *milice*, they were not recruited locally and were even more heavy handed. Guingouin suspected that these probes were reconnaissance operations. In case they were followed up by a full-scale attack involving German armour, he was already making plans to disperse his Maquisards to the hills of Corrèze. After the war, Catesby came to realise that Guingouin had followed the guerrilla tactics of a French Mao: *The enemy advances, we retreat; the enemy camps, we harass; the enemy tires, we attack; the enemy retreats, we pursue.* But it wasn't a way of fighting that made him popular with the Party hierarchy.

Marie's first thought when she heard the door being broken down was for the children of the farmer and his wife. Her job was to look after them and she could see that all five were terrified. She told the two oldest, eleven and nine, to run away as she thought they were cunning and fast enough to make an escape. On reflection, Marie wished that she had told the younger ones to join them. The mother arrived just as the elder two took flight and told them where to go. She gathered the three youngest about her and tried to calm them. It was three o'clock in the morning and they heard the father being shouted at and thrown down the stairs. The bedroom door was kicked open and a German and a *milicien* with pistols drawn entered.

'No one is to leave the house,' said the German in fluent, but heavily accented French. 'We have the house surrounded and anyone who tries to flee will be shot.'

Marie felt a shiver of fear, but tried not to give anything away. *Why had she told the older two to run!* The mother had burst into tears. Marie braced herself to hear shots any second. But there were none. She then coldly calculated that if the running children could manage a distance of a hundred metres in thirty seconds they would reach the woods where they could hide. She counted off the seconds while the German shouted. She got to thirty and there still had been no shots – or shouts – from outside.

'Didn't you hear what I said?' shouted the German. 'Stand against the wall, face to the wall, with your hands above your head.'

Marie did as she was told. Meanwhile, the *milicien* was ransacking the room.

'Where is your carte d'identité?'

'It is in the top drawer of the pine chest. You will find all my papers there – and you will find they are in order.'

'I will be the judge of that.' The German opened the drawer and lifted out a handful of underwear and threw it back in disgust. 'Your British lover certainly doesn't pamper you.'

'I haven't got a British lover. You are confusing me with someone else.'

The German picked up her identity card and laughed. 'Turn around.'

She did and stared at him with defiance.

'According to this document you are thirty-seven years old.'

'Nearly thirty-eight.'

'If you are still in your thirties, I haven't reached sixteen.'

She tried not to react. The affront to her vanity was almost as hurtful as the situation. Meanwhile, there were thumps and screams from the ground floor. The farmer was being beaten.

'As a point of honour,' said the German, 'I would never beat a woman, but there are others who don't share my delicate refinements. Are you fond of music?'

Marie remained silent.

'You remind me of a character in a Strauss opera. People refer to it as a comic opera, but I find it sad and moving. Perhaps I will play it to you on the gramophone.' The German looked at Marie's false papers again and smiled. He then put them into an inner pocket of his tunic. 'I am sure the real you is a more interesting person than Marie Leclerc – there are thousands of Marie Leclercs.'

'And I am one of them.'

'No, you are not. You are a British-trained radio operator who sends messages to London on behalf of the terrorists.' He turned to the *milicien* who was still ransacking the room and pointed to the farmer's wife who was leaning against the wall and sobbing. 'Can you take her downstairs? Her crying is grating on my nerves.' As soon as they were gone, the German turned to Marie. 'Perhaps one day you will realise that you have made a mistake – and you will agree to work for us. It will be more pleasant than what you have been doing with the terrorists.' The German gave a baleful smile. 'And more pleasant than being sent to Ravensbrück where they will treat you like a pack animal and work you to death in the freezing cold. We don't offer this alternative to everyone, only to those who are special.'

Marie stared blankly, but a voice in her mind was pleading for those who were turned into double agents. She prayed that she wouldn't give in.

The German gestured with his pistol towards the stairs. 'Let's go and join the others.'

The farmer was lying on the floor bleeding from face wounds, but still conscious. His wife was sitting in a huddle with her three youngest children. The two *miliciens* were ransacking the house and a thuggish-looking German NCO was sitting in armchair with his pistol aimed at the farmer.

The German officer suddenly shouted, 'Stop all this nonsense now!'

There was an eerie silence. The officer turned to Marie. 'Where have you hidden the radio and the codebooks?'

'I am not a radio operator. I am Marie Leclerc and I am here to look after...'

The officer waved his pistol like a magic wand to dissolve her words. 'Your lies are pointless. Tell me where you have hidden the radio.'

Marie remained silent with a face of stone.

The officer said something in German to the NCO. Marie understood every word and knew what was going to happen next. The NCO grabbed the middle child, a boy of six who struggled bravely against the rough handling, and dragged him to the officer. The NCO held the squirming boy who was trying to bite his hand. The officer pointed his pistol at the boy's temple. 'Tell us where you have hidden the radio and the codebooks.'

The mother screamed.

Marie gave in immediately. 'The radio is buried in the pasture between the barn and the wood.'

'And the codebooks are with the radio?'

'No,' Marie faked a scream of desperation, 'we are never supposed to keep the codebooks with the radio.'

'Where are they?'

'They are not here on the farm.' Marie began to cry, but the tears were genuine ones. 'The codebooks are with the Englishman.'

'And where is he?'

Marie raised her palms in a gesture of futile desperation. 'Somewhere in the woods with Guingouin. He often comes here to make transmissions, but sometimes he takes me to hidden places in the forest or abandoned farm buildings.'

'To avoid the detector vans getting the same fix?'

'Of course.'

'Good. Now let's go find your radio.'

'It won't be easy in the dark – and if we use lights to find the place, the Maquisards might spot them and become suspicious.'

'You have become a very sensible lady – so we shall try in the dark.'

Marie held her breath and prayed that the German had believed her lie about the codebooks. They were hidden in a stack of firewood. The two *miliciens* armed with spades accompanied them into the pasture, while the other German kept watch over the family in the house. Marie decided not to ask the German officer about those who supposedly had surrounded the house to shoot anyone fleeing. He had obviously been bluffing and she didn't want to press her luck by taunting him. But that there were only four of them gave her a ray of hope.

She hadn't intended to waste time trying to find the spot where she had buried the radio, but it was difficult to get her bearings in the pitch dark. Dawn was breaking when they finally unearthed the W/T set in its fake suitcase.

'I am sure you still remember the secret authentication procedures and some of the codes,' said the German.

'Of course I do.' Marie didn't want to pretend she didn't and arouse suspicions about her codebook story. It was obvious that these procedures were ingrained into the brain of any radio operator.

'That may prove useful later,' said the German.

She knew he was hinting that she would be forced to send fake messages to London. During training they had been taught how to include a secret signal – a misspelling, a misplaced word – that would signal that they had been captured and compromised. Some of those receiving the messages in London often failed to spot the signals. As the sky lightened, Marie tried to brace herself for the ordeal facing her.

When they got back to the house, the German officer began by threatening the farmer and his wife. He said they mustn't tell anyone what had happened. If they did, they would be reported by the network of informers that had been sown among 'the terrorists'.

'How did you think we discovered that your childminder was a radio operator? We know everything,' smirked the German officer.

Marie was certain she had been betrayed by Déricourt. Probably in revenge for her having refused him sex. She now began to regret it.

The Germans and the *miliciens* walked her down a farm track which disappeared into a wood. Marie guessed that they had parked their vehicle away from the house to avoid arousing suspicion. Had she heard the sound of a motor in the middle of the night, she would have been up and running. She would have had no qualms about leaving her host family to cope without her. War is a cruel master.

They walked for a couple of hundred metres down the overgrown track until they came to a large lump of vegetation that concealed some sort of structure. Marie noticed grey canvas in the greenery. It was the back of a Renault lorry. The *miliciens* and the German NCO began to strip the truck of its camouflage.

The German officer looked at Marie. 'We've learned a trick or two from the terrorists. We have to cover our tracks. You and I will sit in the back for the trip to Limoges – and I've got a flask of brandy to help you relax. Are you happy?'

Marie remained silent.

'We are now in firm control of the *route nationale*. There will be no danger of terrorist ambushes.'

A fusillade of shots rang out. The bodies of the *miliciens* and the German NCO twisted on the forest floor as automatic fire poured into them. Then all was silent as the Maquisards rose from their hiding places. Marie was surprised that the German officer looked so calm.

A Maquisard called out, '*Lass deine Waffe fallen... Drop your gun and put your hands up.*'

The officer dropped his gun, put his hands up and looked at the Maquisard. 'You speak very good German. I hope I can be of help to you.'

The Maquisard switched to French. 'Keep your hands up and back away from your gun.'

The officer did so as another member of the ambush team dashed forward and recovered the pistol.

The German spoke again. 'I have never been a member of the Nazi party and I am part of an anti-Hitler plot – but I sometimes have to pretend to obey orders. How can I help you?'

'Tell us the names of all your informers.'

'If you need pencil and paper, you will find them in the Renault.'

The leader nodded to a young Maquisard who ran to the truck to fetch them.

The German began with Déricourt, but stopped after two more names. 'I can give you a much fuller account if you take me to your headquarters and give me longer to think.'

'You must prove yourself now.'

A look of fear crossed the German's face. His voice faltered as he continued with the list. He knew he was bargaining for his life, and lies and subterfuge were no longer an option.

'Is that all of them?' said the Maquis leader.

'They are the only ones I can think of at the moment. I need more time to remember.'

'You haven't got more time.'

'Why not?'

'Because we have no facilities to keep prisoners. You are going to be executed.'

Before the German could say another word, the Maquis leader raised his Sten and pulled the trigger.

As the other Maquisards searched the bodies and the Renault, the leader spoke to Marie. 'Do you think he was lying about being against the Nazis?'

'Of course he was.'

'They all lie when facing the barrel of a gun – and I'm not even sure the list of names he gave us is true.'

'How did you know they were here?'

'The oldest boy found us.'

'Where are the children now?'

'They are not far away. I have two people looking after them.'

'Please don't let them see the bodies.'

The farmer and his wife were reunited with their children, but had to leave the farm for safety. Two days later a unit of Vichy police and heavily armed Germans arrived at the abandoned farm. They plundered the house of anything of value and slaughtered the farm animals. They burned down the house and all the farm buildings. It was meant as a warning to any other farmers who gave shelter and sustenance to the Maquis.

The weather was not severe, but the influx of German troops, *milice* and GMR made the winter harsh. The HQ known as Trois-Chevaux had to move back and forth between Corrèze and Haute-Vienne. Sometimes the food ration was one apple a day. There was also a problem with informers, double agents and badly disciplined new recruits to the Maquis. Many of the forest hideaways, now stripped of leaves and dripping with rain, no longer provided adequate cover. Guingouin authorised the use of abandoned farmhouses and buildings to shelter the growing number of Maquisards. They were under strict orders to remain in hiding during the day – and no one was allowed to leave the requisitioned farms without permission. But human longing doesn't always obey the rules. Two of the recruits, young men still in their teens, had formed the habit of slipping away from the farm near Aureil to meet their girlfriends in an abandoned house in Feytiat. They did so once a week at most, so they didn't think it would do any harm. The girls were pottery workers in Limoges and thought it was a great adventure – and they loved the boys.

The widowed and drunken father of one of the girls didn't approve of her liaison. There were unholy rows, but she defied him. The father was also a Pétainist who proudly kept a portrait of the *maréchal* over his mantelpiece. During a drinking session with an old friend who had a minor post at the *préfecture de police*, the father mentioned the problems with his unruly daughter and her assignations with a boyfriend who didn't seem to have a job. The friend from the *préfecture* knew that the information passed on could prove to be gold dust.

It wasn't long before the surveillance team discovered the abandoned house where the girls met their boyfriends. It was a simple mission to trail the young men back to the derelict farm where the Maquisards were lying low. Ironically, the place had been raided a few months before as it was well located to stash supplies and weapons for attacks on Limoges, but it was still empty at the time and a search revealed nothing suspicious – so it was crossed off the list.

Because he was often bored and had little to do when lying

low between actions, Catesby began to write reports which were more diary entries than intelligence documents. They were an excuse for him to try to understand what was happening to himself and others – not as undercover combatants, but as human beings. It was frustrating that the two young lads hadn't employed counter-surveillance techniques. Catesby imagined them as two boys chatting happily to themselves, not a care in the world, as they made their way back to the farm from their love nest.

The attack was led by an SS unit from their barracks in Limoges. The Vichy police who accompanied them were mostly onlookers. The column of vehicles was spotted leaving Limoges and reported to Resistance leaders, but it was impossible to send a warning in time to the eight men hiding in the farm; they were too near Limoges. The attackers had armoured cars mounted with heavy machine guns. The farmhouse and surrounding buildings were pounded with anti-tank weapons and grenade launchers. The young Maquisards put up a brave, but futile resistance with their Stens and rifles before they decided to flee. Five of the eight, including one of the lovers, were cut down and killed instantly by the withering volume of fire. Two of the three who managed to flee were wounded. One, who had a bullet through the buttock, couldn't keep up and begged to be left behind. He was later found by a dog team and executed after a brief interrogation. He wouldn't have told them where to find Guingouin even if he had known – and that was him gone.

The surviving lover had been lightly wounded by wood splinters and glass as a *Panzerfaust* exploded in the farmhouse. He and the others managed to escape the dogs and the SS by crossing a stream. Their eventual aim was to make it to Saint-Léonard-de-Noblat, a small town on the Vienne which sheltered a number of Jews, artists and refugees from Alsace. After two hours of evasion, they decided that the Germans had given up the chase. They continued to the banks of the Vienne and waited until dark before crossing the river to Saint-Léonard. As they lay in the undergrowth, the young lover confessed that he feared the raid was his fault. His companion was too traumatised to comment, but suggested they tell everything to Guingouin.

The young Maquisard broke down in tears before Lo Grand as he confessed to everything. He said he wasn't aware he had been followed, but admitted that he had been careless and foolish. The lad was sent out of the room while Guingouin conferred with three other Maquis leaders. One pleaded that he be punished for a serious breach of discipline, but be given a chance to redeem himself. 'He is not, after all, a traitor or a collaborator, but a foolish young man who fell in love. And, aside from this mistake, he has been a brave and professional fighter. He is skilful with weapons and explosives and tireless when doing difficult tasks.' One of the others said that they needed to make an example of him – and make sure that everyone knew what the sanctions were. The third merely studied Guingouin's face. When Lo Grand finally spoke, his tone was even and decisive. 'Six of our brave fighters have lost their lives because one of their comrades disobeyed a strict order concerning security. Bouts of laziness, occasionally drinking too much and talking back are matters that can be dealt with by non-lethal punishments – but not breaches of security. We have lost six men who would have been heroes in the fight to liberate France. They have lost their lives for nothing. And we have also lost tons of badly needed supplies that were stored in the farm buildings. I know those weapons and explosives were not human lives, but losing them could cost lives when they are distributed to *milciens* and GMR who will use them against us. We must make an example of this young man – and I will carry out his execution.'

A few weeks later Catesby returned to the gravesite when there were others to be buried. He was surprised to see that someone had carved an arrow-pierced heart on the oak tree marking the grave with the young man's dates of birth and death underneath. Catesby later learned that Guingouin, a leader with a human heart, had done the carving himself. The new graves, however, were not for foolish lovers, but for traitors and profiteers. For such crimes, there would be no pity. All three had been found guilty by what the Maquis called a *tribunal militaire.* The first one had been condemned to death for being an undercover *milicien* who had infiltrated the Maquis and become a unit leader. He was also a profiteer who sold Maquis provisions and goods confiscated from collaborators to black marketers. He was stacking up a lot of money and executed a fellow profiteer who was threatening to expose him if he didn't get a larger share. He may have deserved the death penalty, but not for being an undercover agent. It later turned out that he was innocent of that charge. There were also the graves of two peasants from the Creuse who had been tried and executed for being informers. Guingouin hadn't been personally involved, but the *tribunal militaire* and executions had been carried out by Maquis leaders under Guingouin's command.

All three deaths would come back to haunt Lo Grand in the years after the war. The executions were the beginning of the *épuration sauvage*, the unofficial reprisals carried out against those who had collaborated with the Germans or the Vichy government. They continued for several months after the war when they were replaced by the *épuration légale.* In many parts of France women thought guilty of having had German lovers had their heads shaved and were sometimes stripped and tarred with swastikas. Guingouin forbade such reprisals against women, but was accused of having gone too far during the immediate post-war period when reprisals were carried out with quick vengeance. He had presided over tribunals where forty-four people had been sentenced to death and executed. There were also accusations that he and his close comrades had profited from confiscations and extortion. As Maquis leaders emerged from hiding to wed their sweethearts, the costs and origins of their engagement rings became sources of dark rumour. Heroes were slandered as villains.

Many conservatives felt their country had been taken over by a mob and wanted to turn the tables. The battles between the *Pétainists* who had supported Vichy and those who had supported the Resistance continued long after the war had ended. As the 1940s turned into the 1950s and France returned to 'normal', many civil servants reappeared in the same positions of authority that they had held during the occupation. It was no longer a disgrace to have done so. There were many judges and senior police who wanted to dig up the bodies buried by Guingouin and get revenge.

Not all of those out to get Guingouin came from the *Pétainist* right. In the early spring of 1944 Catesby began to hear hushed voices warning that the *polos* were back. Catesby had finally twigged that *polo* was slang for a political officer from the Communist Party. Guingouin was again accused of insubordination for failing to carry the fight into the towns. The Party was pressing for the early liberation of Limoges, but Guingouin knew that such a premature attack would be a suicide mission. Not only would his Maquisards be cut to pieces by armoured SS units, but hundreds of townspeople would be executed or deported in reprisal for such an uprising. The *polos* eventually left Trois-Chevaux after much bitter arguing, but their message was clear and final. If Guingouin continued to defy the Party line, he was in danger of liquidation.

A day after the *polos* departed a new recruit turned up for the Maquis. His credentials were excellent – and he was a tough customer with battle scars to prove it. He was about forty and had been a dockworker in Marseille until he left to fight in Spain. Several of the Maquisards had heard of him, and all of his stories, except one, were true. He had escaped from Gestapo custody on two occasions after being involved in sabotage in Marseille, but after his second escape he decided to head for the hills because his face had become too well known in the port city. His name was Gaston Le Mat. An Occitan-speaking Maquisard whispered to Catesby that *le mat* translated as 'the mad one' in Provençal.

Le Mat was liked and admired by the Maquisards, but his cover story for arriving at Trois-Chevaux just as the *polos* left didn't fool anyone – and even Le Mat could see how feeble it was. The Party had sent him to liquidate Guingouin. Le Mat's mission was obvious, and he had been disarmed and put under guard as soon as he had demanded a meeting with Lo Grand.

After a few generous plum brandies, the truth began to pour out.

'I have been a Party member all my life. I always follow orders. I did the same in Spain. We needed to purge the movement of bourgeois and Trotskyite elements – and the anarcho-syndicalists too. There was only one flag – not a black one, not a red and black one – only a red one.'

'And why were you sent to liquidate Georges Guingouin?'

'I didn't need to know why, but I was told that he was a Titoist who refuses to follow the Party line.'

Catesby exchanged a glance with Paul. They both knew that the Moscow-led Party hated followers of Yugoslavia's Tito more than they did capitalists. Tito was a communist, but Stalin's biggest fear was the spread of communism that wasn't subservient to Moscow – and many suspected that Guingouin was going that way.

'Who gave you the order?'

'The chief *polo*.'

'What is his name?'

'I don't know his name – and I wouldn't tell you if I did.'

'Are you still determined to liquidate Georges Guingouin?'

'I will always carry out Party instructions even if it means losing my own life – and if you were loyal Party members you would let me do so.'

While the interrogation was going on, Guingouin had been sitting in a dark corner of the room looking thoughtfully over his folded fingers. He only exchanged glances with Le Mat once – and there was no emotion in the eyes of either man. After a long silence, Lo Grand made a gesture and Le Mat was led out of the room.

The Maquisard who had been leading the questioning took his pistol out of his holster, chambered a round and looked at Guingouin. 'I'll now go out and get rid of this bastard.'

'No, he is brave and utterly ruthless. He could prove a useful fighter.' Guingouin smiled. 'Just keep him away from me.'

Near Trois-Chevaux: 7 June 1944

The news of the D-Day landings sent a wave of joy through the Maquis camps, but Catesby was cautious about celebrating. The German units in the Limousin finally knew where they were heading. They were preparing for a final round of ruthless and bloody attacks against the Maquisards who were poised to hinder and delay their deployment to the beaches of Normandy. It was do or die for both sides.

The first Jedburgh team to parachute into Limousin landed at midnight. They jumped from a converted American B-24 which made more noise in the sky than any plane Catesby had ever heard – and it looked massive. The drop zone was in the hilly pastureland above Sussac. It was a DZ that had been used before and the Germans and the *milice* knew about it. Déricourt had thought it was perfect. Catesby was comfortable with it too because the area was flooded with well-armed Maquisards who would provide early warning of enemy movements and fight a delaying action until the DZ was cleared. If the Germans wanted to capture teams and supplies as they parachuted in, they needed to be forewarned of the drop in advance so they could take over the DZ with superior force. A compromised DZ was every agent's worst nightmare. Déricourt had not managed it in the Limousin, but only because Guingouin's men were suspicious and never took their eyes off him.

More than a hundred Maquisards were present to greet the Jeds and to help carry away the supplies that would rain down after them. The first Jed that Catesby met turned out to be a Dutch radio operator. Recognising his accent, Catesby answered in Flemish. The Dutchman gave a booming laugh and shouted, *'Oh mijn god, ik ben in...* I've landed in the wrong fucking country.'

'Where's the American?' said Catesby.

'He's the tall one over there.'

The American was getting out of his parachute harness, but as soon as Catesby approached he sprang to attention, saluted and cried out, *'Lafayette, je suis ici.'*

A confused Catesby replied in English, 'I'm not Lafayette, I'm Captain Catesby of SOE. I don't think we have a Lafayette here.'

The American dropped his salute. 'Are you British?'

'Yes.'

'No wonder you don't understand. The Marquis de Lafayette was a French general who came to help us when we were fighting you guys for our independence.'

Catesby could see that they hadn't got off to a great start. 'I am sure that our French colleagues will give you the warmest welcome.'

As Catesby spoke, two Maquisards were busy rolling up the American's parachute. The American turned to them and said, *'Merci beaucoup, mes amis.'*

The drop zone was quickly cleared and the supplies stashed. The Jedburgh team were billeted in a farmhouse some distance from the DZ where Catesby gave a briefing to the American. He explained that Guingouin's tactics were to keep the Maquis as widely dispersed as possible, but able to group quickly for operations.

The American stifled a yawn. 'We've got some really fantastic air-supply drops planned. Not just guns and ammo, but food and uniforms. By the way, what happened to Jacques Dubois?'

'That's my codename. But now that the *période clandestine* is over we're starting to ditch codenames between ourselves – but we still keep them for radio transmissions.'

'My codename is Ollie Opium.'

'We were told.'

'But you can call me Lester.'

'Thanks.'

'The problem with this place,' said Lester, 'is that you're too far from the invasion beaches – even if there's a landing on the French Riviera. We Jedburghs are paramilitary. Our job is to coordinate resistance operations close behind the advancing allied lines and then link up. You guys are in the middle of nowhere.'

Catesby gave a bleak smile. 'Our job is to delay the German units getting to the beaches – especially a big SS division called *Das Reich*.'

'Yeah, I know. We were briefed.'

Catesby was getting increasingly irritated. He was thinking of reminding the American that they didn't get in the war until it was half over – or that Wall Street was pouring money into Nazi Germany while the Luftwaffe was bombing Britain. It also gave him a bitter recollection of the joke about utility knickers, *one Yank and they're off*. It was the British equivalent of *collaboration horizontale*. But he had to keep reminding himself, *they're now our allies.*

'The extraordinary thing about the Limousin Maquis is their numbers. When I first came here in February 1943, Georges Guingouin commanded a tightly knit group of just over a hundred Maquisards. There are now over eight thousand in Haute-Vienne alone.'

'Then why doesn't he take Limoges?'

Catesby was taken aback. The American's words were an uncanny echo of the complaints of the Communist Party *polos*. Before Catesby could answer, the French officer who was part of the Jed team came into the room. His news was an eerie coincidence. The French officer spoke in heavily accented English.

'I have heard a rumour that Tulle is now in the hands of the Maquis.'

Tulle was a small industrial town with a population of about eighteen thousand. It was the capital of Corrèze. Catesby knew that an attack to liberate Tulle had been under discussion since April. A German crackdown in Corrèze had led to more than two thousand arrests followed by hundreds of executions and deportations. There had, however, been no confrontation with the Maquisards. Catesby could understand why the commander of the Corrèze Maquis, Jacques Chapou, wanted to do something to protect the civilian population. Guingouin and the leaders of the *Armée secrète* knew that measures were necessary to protect the civilians, but were against an urban battle. The Party were in favour of it. Catesby, who liked and respected Chapou, could understand why he had launched an attack against German and Vichy positions in Tulle – and, against the odds, he seemed to have won.

Lester slapped the table and laughed. He shouted a resounding *yes* and looked at Catesby. 'That sounds like damned good news, partner. What do you think?'

'Jacques Chapou is an excellent leader and his Maquis are brave and well-trained fighters.'

'But it kinda makes your pal Guingouin look like a pantywaist.'

The French officer gave Catesby a look of enquiry. But Catesby wasn't sure what a pantywaist was either. He replied with a shrug, '*Poltron?*'

The Frenchman frowned and shook his head. It obviously wasn't a word one should apply to Georges Guingouin.

The liberation of Tulle didn't last a single day. As night fell, tanks of the Second Panzer Division entered the town in a crushing pincer movement from three different directions. Faced with overwhelming firepower, the Maquisards fled the town. Any attempt to resist would not just have been futile, but would have resulted in massive civilian casualties because the tanks would have levelled the town to crush Maquis positions. By the morning of 9 June, the Germans had regained control of Tulle. The reprisal massacres began the next day. All the men between the ages of sixteen and sixty were arrested. The SS and *Sicherheitsdienst* ordered a hundred and twenty of them to be hanged in retribution. By early evening ninety-nine men between the ages of sixteen and forty-four were hanging from the balconies and lampposts of Tulle. A shortage of rope left the quota of one hundred and twenty unfulfilled. But the twenty-one who escaped hanging were among the humdred and forty-nine selected for deportation to Dachau. One hundred and one of them died in the camp. Although Guingouin's refusal to commit his Maquis to urban combat was vindicated by the tragedy of Tulle, the Party still pressed him to launch attacks against the German garrisons in Limoges.

The nightmare of Oradour-sur-Glane was a kaleidoscope of toxic images which would haunt Catesby for the rest of his life. It began with the capture of Waffen SS battalion commander Helmut Kämpfe. He was apprehended by a local Maquis leader a few kilometres east of Saint-Léonard-de-Noblat. Kämpfe was leading a column to Guéret to put down an uprising and was frustrated with their slow progress. He drove his requisitioned Talbot-Darracq cabriolet alone down the D941 to see what was causing the delay and got caught in a Maquis ambush. It happened on the same day that other elements of his SS division were hanging civilians in Tulle. The German response to the D-Day invasion was hard and ferocious and Kämpfe was one of those leading it – but, in terms of his own personal security, recklessly. He ended up being the highest-ranking officer the Maquis had ever captured.

Catesby never found out what happened to Helmut Kämpfe and didn't ask Guingouin. When Catesby learned that a German officer had been captured, he suggested that he be used for a prisoner exchange. But after the public hangings at Tulle emotions were running high. When the Germans discovered that one of their respected and highly decorated commanders was now a prisoner of the Maquis, they flooded the area with troops to find him. The search was brutal and civilians were killed in the sweep. It was obvious that Kämpfe had been killed by the Maquis, but the question that haunted Catesby was when. Was the massacre at Oradour-sur-Glane revenge for Kämpfe's execution? Reports circulated among the Germans that he had been burned alive. Or was his execution revenge for Oradour-sur-Glane? Catesby hoped it was the latter.

The tenth of June was a busy day for Catesby. As he set off by bicycle to make contact with 'the Bushell girl', as they used to call the cheeky young Londoner in training, he had no idea what was about to unfold at Oradour-sur-Glane a few hours later.

Violette Bushell was now Violette Szabo. Her Hungarian-born Foreign Legionnaire husband had died of wounds in North Africa and this was her second time working undercover in occupied France. She had been parachuted into a field near Sussac on 8 June, her toddler daughter's second birthday, and been assigned as liaison officer to the Corrèze Maquis. Catesby was desperate to brief her about what had happened in Tulle and the situation in general. He was hoping to poach her for Guingouin's own Maquis. She was a fearless agent – and fun to be with. But when Catesby got to the rendezvous point near Sussac, it was too late. Szabo had already headed off for Corrèze in a Traction Avant. Catesby was unhappy. Not just that he had missed her, but because she was travelling in a car. All use of cars had been banned since the invasion.

A radio operator who had been parachuted in with Szabo met Catesby on her behalf and explained what had happened. 'She's a determined woman. She had a sprained ankle even before she made the jump – and a rough landing made it worse. She can just about cycle and can hardly walk.'

'That's typical of her. She'll never give up.'

It ended in tragedy. The driver spotted a German roadblock, which was part of the search for Kämpfe, and braked the car. They were seen by the Germans and it was impossible to turn the Traction around. Szabo and the two Maquisards bailed out of the car and fled on foot. Szabo could barely walk, much less run. The two men managed to escape, but Violette Szabo was taken prisoner.

News about what had happened arrived late that night while Catesby was sleeping in a farmhouse near Sussac. He helped the radio operator encode a report about Szabo's capture. He stayed up the rest of the night discussing plans to rescue her with local Maquisards. One of the Maquis guessed that she was being held at the Gestapo HQ in Limoges. It was a formidable building in the rue Louvrier de Lajolais in the centre of the city. It would be a risky operation. Catesby knew the talk was largely bravado. He felt heartsick and angry. As dawn broke more bad news arrived. This wasn't about one person facing torture and death, it was about hundreds being burned alive.

The Maquisard who brought the news about Oradour-sur-Glane warned Catesby and the others that Germans were still in the area. The same Maquisard who had proposed the rescue of Szabo suggested that a team go to Oradour to help the survivors. The one who had brought the news shook his head. 'There are no survivors.'

An hour later the W/T operator received an urgent message from London. Following D-Day, radio traffic had increased enormously – and so had the chances of detection. Messages were now sent and received two or three times a day, as opposed to once or twice a week. The incoming message from London was bleak. Baker Street had already heard rumours of a German atrocity at Oradour-sur-Glane. They wanted verification that such a massacre had occurred and details. Catesby knew that SO1, SOE's propaganda section, wanted information about war crimes that they could use as propaganda against the Nazis. Catesby looked at the decoded message and felt the spirit of Violette Szabo stiffen his spine.They needed to use every means possible to defeat the monster. It would be a dangerous trip, but he would go.

It was a long cycle ride through the dark forests of Limousin warmed and scented by the summer sun. Catesby had shed his uniform for the shabby clothes of a schoolteacher on sick leave with suspected TB, but he wasn't sure that his fake identity papers and cover story would fool anyone. If he saw a checkpoint, he would ditch the bike and flee into the woods. Later, he wished there had been a checkpoint and he had fled.

All the buildings were smouldering ruins. Grey smoke was rising from the destruction. He saw charred corpses lying in the middle of the road. There was the body of a woman which hadn't been burnt. Catesby wondered if she could still be alive. He brushed her hair aside and saw a bullet wound in the back of her neck and another in the back of her head. The woman's summer dress was patterned with pink flowers.

Catesby heard someone coughing. A man was coming out of the church. He staggered as if he was drunk, put his hands over his face and shook his head as he shambled off.

The images never went away. A church – a place of peace and reconciliation. How could they do that in a church? The remains of a pram stood before the altar. The canvas and bedding had been burnt away in the flames, but the charred infant rested on the pram's blackened metal base. Its little hands had disappeared, but shards of white bone protruded through the baby's wrists, pointing at Catesby.

The roof of the nave had collapsed in the fire. Most of the bodies among the debris were blackened beyond recognition. They must have been the first to die when the massacre began. Catesby could identify pelvic bones and fragments of skull – but there were other remains that were almost whole. There was a child's foot in a shoe.

The corpses further from the nave were the least damaged by fire, but riddled with holes from gunfire and hand grenades. Behind the altar, Catesby found thirty bodies – all children except for three women who must have herded the children thinking it was a place of safety.

The fire had spread from the main entrance of the church where incendiaries had been ignited to prevent escape. There were two other doors that led outside, both piled with bodies. Many of the women and children had been shot in the back as they tried to escape.

A wooden confessional next to a side chapel was untouched by flames. There were two girls – one aged about eight, the other maybe five – probably sisters. The older girl's body lay to one side of the younger girl whom she had been trying to protect. She had a single bullet hole in her forehead. She must have been tossed aside so that the soldier could finish off the younger girl with two bullets to the chest.

The older girl's eyes were open and staring. Catesby fought back tears. The girl's arms were stretched out in rigor mortis – as if somehow pleading. He picked up the stiff young body and held it. 'I don't know your name, but I will never forget you.'

Someone was calling for him in the church entrance. It was the man he had seen leaving the church. 'What is it?' said Catesby.

'The Germans are coming back. We must now leave this place.'

Suffolk: 10 June 2017

Catesby wiped away his tears and looked at this granddaughter. 'I just can't forget.'

'Does crying help?'

'No, it makes me hate myself for being emotionally self-indulgent. What are my feelings compared to the lives of the six hundred and forty-two people, including two hundred and five children, who were slaughtered at Oradour-sur-Glane? My tears are the whines of a pathetic old man.'

'You are too hard on yourself.'

'I never tried to contact the family of the two girls I found in the confessional.'

'How did you find out who they were?'

'There are photographs of most of the victims. I'm sure I recognised the two sisters. All the immediate family were, of course, murdered.'

'Why didn't you?'

'I didn't want to go back there in any way – and I've never told the story to anyone but you. I still can't deal with the memory. I want to bury it – and please don't say that I should have requested help or counselling.'

'I would never say that. It's something that very few of your generation ever did.'

Catesby gave a bleak smile. 'Instead, we took it out on our families. I could give you a long list.'

Leanna looked at her notes. 'What did you think of Violette Szabo going to fight with the Resistance and leaving her infant daughter behind?'

Catesby could see that it was a difficult question. His grand-daughter's own mother had gone back to Africa to become a human rights activist. She had on occasion been arrested, but the actual cause of her death still remained a mystery. She died when Leanna was fourteen.

'Violette,' said Catesby, 'wasn't the only woman who left young children behind. But I'm not going to judge them.'

'I love my mother for what she did, but I'm not sure that Dad felt the same way.'

'I'm sure he didn't.'

'But if she hadn't gone to fight for a cause, you and Granny wouldn't have shared the parenting.'

'We were both retired and looking for new challenges.'

'And you found them.'

'Indeed.'

'And now I'm discovering a grandfather that I never knew existed.' She looked at her notes. 'Last time, you started telling me about the American who was leader of the Jedburgh team.'

'He was the beginning of a whole new chapter. It began after the war when he joined the CIA.'

'You didn't get along very well.'

'No, but in an odd sort of way I liked him and was fascinated by him.'

'But he was so awful and boorish.'

'The boorishness was largely an act, but he was awful. In fact, he was a criminal.'

'Did he commit crimes in France?'

'Not in occupied France. He cynically used the war to build an honourable and heroic reputation. As American career officers say, "You have to get your ticket punched." This means you need to see a bit of action and win a medal or two before you can settle down to being a corrupt and power-grabbing bastard.'

'What did Lester end up doing?'

'You're jumping too far ahead, let's get through the war first.'

Trois-Chevaux: 14 July 1944

Lester's plan to celebrate the French national holiday infuriated Guingouin, but there was nothing Lo Grand could do to stop it. It was the first parachute supply drop to be delivered in daylight – a security breach that Guingouin regarded as utterly stupid – and it was going to be the biggest airdrop of the war. Realising there was nothing he could do to stop it, Guingouin assembled hundreds of Maquisards and helpers on the drop zone to carry away the masses of supplies and equipment that would soon rain from the sky. The fighters were heavily armed because a daylight drop would attract the Germans and the GMR.

As soon as the first wave of American B-17s passed over the drop zone, it was clear why Lester had insisted on a daytime supply. As the parachutes unfolded they formed an enormous tricolour. The canopies had been dyed blue, white and red – and the riggers stacking the loads organised the coloured parachutes to unfold in the correct order. Lester yelled, 'Liberté, égalité, fraternité' at the top of his lungs. Guingouin couldn't repress a reluctant smile. Three more waves of B-17s passed over. The supplies had landed and the Germans were on their way. Guingouin decided to hold his ground and confront the Germans. It would be the first time that his Resistance fighters and the Wehrmacht faced each other in a pitched battle.

The first day of the battle found Catesby hiding behind a chestnut tree on the slopes of Mont Gargan. They all wanted to revenge Oradour-sur-Glane, but the best way to kill Germans was with tactics and discipline. Giving into rage and embarking on suicidal charges would play into the hands of the enemy. A group of Maquisards was stretched out on either side of him. The fighter closest to Catesby was pointing a Bren light machine gun at a golden field of unharvested wheat at the bottom of the slope. A Maquisard on the other side of the Bren gunner was observing the wheatfield through a pair of binoculars.

'Whenever one of them moves you can see the wheat oscillate.' He passed the binoculars to the Bren gunner who looked and passed them back.

'I've got him lined up,' said the gunner. 'Tell me when he moves again.'

Crouching behind the chestnut tree with Catesby was a Jewish doctor who had come out of hiding in Saint-Léonard-de-Noblat to join the Maquis. The doctor was carrying a rucksack full of medical supplies. 'I wish,' he said, 'they would let me have a gun, but they say my job is looking after casualties.'

'If I get hit,' whispered Catesby, 'take my Sten.'

'The waiting is nerve wracking,' said the doctor.

They didn't have to wait any longer. The Maquisard with the binoculars said, 'Now.' The Bren opened up as did the entire line of Maquis. The Germans in the wheatfield fired back. The fusillade was withering and the Maquis leader gave an order to fall back. They didn't have to withdraw far. There was a ravine behind the chestnut tree which provided protection. The position had been chosen with care. The German bullets stripped leaves from the lower branches of the tree and churned up the ground and vegetation below it. After another minute the German fire lessened, the Maquisards crawled out of the ravine and opened fire on the German soldiers who were now advancing. They again took cover and started returning fire at full pelt. The same pattern continued for another hour. The Germans attempted to pin down the Maquis, while a platoon advanced under the covering fire. But the camouflaged Maquisards were difficult to spot and kept changing position. The Germans finally fell away. An hour later, there was the sound of armoured vehicles moving into the field of wheat. A heavy machine gun mounted on a halftrack began to sweep the Maquis positions. Another halftrack appeared mounted with a 37mm flak gun whose heavy calibre fire began to uproot trees and earth. Meanwhile, the German infantry advanced under the cover of the halftracks. The Maquisards dispersed into the wooded hills.

The next few days were full of confusion and chaos, but the Maquis were accounting for many Germans. They must have killed or wounded a dozen of them when Catesby's unit ambushed a column of trucks bringing reinforcements to Surdoux. The German response to the ambush was fierce and they had to beat a quick retreat to Mont Gargan where, unexpectedly, they met the Jedburgh team. Lester was strutting around with a .45 automatic in his hand and seemed to be enjoying the action – but unaware that the Germans were coming up the hill in force.

The plan was to fight a series of delaying actions so that the bulk of the Maquisards could disappear into the countryside. Catesby found himself in a group of six that included the doctor, the Bren gunner and the Maquisard with the binoculars. The latter had climbed the wall of the ruined chapel that marked the summit of Mont Gargan to get a better view of the advancing Germans. He continued to shout updates about German movements from his precarious perch in a Gothic arch, despite the fact that rockets and heavy machine-gun bullets were impacting into the stonework. Meanwhile, the Bren gunner fired bursts in response to his directions.

The binocular man's next report sent a chill down Catesby's spine. 'There's a platoon coming up on the left side of the road. They're about forty metres away.'

Catesby was about to tell the observer to get down from the ruin, but he was already well on his way. Catesby crawled forward to tell the gunner it was time to withdraw, but the Bren had fallen silent and the Bren gunner had rolled over on his back and was moaning. The doctor was now next to Catesby and they pulled the wounded gunner to a more protected position. Two more Maquisards rushed forward to provide covering fire. The doctor cut off the Bren gunner's shirt and wrapped a dressing around his chest.

'You've got a chest wound that's sucking in air,' said the doctor. 'Don't touch the dressing, it's helping you breathe. Don't worry, we'll get you out of here.'

Another Maquisard arrived and he and the doctor were soon

dragging the wounded gunner down the hill. Keeping his head down, for he could hear bullets popping past, Catesby scrambled to join the two Maquisards who were providing covering fire. They were armed with captured German submachine guns which they preferred to the British Stens, never a popular weapon with the Maquisards. They called the cheaply produced British gun *une saloperie*. Catesby, however, remained loyal to the Sten and joined in with them. He lifted his head up to see if he could pinpoint a German, but none were in sight. The bullets were still cracking overhead, but he couldn't see where they were coming from. The images of Oradour flashed into his mind. He couldn't see a target, but he emptied a magazine in their direction. At least it would keep their heads down.

The Maquisard who had been keeping watch from the tower was now beside them. He shouted, 'Let's get the fuck out of here, now!' It was good advice. The two Maquisards next to Catesby slid backwards and then began to run off the hill dodging and weaving to avoid the bullets. Catesby followed, but something made him turn before he had gone ten paces. The Bren, left behind by the wounded gunner, was still on the hill, alone and bravely defiant while German bullets kicked up the dust around it. What Catesby did next was either the bravest or the stupidest thing he ever did in his life. No way was he going to leave that beautiful British Bren for the enemy. While bullets popped overhead and both sides of him, he raced back and rescued the Bren.

He didn't think Lester had witnessed his foolhardy action, but he had heard about it and recommended Catesby for an American Bronze Star. The award of a US gong embarrassed SOE into putting Catesby forward for a British Military Cross. He didn't think he deserved any medal – more likely a court martial for cowardice and incompetence – but Catesby realised that gongs look good on a CV. He wore all his ribbons when he campaigned in uniform as a Labour parliamentary candidate in the 1945 general election. Although Labour won the election by a landslide, Catesby was contesting one of the safest Tory seats in the country and lost by a wide margin. Nonetheless, he was noticed in other places and Catesby wondered if his undeserved medals were why he was spotted for recruitment by the Secret Intelligence Service. A 'good war' can be a curse.

When it was all over, Catesby realised that the middle of a battle wasn't the best place for knowing what was going on. He thought the skirmishes he had experienced had been part of an action involving a few hundred Maquisards and a similar number of Germans and *milice*. He was astonished to discover that the week-long battle had involved more than three thousand Maquisards and nearly five thousand Germans and *miliciens* – and the Maquis had won. The battle had cost the lives of forty-three Maquisards including five missing. Another fifty-four had been wounded. Less than a hundred casualties. The Germans had suffered three hundred and forty dead and wounded. The Germans were capable of overpowering any Maquis position with the use of heavy weapons. But the cost of eliminating a single Maquisard was three and a half Germans. The *Wehrmacht* commander reckoned it wasn't a price worth paying and withdrew from the area. Meanwhile, Guingouin's Maquis and their helpers had succeeded in recovering and hiding the supplies and equipment dropped to celebrate the fourteenth of July.

During the weeks following the Battle of Mont Gargan the Germans withdrew from Limousin. They weren't fleeing the Maquis, but heading to Normandy. The civil servants and police who had supported Vichy began to feel nervous as the Germans left them to an uncertain fate. Three hundred uniformed gendarmes almost immediately deserted to join Guingouin's Maquis. Switching sides was swelling the ranks of the Maquis all over France. They became known as *les résistants de la dernière heure*. No one, however, was going to call them that to their faces. They were welcomed as comrades because they were going to make the endgame easier and less bloody.

Catesby never forgot the jubilation as he and Guingouin's Maquis crossed the Pont Neuf into Limoges on 21 August 1944. His Sten gun was slung over his shoulder, but Catesby knew he wouldn't need it. It was a bloodless liberation and not a shot was fired. For several days the Maquisards had Limoges surrounded. Three days before the liberation a German armoured column had broken out of Limoges. Although no one knew it at the time, the column included the commander of the Limoges garrison, General Walter Gleiniger, and all the troops who were capable of putting up a fight. The Germans had abandoned Limoges. The delegation that Guingouin had sent into Limoges on the morning of the twenty-first was greeted by a mere captain, the highest-ranking German officer remaining in Limoges, and a handful of conscripts. The surrender document was signed by the captain who ordered the few remaining soldiers to hand over their arms. The captain was a lot luckier than General Gleiniger who was killed in a Maquis ambush the next day.

Guingouin's bloodless liberation of Limoges had vindicated his tactics. The town and its people were still in one piece. Catesby was reunited with Marie and they celebrated long into the night. They were drunk with wine and joy when they tumbled into a hotel bed with clean sheets. They made love all through the night. Neither of them ever had enough. But when Catesby woke in the morning he felt depressed and empty. Something essential was now missing in his life, something he needed desperately. Was it a war?

Suffolk: August 2018

Catesby's granddaughter turned over the final page that he had
written about the Battle of Gargan. She folded her fingers and
stared at him.

'You look like my GP,' said Catesby. 'Are you going to tell me
to stop drinking so much?'

'Maybe your drinking has something to do with survivor's
guilt.'

'I have cut down.'

'But you haven't cut down on the guilt.'

Catesby looked out the window of his studio office, but didn't
see the birds or the trees or the garden. 'I shouldn't be here,' he
said. 'I should be lying in a grave in Normandy next to Strachan.
His tank brewed up near Caen.'

'Wasn't Strachan your night-climbing friend from
Cambridge?'

'He introduced me to that banned sport. I suppose he was my
best friend at university. I didn't make friends easily then – or
now.'

'I bet the soldiers who lived through that battle have survivors' guilt too.'

'We never talked about that sort of thing. But my war was
different from theirs. We fought from the shadows and then disappeared. They fought in the open and died like heroes.'

'You went through a different sort of hell.'

Catesby shrugged.

'Excuse me for prying, but did you carry on much longer
with Marie?'

Catesby smiled. 'Are you going to report me to Granny?'

'She is never shocked by you no matter how much you try.'

'Thanks.' The cat flap rattled. 'And now the Maquis have
arrived for requisitions.' Catesby took a tin of cat food out of

the fridge. 'If I don't feed him, he'll miaow that I'm a collabo and I'll be in line for the *épuration sauvage* – and rightly too. If you don't feed freedom fighters, you don't deserve your freedom.'

'I'm surprised you can joke about it.'

'Joking about it can stop you going mad. One of my uncles who was an infantryman in the first war used to tell a story about a hand sticking out of the wall of a communications trench. As they passed the corpse's outstretched arm, they always shook it and greeted it in an officer's voice, "Lovely morning, sergeant." Or "Great to see you back again, Captain Carruthers, you're looking well."'

'Emotional and mental survival.'

'Yes.' The cat flap sounded again. 'Ah, before Thomas arrived and diverted us, you asked about Marie. I did love her, but not the way that I love your grandmother. I loved Marie as a teacher and older woman – and, dare I say it, that love was mixed with a lot of wild eroticism.'

Leanna smiled. 'I wish President Macron was here. But what happened next?'

'Two days after the liberation of Limoges, Marie dragged me off to Bordeaux, her hometown – which was still under German occupation. Baker Street was furious that I had gone incommunicado. One of their unanswered transmissions was something like: *Thank you for liberating Limoges. When you sober up, contact RF Section London for your next assignment.* But I was more under Marie's command than SOE's. It wasn't easy to get to Bordeaux as the train lines blown up by the Resistance hadn't been repaired, but we managed to get a train from Agen to Bordeaux Saint-Jean.' Catesby shook his head. 'It was a nightmare. Saint-Jean was more a fortified German position than a railway station. It was dominated by a huge concrete blockhouse and there were German soldiers everywhere. Fortunately, we had come without a radio and our bags got through with only a cursory check. But the atmosphere was tense.'

'If it was so dangerous, why did she take you to Bordeaux?'

'Her reasons were both idealistic and selfish. Her family were part of a network sheltering a German naval officer who had defected to the Resistance after blowing up a munitions store and killing fifty of his comrades.'

'How extraordinary.'

'Even more extraordinary was that he was an explosives expert who had been tasked with destroying the port of Bordeaux before the Germans left, but his destruction of a bunker full of fuses and ordnance put paid to that. They hardly had any explosives left. The Germans were baying for his skin and searched the city high and low to find him. Had they got him, his fate would have been unspeakable.'

'Did you meet him?'

'Briefly, that was part of Marie's reason for bringing me to Bordeaux. She was hoping I could persuade SOE to arrange his escape to England, but I couldn't.'

'What was he like?'

'A modest man. He said he refused to obey orders because he couldn't see the point of destroying Bordeaux after the war was already lost, but he regretted having killed so many of his colleagues. On the other hand, his actions saved the lives of thousands of French civilians. He married a Frenchwoman and spent the rest of his life in the city he saved. In fact, blowing up the port would have been more spiteful than practical. The Germans had already blocked the river by scuttling two hundred ships – and they kept a pocket of resistance at Royan which controlled the entrance of the Gironde until the end of the war. Eisenhower was racing towards the Rhine – he didn't want to waste troops and time by clearing out the "Atlantic pockets". It was an odd situation. Guernsey and Jersey were still under German occupation nine months after Paris was liberated.'

'What were Marie's "selfish" reasons for taking you to Bordeaux?'

'She wanted me to help protect her family, their property and their interests. The merchants and growers of Bordeaux didn't regard themselves as wine royalty; they saw themselves as royalty full stop. They considered me like something the cat had dragged in. By the way, where is he?'

'Thomas is sunning himself on the patio bench.'

'Should I put some cream on his nose?'

'I wouldn't disturb him.'

'Where was I?'

'Marie's family.'

'They weren't as idealistic as her. She was a genuine hero. Her family seemed to have feet in both camps. Some were *résistants*, hence the sheltering of the German defector, and some were collabos – or at least did business with the Germans. Protecting their wine empire required some fancy footwork and duplicity. Her estranged husband was, of course, a collabo. Guingouin would have had him executed in the *épuration sauvage*.'

'But he survived.'

'And very well too. He was a great pal of the Abwehr officer, Otto Bömers.'

'The one who met you in Lyon to say your cover was blown?'

'Yes – and that was a frightening moment. Bömers was a selfish shit who wanted safe nests in both camps. As I mentioned before, he was a wine importer who knew Marie and her husband in the 1930s. The husband was, I assume, a willing cuckold, who didn't mind her sleeping with Bömers – either for business reasons or because it gave him some perverted thrill. By the way, that's why I always called her by her cover name, Marie. I couldn't bear to use the name she had when she shared a bed with those two slime buckets. I wanted to put my arms around a different woman.'

'Jealousy is often the dark side of love.'

'Indeed. And we did see Otto Bömers again in Bordeaux. I wanted to shoot him, but he travelled with too much protection. It was at the end, one day before the Germans left Bordeaux. Bömers, with the help of Marie's estranged husband, was looting the wine cellar of a rival merchant. The husband had denounced the merchant to the Abwehr as one of those who had given shelter to the naval officer. False, of course. But it gave Bömers an excuse to raid his cellar and load up a lorry with priceless cases of vintage Bordeaux. The husband was one of those, including the collabo mayor and the *préfet de police*, who tried to broker a safe passage for the Germans out of Bordeaux.

But unlike Limoges, it wasn't a bloodless exit. The Resistance, largely led by Spanish Republican refugees and exiled Basques, fought running gun battles with the Germans as they departed. One of them gave me a pistol and I fired a few parting shots from a safe distance. A symbolic gesture.'

'What happened to Bömers?'

'He went into hiding, but was eventually arrested and put on trial. He was in prison for two years.' Catesby gave a bleak smile. 'When he came out, he went back into the wine trade. I suspect his stash of looted Bordeaux gave him a flying start. I always wanted to put a brick through his shop window and repatriate a few cases of vintage Margaux.'

'You're still angry, aren't you?'

'We were too soft on the so-called "ex-Nazis" – and the collabos too. I blame the Americans. They preferred Nazis and fascists to socialists. After the war, the CIA created a rat run called Operation Paperclip to rescue two thousand Nazi rocket scientists and intelligence officers from the hangman's noose at Nuremberg. One of them was Wernher von Braun who helped put the Americans on the moon. Another was Klaus Barbie, the butcher of Lyon, who helped the CIA slaughter revolutionaries in South America, a continent they jokingly referred to as the "Fourth Reich".' Catesby shrugged. 'Maybe I'm just a bitter old man.'

'You are a very loving person. Anyone can see that.'

'I wonder if Marie saw it. After the Germans left we spent the night in her mother's house, a perfect piece of eighteenth-century architecture frowning on the river with its sunken ships and blown bridges. The interior was all understated elegance – and priceless heirlooms were now emerging from their hiding places with Marie in charge. That evening there were only the two of us in the house and I went to bed first. I was thrilled when I heard footsteps in the corridor and then her hand on the door. She was in a silk dressing gown and her hair, unusually for her, was done up making her look older and even more stately. She came over to the bed, but didn't get in. She kissed me on the forehead and said, "Adieu, my Rosenkavalier." I never saw her again – and can never hear the Marschallin's farewell trio without crying.'

'You're crying now, Granddad.'

Catesby laughed. 'I don't have to hear it, just thinking about it is enough. But life goes on and the war wasn't over. The Bordeaux Resistance put me in touch with a radio operator and Baker Street told me to go back to Limoges and liaise with the Jedburgh team. And when I got back, I got told off.'

'Why?'

'As soon as I arrived Lester shouted at me, in mock anger, "Where's the wine? You go AWOL to the wine capital of the world and you don't bring back a single bottle?" But I felt useless in other ways too. Meaning seemed to have disappeared. The French were busy re-establishing their government and punishing collabos, but they no longer needed us. I don't know why SOE told me to liaise with the Jeds because they were at loose ends too – and I didn't need their Dutch radio operator either because Jimmy Fenn had turned up.'

'How was he?'

'Distant and bitter. His son was safe with his grandparents in liberated Nanteuil-le-Haudouin, but still no news of his wife. Miraculously, she survived Ravensbrück. The couple were reunited with their son, but the marriage lasted for less than a year. Jimmy wanted action again and he joined the French Foreign Legion which sent him to Indochina where he had a leg blown off by a Viet-Minh landmine. He came back to France and drank himself to death on his disability pension. It's surprising and ironic how many ex-Maquisards volunteered for service in Indochina. They swapped fighting against the German occupation to become part of an army trying to re-establish French colonial rule in Southeast Asia.'

'What happened to his wife and son?'

'I don't know. I lost touch. His wife didn't want contact with any of his friends.'

'Did the war destroy more friendships and relationships than it created?'

'I think both in equal numbers. I kept in contact with Paul

who became a renowned art historian – he even met Anthony Blunt.'

'What did Paul think of him?'

'He was impressed by his knowledge, but thought some of his views were eccentric. I didn't press him for more. The saddest piece of news Paul passed on was that Andrée had been killed in the liberation of Lyon. I had a soft spot for her.'

'What about Lester?'

'While waiting for redeployment, Lester kept trying to get pally with me. I think his recommending me for the American medal was part of it – he saw me as someone he might one day find useful. In the end, it backfired on him.'

'What happened?'

'That would be skipping ahead about eight years – and I'm not going to tell you about it now because I don't want to end up in Wormwood Scrubs.'

'You're teasing.'

'Let's get back to September 1944. Lester and I had some long chats while we were waiting for further orders. It turned out that he had met Henri Déricourt and liked him. Lester thought that Déricourt was a sophisticated gentleman and a superb pilot with a taste for adventure and the good life – and they both had an interest in Southeast Asia as a future playground.'

'Did you tell him you thought Déricourt was a traitor?'

'No, I didn't want to put Lester off telling me things in confidence. He went on to say that Déricourt had a lot of enemies who were out to get him for political reasons – but he never said what those reasons were. Our conversations came to an end because Lester was ordered back to the US for further training before being redeployed as an OSS agent in Southeast Asia. He was parachuted into Vietnam in the spring of 1945 where his job was helping Ho Chi Minh fight the Japanese and the French.' Catesby gave a conspiratorial smile. 'Another member of his team was Kit Fournier.'

'Whom we can't talk about.'

'And whose files are still closed under the hundred-year rule. But it was a brilliant sting. Henry Bone's finest.'

'Weren't you part of it?'

Catesby winked. 'Check out the files when they open in 2060. But I can tell you about Déricourt and me. He was arrested by the French authorities in November 1946 on suspicion of treason. When he was put on trial in 1948 I was already an MI6 officer, and eager to go to Paris to testify against him. But permission was refused – and in the strongest possible terms. I was furious about it. But, at the time, I was a junior officer still in training. Not someone in a position to throw a tantrum in C's office and break the crockery.'

'But you did in later years.'

'All the time. And look where it got me: Deputy Director and a pension that would have paid your school fees at St Felix if you hadn't chosen to go to Lowestoft College instead. And thank you. Otherwise, we wouldn't have had anything left to live on.'

'We keep going off on tangents. What happened to Déricourt?'

'He was acquitted, even though it was proven that he had made contact with the Gestapo. The case against Déricourt collapsed when a former SOE officer testified that those contacts had been authorised and encouraged.' Catesby frowned. 'I need a drink.'

'I'll get you one, Granddad.'

'No, stay there. It's not six o'clock yet. The SOE officer who saved Déricourt's neck was the same one who had briefed me before my second deployment and told me that most hush-hush of false secrets. He said that we needed to prepare our Maquis circuits to assist an allied invasion of the Pas-de-Calais in the summer of 1943. The gist was that Déricourt was an important part of an orchestrated disinformation campaign. Once he was freed, Déricourt started spinning half-truths into outright lies. He said he had worked for MI6 which had sacrificed the lives of SOE agents and Resistance leaders in order to deceive the Germans about the allied invasion plan. When it was he himself – as a German double agent – who had betrayed those brave men and women.'

'Do you have any suspicions about the SOE officer who got Déricourt off the hook?'

'Not anymore. I think he was stupid and too arrogant to realise that he was being played for a fool. He was out of his depth – and easily duped by a glamorous alpha male like Déricourt.'

'What did Déricourt do after he was acquitted?'

'He followed Lester to Southeast Asia, which became his new playground. He made lots of money using his flying skills to smuggle opium from the Golden Triangle, the north-western corner of Laos, to drop-off points in Thailand, Cambodia and Vietnam. Quite an adventure: landing and taking off from tiny dirt strips, dealing with dangerous characters. He also got a job flying for the Laotian national airline, a CIA-funded business nicknamed Air Opium. Déricourt's luck apparently ran out in November 1962 when he took off from Vientiane with a load of gold bullion and four Laotian drug dealers. The plane crashed in Sainyabuli province near the Thai border. The charred bodies of the four passengers were found in the burnt-out wreck, but there is no record of Déricourt's remains being recovered. Possibly an administrative error – or because his body was thrown clear and devoured by scavenging animals. Oddly, the date of the crash was the anniversary of his having been arrested for treason.'

'Why are you smiling?'

'I will always be sure of it, but no one believed me. One of my more bizarre assignments for Her Majesty's Secret Intelligence Service involved a trip to Southeast Asia in late 1968. The acting Perm Sec of the MoD had a daughter who was addicted to heroin and revolutionary causes. She had tried to wrangle her way into Vietnam to help in the fight against the Americans – and no one knew what had become of her. I was sent to Vietnam to try to find her and bring her back to the UK. My second stop after pissing off the CIA in Saigon was the coastal town of Da Nang. There was a club near the docks called The White Elephant. It was banned to US military personnel, but a favourite hangout for journalists – and CIA officers. I thought chatting up a few journos might provide a lead to the young woman. It was quite a nice club, any vice you wanted at half the price you would pay in Saigon – but I had a job to do. I found a French female journalist there who proved helpful. I arranged a further meeting with her and as I was leaving the club, I heard a sound that was chillingly familiar. It was an unmistakeable laugh, one that I hadn't heard since 1944. A laugh that was just as warm and infectious as it was false and contrived. It came from a side room where a party was going on. I walked to the door and was barred entry by a burly CIA agent. "You can't come in," he said. "This is a private party." I replied, "Actually, I was invited by an old friend and colleague called Henri." The American said, "There ain't any fucking Henri here. So why don't you fuck off." So I left. But if I hadn't had another job to do I would have hung around.'

'Any idea what happened to him after that?'

'Haven't a clue. Probably survived to a ripe old age surrounded by riches and those naive enough to love him.'

Leanna looked at her notes. 'We seem to have taken a detour from September 1944.'

'Ah,' Catesby began shuffling papers on his desk. 'Here it is. I kept a copy. Baker Street finally pulled their finger out by the end of September and I got this: *Personal for William Catesby [Jacques Dubois] from Squadron Officer Vera Atkins. Return to UK as soon as possible as no further work for you in France. Bring with you all British non-commissioned personnel, codebooks, classified information, lists of agents, W/T crystals and your personal weapon.* And that as they say was that.'

'That smile looks sly.'

'During the four weeks I was cooling my heels waiting for my repatriation orders, one very interesting thing happened. Remember Ewan, the Intelligence Corps officer who was an important figure in the art world?'

'The one who took you to the Café Royal to sip absinthe?'

'That's the one. As France had been liberated, his job was tracking down works of art that had been looted by the Germans. Ewan sent me a message asking if I "would be so kind" as to send him a list of confiscations from the Limousin. I set about the job with vigour and passion, but the list I sent him wasn't long and was largely composed of ceramics. He sent me another message asking if I could track down a "human work of art" and make sure that he was safe. The artist in question was a writer who had been active in the Resistance. He and his partner had been forced to flee Paris and had walked to the south of France. Ewan suggested that they might be in the Luberon.' Catesby smiled. 'Through my Maquis networks I discovered they were in the village of Roussillon. The local Maquisards knew it was him because the writer spoke French with a strong Irish accent. Do you see where this is going?'

Leanna nodded.

'And if you pass it on to one of your Eng Lit colleagues at the uni and they write an article about it, I want to be fully acknowledged.'

'I promise.'

'Well, I went to Rousillon in the company of a grizzled Maquis leader, a former legionnaire, who had spent a couple of years in Indochina. By the way, Rousillon, with its ochre-coloured buildings, red cliffs, lush green pine trees and Provençal sky, is an artist's palette. I can see why the writer and his partner were drawn to it. It was, unfortunately, a brief visit. Neither the ex-legionnaire nor Samuel Beckett were good at small talk – and he did speak French with a pronounced Irish accent. We were assured they were safe and sound. I offered to convey any messages they wished to send to Paris, London or Ireland, but they declined. The ex-legionnaire finally stirred and said, "I suppose we'd better *di di*." For some reason the words attracted Beckett's interest and he said, "What do you mean by *di di*?" The ex-legionnaire huffed. "Only something I picked up in Indochina. *Di di* is Vietnamese for 'go go'. We used to shout it at the native troops all the time to get them off their arses." "How interesting," said Beckett.'

'So, both the main characters in *Waiting for Godot*, Didi and Gogo, translate as "go go".'

'Exactly.'

'And they don't go anywhere. Very impressive. I hope you are proud of your contribution to the world of literature.'

'It was the ex-legionnaire. I was only a bit player. But I sometimes wish I had become an Eng Lit teacher instead of a spy.'

'The undergrads would have loved you.'

'No, nothing so grand as a university. I would have wanted to teach poor ragamuffins like myself and my pals from Roman Hill were in the 1930s. Or maybe at Lowestoft College where you got straight As for your A levels.'

'You exaggerate, Granddad, you know it was two As and a B.'

'I was impressed by the staff and students. That college changed a lot of lives. And how many lives did I change as a spy?'

'You helped prevent a nuclear holocaust in 1962.'

'The Cuban missile crisis? I was only a messenger boy. Why are you laughing, gal?'

'Because you've started speaking with a Suffolk accent again. You're like Ed Sheeran; you've never lost your roots. And neither will I. You've taught me to love this place.'

As Leanna said those words her voice suddenly had the same vowels and cadences as the kids she had known in the state secondary and at the college. A Suffolk accent coming out of a beautiful brown face made Catesby's eyes fill with tears.

'What's wrong?'

Catesby laughed. 'My hid seems to be sloightly on th' huh.'

'Now you're overdoing it.'

'You're right.'

Leanna glanced at her notes again. 'Did you ever meet Georges Guingouin again?'

'Only once. I was invited to France for a ceremony commemorating the fiftieth anniversary of the Battle of Mont Gargan. We only spoke briefly as Guingouin was the centre of attention, but he introduced me to his wife and daughters – none of whom were going to refer to the awful things that happened to Guingouin after the war. I talked to Henriette, his wife, for some time without mentioning the elephant in the room. The conversation was largely about their careers as teachers. Kind of ironic that the greatest hero of the Resistance, one promoted to the dizzying heights of commander of the *Légion d'honneur*, should have ended up a humble schoolteacher in *la France profonde*.'

'Exactly what you would have liked to have been in deepest darkest Suffolk.'

'But Guingouin was mayor of Limoges for two years after the war. He only returned to teaching after being voted out of office in 1947. After that, his relationship with the Party worsened until he was expelled in 1952.'

'Why was he expelled?'

'The Party leadership detested Guingouin for refusing to submit to Party discipline. I suppose you could say he was too bolshie to be a Bolshie. They also accused him of being a Titoist, which, at the time, was worse than being a capitalist and almost as bad as being a Trotskyite. The Party rehabilitated him in 1998 and wrote Guingouin a letter apologising for everything that had happened to him.'

'Did he rejoin?'

'No, he said he had reached the age of *sérénité* and no longer cared.'

'Unlike you.'

'Serenity is for dead people, but to be fair to Guingouin, he experienced something in the 1950s worse than anything the Party ever meted out to him. It was the turn of the right and the former collabos to get their revenge.' Catesby looked away. His eyes were not full of serenity.

'What happened?'

'The Vichyiste collaborating cowards and bastards were waiting to get him and they pounced on Christmas Eve in 1953. He was arrested for complicity to murder and taken before a judge at Tulle. The charges related to the execution of two peasants thought to be informers. The deaths were ordered by a Maquis leader nominally under Guingouin's command, but Georges had known nothing about it. The judge refused bail and ordered Guingouin to be held in custody awaiting trial. The trumped-up charges were a conspiracy concocted by senior police officers who had been outwitted by Guingouin during the war. He was taken to a prison in Brive where he was beaten unconscious by warders. The prison authorities, now fearing for Guingouin's life, had him transferred to a prison in Toulouse where he arrived in a terrible mental and physical state. After a newspaper reported a suicide attempt, a more sympathetic judge ordered a complete mental and physical assessment of his health. Guingouin was sent to a psychiatric hospital where he recovered enough to be sent back to prison. He was freed on bail three months later – but wasn't completely cleared of all charges until five years afterwards. Guingouin calmly went back to teaching. Despite the trauma he had been through, he taught for ten more years before retiring.' Catesby shook his head and then looked at his granddaughter. 'Compare what happened to Guingouin with what happened to the lying traitor René Hardy.'

'The one who escaped prison on a minority verdict and became a successful novelist?'

'With one of his books turned into a film starring Richard Burton. If you don't get hanged for treason or war crimes, you can sell your memoirs.'

'Are you cynical?'

'No, your existence has taught me not to be.'

The cat flap sounded.

'It's already fish-o'clock,' said Catesby picking up a tin opener.

'While you're looking after Thomas, I'm going to start cooking you supper.' She began to gather up her notes.

'You're never to going to finish it.'

'Supper?'

'No, your memoir about me.'

'I'm certainly going to try, Granddad, and with your help we'll get there.'

'It's impossible. There is no such thing as a complete life story – not of anyone's life. There are always chapters left untold.'

Leanna got up to leave for the house. She suddenly stopped and looked at her grandfather. 'Did I hear you singing?'

'No, I was humming.'

'What is it?'

'It's a song the Lowestoft girls used to sing on May Day when they went out collecting. I didn't go with them, but I used to sing it with my sister – who loved it.'

'Can you sing it?'

'No.'

'Please, Granddad, for me.'

'It's only a silly old thing.'

'Please.'

'Well, since you're doing supper and it's a cooking song, I'll sing it.

Climbing up the walls,
Knocking down the spiders,
Cabbages and turnips too,
Put them in your Hallelujah saucepan,
Then we'll have a rare old stew.'

Catesby's eyes had a faraway look.

'What are you thinking about, Granddad?'

'I wonder if she's still alive.'

'If who is still alive?'

'The one who tried to tell me that wherever you go and whatever happens – and no matter how high you climb that wall – you will always regret what you lost.'

'Was she right?'

Catesby smiled at his granddaughter. 'No, she wasn't.'

'Thank you, Granddad.' She leaned forward to give him a hug and disappeared to the kitchen.

Alone now, he watched two young song thrushes foraging in the hedge. They could manage on their own. Catesby wasn't rich, but he loved the luxury of an English country garden. It was a consolation for old age. He knew he was lucky. The faces of those who hadn't been lucky paraded before his eyes. He did the maths that separated him from his war-dead colleagues. Most had bought it in '43 and '44 – seventy-five years ago. More than a lifetime. All that remained of them were the memories of those few of their generation who were still alive – and those memories would soon turn to dust.

Acknowledgements

Once again, warmest thanks to Julia for her support. It isn't easy living with an author at the best of times, but doing so during a pandemic lockdown requires special reserves of patience and selflessness.

Special thanks to my agent, Maggie Hanbury, who has now represented me for more than twenty years. Maggie's guidance and professionalism have led me through many stormy seas. She is a star.

I am grateful to my publisher, Piers Russell-Cobb, for continuing to be an enthusiastic champion of me and my books. Piers also deserves praise for looking after the health and safety of his staff during the pandemic. I also want to thank Joe Harper at Arcadia Books for his ever cheerful help and efficiency.

I am very privileged to have Martin Fletcher and Angeline Rothermundt as my editors. This is the fourth time that Martin has helped turn my raw plots into a polished and coherent narrative. His advice has always stimulated creativity and made me try harder. I want to give a special thanks to Angeline who has now edited seven of my books. She has, over the years, consistently calmed the excesses of my prose and saved me from countless embarrassments.

I am enormously grateful to Tessa Harding for giving me access to the unpublished memoirs of her father, Ewan Phillips, who was a very important and utterly fascinating figure in the art world of twentieth-century Britain. As a young man, Phillips was active in anti-fascist activities during the 1930s. He was a founding member of the Artists' Refugee Committee and worked on the 1938 London exhibition, *German Art of the 20th Century*, to counter Hitler's *Degenerate Art* exhibition. In the aftermath of the war, Phillips, serving as a captain in the Intelligence Corps, was assigned to the Monuments, Fine Art and

Archives unit which was tasked with the retrieval of lost and looted works of art. Although the Ewan Phillips portrayed in my book is a totally fictional character, his memoir was an enormous creative stimulus.

I want to give a note of thanks to Lourina K. de Voogd for looking at and correcting the Flemish phrases in my book. Lourina is a highly skilled linguist whose career speciality was providing library services to multicultural populations.

Finally, I would like to emphasise that this book is a novel. At no point have I tried to be a historian or biographer. A number of real historic events are referred to in this book, but those events are completely fictionalised. Likewise, a few real names are used, but no real people are portrayed. This is a work of fiction. When I have used official titles and positions, I do not suggest that the persons who held those positions in the past are the same persons portrayed in the novel or that they have spoken, thought or behaved in the way I have imagined.

Bibliography

Cobb, Matthew (2009), *The Resistance: The French fight against the Nazis* (London: Simon & Schuster)

Foot, M.R.D. (2014), *SOE: An Outline History of the Special Operations Executive 1940–1946* (London: The Bodley Head)

Kladstrup, Don and Petie with Dr J, Kim Munholland, Historical Consultant (2001), *Wine and War: The French, the Nazis and the Battle for France's Greatest Treasure* (London: Hodder & Stoughton)

Le Dantec, Jean-Pierre (2015), *Un Héros: Vie et Mort de Georges Guingouin* (Paris: Gallimard)

Phillips, Ewan, unpublished memoir

Piquet-Wicks, Eric (1959), *Four in the Shadows: A Tmaquisrue Story of Espionage in Occupied France* (London: The Adventurers Club)

Special Operations Executive and The National Archive (2014), *Special Operations Executive Manual: How to be an Agent in Occupied Europe* (London: William Collins)

Stroud, Rick (2017), *Lonely Courage: The True Story of the SOE heroines who fought to free Nazi-occupied France* (London: Simon & Schuster)

Taubmann, Michel (2011), *L'affaire Guingouin: La véritable histoire du premier Maquisard de France* (La Geneytouse: Editions Lucien Souny)

THE ENVOY

London, 1956. The height of the Cold War.

On the face of it, Kit Fournier is a senior diplomat
at the US embassy in Grosvenor Square. But that's
not the full story. He is also CIA Chief of Station.

With the nuclear arms race looming large, Kit goes
undercover to meet with his KGB counterpart to pass on
secret information about British spies. In a world where
truth means deception and love means honey trap, sexual
blackmail and personal betrayal are essential skills.

As the H-bomb apocalypse hangs over London, Kit
Fournier faces a crisis of the soul. The unveiling
of his own dark personal secrets will prove more
deadly than any of his coded dispatches.

~

'A glorious, seething broth of historical fact
and old-fashioned spy story' *The Times*

'A sophisticated, convincing novel that shows
governments and their secret services as cynically
exploitative and utterly ruthless' *Sunday Telegraph*

THE DARKLING SPY

August, 1956. A generation of British spies is haunted by the ghosts of friends turned traitor.

Whitehall spymaster Henry Bone has long held Butterfly to be the Holy Grail of Cold War Intelligence. His brain is an archive of deadly secrets – he can identify each and every traitor spy as well as the serving British agents who helped them. And now Bone learns that Butterfly plans to defect to the Americans. Unless Bone gets to him first.

William Catesby, a spy with his reputation in tatters, is pressured into posing as a defector in order to track down Butterfly. His quest leads him from Berlin, through a shower of Molotov cocktails in Budapest, to dinner alone with the East German espionage legend Mischa Wolf.

~

'A gripping Cold War story centred on a Berlin seething with agents and counterspies' *Mail on Sunday*

'More George Smiley than James Bond, Catesby will delight those readers looking for less blood and more intelligence in their spy thrillers' *Publishers Weekly*

THE WHITEHALL MANDARIN

**London, 1957. Lady Somers is beautiful, rich
and the first woman to head up the Ministry of
Defence. She also has something to hide.**

Catesby's job is to uncover her story and bury it
forever. His quest leads him through the sex scandals
of Swinging-Sixties London and then on to Moscow,
where a shocking message changes everything.

His next mission is a desperate hunt through the war-
torn jungles of Southeast Asia, where he finally makes
a heart-breaking discovery that is as personal as it is
political. It's a secret that Catesby may not live to share.

~

'We attempt to second-guess both Catesby
and his crafty creator, and are soundly
outfoxed at every turn' *Independent*

'Espionage and geopolitical history rewritten
by Evelyn Waugh' *Sunday Times*

THE MIDNIGHT SWIMMER

**October, 1962. If the Cuban gamble goes wrong
and war breaks out, Britain will cease to exist.**

Whitehall dispatches a secret envoy to defuse the
confrontation. Spawned in the bleak poverty of an
East Anglian fishing port, Catesby is a spy with an
anti-establishment chip on his shoulder. He loves
his country, but despises the class who run it.

Loathed by the Americans but trusted by the Russians,
Catesby is sent to Havana and Washington to make
clandestine contacts. London has authorised Catesby
to offer Moscow a secret deal to break the deadlock.

But before it can be sealed, he meets the Midnight
Swimmer, who has a chilling message for Washington.

~

'An excellent spy novel ... Fast-paced and capable
of keeping the reader guessing. It belongs on the
bookshelf alongside similarly unsettling works by le
Carré, Alan Furst and Eric Ambler' *Huffington Post*

'An intellectually commanding thriller' *Independent*

A VERY BRITISH ENDING

**March, 1976. A secret plot unfolds on
both sides of the Atlantic to remove the
British prime minister from power.**

1947: As a hungry Britain freezes through a harsh
winter, a young cabinet minister makes a deal with
Moscow, trading jet engines for grain and wood.

1951: William Catesby executes a Nazi war
criminal in the ruins of a U-boat bunker.
The German turns out be a CIA asset.

Both men have made powerful enemies in Washington,
and their fates become entwined as one rises through
MI6 and the other to Downing Street. Now the ghosts
of the past are returning to haunt them. A coup d'état
is imminent, and only Catesby stands in its way.

~

'Le Carré fans will find a lot to like' *Publishers Weekly*

'Probably the best espionage story you'll read
this year or any other' *Crime Review*

SOUTH ATLANTIC REQUIEM

April, 1982. The British prime minister and the Argentine president are both clinging to power.

Downing Street, having ignored alarm bells coming from the South Atlantic, finds itself in a full-blown crisis when Argentina invades the remote and forgotten British territory of the Falklands Islands.

Catesby is dispatched urgently to prevent Argentina from obtaining more lethal Exocet missiles, by fair means or foul. From Patagonia to Paris, from Chevening to the White House, he plays a deadly game of diplomatic cat and mouse, determined to avert the loss of life.

The clock is ticking. Diplomats and statesmen race for a last-minute settlement while the weapons of war are primed and aimed.

~

'Absolutely fascinating' *Literary Review*

'All too often, amid the glitzy gadgetry of the spy thriller, all the fast cars and sexual adventures, we lose sight of the essential seriousness of what is at stake. John le Carré reminds us, often, and so does Edward Wilson' *Independent*